HIDDEN POWER

KATHRYN ROYSE

Printed in Australia

Cover by Elizabeth McCracken @lizzacreative

Internal design by Book Burrow www.bookburrow.com.au

First printing: July 2025

Paperback ISBN 978-1-7640-3060-1

eBook ISBN 978-1-7640-3061-8

Hardback ISBN 978-1-7640-3062-5

Distributed by Lightning Source Global

A catalogue record for this work is available from the National Library of Australia

DEDICATIONS

To all those who believed in me and encouraged me when my strength and belief in myself was at its lowest ebb, thank you doesn't seem like enough.

ALSO BY KATHRYN ROYSE

Secret Alpha

PREFACE

For years I dreamed of writing the stories that would flow around in my thoughts. When I started reading Terry Spear's shifter stories and discovered her online writing workshops my dreams became a possibility, and with Terry's encouragement, they took flight. With further inspiration from a photo of my favourite knight and the support and belief of a special few, including Terry, my stories went from dream to reality.

A huge thank you to everyone who took an interest in the progress of my work and supported me through the ups and downs. I couldn't have done it without you.

CHAPTER 1

Raef's warning slid into Tarienne's thoughts, the sudden intrusion causing her to jump and yank on her mare's reins.

'Riders, hold!'

Her gaze sought her brother, ever vigilant on the back of his black stallion. Raef's hand rested on his sword. Not the fae weapon gifted to him by their father, but one made by a master swordsmith. A weapon befitting the consummate warrior—powerful and deadly. They were on their way to Castle Therin to see the king, a man who loathed magic and those who wielded it. It would not serve them to reveal their fae heritage to anyone during this journey.

Tarienne peered between the thick trunks of the elm trees supplying cover, the grey-brown, fissured bark a stark contrast to the vibrant, green leaves and buds of reddish-pink, tasselled flowers heralding the beginning of spring in the kingdom of Therin. Her mount, Lacey, shifted restlessly beneath her. The sound of hooves thundering across the grassy plain ahead told Tarienne there was more than one rider.

The *twang* of an arrow, the shrill squeal of a pig, followed by shouting indicated the riders hunted a wild boar. A curse rent the air as the boar crashed through the undergrowth not twenty feet away.

Raef's stallion did not flinch, but Tarienne's mount let out a startled whinny. Tarienne quickly leaned forward, whispering soothing words into Lacey's ear.

'*Cionnaith*, dear heart.'

The mare instantly settled, but her ears continued to twitch nervously.

The shouting stopped, and a male voice carried in the stillness.

'Sire, the boar was wounded.'

The deep voice, laced with concern, caught Tarienne's interest, and she strained to see its owner. A flash of maroon and gold moved across her line of vision, but she was unable to see the face of the person who spoke.

Raef's voice in her mind diverted her attention. '*Sire? Could this be the king we seek?*'

Moments later, they knew the answer. The voice of a young man – authoritative yet displaying an unexpected air of relaxed friendliness – answered. Definitely not the king. Perhaps this was the prince?

'I will not be a moment, Daien. I just want to check the boar's tracks. Orien, did you see where my arrow hit the animal?'

'No, sire. It reached the undergrowth before I could glimpse its injury.'

'There's a great deal of blood. Perhaps the creature has gone somewhere to die.' The man they assumed was the prince dismounted and disappeared from view.

Raef urged his stallion forward several steps, and Lacey followed. They stopped in a small clearing that afforded a better vantage point but still hid them from view. Through the swaying branches, they saw three men garbed in maroon and gold cloaks moving around close to the forest's edge, two were still mounted on their stallions. Another, the one Tarienne assumed was the prince, crouched on the ground, presumably over the boar's tracks. His hair was short, blond, and tussled, a lock hanging loosely over his forehead.

When he stood, Tarienne realised he was taller than she had

first thought, around six feet, and lean but muscled. His eyes were a brilliant azure blue that sparkled with both intelligence and emotion. She guessed he was around twenty, which would fit with what they knew of Prince Aidan. His black breeches were tailored, leather boots polished and obviously expensive. The jewelled sword hanging at his side spoke of his privileged life.

The prince started toward his mount when a rustling to Tarienne's left drew her attention. Bellowing its fury, the boar hurtled through the bracken toward the clearing. Tarienne cursed and nudged Lacey forward, fear for the young man constricting her throat. It did not matter she didn't know him. She respected the way he talked to his men, and he was the key to the prophecy even though he did not yet know it.

Raef's hand shot out and grabbed Lacey's reins, halting the horse. He shook his head. Tarienne scowled at her brother, knowing he was right but unable to bear what would happen next.

Turning her attention back to the scene playing out before them, she watched the prince's expression harden. He straightened, drawing his sword. She couldn't let this happen.

Tarienne began gathering the strength of her fae magic, grateful for the power her royal blood afforded her. Just as she was about to unleash it to halt the boar's trajectory, her attention was drawn to the one called Daien leaping from his mount.

'Sire!'

The boar crashed into the open as Daien darted in front of the prince, his sword raised. Tarienne gasped as the creature lowered its deadly tusks, an unearthly shriek filling the air.

Daien's stance was wide, his face a mask of concentration as he timed the killing strike of his blade. His sword plunged through the boar's head. At the same time, the creature flicked its head sideways, ripping open Daien's thigh. He crumpled to the ground, blood pouring from the gash, a grunt of pain the only sign of his injury.

Unable to stop herself, Tarienne cried out, jumping to the ground.

Raef reached out, attempting to stop her, but she sidestepped his grasp. Something elemental pulled her to the warrior.

'Help me, Raef. We can't let him die.'

Raef sighed, then dropped to the ground and grasped both animals' reins, running after her.

Tarienne cursed her dark green, ankle-length gown as she hurried through the rough, scratchy undergrowth that relentlessly tugged and ripped at her hem and soft, silk shoes.

Sliding to a halt at the edge of the plain, Tarienne eyed the bloody scene. The prince's eyes snapped up as she and Raef entered the clearing. Both he and his remaining companion leapt to their feet, drawing their swords as they moved in front of Daien.

Tarienne drew in a deep breath. 'We saw what happened. We can help.' Her eyes drifted to Daien. His face was drawn and pale, eyes closed. His lifeblood pumped onto the grass, spreading in an ever increasing, bright red circle, his breathing shallow and rapid. Turning her gaze back to the prince, she saw the moment he made his decision. With an almost imperceptible nod, he sheathed his sword and stepped aside, dropping to his knees beside Daien, his forehead crinkled with concern.

Tarienne rushed over to Lacey and yanked her satchel of herbs from the saddlebag, then returned to kneel beside Daien on the cool, damp grass, now slick with his blood. Withdrawing a clean cloth, she packed the wound, then leaned her weight onto it to stem the bleeding. Daien groaned, his jaw clenched.

Tarienne leaned closer, resting her cool hand on his heated forehead, and spoke in a soothing voice. 'I'm sorry, but we must stop the bleeding.'

Prince Aidan watched her intently, his expression one of deep concern. 'I can do that.'

Tarienne blinked in surprise. *A prince who cares about his men... Maybe fulfilling the prophecy will be easier than expected. But if this is any indication, I fear keeping him safe will be another matter.*

'Forgive me, my lord. I do not know your name.'

He waved her off impatiently. 'Aidan. Tell me what to do to help. Please.'

His azure eyes held hers, and Tarienne smiled, his genuine concern touching her heart. He was right not to introduce himself as Prince Aidan. Her admiration for him escalated another notch.

'You need to put as much pressure as you can on the wound to stop the bleeding. I'll prepare an herbal tea to help the pain and hasten the healing.'

Aidan moved closer and knelt beside Daien, placed his hands over the wound and pressed firmly, talking quietly to him.

Tarienne stood and looked at the third man. 'Can you please build a fire so I can steep the herbs...' She raised her eyebrows at him.

'Orien. My name's Orien,' he supplied, genuine concern creasing his brow. 'Can you save him?'

'Thank you, Orien. We were able to start his treatment immediately, so I believe so. I am Tarienne.' She gestured behind her. 'My brother, Raef, will help you.'

Orien nodded, glancing at Aidan. Raef raised one eyebrow at her, then began helping Orien collect wood, speaking with him in the calming voice he used on her when she was upset.

Tarienne moved beside Aidan, showing him the herbs as she placed them into a linen bag, explaining the purpose of each. Aidan asked a few questions to clarify their effect, seemingly satisfied by the time she was ready to drop them into the water Raef had brought to a boil on the fire he and Orien had started.

Tarienne motioned to Aidan to lift his hands from Daien's wound, pleased to see the bleeding had slowed significantly. As she cut away his ripped trousers with a small knife she kept hidden in her boot, Aidan sat back on his heels, watching. She cleaned around the deep gash, inspecting the damage caused by the boar's long, curved, razor-like tusk.

'I will need to close the wound with some stitches, but if he doesn't get an infection, it should heal well.'

Aidan nodded. 'Can we move him? I'd like to get him back to the castle.'

'He'll need to rest for a few hours, so the bleeding doesn't start again. He has already lost a great deal of blood.'

Tarienne began packing and bandaging Daien's wound, her gaze straying. His muscled thigh had a light smattering of dark hair. The gash was high, close to his groin, and Tarienne's eyes took in the bulge between his legs.

Her eyes slid to Daien's face. He was incredibly handsome, even with his pained expression. A shadow of a beard darkened his chin, and his wavy, brown hair hung limp, dampened by the beads of perspiration induced by the incredible pain he must be suffering.

As Tarienne worked, she silently chanted a spell of healing. Raef squatted beside her, placing his hand on her shoulder.

'How is he?'

She felt the tingle of his magic infusing her, strengthening her own. Tarienne smiled gratefully at him.

'A little better, I think.'

Having finished bandaging the deep wound, she shifted up his body so she could rest Daien's head in her lap. Dampening a clean cloth, she dabbed his forehead, working a spell through her mind to bring Daien to full awareness so he could drink some of the tea.

His eyes flicked open, confusion crinkling his brow for a brief moment. Glancing around, he focused on Aidan and Orien, then tried to sit up. A hiss slid from his lips as he moved his injured leg.

Tarienne brushed her fingers across his forehead.

'Do not try to move, it is too soon. Drink this, it will take away some of the pain.'

Daien tipped his head back slightly to see who spoke. His chocolate brown eyes widened, and the most gorgeous smile Tarienne had ever seen lit his face. She sucked in a sharp breath, her heart thudding loudly. She'd thought him handsome before, but when he smiled, he was breathtaking.

Taking a deep breath to calm herself, she helped him lift his head a little. He managed to drink most of the tea before falling back into her lap. Daien gifted her with another smile, sending her pulse racing, before he dozed off again.

Aidan placed his warm hand on her arm.

'Thank you. If you hadn't been here, we might have lost him. He's one of my father's guards… and a dear friend. We were hunting to supply food for the Spring Festival.'

He glanced at the boar Orien and Raef crouched over, cleaning and butchering it. Aidan still hadn't mentioned he was the prince of Therin.

Tarienne smiled at him.

'We were on our way to meet your father. You are the crown prince of Therin, are you not?'

Raef's warning growl penetrated her mind. *'Tarienne!'*

Aidan's expression hardened. Gone was the man concerned for his friend, replaced by the prince. His air of authority snapped back into place.

'I am. What business have you in Therin?'

The boar forgotten, Raef quickly moved to join Aidan and Tarienne.

'Forgive my sister's impertinence, sire. That is exactly why we are travelling to Therin. To ask your father if he might allow her to stay with you to learn the ways of a high-born lady at court.'

Raef pinned Tarienne with a scowl, warning her to hold her tongue.

Aidan stood, eyeing them both.

'Ah, yes. He mentioned your missive.'

His shoulders relaxed slightly.

'When Daien is well enough to move, you can accompany us back to Therin. Perhaps the lady can continue her care of him?'

Raef glared at Tarienne. She decided it best to follow her brother's lead. Lowering her eyes, she gently moved Daien's head from her lap and laid it on her pack, stood, then dropped into a small curtsy.

'I would be honoured to continue your warrior's care, sire.'

Aidan shifted uncomfortably.

'Please, call me, Aidan.'

Lifting her eyes to meet Aidan's, she smiled. His flashes of kindness and insecurity, in between displays of authority, were quite charming. She promised herself she'd work hard at being friends with him.

'Thank you, Aidan. I can do that, if you'll call me, Tarienne.'

Aidan nodded and smiled, his blond hair, vivid blue eyes, and classically handsome face reminding Tarienne of elven royalty, but there was no way a magic-hating king would sire a child with an elven princess.

Several hours later, Daien was well enough to travel, yet still not strong enough to ride his own stallion. Aidan would not allow anyone else to take him, so Raef and Orien helped him mount in front of Aidan. She knew Daien had to be in tremendous pain and was impressed with his ability to school his features and not cry out. As they began their journey back to Therin, Orien rode ahead, leading Daien's horse, Tarienne stayed beside Aidan, keeping a watchful eye on Daien, and Raef brought up the rear.

It wasn't long before the imposing grey and black stone of Castle Therin, which had been carved into the side of Mount Avalon, loomed before them. The cold, stark effect of the fortress was softened only by the clusters of tiny cottages nestled in the vibrant green, rolling hills surrounding it.

Along the side of the well-worn, gravel path, the first lily of the valley nodded their tiny white, fragrant heads. Tarienne was fascinated by the contrast, a smile spreading across her face as she drew in a deep draught of the sweet scent.

When the gates of Castle Therin opened, a handful of men, wearing the same mantles as Orien, Daien and Aidan, rushed forward, carefully lowering Daien from Aidan's stallion, and carrying him into the castle. As soon as their mounts were led away to the stables, Tarienne and Raef followed Aidan to the infirmary. After he had ensured that Daien was as comfortable as possible he left to inform his father of their arrival and the unexpected events of the hunt. He promised to return quickly and show them to the guest rooms, where they could bathe and rest. He left Orien with them to help with anything they needed... and, Tarienne suspected, to keep an eye on them.

When Aidan returned an hour later, seeing Daien sleeping comfortably, he showed them to the guest rooms, where baths were already drawn, and a light meal awaited. Their belongings had been retrieved from their horses and placed beside the huge, four-poster beds. Aidan left them to rest, letting them know he'd return in a few hours so they could meet with the king prior to the evening meal.

Raef hugged Tarienne and disappeared into his room, leaving her to bathe.

Anxious to remove the grime and blood, she stripped as quickly as the cumbersome dress would allow, having already refused the assistance of a lady's maid, and stepped into the steaming water. Sighing, she sank beneath the surface to rinse the dust from her hair. She lathered her hair and body, rinsed the suds away, then relaxed back in the water until it grew cool.

Stepping out of the tub, a shiver raised goose bumps on her skin before she wrapped herself in the soft, warm towel the maids had left beside the open fire before their reluctant departure. She tucked it around her body, then dug into her pack to find a dress suitable for a meeting with the king. She chose a deep green one she knew enhanced the colour of her eyes, slipped into it, then began brushing her hair, feeling her anxiety escalate at the prospect of meeting the king.

Dragging in a deep breath to calm herself, she let her thoughts drift to the handsome knight, Daien.

A knock at the door startled her from her musings. Rising, she padded on bare feet to open it. Raef smiled at her, looking clean and refreshed as he stepped into the room. He dropped on her bed sitting with his long legs crossed at his ankles as she returned to combing her hair.

'Feeling better, sweetling?'

'Yes, much better. Before we meet with the king, I must check on Daien.' Struggling to draw the brush through a knot in her long hair, she swore colourfully.

Raef chuckled as he moved up behind her, taking the brush from her hands and running it through her hair in a gentle, practiced way.

'That's no way for a lady to talk, little sister.'

She twisted around and punched Raef playfully in the arm, then sobered. 'I am going to miss you so much, Raef. Can't you stay here with me for a while?'

His dark eyes softened.

'You know I can't, sweetling. But I won't be far away, and we can converse across the distance through our mindspeak.'

Tarienne's eyes misted with tears. Raef's arms wrapped around her shoulders hugging her tightly before he kissed the top of her head, then continued brushing her locks in silence.

Moments later, Aidan knocked softly and stepped into the doorway, running his gaze over Tarienne, who looked every inch a lady at court. He eyed her approvingly as she stood, smiling, and offering his arm. They walked down the corridor, Raef strolling behind them, the eyes of every woman they passed roving toward Tarienne's strikingly handsome brother.

Tarienne grinned, knowing Raef disliked the attention.

Aidan turned his head, his gaze meeting hers.

'I thought we'd visit Daien after dinner, if it pleases you.'

'That would be wonderful. I'd like to check on his wound and possibly stitch it given it has been thoroughly cleaned, before it begins to heal too much.'

Aidan nodded as they swept into the great hall, delicious aromas of the evening meal wafting around them.

As the king approached, Tarienne curtsied low, and Raef dropped to one knee, his head bowed.

'Rise.'

Stopping in front of Tarienne, the king visually assessed her, but no smile graced his face. She shivered, lowering her head and eyes in deference, then lifted them again to follow his progress toward her brother. As Aidan formally introduced them, King Eldan assessed them both, his steely grey eyes cold, making Tarienne want to fidget.

'I thank you both for assisting my son and his hunting party this afternoon. Aidan has told me of your care for my guard, Daien. He shall be rewarded well for protecting his prince. Aidan also tells me you are willing to continue tending Daien's wound.'

Without waiting for her to answer, King Eldan turned his piercing gaze on Raef.

'I hadn't previously decided whether to accept your sister as a guest at Castle Therin, but now I have evidence of her honour, I would be happy to have her stay and learn the ways of a lady at court.'

Raef nodded.

'Thank you, sire. We very much appreciate your agreement in this. May I ask to be allowed to visit occasionally, and my sister be allowed to visit my modest holdings at Ferngrove when time allows?'

Eldan clapped Raef on the shoulder, but his smile did not reach his eyes.

'Of course. However, she'll be busy. There are numerous tasks she will undertake as chatelaine. It has been many years since we've had someone around to take care of the tasks a high-born woman is responsible for.'

Tarienne opened her mouth to respond, snapping it shut again when Raef shot her a quelling glare. She growled into her brother's thoughts, the sweet smile on her face belying her anger.

'This had better be necessary for the fulfilment of the prophecy. The king has just commissioned me to run the castle, rather than providing

me experience of life at court! I may as well have applied for a position as his housemaid.'

She felt, rather than heard, Raef's silent chuckle. Spotting the twinkle in his eyes, she barely suppressed the urge to punch his arm again.

During the meal, which now tasted like ash in Tarienne's mouth, the king cheerfully explained the duties for which she would be responsible. Apart from management of the kitchen, menus, larder, accounts, and supplies, she was expected to supervise the household staff and any repairs, including the purchase of new materials. The one thing she was familiar with that would become part of her duties was making medicines and caring for the sick in the castle and the surrounding villages. At least she knew she could perform one task adequately. She sighed quietly.

After the torturous meal, during which she was forced to smile and appear pleased with her new duties, they visited Daien in the infirmary. The fire in the hearth had been stoked to chase the chill of the evening from the stark room. Daien's colour had returned, and he looked much better. The smile lighting his face when she entered went a long way to cheering Tarienne up.

'May I check your wound, Daien?'

'Of course, milady.'

His deep, rich voice washed over her, sending her pulse racing.

Her hands shook as she removed the bandage, and he sucked in a breath when she accidentally grazed his groin. Her eyes shot to his, her cheeks heating.

'My apologies,' she mumbled, heart hammering. *Damn.*

Careful to avoid his manly parts, she pulled the last of the bandage away. The wound looked clean and was ready to be stitched. Meeting Daien's eyes, she pulled in a deep breath.

'The wound looks clean, and the bleeding has almost stopped. I think it's time it was stitched.'

Daien nodded his assent.

At Tarienne's request, Aidan asked a maid to fetch boiling water. Raef left to retrieve her satchel of herbs from her chambers. Shivers ran along Tarienne's spine as she busied herself examining the wound.

Daien's warm, calloused hand suddenly covered hers.

'Thank you for saving my life today.'

Tingles shot up Tarienne's arm, heat coiling in her stomach. Daien yanked his hand away, as if similarly affected, an odd look of confusion briefly passing across his face.

Pulling her self-control around her like a protective blanket, Tarienne smiled sweetly.

'You are very welcome. I am glad that we were close by and able to assist.'

Daien relaxed back onto the bed, watching her intently, a tiny, mischievous smirk curving the corners of his mouth. His languorous perusal made Tarienne nervous, so she moved away, picking through the small vials on the infirmary shelf to calm the spiralling awareness he had awakened in her.

When Aidan and Raef returned, one holding a steaming pot and the other her herbs, Tarienne focused on brewing a tea to dull his pain and relax Daien so she could begin stitching the wound. She then sanitised the needle and thread in boiling water steeped with Calendula leaves as a mild antiseptic, which would also promote healing.

When Daien's eyelids drooped, Tarienne pulled in a deep, calming breath, placed an apron around her middle, to prevent her best gown from ruin, and began stitching.

Reciting a healing spell through her thoughts as she worked, Tarienne startled a little when Daien's eyes snapped open. His eyes searched hers, forehead creasing into a tiny frown. As she held his gaze, his lips twitched into a cheeky smile, and he relaxed again. Tarienne's pounding heart eased.

Working methodically, she took great care to ensure the wound was neat and would not leave much of a scar, even though she knew men wore scars as marks of honour.

Pleased, Tarienne gently wiped the wound with a clean cloth soaked in the now cooling Calendula tea, then rebandaged Daien's swollen, bruised thigh.

She sat beside him for longer than necessary, fussing with the bandage, hoping he'd open his eyes and bestow another of his devastating smiles on her. But she knew her herbal tea had been strong enough to ensure he slept for some time.

Aidan and Raef escorted her back to her chambers. When they reached her room, she thanked them and closed the heavy wooden door. Sighing, she quickly undressed, slipped a light gown over her head for propriety's sake, even though she preferred to sleep naked, and fell onto the bed, exhausted.

The rising sun streaming through the window woke Tarienne early. Slipping on her soft, pale green dressing gown, she secured it at the waist and padded to the window, curious to see the hustle and bustle of life at Therin. The glorious scent of freshly baked bread wafted through the air as she watched people hurry about the market, buying wares and fresh food.

Her stomach rumbled loudly, reminding her she had not eaten much the night before. Dropping her dressing gown to the floor, she used a quiet spell to warm last night's bath water and climbed in. She washed quickly, then dried herself on a fresh towel the maid had left over the chair near the open fire.

Before wandering over to peruse her belongings, she tossed a log onto the fire and pushed it into place with the heavy iron poker that rested against the outside of the stone fireplace. She picked out a deep blue dress with a square-cut neckline, which didn't reveal too much of her bosom.

Sighing, she brushed her hair and pinned it on top of her head, allowing some of her curls to tumble down her back.

Pleased with her appearance, she slipped on her soft, deep blue, jewelled slippers and wandered out of her chambers down the long, stone corridor, trying to remember the way to the dining hall.

Finding herself at the stairs leading to the courtyard, she caught sight of Aidan speaking to several men, all of whom wore the maroon and gold colours of Therin, the men laughing at what he had said. She watched, a small smile on her face, admiring the easy banter between Aidan and his people.

As if sensing her presence, Aidan turned and strode over, greeting her with a huge grin.

'I trust you slept well?'

Tarienne smiled back. 'Yes, thank you. I was looking for the dining hall,' she looked around with a small frown, 'but couldn't remember how to find it.'

Aidan chuckled. 'Therin can be difficult to navigate until you grow accustomed to its corridors. I have not broken my fast yet. If you'd like, I'll show you the way.'

Aidan held his arm out, and Tarienne slipped hers through it, noting that she did not feel the same prickle of awareness as when she touched Daien.

As they made their way to the dining hall, Tarienne became aware of the hostile stares from some of the ladies they passed. She assumed they thought she was here to be courted by their prince. Lifting her chin, she chatted and laughed with Aidan as they traversed the long, stone corridor, doing her best to ignore them.

Raef joined them shortly after their arrival in the dining hall, the two men greeting each other with friendly smiles. Tarienne marvelled that Raef had been able to find his own way there after being shown it just once. She greeted him with a quick hug, and they all sat as the food was served.

As they filled their plates with the delicious cold pork and sweet, berry pastries set out on the heavy, wooden tables they chatted as though they'd known each other for much longer than one day. Aidan asked them about their home at Ferngrove. Raef and Tarienne answered his questions carefully, cautious not to reveal anything of their true heritage, or the fact they'd only lived at Ferngrove six months. If Aidan learned they were fae and born in the forests of Darewood, they'd be imprisoned in the dungeon or banished, unable to fulfil their purpose.

The prophecy had brought them to Therin to protect Aidan until, ironically, he could return the balance of magic to the kingdom. They had no idea how it would play out but were sworn to keep him safe until it did. However, given the recent news from their fae scouts of fell creatures terrorising remote farms and murdering livestock, they didn't know how long it would last. It was only a matter of time before the beasts started killing people.

After breakfast, they made their way to the infirmary, finding Daien propped up on a pillow, eating a sweet pastry.

Aidan grinned. 'You look much better. I thought we'd lost you to that damned boar, Daien.'

'I'm feeling much better, sire. Thank you.' Daien's eyes followed Tarienne as she bustled to his side, anxious to check his wound. 'It seems I am indebted to the lady whose name I do not yet know.'

Aidan chuckled, moving forward to make the formal introductions.

'This is Lady Tarienne and her brother, Raef, without whom we would have been ill-prepared for the treatment of your wound.'

Daien sobered a little. 'I thank you again, milady. I owe you a debt of gratitude.'

'You are welcome and owe me nothing.'

Tarienne didn't mean to sound so snappy, but as soon as she had begun unwrapping the bandage, her hands started to tremble again. She was frustrated by her reaction to Daien.

When he shifted his leg in an attempt to aid her ministrations, a grunt of pain rumbled through him. Tarienne reacted instinctively, grabbing his leg to support its weight. Daien's eyes snapped to hers, and she heard a tiny hiss slip from his lips. She held his gaze for a moment, only distantly aware of the others in the room. Reluctantly tearing her eyes away, she asked Aidan if he could arrange some boiling water so she could make some more tea.

The rest of the cold Calendula tea sat on the table where she'd left it last night. Carefully tucking a pillow under Daien's leg to support it, she retrieved the tea to cleanse his wound again. Pleased with how well the skin was healing around the stitches she'd so carefully woven through his torn skin, she began gently dabbing the antiseptic brew onto them.

*   *   *

Daien

Daien watched Tarienne cleanse and rebandage his wound, his heart almost leaping out of his chest each time she accidentally brushed his groin. He was certain she must be aware of his arousal burgeoning underneath the thin blanket.

He dropped his hands into his lap, surreptitiously covering it. His body ached, and he knew it wasn't entirely due to the injury. He needed to get his reaction to this stunningly beautiful redhead with deep green, beguiling eyes under control. She was a lady, out of his reach.

An audible sigh escaped. He couldn't help but smile at the curious look Lady Tarienne sent him as she tied the ends of the bandage.

He promised himself he'd visit the tavern when he was well enough. There were plenty of attractive women there willing to lay with a king's guardsman. Not that he indulged as often as everyone thought.

He allowed himself another glance at Tarienne. Suddenly, the thought of a tavern wench beneath him wasn't as appealing as it used to be.

CHAPTER 2

THREE YEARS LATER…

Tarienne looked up from her tapestry when Daien knocked on her open door. She was pleased yet surprised to see him. Her body warmed involuntarily, heart thumping against her ribs. Her reaction to his presence hadn't changed in the three years she'd been in residence at Therin. Daien seemed uncomfortable, shifting from foot to foot, as he passed on the message that she'd been summoned to the throne room for an audience with the king.

Fleetingly, icy shards of fear skittered down her spine. Heart pounding, Tarienne stood, smoothing the front of her dress, her hands trembling. She walked to where Daien waited, closing the door behind her. The heavily decorated corridors of the inner citadel closed in around her as they walked, almost crushing the breath from her lungs. She scrambled to think of a reason for the formal summons. Could the king have discovered her fae heritage?

To calm herself, she glanced at the king's guardsman beside her. Despite her inner turmoil, she smiled to herself. Extremely handsome and known as a bit of a rogue, Daien marched purposefully down the corridor, alongside her, his expression stern.

His presence calming her, as it always did, a modicum of rational thought returned. If King Eldan had discovered her magical abilities, she would surely already be in irons, either being dragged to the throne room or into the depths of the castle dungeons.

Tarienne had been using magic for some time now in to heal villagers' wounds and ailments. She could not turn them away, drawn to help the simple people who were so grateful, so kind. But she had been extremely careful. Everyone believed it was the herbal remedies that helped them, which was partially true. But without the magic many of the illnesses and injuries they suffered would have been fatal.

Only yesterday, she had visited a family of seven in a tiny cottage on the outskirts of the city. The father was bedridden with what Tarienne suspected was pneumonia. She had made a tea from elecampane root, coltsfoot and juniper to help clear his lungs and reduce the fever.

After sponging down the farmer's upper body she had administered the tea, all the while working a silent incantation. Before she left, she instructed the family on administering the tea regularly and told them to sponge him down often until the fever broke. Glancing back as she left, she noted he was sleeping peacefully. It was such a simple use of the immense magical power she held; it would be ironic to be punished for it.

Breathing deeply to settle her churning stomach, Tarienne touched Daien's arm to draw his attention. She could not resist tempting his resolve.

'Not going to the tavern today, Daien?'

He raised a questioning eyebrow, playing along with her teasing, he slowed his pace a little.

'The tavern, milady?' He shook his head. 'It's forbidden while I'm on duty.'

In contrast to his solemn declaration, his face lit in a smile fit to melt the heart of any maiden. Tarienne sucked in a sharp breath.

Daien lowered his voice, leaning closer. 'This afternoon, as long as no one catches me.' Then he quickly schooled his features into the same serious look as before.

Tarienne chuckled, then sighed quietly, wishing things could be different. She had felt a connection between them since they had first met three years earlier. However, he had never shown any real interest beyond propriety. There were times she felt his eyes on her, the heat of them warming her skin. Other times, she was certain he made himself scarce as soon as she entered a room.

She had watched Daien practice his swordsmanship with Aidan and the other guards. He was a strong, formidable warrior. She had seen his bravery, honour, loyalty. Witnessed his sweet nature when he had comforted a child who had fallen in the street, then carried the small boy back to his parents.

His deliciously expressive, chocolate brown eyes twinkled when he laughed, and it did not hurt that his lean, muscled body was honed to perfection. Her heart fluttered and a tiny flame of warmth trickled through her.

They stepped into the throne room. Tarienne pulled in another calming breath, steeling herself for the interaction with the king. She missed Daien's warmth the moment he stepped away from her, snapping to attention as he awaited the king's orders.

Standing at the window with his back to her, King Eldan turned. 'Thank you, Daien.' He dismissed him with a wave of his hand as he walked toward Tarienne. She was almost certain that Daien sent her a look of concern as he left.

Halting no more than an arm's length away, Eldan's piercing, grey-blue eyes assessed her for a moment. Forcing herself not to fidget under the king's scrutiny, she waited.

'Tarienne.'

She bowed her head slightly, squeezing her clasped hands together.

'Sire, you wished to speak with me?'

Powerfully built, the king dwarfed most men. His weathered, yet still handsome features and greying hair afforded him a distinguished appearance. His eyes held intelligence, promised intimidation. Eldan commanded respect, instilled fear in his people, yet showed a measure of fairness where human folk were concerned. His major fault was his stubborn refusal to tolerate the existence of magical beings.

Anyone thought to be practising a form of magic in the kingdom of Therin would, at the very least, be banished into the wilds where vicious thieves, murderers and vile creatures lived.

Tarienne was fortunate. If she were banished, she would still have a home in her birthplace of Darewood or in Ferngrove with Raef. But it would mean she could not protect Aidan so he could fulfil the long-ago written prophecy. That would mean the demise of magic in the light. The kingdom would be consumed by dark magic and the evil that wielded it.

For an intelligent and courageous man who was a brilliant strategist, Tarienne wondered at King Eldan's emotional response to magic. A frisson of anger chased away some of her worry. Many others, including Aidan, did not agree with Eldan's harsh decree. But no one, herself included, would ever openly question the king's ruling on any matter, especially this.

At his gesture for her to sit Tarienne demurely lowered herself onto the ornate chair beside the throne, as she had many times before, awaiting the king's words. He strode over to the throne and sat, turning toward her and leaning forward, his elbows resting on his knees.

'Tarienne, I've noticed you spending time with Aidan as of late. This pleases me greatly.'

Tarienne let out the breath she had not realised she'd been holding. Relief flooded her as she smiled. 'Yes, sire. We are enjoying each other's company.' It was not a lie. Just not the whole truth.

A few months ago, it had become clear King Eldan was determined to find a suitable bride to rule at Aidan's side and produce an heir to the throne. Against tradition, Aidan wished to marry for love, not duty, so he had begged Tarienne to help. She loved him like a brother, the pair having become close friends, so she'd agreed, but they both knew the ruse couldn't continue indefinitely.

Her attention returned to the king.

'Well, know this, my dear. Seeing you together warms my old heart. I have despaired of Aidan ever seriously courting anyone, let alone a most suitable choice such as yourself. My time as king will not last forever. Soon, Aidan will rule this kingdom. He'll need a strong woman of royal breeding to rule by his side.'

If he only knew my true heritage, he would think of me as anything but suitable.

She felt guilty for deceiving the king, now fearful he'd force them into marriage. She must find Aidan to discuss this new development.

'Thank you, sire. Have you also spoken with Aidan on this matter?'

'I will on the hunt this afternoon.'

'Very well, sire.'

Her heart hammering, Tarienne quickly changed the subject.

'It is almost time for lunch. Would you care to accompany me to the dining hall, milord?'

Eldan nodded, a conspiratorial smile playing across his lips.

'We'll collect Aidan on the way.'

She looped her arm through his, and they headed for Prince Aidan's chambers.

'Aidan,' the king called as he entered without knocking. 'It's time for lunch.'

Aidan looked up from the sword he meticulously polished, a smile transforming his already handsome face. Tarienne admired that he always cleaned his own weapons. As the future king, he lacked the self-absorption and snobbery evident in his father.

'Father, milady, I did not realise the time. I have not long returned from training with Orien and Daien.'

Tarienne's pulse skipped at the mention of Daien, but she

carefully schooled her expression into a joyful smile. When Eldan released her arm, she scooted over to Aidan's side, threading her arm through his. Eldan smiled indulgently, and any happiness Tarienne had felt at the thought of Daien slipped away as they made their way along the long, chilly corridor.

A delicious lunch of beef pies and apple pastries was served in the informal dining area beside the enormous kitchen. Aidan, Tarienne and Eldan chatted companionably about the upcoming Spring Festival, the impending changes to the weather as the season of growth took hold and the delicious food.

Aidan complimented her on her management of the kitchen and the varied, pleasing menus. Since arriving at Therin, she had learned that an efficiently run kitchen, with various and well-prepared food, was central to the running of the castle, and Therin was fortunate to have a very talented cook. Pleased he had noticed, she smiled, adding a shy little flutter of her lashes to further fulfil her role as Aidan's sweetheart. Her eyes met his when Aidan lifted her hand to his mouth and kissed it tenderly, playing his part for his father.

When the conversation turned to the afternoon's impending hunt, Tarienne asked the king if he would mind excusing her to work on the menus for the next month.

Curtsying, she made her way to the large, bustling kitchen, where several scullery maids were preparing vegetables for the evening meal. She left a copy of the menu with the head cook, then checked the larder to ensure the food supplies were adequate. After running her practised eyes over the accounts, she returned to her chambers to continue her sewing.

Tarienne busied herself with her needlework, making something she hoped she might eventually have the courage to gift to Daien. Her pulse fluttered at the thought of him—his lean, muscular frame, confident swagger, heart-stopping smile. How could she let him know she cared for him now?

Daien would never do anything to hurt Aidan. They were more

than a prince and his guard. They were friends. Their friendship was built on trust and the knowledge they had each other's back.

Sighing, Tarienne turned her attention back to her sewing. But thoughts of Daien, his ready smile, his toned body, his thoughtful nature, continued to distract her.

A knock sounded on the door of her chambers; a muffled voice called to her from the corridor.

'Tarienne?'

'Come in, Aidan.'

She smiled as he entered the room, noticing he had taken the time to bathe and change his clothing after the hunt. Tarienne liked that cleanliness was important to him. He always smelled fresh and clean, unlike some of the other courtiers, who tried to cover their lack of hygiene with heavy scents, albeit unsuccessfully.

Melodramatically, Aidan flopped into the chair beside her, almost knocking her sewing from her hands. Tarienne calmly gathered the needlework into her lap, focusing on the next stitch.

'How was the hunt?'

She lifted her eyes to meet Aidan's.

'It went well. My father mentioned his happiness at our spending time together.' Aidan raised an eyebrow, lowering his voice conspiratorially. 'So, our plan is working just as we hoped, although, I truly dislike having to lie to him.'

'Now that he has acknowledged our supposed interest, my concern is he'll expect a betrothal and wedding soon. What can we do, Aidan?' Little frissons of panic darted across Tarienne's chest, tightening it uncomfortably.

'Don't worry. I will just tell him we're taking it slowly.'

Tarienne was frustrated he didn't seem to be taking the situation seriously.

'But in time, he'll expect a wedding, Aidan. What then?'

'Hopefully by then, I will have had enough time to find someone. If not, I will tell him we have decided we are not as suited as we first believed,' he sighed, 'and I'll be back to entertaining every eligible maiden of suitable lineage in the area.'

Tarienne chuckled at the despondency in his voice, though she knew how frustrated Aidan had become at the constant stream of high-born females his father had invited to Therin for him to court.

Aidan raised his eyebrows mischievously, a cheeky grin spreading across his face. 'Until then, to make our feelings appear real, perhaps we should share a kiss now and then.'

Tarienne snorted softly.

'Aidan, you may be the most handsome and eligible bachelor in the kingdom, but you are more like a brother to me. I'm only doing this to save you from your father's matchmaking.' A tiny smile curled the sides of her mouth.

Aidan preened a little as he stood, a huge grin splitting his face.

'You think I'm handsome?'

She rolled her eyes, chuckling.

'That's *all* you heard from what I said?'

Like Eldan, Aidan stood around six feet tall, but unlike his father, he had a sunny, thoughtful disposition. It was his charisma, good looks, and the natural compassion he possessed that set the ladies' hearts aflutter.

However, Aidan took his responsibilities very seriously. He trained hard, building his strength and endurance to ensure his readiness when the battle for Therin finally erupted, as they all knew it eventually would. His focus was to be the best swordsman and future king he could, to defend the kingdom, to lead by example. He was actually quite shy and not conceited. Most of the time.

Again, just as when they'd met, Aidan's short, unruly blond hair, clear, blue eyes and angelic face reminded Tarienne of elven royalty. Combine that with a smile that would set any woman's heart racing, and Aidan was, indeed, extremely easy on the eye. She genuinely loved him... like a brother. He did not, however, stir her body as Daien did.

Daien's rich, deep voice reminded Tarienne of warm chocolate. His dark brown eyes, set in a ruggedly handsome face that often struggled to contain a grin, constantly twinkled with mischief. In contrast, his fighting skills were unmatched, his unusual style unhurried, almost relaxed.

Tarienne's reaction to Daien disconcerted her. When the king's guardsmen trained, the sight of Daien, shirtless, muscles rippling, took her breath away. However, to her chagrin, he generally treated her no differently than any other member of the royal household.

A sigh escaped her lips. Given her ruse with Aidan, she couldn't make him aware of her feelings. They had agreed not to reveal their deception to anyone, not even Daien. She forced her attention back to Aidan.

He watched her intently. A tiny frown of concern wrinkled his forehead.

'You know I appreciate what you're doing, right?'

He grasped the fingers of Tarienne's free hand, gently urging her up. She allowed him to lift her from the chair, placing her needlework on the arm with her other hand.

Aidan leaned in, kissing her lightly on the cheek.

'Will you come for a walk with me?'

His innocent expression caused a chuckle to bubble up within her. She acquiesced to his insistent tug on her hand as he walked toward the door.

'Where are we going?'

'Around the grounds to check on the festival preparations, then to the practice yard to speak with Orien about setting up the jousting tournament.'

Tarienne quickly brightened at the prospect of bumping into Daien. Their hands clasped, supporting the deception they were in love, Aidan and Tarienne walked through the palace and out into the courtyard. She revelled in the familiar feeling of Aidan's warm hand holding hers. It gave her comfort, a sense of caring not apparent in the usual austerity of royal life.

Arrangements for the week-long Spring Festival were well underway. The delicious aroma of food cooking in preparation for the festival reached Tarienne's nostrils. Her mouth began to water at the delectable scents of roasted meats and sugary treats wafting around her as they walked along the cobblestone streets.

Aidan stopped to chat briefly with the merchants bustling around their stands, all eager to talk to their prince. Tarienne watched, smiling at his genuine interest in each and every one. The people loved Aidan. Things would be so much different if he were king.

Be careful what you wish for.

Leaving the bustle of the courtyard behind, Aidan and Tarienne approached the practice yard, the unmistakable ring of clashing swords echoing around them. Tarienne's pulse escalated at the possibility of seeing Daien.

When they rounded the corner, she saw the king leaning casually on the rough, wooden rail separating the viewing stand from the training arena, observing the practice session. Seeing them, Eldan's eyes slid down to their joined hands. He beamed. Tarienne suppressed a sigh, shifting her attention to the arena.

Once Tarienne's attention landed on the two men training, she found it difficult to tear her eyes away. The dust rose from the sun-dried soil of the arena as the two men jumped and slid around. Their focus was solely on each other, waiting for their opponent's next move. Their blades viciously sharp, a deadly dance where one error of judgement could result in a severe injury.

Orien and Daien fought, unaware of their audience. Daien's shirtless torso glistened with perspiration. His sculpted muscles flexed and rippled as he blocked and parried Orien's blows.

Tarienne's heart clenched, her thundering pulse erratic. Gasping quietly, she fought the urge to lift a hand to her chest. She chewed on her bottom lip instead, trying to control her reaction.

Gods, what a gorgeous man.

Breathing deeply, she managed to reclaim some much-needed air.

Fortunately, the king did not see her reaction; otherwise, he would be swift to anger. Aidan, however, did notice, eyebrows lifted as his gaze followed hers. He grinned, knowing how she felt about Daien, having pried the information from her during one of their many deep and meaningful conversations.

Tarienne jabbed her elbow into his ribs, sending a glare his way.

Aidan let out a quiet 'oof', rubbing the spot. Yet his annoying smirk stayed in place.

Struggling to prevent her eyes from straying back to Daien, Tarienne swallowed hard. With significant effort, she forced her focus back to king Eldan.

Plastering a smile onto her face, she politely enquired, 'Sire, did you enjoy the hunt today?'

Eldan turned toward her, his deep brown, leather jerkin a stark contrast to the crisp white of the shirt tucked into his black, leather trousers.

His eyes lit up, his passion for hunting obvious.

'Yes, very much. We brought back a large stag for the feast tomorrow. The chase was exhilarating, the stag a worthy adversary.'

Glancing between them, he smirked.

'But it appears Aidan couldn't wait to get back to you. I'll leave you to enjoy each other's company.'

Frustration welled inside Tarienne. Why did she ever agree to this ruse?

Aidan lifted her hand to his lips, dropping a light kiss onto her knuckles. He gazed into her eyes and leaned closer, but once Eldan disappeared toward the inner citadel, Aidan sighed heavily and stepped back. Their hands still entwined, he hauled Tarienne down the steps to the practice yard.

*   *   *

Aidan

Aidan knew his father loved him, but also that he struggled with showing his emotions. A legacy of being the king, Aidan supposed. His father had done his best to raise him on his own after his mother's death when Aidan was a small boy. When he had children, Aidan hoped he would be a loving and patient father, as well as a good king.

He often found himself craving the sisterly affection Tarienne bestowed upon him. If he were being honest with himself, it was why he'd suggested they pretend to love each other in the first place. Now, though, he could see how selfish it was to expect her to continue with their ruse, given how Daien and Tarienne felt about each other.

He chuckled quietly at the irony that neither knew the other's feelings. He desperately hoped someone would look at him one day like Tarienne looked at Daien, and vice versa, as if he were the most special and desired person in the world.

Aidan led Tarienne to the edge of the practice yard, absently caressing the back of her hand with his thumb. Realising what he was doing, he stopped abruptly, giving her a sideways glance. Perhaps it was time to tell his father his feelings and let Tarienne have her chance with Daien.

Even though Daien hadn't confessed he had feelings for Tarienne, Aidan had seen his eyes smoulder with desire for her, albeit when she wasn't looking. Aidan assumed he kept his distance out of respect for their situation. Though Aidan had pried and prodded enough during their companionable chats, trying to get him to admit it. It was fortunate for him his friend didn't have a quick temper. He'd just evaded the questions by laughing and changing the topic.

As a guardsman, Aidan knew Daien felt he was unworthy of Tarienne. The king would feel the same, never allowing her to consort with a guard. Aidan decided he could at least give Daien and Tarienne a legitimate excuse to spend time together. Pleased, he grinned to himself.

*　　*　　*

Tarienne

Tarienne's eyes lowered as they approached the two guards, stealing brief glances at Daien as he and Orien spoke with the prince.

Daien's eyes flicked down to their clasped hands, and Tarienne had an undeniable urge to untangle her fingers from Aidan's. She fidgeted, wishing he would let her go. They had no need to continue their ruse now the king could not see them.

Tarienne's slight fidgeting drew Aidan's attention. He turned toward her and dropped her hand, as though reading her mind.

'I have quite a lot to discuss with Orien regarding the jousting match. Perhaps Daien can accompany you back to your chambers.'

Tarienne shot Aidan a surprised look, eyes wide.

Aidan grinned, turning back to Daien.

'You don't mind, do you, Daien?'

'Of course not, sire.'

His rich voice curled around Tarienne like an intimate caress. Daien slipped his soft, grey shirt over his head, allowing the wrinkled hem to hang loosely over his black training pants. Eyebrows raised in invitation, he offered Tarienne his arm.

Feeling warmth creep up her neck as she linked her arm with his, inadvertently brushing the heated skin of his side. She heard Aidan chuckle.

Tarienne narrowed her eyes at him, then glided away with Daien as gracefully as she could, hoping he couldn't feel her trembling or hear her heart thumping against her ribs.

Daien smelled musky and deliciously masculine. Tarienne thought she might faint from the onslaught of emotions swirling through her at the physical contact with the virile man at her side. Involuntarily, she swayed into him. Her body heated, chest tightening as she struggled to breathe.

Clearing her throat, she desperately hoped a conversation might settle the butterflies fluttering wildly in her stomach.

'Did you enjoy your training session, Daien?'

Her voice had a huskier quality than usual.

He turned his head toward her.

'It went well, milady. We are teaching each other special techniques, honing our abilities in the process. It helps us stay in top condition.'

Did he just focus on my lips?

His closeness and the timbre of his voice sent heat spiralling through her. Desire pooled low in her belly, and her nipples peaked against the soft material of her bodice.

Losing herself in the sensations coursing through her, she responded in the moment.

'Mmmm, I noticed.' At his raised brow, she cursed her boldness, horrified at her lack of control. Heat crept up her neck again.

'I... I noticed you all appear to be using each other's signature moves, though none appear to be able to execute yours quite as well as you.'

She forced a smile. Mortification filled her. Even more so when she saw a grin fleetingly play across Daien's lips. She looked away, trying to regain her composure and when she finally dared to look at him again, his expression held only polite interest.

All too soon, they reached the door to her chambers. Tarienne wanted to spend more time with him, enjoying his warmth as they walked. She suppressed a sigh when Daien untangled her arm and took her hand in his, his touch exquisitely gentle. Her heart thundered as his gaze held hers. Moving closer, a moment of indecision flitted across his face. Tarienne fervently hoped he was considering a kiss.

Holding onto her hand a little longer than entirely proper, Daien leaned in, close enough that his warm breath caressed her cheek. He whispered, 'Thank you, milady.'

Tarienne frowned and pulled back, brows furrowed in question. Daien smiled slightly. 'For noticing my... condition...'

Tarienne gasped. He *had* heard her.

Laughing heartily, Daien bowed and strode away.

A retort on her lips, held back by her forced sense of propriety, Tarienne huffed crossly, glaring at his disappearing form. Slowly, a smile curved the corners of her mouth as she entered her chambers, shaking her head and chuckling quietly to herself. She found it impossible to stay annoyed with him, especially when her body still hummed with the memory of his touch.

*   *   *

Daien

Daien hurried down the hallway, his pulse racing, trousers tighter than they were earlier. He was grateful his shirt was long enough to cover the bulge in the front of his pants. He'd barely stopped himself from tasting those full, soft lips. He groaned.

She's a lady, not some tavern wench, and under the king's care. A mere guard cannot consort with a lady of the court.

The problem was, each time he touched Tarienne, no matter how innocent, it became increasingly difficult to maintain any semblance of self-control.

Daien headed toward the stables. His black stallion nickered at his approach. Taking a moment to run his hands down the horse's muzzle, Daien hauled in a deep breath, then hefted the saddle onto the animal's broad back. He quickly tightened the leather straps around the horse's girth and leapt up. He needed to get out of the castle walls.

Once through the heavy castle gates, Daien urged the animal into a run, bending low over his steed's neck. They thundered across the open plain, toward the lake. Exhilaration pumped through his veins, his pulse racing. He finally slowed his destrier as they entered the edge of the forest. Although Daien knew the woods so well he could travel through them blindfolded, he did not want his mount injured tripping on a stray root or catching its hoof in a rabbit hole. The lake appeared to his right, glistening invitingly. It beckoned for him to dive beneath its smooth surface, cool his overheated body.

Barely waiting for the stallion to stop, Daien slid from its back. Loosely draping the reins around a sapling, he began stripping off his clothes as he walked. He left a trail of garments leading to the lake's edge and strode into the water, its biting chill easing the ache in his loins. Hauling in a deep breath, Daien dove beneath the surface, pulling his body through the inky depths. After several moments, he burst up into the warm sunshine once again, raking his fingers through his dripping hair. His feet touched the muddy bottom, the water lapping around his waist. If only the lake could cool the impassioned thoughts created by the mental image of Tarienne, naked, legs wrapped around him. Daien swore.

Ducking beneath the surface once again, he swam until he thought his lungs might burst. He'd been here before, with Aidan, training for the battle they knew was coming, but it was nothing like this.

He wondered if Tarienne liked swimming, and his body responded to the thought. He swore silently again and pulled himself through the water until his arms, chest and body ached.

When the sky began to darken, Daien dragged himself out of the water and dressed, not bothering to dry himself. Mounting his stallion, he headed back to Castle Therin, Tarienne's beautiful, silky red hair, compelling green eyes and body that would inflame any man, consuming his thoughts.

Unbidden, his body filled with a possessive fire he'd not previously experienced. Leaning low, he urged his horse into a run.

CHAPTER 3

The next morning heralded the beginning of the Spring Festival. Castle Therin was a bustling hive of activity, a riot of colour adorning every black and grey stone wall. The castle rose through the morning mist, like a silent sentinel. Small villages of a hundred or so families, each composed of merchants and tradesmen of all kinds, surrounded the fortress.

The castle afforded an almost impenetrable stronghold in times of war and could feed and house many refugees in need. It stood for protection, justice, and security. Today, entertainment and food of innumerable variety filled the brightly coloured stalls. People gathered on the cobblestone streets, chatting, and bargaining animatedly. Tarienne's attention drifted around as she and Aidan walked through the streets, dutifully greeting the villagers, tasting various foods, applauding the entertainers.

They turned into an adjoining street and her steps faltered; certain she'd seen one of the elven folk. She scanned the crowd, but the tall, slim man with long, blond hair had disappeared. Unsure if her mind was playing tricks, she returned her focus to Aidan.

Slipping her arm through his again, she smiled brightly when he turned to her, sending her a questioning look. She squeezed his arm lightly, and they continued through the streets.

Around lunchtime, Aidan excused himself to prepare for the jousting tournament. Tarienne seized the opportunity to stroll around the streets on her own. She enjoyed getting away from what she termed 'the stuffiness of royal life'. Poking around some stalls far from the main street, she bought a few small trinkets to take to Ferngrove on her next visit.

As she walked away, she felt the tingle of magic skitter across her skin. Her eyes snapped up, searching for the source. Unable to locate its origin, frustration welled within her. She decided to contact Raef after the tournament and let him know what she'd felt.

She stopped to chat briefly with villagers she'd met either when helping tend wounds or illnesses or when she'd heard they were in need and taken them food or supplies. At first, they'd been reserved around her, but over the three years she'd lived at Therin, they all now considered her their friend, greeting her cheerfully. It wasn't the same as being at Darewood or Ferngrove, but it helped to know they were pleased to see her.

Throughout the years, Tarienne had returned to Ferngrove as often as possible, partially because the people were so tactile and affectionate. She craved the gift of touch so sorely missing from life within the castle walls. The royal household was very austere. No one touched unnecessarily. The one exception was Aidan. He did show her some affection, holding her hand and occasionally giving her a quick hug... all for the benefit of his father. Yet those displays of fondness did not truly fulfil her primal need for contact.

Daien, on the other hand, was not like the others. She'd initially thought him indifferent, but she'd recently noticed he often ensured they surreptitiously touched in some way. She drew strength from him in a way that was difficult to explain. Warmth spread through Tarienne, and she wondered how it would feel to have his strong arms wrapped around her, his lips on hers. Would he be as passionate as she suspected?

Pulling in a deep breath, Tarienne attempted to settle her heated thoughts and turned to head back for the tournament.

'Milady, are you enjoying the festivities?'

The familiar voice sent a shiver of awareness skittering through her body. She turned to see Daien striding purposefully toward her, his smile making her heart drum against her ribs. His dark eyes swept over her appreciatively, sending tingles all the way to her toes.

Gods, he's gorgeous.

When Daien turned the full force of his devastating smile on her, Tarienne's knees threatened to buckle.

'Ye-Yes,' she stammered, then swallowed hard, struggling for coherent thought. 'I've managed to purchase a few gifts to take home to Ferngrove when next I visit.'

She held up the tiny carved black horse, which reminded her of Raef's first stallion, Noir, and the red and gold serrated leaf, which filled her with longing for autumn in Darewood, captured in a ball of clear resin. Daien grasped her hand between his to look at the horse. Tarienne drew in a sharp breath, feeling a flush heat her cheeks. If he could do this to her with only a touch, she just might pass out if he ever kissed her.

He spoke, shaking her from her reverie. 'It's beautifully carved. I'm certain your brother will appreciate it.'

He held onto her hand for a long moment, seeming reluctant to relinquish it. 'I'm heading back for the jousting tournament.' He offered his arm, his dark eyes holding hers. 'Would you care for an escort to the royal box?'

Is that desire in his eyes?

Tarienne's entire body heated, libidinous flames licking through her. Her heart thudded erratically. With all the grace and self-control she could muster, Tarienne smiled and nodded, not trusting her voice.

Loosely draping her arm through Daien's, they glided through the streets, chatting companionably, many envious eyes following. Tarienne almost sighed with the pleasure of his touch. The hard muscles of his arm bunching under her hand made her wonder how his sculpted chest would feel beneath her fingers. The direction of her thoughts once again unsettled Tarienne, and she had to consciously control her breathing, so Daien didn't notice her chest heaving.

He took his leave at the entrance to the royal box, kissing her hand lightly, maintaining eye contact for a long moment. Propriety demanded she lower her gaze, but the tenderness evident in Daien's eyes held her, sweeping her through a maelstrom of emotions.

Tarienne watched him turn and stride away, her heart continuing to thump erratically. The loss of his warmth and presence left her inexplicably bereft, at odds with the excitement coursing through her. At least now she knew Daien felt the connection between them, as well. That knowledge gave her comfort and filled her with hope.

Running her hands down her deep green, velvet dress, she took a few moments to compose herself, taking several deep breaths. Somewhat more in control, she stepped demurely into the royal viewing box, seating herself to the left of the king. Eldan nodded a greeting and signalled the start of the competition.

Folding her hands in her lap, Tarienne feigned interest in the tournament, her stomach swirling with concern each time a rider was felled. She considered jousting to be a barbaric sport. It upset her to see the less experienced competitors sometimes sustaining horrific injuries. Even the experienced ones, like Aidan and Daien, were occasionally seriously hurt. Nonetheless, Tarienne smiled and applauded enthusiastically when Aidan won his round, then again when Daien won his.

When Aidan and Daien faced each other in the final round, mounted on their stallions, armoured and ready, Tarienne squirmed nervously. Rubbing her arms against the goose bumps standing her hairs on end, she hardly dared watch as they thundered toward each other. The dirt scattered beneath the pounding hooves of their armoured mounts. The maroon and gold standard of Therin flapped against the horses' rumps like sheets in the wind.

The crowd quieted as they lifted the long, colourfully decorated, wooden lances. Nothing moved but the riders and their horses. The only sounds were the snorting of the huge stallions, the thundering of their hooves, the metallic clang of armour.

Tarienne closed her eyes, reaching for inner calm, then opened them moments before the prince's lance connected heavily with the armour protecting Daien's right shoulder, unseating him. A cheer rose from the crowd as he fell heavily to the ground, a deep dent in his armour. A small cry escaped her lips, and she almost leapt to her feet. To her, it looked as though Daien purposely lowered his weapon just before Aidan's lance slammed into him.

Why would he do that?

To his credit, Aidan reined his horse around, lifting his visor to check on Daien. Tarienne's heart thumped erratically as she waited for Daien to rise to his feet. His awkward, slow movements showed he was injured. A desperate need to know how seriously had her eyes locked on his every move, but she lost sight of him as the guardsmen crowded around Aidan to congratulate him on his win. The last glimpse she'd caught was of Daien being helped back in the direction of his tent.

Plastering a smile onto her face, Tarienne applauded as Aidan accepted the trophy from his father. The king's guardsmen quickly crowded around again to congratulate their prince. All Tarienne wanted was to ensure Daien was not gravely injured.

She slipped, unseen, from the royal box and through the crowd, something powerful she couldn't identify driving her toward Daien's tent. At the entrance, her determination wavered. She pulled in a deep breath to boost her confidence and calm her nerves.

'Daien?' she called softly.

Her heart thumped as she waited for a response.

'You may enter, milady.'

His voice rolled over her, spreading relief through her body as she stepped inside.

Wearing only black, leather trousers, his sculpted abdomen bare and glistening with perspiration, he stood in the centre of the tent, barefoot and unbelievably handsome. Tarienne couldn't drag her eyes from him.

Pulling in a shaky breath, she managed to speak. 'How badly were you injured?' She couldn't hide the edge of concern in her voice and didn't want to. She attempted to assess his injuries, focusing on the bandage tightly wrapped around his middle.

Broken ribs.

Moving toward him, she gently touched his shoulder, where a blue-black bruise had already started to develop. Tarienne heard him suck in a quick breath, then saw him wince slightly when her cool hand gently covered the bruise. She didn't pull her hand away, even though she knew she should. Her focus slid down to his toned stomach, a line of dark hair disappearing enticingly beneath the top of his leather trousers. Her desire ramped up. Swallowing, her eyes lifted back to his.

A brief moment of uncertainty played across Daien's face, then he gifted her with his gorgeous smile, stealing her breath.

The moment Tarienne entered the tent she sensed Daien's growing desire along with a measure of uncertainty. Without meaning to she entered his thoughts catching only a flash of a memory before she realised and snapped the connection shut.

One evening, when he and Aidan had partaken of too much mead, he'd discovered Tarienne and Aidan's love was not real. His friend had asked Daien not to tell Tarienne he knew of their secret.

Shaking his head a little his eyes briefly met hers before he stepped away and shrugged into a clean linen shirt to maintain propriety, though he left it unfastened. She knew he struggled to maintain his composure. When he held his breath and clutched his ribs in pain,

Tarienne moved closer, smiling when she heard him inhale and sigh quietly. His pulse skipped against her fingers as she laid them gently on his bruised shoulder. She watched as he forced himself to breathe, the sharp pain of his ribs probably the only thing keeping his thoughts focused.

Tenderly, he rested his fingers over hers.

'It's nothing a few days won't heal, milady.'

His low, husky voice and liquid brown eyes pulled her in like a whirlpool sucking her into its vortex.

She stepped closer. 'You lowered your lance.'

Daien didn't respond, lowering his head until his mouth stopped only a whisper from hers. His breathing quickened slightly, his warm breath fluttering across her cheek. Tarienne's tongue flicked out, dampening her lips.

'You should leave, milady.' His words floated to her on a deep, regretful sigh.

'Mmm... Yes, I should.' *Kiss me, Daien.*

His eyebrows lifted as a tiny grin tugged at his lips.

Did I say that out loud?

Already lost in Daien's eyes and his delicious, spicy, masculine scent, she couldn't move. He let out a small groan, dipping his head to brush his lips against hers. Her arms snaked around his neck, her body melted into his, but something suddenly prickled at the edges of her awareness.

Without warning, she straightened and jerked away from him, declaring in a loud and formal voice, 'Well done, Daien. You fought well. If you require any aid with your injuries, I would be pleased to assist.'

Tarienne wobbled as she stepped back. Daien instinctively reached out to steady her, then snatched his hand back when Aidan and his father walked into the tent.

She rushed, somewhat unsteadily, to Aidan, kissing him on the cheek with what she hoped looked like great enthusiasm.

'Well done, Aidan!'

Daien's eyes flicked to Tarienne, a small frown creasing his brow, before he quickly refocused on the royal visitors. Aidan hesitated, obviously perplexed by Tarienne's uncharacteristically affectionate reaction. Temptation to jab him in the ribs filled her, then a knowing grin curved his lips, and he pulled her firmly to his side.

'We came to congratulate you on competing in the final,' Aidan offered brightly.

'Well done,' the king added. 'I knew you could never best your prince, but well done.'

Aidan slid Tarienne a sideways glance, rolling his eyes.

Daien bowed his head slightly in acknowledgment.

'Thank you, sires. It was an enjoyable match.'

Turning to leave the tent with the king and Aidan, Tarienne risked a glance back at Daien. To her relief, he rewarded her with a wink and a smile. Her heart swelled, but she tempered the joyful grin tugging at her lips. What she really wanted was to blow Daien a kiss. Instead, she returned an almost imperceptible nod, exiting the tent on Aidan's arm.

He escorted her to her chambers, kissed her hand, then paced away in his father's company. Safely ensconced in her room, Tarienne touched her fingers to her lips, remembering Daien's kiss. She couldn't hold back a smile.

Then she sobered, remembering what she'd felt in the crowd, and pushed her thoughts out to Raef, grateful for his strength with mindspeak over great distances. She was certain seeing one of the elven kind in Therin and sensing the presence of magic was something her brother needed to know. If she were correct, it meant the balance of magic was in peril and the prophecy was in motion. A stab of fear gripped her.

CHAPTER 4

The days following the Spring Festival passed quickly, Tarienne accompanying Aidan to official events and aiding with the running of the castle. This meant she hadn't seen Daien since the jousting tournament, though memories of the brief kiss they'd shared hadn't been far from her thoughts. She missed the warmth and contentment his presence provided.

Deciding to check on how his shoulder and ribs were healing – in her official capacity, of course – Tarienne glided down the corridor, fervently hoping she'd find him alone. Her heart thumped in anticipation.

Lost in her thoughts, she almost bumped into Eldan and Aidan, who strode along the corridor, deep in discussion. They barely acknowledged her presence as they swept past, their brows furrowed. Tarienne frowned, catching a few, troubling words of their conversation.

Army... Siege... Battle... River Arnon...

Tarienne now had an excuse to find Daien, hoping to learn what transpired to evoke such a conversation. She eventually found him in the stables, checking his saddle. A familiar tingle spiralled through her body, every inch of her aware of his presence. Watching her approach, he rewarded her with a smile. His pure, virile masculinity sent heat spiralling through her. Tarienne's thoughts scattered momentarily, but she managed to yank back her focus.

'Daien.'

He bowed slightly. 'Milady.'

His formal tone ignited a spark of anger. Tarienne moved closer, glaring up at him.

'I do wish you would use my name.'

His molten gaze made her feel exposed, naked. A carnal shiver rippled through her body, chasing away any trace of anger. Her heart slammed against her ribs as Daien's eyes flared with desire.

Despite being taller than most females in Therin, Tarienne still needed to stand on tiptoes to come even close to looking Daien in the eye. The emotion she saw there turned her legs to jelly, making her sway slightly. His hands moved to her waist to steady her before he spoke her name, his voice deep and sensual.

'Tarienne.'

Tarienne sucked in a breath, the timbre of his voice causing shivers to skitter along her spine. She sensed a moment of indecision before he closed the gap, gently capturing her mouth.

A little sigh of pleasure escaped her as his warm, soft lips moved over hers. When his tongue traced the seam of her mouth, she couldn't deny him entry. Daien wrapped his arms around her, pulling her closer and deepening the kiss. All sensible thought fled as the evidence of his desire pressed into her belly.

Daien finally lifted his head, and Tarienne managed a breathless, 'Daien, we need to take care. The king believes—'

He placed his finger on her lips, silencing her. 'I am aware of what the king believes.'

He dragged in a ragged breath, not releasing his hold on her hips. 'Tarienne, you wished to ask something of me?'

Like an intimate caress, the rich, slightly husky timbre of his voice caused a damp warmth between her thighs. Several things she would like to ask skittered through her thoughts, making her blush. But she settled on the most pressing one at the moment.

'Y-Yes... Do you have any idea what the king and Aidan are planning?'

He nodded, still not releasing her. 'They are gathering the army of Therin. Lemere has demanded Therin surrender to him and name him king. It is as we've suspected for some time. We are ready.'

Daien waited for a response, caressing her hips with his thumbs.

'I'm coming with you.'

He blinked, pushing her back to hold her at arm's length, sighing.

'Tarienne... I've witnessed your fighting prowess, but this will be a full-scale battle. You'll be...' He hesitated, not wanting to offend her.

'I'll be what, Daien?' she asked, scowling. 'In the way? Frightened? I was raised to fight. My father and brothers trained me for—' She snapped her mouth shut.

'Tarienne, please...' He trailed his fingers down the side of her face.

She grasped his hand.

'This is something I must do, Daien.'

Releasing him, she glided away, blowing a kiss over her shoulder. Tarienne felt his eyes follow her, so she added a sensual sway to her retreat. Hearing him sigh, she stole a glance over her shoulder as he turned back to his saddle, seemingly deep in thought. When a page dashed up, startling him from his reverie his hand flew to his sword before the boy stammered out a message summoning him to the great hall.

Tarienne hurried along the long corridor deep in thought, wondering why Daien had been summoned so urgently. Hearing footsteps she looked up as Aidan strode toward her, his expression one of fury. Before she could ask what was wrong, he shoved her against the cold, hard wall.

'What are you doing?' he hissed between clenched teeth. 'My father is not far behind me.'

She looked at his angry face, confused, but had no time to respond before Aidan slammed one hand above her head, grasping her waist with his other and kissing her, hard. Too shocked to react, she registered a chuckle from the king as he passed.

Finally, clarity returned. Tarienne thumped her hands onto Aidan's chest and forced him to step back.

She swiped the back of her hand across her lips, wiping away the unwelcome intimacy. 'What do you think you're do—'

'What do you think *you* were doing?' Aidan growled. 'Do you think I'd let my father see you with swollen, red lips when I hadn't been near you all day?'

Tarienne's temper ignited, she slapped him.

'How *dare* you speak to me so when I do this for you.'

Aidan dragged his fingers through his hair, cursing softly.

Not waiting for his response, Tarienne stomped off after the king to inform him she would be going with them into the battle.

Tarienne's audience with the king did not go well. Aidan made no attempt to support her, glaring sulkily at her as she argued with Eldan. Finally, after a blazing row during which the king threatened to throw her into the dungeon, she swept out of the hall. Waiting in the corridor with the other guards, Daien sent her a look of concern and compassion as she stormed past. It was almost her undoing.

Stomping into her chambers, Tarienne slammed the door so hard, the hinges protested. Tears threatened. Her throat burned and head ached. How could she keep Aidan safe if she wasn't with him? Frustration spiralled through her as she yanked her shoes off and threw them aside. She angrily stomped one foot onto the hard, wooden floor, hating she was forced to hide her true nature. She was not a silly, useless female who wouldn't know one end of a sword from another. She'd fought in battle with her brothers and possessed magic more powerful than

Eldan and Aidan could conceive. Cursing colourfully in fae, she clomped to the window.

Tarienne watched a few of the king's guardsmen and a small contingent of the gathering army prepare for the impending journey and the battle to follow.

A knock on the door made Tarienne jump. Her response was waspish. 'Enter.'

The king and Aidan moved stiffly into her chambers. Their serious expressions told her they had not reconsidered their decision. Tarienne said nothing, curtsying formally. She couldn't stop herself from raking them both with a peevish glare.

'Tarienne,' Eldan began, his tone annoyingly condescending, 'we understand you feel the need to be with Aidan, but this battle will be bloody and brutal. It is no place for a woman. Aidan will be safer if he doesn't have to worry about you.'

Her indignation rising, she desperately wanted to tell them who she was and of what she was capable. Tarienne pressed her lips together, swallowing her tart response.

Eldan continued. 'We need you here to keep everything running smoothly until our return. Can you accept this and look after things while we're away? It is a huge responsibility and an honour we bestow upon you.'

Far from mollified, Tarienne was insulted by the king's demeaning tone. One glance at Aidan's sad and remorseful face, however, took the edge off her anger. Turning to Eldan, a battle raged in her mind. He wore a look of steely determination, a contradiction to his gentle words. Tarienne decided to acquiesce. She knew better than to push him too far, especially after their earlier argument. After all, he was the king of Therin.

Tarienne lowered her eyes in a show of deference she did not truly feel.

'Yes, sire. I can.'

'Good. I'll leave you two to talk.'

She glared at the king's disappearing form.

Aidan reached out, gently capturing her hand, and lifting it to his lips. His expression held gratitude that she'd backed down from another argument with his father.

'I'm so sorry, Tarienne. I can see you care deeply for Daien. When we return from this battle, I'll tell Father the truth. I promise. Forgive me?'

He looked so wretched, Tarienne couldn't resist wrapping her arms around his waist.

'Of course, I forgive you. I'll be more careful, and... and I'm sorry I slapped you.'

Squeezing Aidan firmly, she pulled back, dropping a tiny kiss on his still red cheek. Guilt assailed her. Reciting a healing spell through her thoughts, she placed her fingers gently over the mark on his cheek, diminishing the redness to little more than a tinge.

Aidan held her waist.

'We're leaving at daybreak, so we'll talk more when I return. All right?'

He placed a quick kiss on her cheek, then spun and headed for the door.

'Stay safe, Aidan. Please.'

He turned back to her, his expression softening. He nodded, smiling reassuringly, then closed the door behind him. Tarienne sadly watched him leave, her heart heavy with dread.

I can't protect you when you're so far away, Aidan. Stay safe.

Sighing, she picked up her needlework, throwing it down again almost immediately. Unable to concentrate, she walked to the window, watching the soldiers prepare. A knock on the heavy wooden door interrupted her thoughts.

Padding to the door on bare feet, Tarienne opened it to find Daien, wearing the same concerned look he had after her argument with King Eldan.

'I'm sorry if I disturbed you, but I needed to see if you were all right.'

His deep voice and the worry in his eyes shattered the control she'd clung to. She grabbed his arm and pulled him into the room, closed the door and swept her arms around his neck.

Burying her face in Daien's shoulder, Tarienne couldn't hold back the tears any longer. The maelstrom of emotions, which had built through the day, spilled out. Daien hesitated for a split second, before his strong, warm arms snaked around her. He stroked her hair, holding her close, until the sobs subsided.

Tarienne took a deep breath, intensely aware of his very enticing, masculine scent. Her heart thumped as she lifted her face. Daien cupped her cheeks, using his thumbs to tenderly wipe away the remaining tears. Gazing into her eyes, his glistened with such intense emotion her breath caught in her throat.

Tarienne reached up, pressing her lips to his. Passion ignited within her, and she poured every ounce of it into the kiss. A low growl rumbled deep in Daien's chest. The evidence of his desire pressed against her. His hands made an agonisingly slow journey down Tarienne's back, finally cupping her buttocks and pulling her firmly against him.

Daien groaned. 'Ah, sweetheart.'

Tarienne smiled against his lips. He nibbled gently at first, then deepened the kiss, sending heat swirling through her body. Daien lifted her off the floor, embracing her firmly. Tarienne tightened her arms around his neck, her full, round breasts straining against the soft material of her low-cut dress.

*　*　*

Daien

His pulse raced. His body hummed with need.

Lifting his head, he gazed into Tarienne's expressive, deep green eyes, still watery from her tears. Her ethereal beauty took his breath away. For so long, he'd wanted to touch her, kiss her. He'd believed her to be out of reach, but now here he was, Tarienne in his arms. He lowered her feet to the floor, tightening his arms around her.

Daien brushed a stray strand of hair away from Tarienne's face and bent to kiss the side of her mouth, nibbling his way down her neck, his heart clenching with emotion.

'You are so beautiful.' His hand slid slowly from her waist to the underside of her breast.

Daien's groin tightened further when she wriggled wantonly against him and arched into his touch. He nibbled her ear, focusing on the tiny moans slipping from her full, moist lips. His body hummed with desire, but he refused to rush. He wanted to savour the moment, to pleasure her as she deserved. When his thumb brushed over her breast, he smothered her cry with a kiss.

Even though he didn't think it possible, her sweet, vanilla taste made his body harden more, her tongue duelling with his. Daien burned with the pleasure of her response to him. It took all his resolve to hold on to the thin shred of self-control.

This is no tavern wench. This woman is special.

A moment of shock sliced through him as he wondered where the thought had come from.

Daien lifted his head, smiling, then moved back to her mouth to kiss her senseless.

She trailed her hands over his body, causing him to draw in a sharp breath when she slipped her fingers under his shirt. He revelled in the sweet passion of her kisses.

Stilling he pulled back a little as Tarienne let out a half-suppressed sob.

'Sweetheart...'

She met his eyes and gave him a little sad smile.

'I must go.'

Raking his hands through his hair, he exhaled loudly, his heart filled with regret.

Letting out a deep sigh, Tarienne pulled back. 'I know. Before you go, though, I wanted to ask you something. When I found you in the stables and told you I was going with you to battle Lemere, you said you'd witnessed my fighting prowess.' She cocked her head. 'How could that be when you've never seen me fight?'

Daien hesitated briefly, then dragged in a breath, smiling.

'I've watched you practice with both your twin knives and short sword when you thought no one was around.'

Tarienne held his gaze. 'Why?'

Daien looked down at the floor, then lifted his eyes to meet hers.

'The first time was an accident. I was walking through the garden and saw you in the forest.' He shook his head. 'I couldn't take my eyes off you, Tarienne. You were so graceful, so beautiful, yet so obviously deadly... I returned to the spot often, hoping you'd be there.'

Tarienne smiled, then flung her arms around his neck and kissed him... a long, deep, soul-searing kiss.

When she finally pulled back, Tarienne looked deep into his eyes, making his heart thud.

'Come back to me, Daien. Please.'

'I will, sweetheart.'

He leaned down, capturing her lips again, a kiss filled with passion and promise that had them both gasping for breath as he pulled back.

Daien walked to the door, turned back, and blew her a last kiss, watching for a moment as Tarienne flopped back onto the bed, her fingers drifting to her lips.

Daien turned and strode down the corridor, unable to contain a grin. He could barely believe Tarienne had been so bold as to drag him into her chambers and kiss him. It was just as well he had to leave, because if he'd stayed any longer, he wasn't sure he could have stopped himself from ravishing her. Her delicious curves pressed against him, the way her breasts heaved in the low-cut dress, had his control hanging by the barest of threads.

Since the first time he'd woken to see her tending to his wound three years ago, Daien had wondered what it would be like to kiss her, have her under him in the throes of passion. His body hardened again at the thought of making love to her. With Tarienne, it would not just be a quick tumble. He wanted her so much, it unsettled him.

Propriety dictated he couldn't take this any further, that he should walk away. But for the first time in his life, he realised he didn't *want* to walk away. Tarienne was different than anyone he'd ever known, and he wanted – no, *needed* – to learn more about her, to wake with her in the morning.

Daien stopped midstride, stunned at the direction his thoughts had taken, a slow smile spreading across his lips.

Stay all night? Hmmm...

He strode into the guardsmen's sleeping quarters, his grin wide. After packing what he would need for the impending journey he lay on his pallet, his hands behind his head. Lustful thoughts of Tarienne refused to let him sleep until the wee hours of the morning.

*   *   *

Tarienne

Tarienne woke early to the clatter of hooves on the cobblestones in the courtyard below. Leaping out of bed and running to the window, she scanned the crowd of men and horses, her heart thumping wildly. Finally, she spotted Aidan, knowing Daien would be close. Locating him at the head of the column, clad in chainmail and a long, deep red cape bearing the royal crest, her pulse escalated.

As if sensing her watching, he turned in the saddle, eyes seeking the window where she stood. A smile curved his lips. A deep sense of happiness welled up within Tarienne. She brought her fingers to her lips and blew him a kiss. Daien nodded almost imperceptibly, extending his gloved hand a little, as if catching the kiss, and held it over his heart.

Tarienne felt a tingle start in her toes and spread upward, flooding her entire body with a torrent of emotion. *I love him.* Her heart swelled, then immediately clenched with worry.

Daien turned away, urging his black stallion through the gates. Hooves clattered and armour clanged for what seemed like hours, until the last soldier had left the walls of Therin. An eerie silence settled over the courtyard.

'Keep safe, my Daien. Keep safe,' Tarienne whispered.

*　　*　　*

Daien

Daien's horse cantered away from the castle, close to five hundred soldiers trailing behind him. Hearing what sounded like Tarienne's voice whispering on the wind, Daien smiled at the mental image of her warm, soft body pressed against him last night. It was a memory that would keep him warm on this long, cold journey... along with thoughts of her in his arms upon their return. His body tightened with need and his heart thumped erratically.

Reluctantly pushing all thoughts of Tarienne aside, he focused on Aidan, his destrier cantering up ahead. Daien mentally prepared for the impending battle. A battle that would forever change the kingdom of Therin.

CHAPTER 5

Tarienne called out, her heart pounding as she searched the battlefield for Aidan and Daien, unable to find them in the aftermath of the bloody conflict. Her stomach churned at the sight of broken and bleeding bodies strewn across the battlefield. The river ran red. Tears flowed down her cheeks for the soldiers she knew, their limp, lifeless bodies crumpled on the muddy ground. Was anyone left alive?

She spotted Daien's lifeless body, his battle garb slick with blood, his brown eyes open, yet empty of their usual warmth and laughter. She cried out, rushing to him, stepping over the corpses, almost slipping in the slimy mixture of blood and mud. The stench of death threatened to overwhelm her as she sank to her knees at Daien's side. Her body racked with sobs, she grasped his now ice-cold hand, then flung herself over his chest.

'No! No! No!' she screamed, unable to stop.

Tarienne woke in a cold sweat, sitting bolt upright, her heart pounding. She fought to retain the contents of her stomach, her breath coming in short gasps. It took her a few moments to realise it had been a nightmare.

She shivered and took a deep breath, the first shafts of sunlight peeking around the edges of the heavy curtains that covered the thick, glass windows doing little to warm the room. Wrapping her arms around herself, she shook her head to dispel the disturbing images. A tear escaped, trickling down her cheek. It felt too real.

It had been two weeks since the king and Prince Aidan had marshalled the army of Therin and thundered through the gates to battle the bloodthirsty warlord, Lemere. Why hadn't she heard any news yet? Time should have passed quickly, considering she'd been tasked with the day-to-day running of the castle. She all but collapsed into bed each night, exhausted from meeting with the villagers to hear their grievances, managing the servants, visiting the sick and checking on food stocks. However, sleep still did not come easily. She couldn't dispel the feeling something was wrong.

Gods, let them be safe.

Unable to sleep, Tarienne dressed, stomped into the corridor and down to the great hall. Her eyes swept around the room. She couldn't suppress a shiver at the cold emptiness without the presence of Aidan and his guards.

The staff busied themselves thumping the huge tapestries hanging on the walls with thick, wooden bats to dislodge the dust clinging to them. Tapestries that told stories of the kings of old and their final battles. Tapestries that had hung on these same stone walls for hundreds of years, through many generations of Therin royalty.

A movement outside the window facing the courtyard captured her attention. A lone rider thundered across the cobblestones and reined his horse hard, the animal skidding to a halt. The steed's heavy breaths blew white clouds into the cold, winter air. The rider leapt down, sprinting up the wide, stone stairs to the castle's inner sanctum. The maroon and gold cape flowing behind him told Tarienne he was one of the king's guardsmen.

Please, no...

Tarienne's breath hitched, and heart thumped as she turned,

waiting to receive the news he brought. She barely stopped herself from rushing out to meet him. She heard his footsteps hurtling through the corridors before he finally burst into the great hall.

Immediately recognising him, Tarienne rushed forward. She gasped at the grim expression on his face. Fear gripped her.

'Orien, what's wrong? What has happened?'

Don't let it be Aidan or Daien.

Several long moments passed as Orien tried to catch his breath, bent over, hands on his knees. His face creased with worry, he panted, 'The king has been... gravely injured. Prince Aidan has asked... for yourself and the healer, Garneth... to return with me. Time is... of the essence.'

'Dear gods, I knew I should have gone with them. Is Aidan injured?' Her heart thundered, pounding in her ears. She wrung her hands, her brow furrowed, and tears pricked the backs of her eyes.

'No,' he managed, still struggling for air.

Tarienne's hand drifted to his back, rubbing small circles, offering comfort, allowing an imperceptible trickle of healing essence to flow through her fingertips to ease his distress.

'Thank you, dear friend. Have some food and rest a while as we prepare to leave.'

She flew into organisation mode, calling orders to the staff. Her mind raced, considering all the necessary preparations. All the while, her fear for those she loved grew, threatening to overwhelm her capacity for rational thought.

Summoning one of the servants, she asked him to find Garneth and have him prepare to leave. Passing the kitchen on her way upstairs, she stopped to ask the cook to prepare something for Orien, plus some provisions for the journey.

Lifting the hem of her pale blue dress off the floor a little so it did not trip her as she hastened up the winding staircase, her thoughts tumbled over possible scenarios. Her heart ached for Aidan, and she desperately wanted news of Daien.

Tarienne quickly changed into her riding clothes, her hands shaking so much, she fumbled with the clasps of her soft, rust-coloured shirt. She hastily yanked several changes of clothes out of her wardrobe, grabbing her satchel of healing herbs at the same time. Dragging in a few deep breaths to calm herself, she stuffed the clothes into a soft, leather travel pack and slung it over her shoulder. At the last minute, she retrieved her dagger and slid it into the top of her boot, within easy reach should she need it.

Her thoughts returned to Orien's words. If Eldan's injuries were as grave as he had reported, the only thing likely to help him would be magic. Yet the king would never willingly accept that kind of help. If he discovered her gift, she would be banished... at the very least.

If he lived.

She may not always agree with the way he ruled, but overall, Eldan had been kind to her. She certainly did not wish him harm, and his death would devastate Aidan. This was something she had to do, no matter the cost.

While she gathered what she needed for the journey, she used her fae magic to contact Raef at Ferngrove. His deep, calm voice slid into her consciousness, soothing her. Momentarily, she wondered if he'd done it intentionally, or if just being in contact with him was enough, as it had been when they were children.

Explaining the situation, she was unable to keep her worry from tumbling through her thoughts. He counselled Tarienne, telling her to contact him again when she knew the full extent of King Eldan's injuries. Raef would then project his magical strength through their sibling bond, adding it to her abilities, in an attempt to heal the king's wounds.

His presence faded. Tarienne fervently wished their sister, Arivaelle, wasn't so far away. Arivaelle possessed the strongest magical healing abilities anyone had encountered over the last few centuries.

Gods, I miss you, Rivi.

Their home at Darewood was, unfortunately, too far away to reach Arivaelle through mindspeak. Tarienne would have to work with what she had. Combined, Raef's and her own abilities were powerful, but would they be enough? She considered how she might use her power on the king without anyone's knowledge.

Hands shaking, she pushed her worry aside, focusing on the task at hand. There would be time enough during the journey to think on how best to use her magic undetected.

Several hours later, Orien was fed and rested, their horses were saddled, and their supplies were strapped on. Orien, Tarienne and Garneth mounted their steeds and thundered through the castle gates. Small, white clouds puffed from the horses' nostrils in the chilly air, their hooves crushing the grass as they carried their riders on a mission to save Eldan, king of Therin.

Tarienne desperately wanted to ask if Daien had been injured, but instead inquired, voice raised over the drum of the hooves,

'How bad was it, Orien? What happened?'

He shook his head. 'We rode into a trap. Without Prince Aidan, we'd all be dead. They had a sorcerer with them, who struck without warning. I've never seen anything like it. I'd say about one-third are dead or injured...' He sighed. 'We lost three king's guardsmen.'

Tarienne yanked on Lacey's reins, almost causing her mare to rear in fright as she skidded to a stop. Orien and Garneth quickly reined their horses, turning them to face her. 'Three?!' She clapped a hand over her mouth, in shock. Not sure she genuinely wanted to know, she lowered her hand, her voice quivering, 'W-Who?' Her chest constricted, waiting.

Orien walked his mount over to her. When he responded, his voice was so low and despondent, she could see he was struggling to control his emotions.

'Enidar, Janek and Rouan.'

'Gods, no...'

She knew them all well. Her body shook with the effort of holding back tears for the loss of three brave men she considered friends. Tarienne bit back a sob.

Enidar was a big, friendly man, a formidable enemy, and fiercely loyal. Janek was smaller and wiry, always smiling, the best hand-to-hand fighter she'd ever seen, other than Daien. And Rouan had just married his sweetheart. They were expecting their first child. He had talked to Tarienne endlessly about his dreams for their life.

Her heart clenched at the thought of never seeing them again. Despite her best efforts, a tear escaped and rolled down her cheek. She swiped it away. There would be time enough for mourning later. She needed to concentrate on reaching those still alive.

They pushed the horses and themselves long into the evening, eventually stopping to rest. Tarienne harboured deep concern for Orien. He'd travelled hard and fast to reach Therin, and now they raced back in a bid to save Eldan's life. Despite Orien being a hardened warrior, Tarienne had convinced him they should stop for a few hours so he could rest, then press on to reach the encampment at first light.

Her back against a tree, Tarienne drifted into a fitful sleep, her dreams haunted with visions of a bloody battle and the deaths of so many, their once bright, laughing eyes now empty and lifeless.

Several hours later, Orien woke them. Tarienne wondered at his stamina, tiredness hampering her own thoughts and movements. Gathering her belongings, she prepared to leave, looking over at Garneth.

He rose stiffly and shuffled toward his horse, pulling his coat tightly around himself. They would never hear him complain, but Tarienne sensed his struggle, his age working against him in the bitter chill of the early morning.

Wrapping her woollen shawl around her shoulders, Tarienne moved to be beside Garneth. Placing her hand lightly on his arm, she sent a gentle stream of healing magic into him, chatting to distract him from her ministrations. When he straightened a little and sighed, she withdrew, smiling.

After Garneth mounted his steed, she lifted his heavy, leather medical bag across the saddle and patted his hand, seizing the opportunity to impart one last pulse of magic into his body.

Tarienne's thick, green, woollen shawl helped ward off the cold but did nothing to dispel the shivers of fear racking her body. Fear of what they'd find when they reached camp.

They set off, sleepy, dirty, and hungry, having decided they needed to reach the king more than they needed to eat.

Tarienne was glad for the warmth of the animal beneath her, though with the biting wind whipping around her, her upper body suddenly felt like ice. Garneth bent over his mount, trying to prevent the worst of the wind from chilling his body. When icy rain began to fall, Tarienne gathered her cloak closer and tightened the strings of her hood. They must make haste before the king's condition worsened... or the bitter weather claimed one of them.

Thankfully, the rain didn't last long, the clouds quickly parting. The fresh, pure scent of the forest reached Tarienne's nostrils as they galloped through its leafy cover. Many varieties of trees in multiple hues of green hugged the well-worn track. The rising sun revealed a multitude of fragrant flowers, the last before winter, adorning the bases of the trees and spilling over the edges of the trail. She drew in a deep breath, smelling lemon balm, lavender... and grass, which was crushed under the pounding hooves of their horses. Birds sang their sweet melodies, and small animals skittered out of the way, lest they be trampled. Tarienne allowed the calming scents and sounds to soothe her frayed nerves.

After many hours of hard riding, the smell of damp, rich soil reached her, heralding the distant echo of the falls feeding the River Arnon. Despite the urgency of their journey, a tiny smile curved her lips at the mingling fragrances of the forest and the river. Images of her childhood in the beautiful forest of Darewood, where she'd played happily with her siblings, crept into her thoughts.

The unmistakable sounds of the army of Therin – clanging of

steel, stomping, and snorting of horses, murmur of men going about their business – pulled her back to the present. When they entered the campsite, a wave of misery struck Tarienne like a physical blow to the chest. Dragging in a long breath, she slowed Lacey and peered around, trying to identify the origin of the despair festering amongst the men.

A few of the soldiers tended those with minor injuries, some busied themselves feeding and grooming the horses, others cleaned their weapons despondently. Death hung over them, their movements sluggish, without real focus. They seemed – she struggled to categorise the feelings radiating from them – directionless, without hope. Tarienne fought the misery, its groping fingers threatening to pull her down into the murky depths of despair.

Could magic be at work here? She didn't have time to ponder the thought.

The main tent loomed into sight and the melancholy intensified. Tarienne dismounted, asking a passing soldier to take care of her mare. The man appeared startled by her presence, as though he hadn't noticed the group's arrival. His eyebrows raised in surprise when he recognised her, and he managed a tiny smile that didn't reach his eyes. Tarienne patted Lacey affectionately, scratched behind her ears for a brief moment and whispered her thanks, as was her custom after any ride.

She turned toward the king's tent, Garneth close behind. Her heart heavy with dread, Tarienne could barely form a clear thought. She moved the tent flaps aside, and her breath caught in her throat.

Tarienne fisted her hands at her side to force herself to appear outwardly calm, while her heart thumped, and chest tightened. Fear ripped through her as she assessed the king. Blood covered his body. Barely an inch of clothing or skin remained unstained by his deep red, viscous lifeblood. *Gods...* She didn't know where to start to heal him.

Pulling in a deep breath, her eyes slid to Aidan crouching at the head of his father's makeshift bed. He was so quiet she hadn't even realised he was there. His face ashen, Aidan appeared not to have slept or eaten for days. Tears welled in her eyes. Never before had she seen him so distraught, so vulnerable. It broke her heart.

Reaching into her pack, she took out a cloth and her waterskin, then bent, wiping the blood off Eldan's face as best she could. His breathing was shallow and uneven, his chest barely rising and falling. Forcing herself to focus, she withdrew the knife from her boot, cutting his clothes away. Though she doubted he was aware of anything, she quietly apologised to him as she bared his upper body, explaining it was necessary to allow her to tend his wounds properly.

She gasped at a deep, gaping wound in his side, yellow fluid trickling from an arrow wound in his shoulder and dark blood oozing from a viciously deep cut in his thigh, probably inflicted by an axe. Tarienne shuddered involuntarily.

Rising unsteadily, she left Garneth to assess Eldan's wounds. She pulled in every speck of control and calm she had and crouched beside Aidan, wrapping her arm around his shoulders. He turned to her; his eyes hollow, dark, despondent. Anguish washed over her when his shoulders shook with the sorrow consuming him.

She barely managed to hold herself together when he stood, pulling her up with him. His arms snaked around her in a crushing embrace. One born of desperation. The proud, self-assured prince broken. Aidan buried his face in her shoulder. Feeling the dampness of his quiet tears, she held him tightly.

Eventually pulling back, she brushed the mud-caked tendrils of hair from his face. 'Aidan, listen to me.' Tarienne's quiet words were laced with compassion yet commanding. 'I know this is terribly difficult, but you need to clean yourself up and eat something. Show your people they still have someone to lead them. Garneth and I will tend to your father.'

Aidan glanced at him, reluctant to leave. Tarienne grabbed his cheeks gently, bringing his attention back to her.

'I love you, Aidan. You are like a brother to me. You need to do this… for your father. I promise. I'll come get you if anything changes.'

He stared blankly at her for a long moment, then turned, shuffling disconsolately from the tent. Tarienne poked her head through the tent flap, calling to Orien, who leaned against a tree, talking to a soldier she didn't recognise. Turning to her, he quickly strode over.

'Would you make sure he cleans himself up and eats something, please?'

Orien nodded, trailing after Aidan.

Tarienne turned back to Garneth. Meeting her eyes, he shook his head. His expression betrayed his distress.

'Thank you, Garneth. Could you leave us, please? You may be able to help others.'

Bowing slightly, Garneth left to seek out the many injured they'd noticed on pallets as they rode in.

Tarienne contacted her brother as the tent flap closed behind him. *It's bad, Raef. I'm not sure we can help him.*

She carefully lifted Eldan's eyelids. He was unconscious, the skin surrounding his eyes sallow. Mustering all her courage, determined not to let panic overwhelm her, Tarienne knelt beside him, gently placing her hands over the wound in his side.

She breathed deeply and began silently chanting the healing spell. The warm tingle of Raef's magic infused her, strengthening the spell and filling her with a gentle, determined calm.

Moving down, Tarienne's hands hovered over Eldan's ravaged thigh, beginning the spell anew.

Through her focus, Raef's voice pushed insistently at her thoughts. Forcing her attention back on her brother, his words told her what she already knew but didn't want to hear.

Sweetling, his injuries are too severe. The king is dying.

No, Raef. I must help him. I have to do this for Aidan.

Panic almost overwhelmed rational thought. She couldn't let Aidan down.

'Ren... His wounds are too deep and the blood loss too great. Anything we do won't make any difference. Deep down, you know that.'

Raef's voice was gentle, the use of her nickname softening his words.

Compassion flowed through their connection. A small sob escaped her lips, but she gritted her teeth, pulling herself together for Aidan's sake.

'Thank you for trying, Raef.'

'Be strong, sweetling. I love you.'

'And I you, dear heart.'

When their connection dissolved away, sorrow tugged at her. Her throat ached with the effort of holding back tears, her breathing becoming fast and shallow.

Pulling at the tattered edges of her control, Tarienne realised what must be done. She made an herbal tea to ease Eldan's pain, then softly chanted a spell to help bring him to consciousness.

Exiting the tent, she found Garneth nearby, tending a wound on a soldier's hand, and asked him to tend to the king. 'If he wakes, please give him some of the herbal tea cooling beside the bed,' she instructed. 'I need to find Prince Aidan.'

Garneth nodded, entering the tent.

Tarienne found Aidan bathed, and gripping a small mug of broth. Her heart clenched at the sight of him sitting dejectedly with his back against a tree, his elbows resting on his knees, eyes downcast. Daien and Orien stood watchfully nearby.

Tarienne felt guilty at the relief flooding her when she saw Daien. She barely managed to stop herself from running into his arms. His gaze met hers, and his lips curved into a small, reassuring smile. Even he appeared fatigued, dispirited.

Tarienne returned her attention to the prince. 'Aidan, you need to come with me.' Curling her fingers around his hand, she gently urged him up. Aidan's eyes sought hers. The hollow sadness she saw made her heart ache. His chest heaved in a deep, sorrowful sigh, as if he already knew the answer to the question he was going to ask.

'Were you able to help him?'

*   *   *

Aidan

The grief in Tarienne's eyes told him the answer. Aidan swallowed hard, fighting back the urge to cry out in desolation. Holding onto Tarienne's hand as if it were a lifeline, he allowed her to lead him toward the tent where his father lay. Denial consumed him. This could not be happening. Aidan struggled to understand how quickly everything had changed in only a few days.

Chest tight, heart aching, he could not form a rational thought. If his father died, how would he be king? His father had always been at his side. They didn't always agree, but they'd always talked things through. How could he do this without him? He swallowed a sob. He didn't feel like a king. Instead, he felt like a small boy, alone and afraid, surrounded by people who would look to him for direction.

I can't do this.

Tarienne led him into the tent. Aidan instantly recognised the odour of death pervading the air. Legs shaking, he knelt beside his father as grief tugged at him.

Eldan opened his eyes. 'Aidan,' he whispered weakly and grabbed Aidan's hand, holding it tightly. 'My son...' He coughed. Specks of blood stained his spittle.

Aidan looked up at Tarienne, pleading. She leaned down to wipe Eldan's face with a damp cloth. Shaking her head almost imperceptibly, Tarienne lowered her eyes, tears dampening her cheeks.

Aidan turned back to Eldan. 'Father, I—'

'Shh, Aidan. I need to tell you some things before I die.'

He opened his mouth to protest, but his father continued.

'Aidan, I am very proud of you, of who you are and who you will become. Please, do not forget that. I've never been very good at expressing my feelings, but I need to tell you… I love you, my son. You will be an excellent king.'

Aidan rubbed his sleeve across his damp face. Only a few days ago, this fragile, broken man in front of him was a proud and formidable warrior. Aidan had seen men die before. He had experienced sadness and compassion for them and their loved ones, but nothing could have prepared him for this. For the loss of his mentor, his father, his king.

Aidan choked back a sob of despair. 'I can't do this without you. I need you. I love you, Father.'

'Yes, Aidan, you can, and you will. You are strong, and the people need you.'

Eldan's entire body shook with a deep, hacking cough. His face contorted with pain and the effort of remaining conscious. His eyes sluggishly lifted to meet Tarienne's.

'Promise me you'll look after him. Help him be the king he can be. The king he needs to be.'

Tarienne's voice was barely a whisper through her sorrow.

'I promise.'

Turning to Aidan, her voice wavering, she asked, 'Shall I leave?'

Aidan nodded, unable to speak. Tarienne held his gaze for a moment, the unspoken support and love flowing between them. Aidan could not express how grateful he was for her presence. He had no idea how he was going to get through this, but he knew Tarienne would be there for him.

His chest ached with the intensity of the emotions swirling through him. It was difficult to form a clear thought. He reached out and hugged his father for the last time.

*   *   *

Tarienne

Tarienne walked out of the tent, deep sadness threatening to overwhelm her. Once she stepped between the flaps, her knees buckled, unable to hold her emotion back any longer. Daien rushed to her side. His strong arms snaked around her, arresting her fall, and pulling her close. She leaned into him, violent sobs racking her body. His arms tightened around her, cradling her against his warmth, as he stroked her hair, muttering soft words of comfort.

Finally gaining control of her emotions, she leaned back slightly, looking up into Daien's eyes. He scanned her face, worry swirling across his. The maelstrom of emotions rushing through her body set her shaking involuntarily. She shivered, the spectre of death chilling her. Leaning his forehead against hers, he rubbed his hands up and down her arms.

Aidan emerged from the tent and whispered, 'He's gone.'

Tarienne stepped away from Daien to comfort Aidan, suppressing a sob as she held him. They stood quietly for a long time, Aidan's face buried in her hair, his shoulders shaking with grief. Daien and Orien waited silently, heads bowed.

Finally, Aidan stirred and spoke, his voice flat, devoid of any emotion. 'I need to tell my people.'

Tarienne knew his heart was broken, but duty called. Aidan was now king. He must show strength and leadership, no matter the circumstances. Tarienne did not envy him at that moment.

He took a deep breath and strode away to gather the rest of the army of Therin to inform them of the king's passing. Daien moved beside Tarienne, wrapping an arm around her waist. She leaned into him, absorbing his strength and compassion, unable to voice how much the contact and his unspoken support meant to her.

She ignored the tears sliding down her face, wetting his sleeve. Daien turned her to him, tenderly wiping away the moisture with his thumb. She'd never needed anyone's support as much as she needed his right now.

Wrapped in his warmth, they made their way to where Aidan had gathered the army. The soldiers quieted as he prepared to address them.

He spoke in a loud, strong voice. 'You are all aware my father, your king, was gravely injured in the battle... Sadly, he has passed on.'

Aidan paused while murmurs of disbelief rippled through the crowd. Tarienne watched him struggle to maintain his composure. She pushed a tiny pulse of magic his way. Just enough to help him through.

Aidan straightened, pulling in a deep breath. 'My father was not the only one lost in this battle. Many have died to ensure we defeated Lemere's army. You have all done well. Be proud of the valour with which you fought. Sleep well tonight, for we ride for Therin tomorrow. In the days to follow, we will mourn and bury our dead.'

Aidan made eye contact with many of those close to him and waited, his back ramrod straight, until the crowd began to disperse.

Tarienne knew what it must have cost him to speak to his soldiers so soon after his father's death. She briefly grabbed his hand in a sign of support as he passed on the way to his tent, alone. He needed time to accept Eldan's death and the fact he was now king of Therin. He pushed through the opening of his tent, his shoulders slumped.

Tarienne turned back toward Daien, then whirled around again when the hairs on the back of her neck stood up. A tiny sliver of magic tingled across her awareness so quickly, she almost missed it. Her eyes snapped back to Aidan's tent, searching for its source, but the feeling dissipated. Deciding she was merely tired and overwrought, she turned back to Daien, who watched her, concern etched across his face.

*   *   *

Daien

Daien wrapped his arms around her, willing his strength into her. She seemed so vulnerable and fragile. Her skin was paler than usual, almost gossamer over the vibrance of her inner strength. She sagged against him, utterly spent and ready to collapse. He slipped one arm under her legs, scooping her up into his embrace. Too tired to protest, she simply rested her head on his shoulder.

Daien carried her over to the fire. He lowered himself to the ground, his back resting against a small tree, Tarienne settling on his lap.

She snuggled into him, lifted her head to place a tiny, tired kiss on his lips and murmured, 'Thank you, my Daien.'

Daien's heart thumped in response. He dropped a kiss onto her forehead, a smile playing across his lips.

Moments later, a soft snore escaped her. Despite everything that had happened over the last few days, this woman curled up on his lap was the best thing that had ever happened to him, and he had no intention of letting her go. Daien closed his eyes, contentment seeping through him.

When he woke the next morning, Tarienne was still snuggled against him. He smiled and when she finally stirred, Daien unlocked his arms from his protective hold around her soft, warm body. Looking up at him with sleepy eyes and mussed hair, she looked incredibly sensual. She smiled, making his pulse skitter and stretched up.

'Good morning,' she whispered close to his lips.

It took all his resolve to not dip down to taste those sweet, damp lips. Despite the fact they had slept cuddled together, he wasn't certain she'd be pleased if he kissed her in plain view of everyone.

Moving out of his lap, she stretched like a cat, ran her fingers through her hair and scrubbed at her face. Daien stood, arching his back to loosen his stiff muscles, then he grasped her hand, kissed it, and curled his fingers around hers. She smiled and stepped closer, touching her lips to his.

Her eyes held his for a moment before she ran her fingers along the stubble on his chin. 'I need to check on Aidan.'

Daien watched the sensual sway of her hips as she moved away, gliding like a swan on a lake. He shifted slightly, trying to relieve the sudden tightness of his trousers. Grinning, he shoved his gear into his saddlebags.

*   *   *

Tarienne

Tarienne found Aidan in his tent, packing. He looked up as she entered, his sad eyes tearing at her heart. He opened his arms, and she walked into his embrace.

'Thank you for coming, for trying to help Father. I couldn't have gotten this far without you.'

'I will keep my promise,' she whispered.

He pushed her back slightly, holding her at arm's length, managing a small smile.

'At least you don't have to pretend you love me anymore.'

'Aidan, I *do* love you but like a brother. I'll always be here for you whenever you need me.'

'Thank you. I'm going to need you all.'

'Your people would follow you to the depths of hell itself. You must know that.'

'They already have.' His voice was strained and filled with emotion.

Tarienne watched him shoulder his pack and leave the tent, realising just how far he'd come since she'd first met him. Back then, he would never have sought comfort in her arms or anyone else's. If nothing else, she had given him the gift of touch.

She walked out into the gloomy, grey day to gather her belongings and find Lacey for the journey back to Therin. A myriad of emotions swirled through her. Bone-deep sadness, pride at the way Aidan had rallied for his people combined with the burgeoning affection between Daien and herself, made her feel emotionally fragile and exhausted, despite the dreamless sleep she'd managed in Daien's arms last night.

CHAPTER 6

After his father's interment in the tombs beneath the castle, Aidan waited several weeks before allowing his coronation ceremony. When he eventually gave the go-ahead, the preparations kept both him and Tarienne extremely busy. Tarienne wanted everything to be perfect, working hard to ensure it would be.

Though she was occupied selecting the menu, ensuring there was sufficient food in the larder and organising the decorating of the great hall, she couldn't prevent her thoughts from wandering to Daien. She missed his warmth and good humour, aching to feel his lips on hers, his hard body pressed up against her. She had not caught more than a glimpse of him since they returned to the castle. She wondered if he missed her, too. A long sigh escaped her lips as she forced her attention back to the preparations.

Tarienne had just finished dressing and applying her makeup when there was a knock on the door. Her deep cream-coloured dress, beaded with ruby-red gemstones around the bodice, sewn especially for the occasion, rustled as she glided to the door.

She caught her breath at the sight of Daien, looking devastatingly handsome in the royal colours of maroon and gold. His hair was combed back neatly, and he had shaven. When he smiled, her heart almost stopped beating. Drawing him into the room, she quickly pushed the door closed.

Daien eyed her appreciatively. His voice was low and husky with desire when he spoke.

'You are so beautiful. I've missed you, sweetheart.'

His declaration simultaneously stole her breath and filled her with joy. She wished she could spend some time tasting those delicious lips, but the ceremony was scheduled to begin soon.

She leaned in for what she meant to be a quick kiss, a promise for later, but his masculine scent teased her senses, and she swayed closer. Daien sucked in a sharp breath, arousal flaring in his eyes. Tarienne gave in to her desire. Rising up on her tiptoes, she kissed him, moulding herself against his heated torso.

*   *   *

Daien

After several moments, Daien lifted his head and gazed down at her beautiful face. He breathed deeply.

'You smell so good.'

Their lips met again, tongues dancing and bodies intimately close. Her breasts heaved against his chest, and his body thrummed with need.

A niggling memory fought to surface. He shoved the feeling aside, splaying his hands across Tarienne's lower back, pressing her body against his aching loins. Desire spiralled through him, causing his heart to thump wildly. When he slipped one knee between her thighs, a breathy gasp nearly brought him undone.

Slowly, they both pulled away, breathing hard. Standing quietly, they held each other for a few moments, their foreheads touching. Then Tarienne gently pushed him away with a sigh.

The coronation.

Daien's eyes followed Tarienne as she walked over to the mirror to repair her makeup. Her dress clung sensuously to her hips, accentuating her curves. He ached to touch the creamy white skin around the low neckline, kiss her soft, delicate neck beneath her silky, red hair, nibble at her luscious lips. Hauling in a deep breath, Daien clung to his tenuous control.

When she turned back and gifted him with a dazzling smile, his passion ignited and loins tightened even more, pulling a groan from his lips. 'Sweetheart…'

Gliding back over to him, she grabbed the front of his shirt and pulled his face down to hers.

'Later, my Daien. Later,' she purred softly, kissing him tenderly.

His body jumped in response, heart slamming into his ribs.

'Woman, you're going to kill me,' he ground out.

'I was just thinking the same thing, but what a sweet death.'

They both chuckled, easing the sexual tension a little. Taking a moment to collect themselves before Tarienne looped her arm through Daien's, they glided along the heavily decorated corridor to celebrate the crowning of Aidan as king of Therin.

Daien's entire body sparked with desire. How the hell he was going to get through the evening without ravishing her, he had no idea. Grateful he was no longer forced to hide his feelings; he placed his hand possessively over hers as they walked and chatted.

He'd never before felt so accepted, so cared for. His heart swelled with pride for the stunning, sweet woman at his side. But something else surged through him, too. Something he had yet to identify.

*   *   *

Tarienne

When they arrived in the great hall, Tarienne looked around approvingly at the decorations and the huge royal banners adorning the area. The servants had followed her instructions to the last candle. She made a mental note to thank them.

Sharing a glance with Daien, her heart felt like it might burst with love when he gave her a nod of pride for the beautiful decorations she'd organised. Resolved, she decided to bare her soul and tell him everything about herself later tonight, not wanting to start their relationship keeping secrets. She only hoped he could accept everything about her.

Tarienne released Daien's arm, moving to the right of the royal carpet. Daien moved to the left to assemble with the king's guardsmen, as was the custom for all official events. This ensured their sword arms were free and close to the aisle if they should have the need to protect their king. Tarienne fought to stop her eyes from sliding back to Daien. He was breathtakingly handsome, and she couldn't believe they were finally together, though their future was still uncertain.

The court musicians commenced the Royal Anthem, bringing her focus back to the moment. Tarienne turned to see Aidan sweeping up the centre of the hall, along the rich, red carpet edged with gold. He looked so regal. The royal cape, the deep maroon and gold of Therin, was clasped with gold at his neck, flowing for many yards behind him, the small circlet on his head designating him as the prince of Therin. His father's sword hung at his side in a heavily decorated, golden scabbard.

Every person in the hall bowed or curtsied as he passed. He beamed at her as he moved up to the dais. She returned the smile and held her hand over her heart, a gesture of loyalty and love. Aidan returned the gesture, his smile reflecting his gratitude. Tarienne's eyes misted a little.

Aidan looked incredibly handsome, and it was obvious he enthralled many of the women courtiers, their eyes conveying adoration. Tarienne hoped he would find true love one day soon. He deserved it. But she also knew none of the women fawning over him this evening would be the one. He'd often bemoaned to Tarienne of their gushing, silly attitude. Holding back a smile, her attention strayed to the enraptured women, and she barely stopped herself from shaking her head at their ridiculous behaviour.

As the ceremony began, all attention was focused on Aidan. He stood very still and solemn throughout. Tarienne knew he was thinking of his father. Being crowned king like this was bittersweet.

When the high priest of Therin removed the gold circlet from Aidan's head, replacing it with the ornate, gold crown of his kingship, a cheer rose from the crowd.

'Long live the king!'

Aidan turned to face his court, a huge smile curving his lips. 'Thank you all. My first act as the king of Therin is to proclaim,' he held his arms up, 'let the feast begin!'

Another cheer rose. Tarienne chuckled to herself. Trust Aidan to think of food first. He swept off the dais and through the great hall, beaming at everyone flanking his exit.

Tarienne, as part of the royal procession and now the closest family he had, followed after Aidan. The king's guardsmen were next, then the rest of the guests. Feeling Daien's heated gaze on her, Tarienne added a little extra sway to her hips. She smiled mischievously to herself. Daien caught up to her in the hall.

'Witch,' he whispered into her ear.

She chuckled softly, an expression of mock horror on her face.

'You shouldn't be looking! Such impropriety.'

Her heart brimmed with love at their easy banter. Her body warmed in anticipation of his touch later.

During the meal, they sat at long, wooden tables, Aidan at the head, Tarienne to his right and the king's guardsmen to both the right and left. Daien sat so close, Tarienne thought the heat of his body would ignite her clothes. His proximity did nothing to ease her pounding heart. He made physical contact with her at every opportunity, touching her arm or hand to draw her attention to something being discussed.

Tarienne was wound so tightly, she wished Daien would whisk

her off to her chambers so they could explore their desire. When he stood and offered his hand to her, bowing gracefully, he betrayed no sign he was similarly affected.

'Would you do me the honour of this dance, Lady Tarienne?'

Taking his hand, she shot him a questioning look and tried to control her rapid breathing. He swept her onto the dance floor, at which point she gave up any hope of calming herself. He whirled her around, his eyes never leaving hers. She could hardly believe this skilled warrior was also an accomplished dancer. Was there anything he couldn't do?

Tarienne and Daien moved in unison around the polished dance floor. Their bodies swayed in a sensual motion, escalating their already hypersensitive awareness of each other. By the time the music stopped, the tension between them was so palpable, Tarienne was certain everyone in the room was aware of it.

Aidan stepped up and bowed low, asking her for the next dance. Reluctantly, Daien relinquished Tarienne's hand, moving back to chat with the other guardsmen. His molten gaze followed Tarienne around the room, like a predator stalking its prey.

Dancing with Aidan allowed Tarienne time to regain a modicum of composure. At least now she was aware Daien's emotions were as ragged as hers. She groaned at Aidan's teasing comments about her flushed cheeks and Daien watching their every move. His taunting grin made her want to punch his arm.

When the dance ended, Aidan released Tarienne and bowed, his annoying grin still in place, faltering only when he was surrounded by several giggling young women. She considered rescuing him from them, but just smiled sweetly and winked at him before walking away.

Daien's heated scrutiny held her focus as she walked toward him. No one else existed. She wrapped her arm around his waist, urging him toward the hallway. His arm curled possessively around her shoulders, and he trembled slightly as they swept through the doors.

They had barely reached the corridor when Daien hauled her into the shadows of an alcove, claiming her lips. The intensity of the kiss stole her breath. Snaking her arms around his neck, she returned his passion, tongues tangling. When Tarienne pushed him away a little to catch her breath, Daien groaned softly.

She captured his face between her hands, her heart pounding.

'I wish I didn't have to say this, but we must return to the hall before we are missed.'

Daien nodded, scraping his hand through his hair, regret in his eyes.

'Forgive me. I—'

Tarienne placed a finger to his lips to silence him.

'Will you escort me back to my chambers later, my Daien?'

She held his gaze, hoping to convey the promise of later pleasures. His eyes widened slightly, then he swallowed and nodded, drew in a deep breath, claimed a quick kiss, and offered his arm to escort her back to the hall.

They talked, laughed, and danced late into the evening, acutely aware of each other the entire time. The anticipation was exquisite torture.

Well after midnight, Tarienne approached Aidan to bid him good night. She kissed him on the cheek and congratulated him, hugging him fiercely as Daien moved up beside her, ready to escort her back to her chambers... as she'd requested.

Her entire body hummed. Barely managing to maintain a façade of control, she linked her arm with Daien's. Many envious, female eyes followed them. Tarienne leaned closer, a spike of unbidden jealousy coursing through her.

When they reached her door, she turned to him, the molten passion in his eyes stealing her breath. She slowly drew him inside, sliding the heavy iron bolt into place to lock the door behind them. Daien pulled her close, claiming her mouth in a searing kiss. His strong, warm arms circled her, their passion flaring.

Daien tasted of mulled wine, spicy and sweet at the same time.

Tarienne's heart thundered mercilessly as he eased her toward the bed, she did not – *could not* – resist. Gently lowering her, he covered her body with his, the evidence of his desire pressing at the juncture of her thighs.

Resting on his elbows, Daien's entire focus was on her as he tenderly brushed her hair away from her face. 'Have I told you tonight how incredibly beautiful you are?'

He hesitated and she sensed he had something important to say. She watched as he pulled together the tattered edges of his resolve and placed her hands on either side of his face.

'Daien, what is it?'

'Sweetheart, do you trust me?'

She answered without hesitation. 'With my life.'

Again, he faltered, a myriad of emotions playing across his face.

She witnessed the moment he made up his mind.

'Tarienne...'

She waited expectantly. His eyes betrayed a vulnerability she'd never seen in him before.

'Over the course of the evening, I realised why being with you feels different. From the first moment I met you, I knew you were different. You not only fuel an impossibly intense desire within me and filled a hole in my life I hadn't realised was there, but I treasure every moment with you, and I'm unreasonably jealous whenever you laugh and chat with any other man. I've fallen in love with you.'

She sucked in a breath, her heart racing. *He loves me...* Moisture gathered in her eyes. His face held such hope, she opened the final piece of her heart to him.

'I love you, too, my handsome, funny, sweet Daien.'

Daien captured her lips in a soul-shattering kiss, his tongue sweeping into her mouth, claiming her as his. Her heart sang with joy, but a tiny sliver of fear tempered her happiness.

She gently pushed on his shoulders to break the kiss. 'Daien, allow me up for a moment, please.'

His forehead creased into a frown. Uncertainty clouded his eyes as he slid off the bed to stand.

'Have I done something to upset you?'

Tarienne slid to the edge of the bed and stood facing him. She captured his face between her hands and kissed him with every ounce of passion in her, then walked a short distance away. Turning to face him again, her eyes held his.

'I need to tell you something, Daien. Something that may test what you've just told me.'

She trembled slightly, fearful she'd lose him once he knew who and what she was.

He nodded, dropping onto the edge of her huge, four-poster bed his brow creased in a frown. She walked to the window, struggling for the right words. Finally, she turned and drew in a fortifying breath.

'A moment ago, you asked me if I trusted you. I need to know now if you also trust me.'

His rich voice sliced away a little of her fear.

'I have seen your strength, your valour, your compassion and loyalty. I would trust you with my life.'

She swallowed. 'This may take more than mere trust to accept. Please remember, I love you with everything I am and will be.'

He nodded again, his, hands clasped between his knees awaiting her next words.

It was time to give him more of herself. She prayed he truly was the man she imagined him to be. Taking a deep breath, she met his eyes.

*　*　*

Daien

'Where I was raised, emotion and passion are encouraged, not hidden like here. I have long struggled with wanting to touch you, let you know how I feel, yet not being able to.'

Daien ached to touch her, to let her know whatever it was he would love her, but he could tell she had more to say, so he forced himself to stay seated. Fear radiated from her. He could almost feel it. If he concentrated, a palpable connection pulsated between them. Was that what she was trying to tell him?

'Where were you raised, sweetheart? By whom?' he asked in a calm voice.

Moving away from the window, she approached, dropping to her knees in front of him. Placing her hands on his knees, she looked into his eyes. He swallowed hard, sliding his hands over hers, waiting.

'I was raised in the forest of Darewood, where my family still lives.'

'Darewood... It is rumoured the fae folk make their home there,' he mused.

She didn't respond, but her eyes held his.

Realisation dawned. 'You are fae?' he whispered, incredulous.

'Yes.'

A slow grin spread across his face.

'You have lived in this castle for nigh three years, under the king's roof, and you are fae?'

This is her secret?

He smiled encouragingly as she continued. 'My brother, Raef, and I are crown prince and princess of the fae...' She trailed off, and he witnessed her surprise as he whooped softly.

'I am in love with a fae princess?'

Tarienne's entire body sagged momentarily displaying her relief at his reaction to her confession. He reached out to her but stopped, dragging in a deep breath as she allowed her hand to trail up his leg. Her thumb grazed his inner thigh, his muscles bunching under her touch. Jumping slightly at the intimate contact, Daien's hand shot out, grabbing her wrist. Hauling Tarienne onto his lap, his lips captured hers, pouring every ounce of his passion into the kiss.

Pulling away, leaving Tarienne gasping for breath, Daien trailed kisses down the side of her neck to the sensitive area behind her ear. Shivers of pleasure raised goosebumps on her exposed skin. She wiggled impatiently showing her desperation for his intimate touch.

A low growl rumbled through him as he gently pushed her back onto the bed. Positioning himself above her he explored the skin around her bodice, his fingers trailing just beneath the neckline of her dress.

Tarienne sucked in a breath.

'Daien, I... I want to touch you, too.'

He paused, her words almost bringing him undone, his eyes sweeping over her appreciatively. Lifting himself off the bed he grabbed the edges of his shirt, sweeping it over his head in one smooth motion. Tarienne drew in a sharp breath, and she smiled appreciatively.

She sat up and reached for him, trailing her fingers across his stomach. His body reacted accordingly as she leaned forward, her hands coming to rest on his hips and circled his belly button with her tongue.

His muscles flexed under her touch as she kissed her way to the top of his leather trousers, which hung low on his hips. She looked up, and with a smile began undoing the buttons restraining his arousal.

Daien placed his hands on either side of her head, halting her progress. 'Sweetheart...'

Tarienne held his gaze, then stubbornly continued her exploration of his now overheated skin. He groaned, his body trembling. He knew she enjoyed that she had the power to destroy his control.

Tarienne trailed kisses along the skin at the edge of his trousers. Daien bit back another cry, firmly pushing her away. Dropping to his knees, he captured her mouth.

'You really are trying to kill me,' he breathed against her lips.

'I want you, Daien.'

His heart stuttered. He hauled her to him, the honesty of her comment severing the last filaments of his self-control.

'Do you have any idea how beautiful, how sensual you are? Gods, sweetheart. Are you sure about this? Because if we continue, I'm not sure I could stop even if I wanted to.'

'Yes, Daien, I'm sure. Now, please stop talking.' The wild desire in her eyes convinced him.

Daien eased her back onto the bed. He covered her body with his, tasting her lips, nibbling the sides of her mouth, flexing his hips into hers, until they both panted for breath. His heart thundered, loins aching with need, but he refused to hurry even though his body shook with the effort of holding back.

Slowly sliding Tarienne's dress off her shoulders, Daien kissed his way along the top of her breasts, releasing them from the confines of the silken material. *Beautiful.* His tongue circled the soft skin of her areola. Tarienne moaned. When he suckled her nipple, she cried out and wriggled impatiently.

He stood, pulling her up and turning her so her back faced him, allowing him access to the tiny buttons of her dress. He slowly unfastened them. Tarienne let it fall to the floor, then turned toward him, her long lashes flickering open to reveal deep green eyes glazed with desire.

Daien waited, motionless, holding his breath, the anticipation almost too much. He'd never wanted anyone as much as he did Tarienne. Everything in his past paled, as if this were the beginning of who he was meant to be.

Tarienne watched Daien's gaze rake over her. She stepped away from the pile of material and toward him. He stooped, grabbing the hem of her gossamer chemise, his breathing ragged. Tarienne lifted her arms, allowing him to draw it over her head as he stood, then tossed the garment aside.

Wrapping his arms around her, he lifted her off the floor and eased her back onto the bed, gazing down at her for a moment, his chest heaving. He captured her lips as his finger drew little circles over each breast in turn. Tarienne's body shook with need.

She moaned. 'Daien...' She arched her back into his touch, begging, 'Please...'

He lifted his head, eager to comply with her wishes and watched her raptured expression as he slid his hand down her stomach, to the juncture between her thighs. He groaned as he slid his finger beneath her undergarments and into her slick core. He had no idea how he was going to survive this. His heart threatened to burst through his chest. His arousal throbbed, aching to be free from the constriction of his now overly tight trousers.

When Tarienne's hips lifted, pushing into his hand, and begging him for release, something inside him snapped. He slammed his lips down onto hers, pumping his fingers rhythmically into her warm wetness. Tarienne moaned and thrashed, then shattered on a cry. Daien smothered her shout with another long, passionate kiss. His climax was so close, he knew if she touched him, he'd be lost.

Slipping his fingers from her pulsating sheath, he slid off the bed and hooked his fingers around the top of her knickers. 'Lift for me, sweetheart.'

Panting, Tarienne complied. Daien dragged them down her legs, tossing them aside. His breath caught at the beauty of her naked body, waiting for him.

Dropping to his knees, he hauled her to the edge of the bed, so her legs dangled over the side. The sweet scent of her arousal drove him wild. He dipped his head to taste her, hearing her cry out softly. He brought her to the edge of another climax, then stood, dropping his trousers to the floor, and kicked them aside.

Hauling in a deep breath, his eyes met Tarienne's. She was propped up on her elbows, her eyes devouring him. She looked tousled and so sexy as she sat up. His hands dropped to her silky, red tresses, allowing himself a moment to find calm in the torrent of emotion.

Her fingers trailed over his stomach and down to his braies, caressing his arousal through the thin fabric. Daien moaned, gritting his teeth against the climax that hung perilously close. Tarienne twisted her fingers in the material and slid them down his legs. He held his breath as her soft hair drifted across his erection.

When Tarienne lifted her eyes to him and curled her fingers around his hard length, he thought he might die from pleasure. Daien's eyes drifted closed, savouring the moment. When her lips closed around him, he sucked in a breath, almost jerking away from her.

'Gods, Tarienne. You're going to kill me.'

The look in her eyes was so sexy as she took him in, he swallowed hard and fisted his hands by his side. Unable to stop his hips pumping, his climax built quickly with the exquisite sensations racking his body. Close to losing control, Daien quickly pulled away, hauled her up onto the bed and positioned his body over hers.

Tarienne wrapped her fingers around him, guiding him inside her. He moaned, holding back the urge to plunge deep inside her welcoming warmth. Pushing slowly to give her time to adjust, he reached what felt like a barrier. Shock slid through him.

She's a virgin?

In the heat of passion, he hadn't considered the possibility. Teetering on the edge of reason, he swore quietly. With a supreme effort he hadn't thought he was capable of, Daien stopped moving. Bracing himself on his elbows, he clamped down on his desire, barely clinging to his last shred of self-control. He shook with the effort of holding back.

'Sweetheart?'

Tarienne didn't respond. Instead, her hips surged up. He felt the pop as he broke through her maidenhead, heard her hiss in pain. He started to pull away, but Tarienne wrapped her legs around him, dragging him closer and rocking invitingly beneath him. She smiled and moved, tears clinging to her lashes, pulling him deeper.

Tentatively, he slid rhythmically into her tight sheath. Her moans of pleasure encouraging him, he increased the pace, sweat beading on his forehead. Tarienne began thrashing, crying out his name. When her muscles clenched around him, a tingle shot up his spine, an earth-shattering climax exploding through his body, making him moan loudly.

He pumped a few more times into her moist heat, then collapsed on top of her, spent, sated – for now – and a little bewildered.

Rolling to the side, he pulled her to him, kissing her with supreme tenderness bordering on reverence. He had been her first. His chest swelled with joy, then tightened with a fierce stab of possessiveness.

The next morning, Daien propped himself up on his elbow, watching her sleep. When she woke, he smiled lazily, gently claiming her lips.

'Good morning, beautiful. You gave me an incredible gift last night. Thank you. I am honoured to be your first.'

Tarienne beamed back at him, reaching up to caress his face.

He kissed her again, a thank you and a claim wrapped into one long, searing melding of their mouths. Another wave of warmth and deep protectiveness rolled through him. He shifted, his body half covering hers, revelling in the feel of her soft skin against his. Even after making love many times during the night, his body hardened with the desire consuming him. Gently, he wiped away the tear running down her cheek.

'I could not have asked for more from you. You are a sweet and generous lover, my Daien.'

He nibbled his way across her soft, swollen lips, gathering her close. Burying his face in her soft hair, he inhaled the delicious vanilla and cinnamon scent, until she wiggled beneath him.

Reluctantly, Daien released her, rolling onto his back.

'I'm starving,' she declared.

He chuckled. 'Me, too, but we can't go down like this. Do you have any water to bathe in? I'll clean up, then fetch us something.'

Smiling, Tarienne leapt out of bed, ignoring her nakedness.

Daien eyed her appreciatively, a sensual smile pulling at his lips. He patted the bed, his voice deep and husky. 'I'm not *that* hungry.'

Tarienne returned to the side of the bed. Daien's eyes widened, hope surging. Smiling, she grabbed his hand and pulled him up, hauling him to the screen she used to dress behind. He groaned; his hope dashed. There sat the bath she had used to prepare for Aidan's coronation.

'That will do.' Daien moved to step into the tub of icy water.

'No!'

He jumped back, startled.

Clutching his hand, Tarienne urged him closer to the water, dipping their entwined hands into its cold surface. A confused frown wrinkled his brow. Tarienne softly murmured some unfamiliar words, and the water warmed around their fingers.

*   *   *

Tarienne

Daien's face lit with wonder and amazement. He curled one hand around the nape of her neck, hauling her closer. His kiss heated her and rekindled the ache low in her belly.

She smiled. 'Well, if that's all it takes for you to kiss me like that, I should have done it a long time ago.'

They laughed, easing the desire between them, despite their naked bodies touching intimately. Daien slid into the steaming bath on a sigh. Tarienne admired his toned body.

He's gorgeous... and all mine.

She padded over to the wardrobe and slipped on a loose robe, then grabbed some unscented soap from the basket and glided up behind Daien. Tenderly, she lathered his wet hair, then carefully rinsed his wavy brown locks until they were squeaky clean. He dipped beneath the water to wash the soap from his skin, then surfaced, little rivulets of water drizzling enticingly through the light smattering of dark hair on his muscled chest.

Tarienne dropped her hands to his shoulders and began massaging the knots. A relaxed and contented sigh tumbled from Daien's lips. He leaned back, craning his neck to look at her. Hooking his arm over her neck, he pulled her down, plundering her mouth with a fervour that spoke of his renewed desire.

Tarienne anchored herself on his shoulders, contemplating climbing into the bath with him.

Eventually releasing her, Daien smiled and rose from of the water, his desire for her clear. When he stepped out of the tub, Tarienne's mouth went dry as water trickled down his sculpted stomach. His lean, muscular body did nothing to alleviate the escalating lust rising within her. She tore her eyes away and handed him a soft towel, her hands shaking.

Drying and dressing quickly, Daien drew in a deep breath and opened the door. He peeked out to ensure no one was in the corridor, then headed toward the kitchen to find something to eat.

Deciding to take the opportunity to freshen up while he was gone, Tarienne reheated the water with a quietly spoken spell and lowered herself into the tub.

Sighing when the warmth enveloped her, the heat soothed the achiness in places she'd never ached before. Tarienne smiled and closed her eyes, sinking beneath the water. She washed herself carefully, rinsing her hair, then her body.

Once finished, she rested her head on the back of the tub, closing her eyes. As she dozed, memories of her night with Daien – delicious images replaying through her mind – sent tingles of arousal through her already overly sensitised body.

Waking with a start, she dipped below the cooling water to clear her head. Surfacing, Tarienne stood, water running down her face and over her shoulders, dripping down her body. She moved around the screen to grab a fresh towel, jumping slightly as the door clanged shut. Tarienne spun around to see Daien, holding a tray filled with fruit and pastries, wide eyes dark with desire.

Placing the tray on the bedside table, he prowled toward her, his gaze drifting over her naked, wet body, a predator ready to pounce.

Goosebumps rose on Tarienne's wet skin. Daien stopped a

whisper from her and captured her dampened lips, then swept his shirt over his head, dropped his trousers to the floor, lifted her into his arms and carried her to the bed. There was no mistaking the power of Daien's desire as he swept her to the heights of ecstasy again.

The sun had risen high in the sky, its warm rays filtering through the high windows of Tarienne's chambers, before they finally settled into the large, comfy chairs, eating the fare Daien had filched from the kitchen. He paused, a pastry halfway to his mouth.

'Would you like to ride with me later today?'

Tarienne looked at him for a long moment, her heart doing little flips at the thought of taking a leisurely ride with him.

'I'd like that very much.'

He smiled and finished the apple pastry, then stood and placed his hands on the arms of her chair, leaning over her. She could feel the heat from his skin, his breath caressing her swollen lips, elevating her heart rate even more. She licked her lips in anticipation of his kiss, her eyes locked with his.

'I'd best make an appearance downstairs. I'll meet you in the courtyard, mid-afternoon.'

Daien closed the gap between them, plundering her mouth, sending her pulse skittering. With a reluctant sigh, he pulled away, his breathing ragged.

Gently capturing her chin between his thumb and forefinger, Daien's molten gaze delved deep into her eyes. Tarienne leaned forward to steal another kiss. He obliged, nibbling on her lip, his tongue duelling with hers.

He sighed again as he dragged himself away and turned to exit her chambers. Tarienne's eyes followed, admiring his lean, muscular build, certain there was a new swagger to his gait as he turned, winked, and pulled the door closed behind him.

Sighing with a smile, Tarienne wandered over to her wardrobe, wondering what she should wear. She wanted to look her best.

About an hour later, satisfied with her choice, Tarienne freshened up using the water from the bath and a soft cloth to wash her face.

Once finished, she dressed, braiding her waist-length hair, then decided to check in with Aidan. She couldn't wipe the smile from her face as she walked down the corridor.

Arriving at Aidan's chambers, Tarienne knocked, waiting.

'Come,' he called in a gruff voice.

She entered to find him sitting up in his bed, looking tired and scruffy, one hand rubbing his eyes. However, his face still lit in a small smile when he saw her.

'A little too much mead, sire?' she teased, laughing softly.

Aidan swung his legs over the edge of the bed with a moan. Tarienne noted he hadn't quite finished undressing before he fell asleep. She chuckled. He had obviously celebrated until early this morning.

'Don't you "sire" me.' Aidan laughed, then grabbed his head, groaning loudly.

Deciding she'd teased him enough she gentled her tone.

'Would you like me to prepare something to help with your headache?'

A sheepish grin spread across his face. 'Yes, please.' He flopped back onto the bed, groaning again.

Tarienne felt the edge of his thoughts flutter across her consciousness, letting her know he wished he'd indulged a little less last night. Chuckling to herself, she hurried to her chambers to mix an herbal brew for him.

No more than fifteen minutes later, carrying a mug of tea, Tarienne headed into the kitchen to organise a tray of fruit and oatmeal for the newly crowned king.

By the time she returned to his room, Aidan was washed and dressed, sitting in the chair beside the open window, overlooking the courtyard, yet he still looked pale and sickly. She took the tea off the tray and handed it to him.

'Thank you.' He managed a small, pained smile as he sipped it, scrunching up his face at the taste, although he refrained from commenting.

Tarienne placed the tray on the small table in front of the fireplace, then moved behind Aidan to massage his neck and temples. She silently murmured a healing spell, kneading his tight muscles with her fingers, making him groan. Images of massaging Daien's shoulders while he lounged in the bathtub, naked, filled her thoughts, heating her body. She focused on Aidan to calm her thudding heart, eventually moving to sit beside him.

Handing him pieces of fruit, which he nibbled absently, they chatted about the events of the previous evening. Tarienne wondered if Aidan would tease her again about how attentive Daien had been last night. However, he refrained from commenting.

Eventually, Aidan's colour began to return. He grinned. 'I feel much better.' He stood, pulling her into a hug. 'Thank you.'

Tarienne smiled, excusing herself. When she turned to leave to meet Daien in the courtyard, Aidan's focus swept over her attire.

'Are you going riding? Would you like some company?'

Her eyes flicked a little nervously to him. Should she confess with whom she would be riding? Aidan's promise to her before he rode out to battle Lemere's army tumbled through her thoughts. She straightened, her chin rising defiantly in preparation for his judgment. Her eyes held his for a moment, a silent challenge.

'No, thank you. Daien is riding with me.'

Aidan's eyebrows rose, a knowing smile playing across his lips.

'Oh, well... Enjoy yourselves.'

Surprised he did not voice disapproval, Tarienne's cheeks flushed as she left his chambers. Hurrying along the empty corridors and out to the courtyard, Tarienne's heart fluttered with anticipation. Daien waited for her, scratching the ears of his stallion. He looked so devastatingly handsome wearing a black shirt that stretched tightly across his muscular frame, chocolate brown riding pants clinging enticingly to his firm backside and black boots, his hair brushed into shiny waves, the faint shadow of a beard already darkening his chin. The sight stole her breath.

Pulling in a deep, calming gulp of air, Tarienne nervously ran her hands down her clothes, her cheeks heated. She'd chosen her light brown riding pants, cream ankle boots and a soft, lacy, cream blouse, a white, collarless shirt underneath to keep her warm.

Daien seemed to notice her discomfort, his forehead creasing in a questioning look. Tarienne just smiled, mounting her mare, Lacey, in one swift, easy movement. Daien swung into his saddle, and they cantered along the street and out through the castle gates.

Riding side by side along the well-worn, dusty track, they talked and laughed about the day-to-day events around the castle, until they reached a lush, green clearing at the edge of a large pond. Daien slid from his steed, hurrying around to help Tarienne dismount, a mischievous glint in his eyes as he grasped her waist.

Pulling her close, he slid her down his hard body. Heat suffused her at the intimate contact. Daien captured her lips for a long kiss, sending desire curling through her.

When the kiss ended, Tarienne gulped in a few much-needed breaths. Daien released her and, for a moment, she wasn't sure her legs would hold her.

Yanking a blanket from his pack, he spread it on the ground beneath an old, shady tree close to the water's edge. He gave her a dramatic bow and gestured to the blanket, urging Tarienne to sit. Chuckling and giving him an equally flamboyant curtsy, she dropped as gracefully as she could onto the thick, woollen blanket.

Daien pulled a pannier full of delicious treats from behind his saddle, then plopped down beside her. They sat there, legs touching, nibbling on pastries filled with sweet, cooked berries.

Daien paused, looking at her. 'I still can't believe the gift you gave me last night. How can it be a beautiful woman like you has never, um… been with a man before?'

Tarienne laughed. 'Daien, I said my people are passionate and affectionate, not of loose morals.'

His easy smile disappeared. 'I didn't mean to imply—'

Tarienne leaned closer, hushing him with a finger to his lips. He kissed it, then grasped her hand and kissed her palm. Liquid heat pooled low in her body. She breathed deeply to settle the butterflies dancing in her stomach, then cleared her throat.

'I know, Daien. Don't fret. Truthfully, I had a few suitors in Darewood, but I never let any of them go too far. As a princess, these things are difficult. I had to be circumspect, especially with three over-protective brothers around.' She lowered her eyes for a moment, then lifted them to meet Daien's again. 'Truthfully, ever since I arrived in Therin, I have been waiting for you.'

Daien's eyes twinkled, a deliciously sensual smile curling his lips. He swooped toward her for a long, passionate kiss, pinning her body beneath him on the blanket. Tarienne wondered if it would always be like this with him.

They spent the rest of the afternoon walking through the lush green of the forest, pausing often to kiss. As they relaxed on the blanket in each other's arms, Daien propped himself up on his elbow. He tenderly brushed a stray strand of hair from her face.

'You have occupied my dreams as of late.'

Tarienne let her eyes drift over his handsome face. Her heart thumped erratically.

'Tell me about them.'

Daien's eyes gleamed with an emotion Tarienne could not identify.

'One in particular revisits me almost nightly. We are in the throne room. You sit beside Aidan, as you often do. When you beckon me forward, I kneel before you and you drop to your knees and kiss me in front of everyone.' He paused.

'Is there more, my love?'

Tarienne's heart fluttered at Daien's brief moment of insecurity. His need for acceptance surprised her. She'd rarely seen him as anything less than confident. It tore at her heart. She ached to give him what he desired, secretly vowing to fulfil Daien's dream.

His emotion-filled eyes lifted to hers.

'No. More... graphic dreams visit me, but this one always ends with you kissing me in front of the king and the other guardsmen.'

She scooted closer and planted a searing kiss on his lips, snuggling close. A deep growl rumbled through him, the moment passing.

Wrapped in each other's arms once again, they watched the fluffy white clouds change shape, nudged along by the warm zephyr. Tarienne could feel little beads of perspiration on her forehead as the long fingers of the afternoon sun reached across the blanket, heating her skin.

Suddenly she sat upright. 'I feel like going for a swim.'

*   *   *

Daien

'You don't have any swimwear with y—' Daien stopped as she began to unlace her blouse. His mouth went dry at the realisation.

He groaned, his body hardening. 'Woman, you'll be the death of me.'

'Swim with me, Daien.'

The heated look she sent him made his body ache and heart race. He fought an internal war.

I should remain dressed. If anyone approached, her honour would remain intact. I can say I am guarding her.

Her eyes held his, desire flaring between them. Tarienne removed her clothes, slowly, sensuously, every movement escalating his hunger for her. Daien could neither speak nor move, transfixed by her ethereal beauty. His breath caught in his throat when the last of her clothing dropped to the ground.

She looked back over her shoulder, invitingly, as she waded into the clear, cool water. Her creamy white skin disappeared beneath the veil of the water's surface.

Daien moistened his lips, hesitating only moments before he cursed his crumbling resolve. *To hell with it. She's mine!*

He yanked his shirt over his head, then tugged off his boots, flinging them over his shoulder. Pulling his trousers down his legs, he almost tore them in his haste.

Daien dove into the water, emerging and swimming to where she floated. His world closed in, Tarienne at its centre. She swam away playfully, laughing. A strong swimmer, Daien dove under the water, capturing her in his arms as he erupted up through the liquid veneer. Tarienne shrieked, trying to escape, but he hauled her close, silencing her with an impassioned kiss.

She nearly brought him undone when she wrapped her legs around his waist, centring her body over his rock-hard manhood. Daien growled as he entered her, allowing himself to be enveloped by the passion this woman aroused in him, shouting her name when her clenching muscles catapulted him into sweet oblivion.

*　　*　　*

Tarienne

Fully dressed again, they sat on a smooth rock at the edge of the water, Tarienne attempting to brush the tangles from her hair with her fingers.

'Let me do that,' Daien offered, sitting behind her, his legs on either side of her body. He ran his fingers carefully through her damp locks, gently teasing the knots loose. 'Would you like me to braid it for you?'

Amazement that he knew how to braid hair, along with a myriad of other emotions generated by his tender gesture, spiralled through her. Not trusting herself to speak, Tarienne nodded, moisture accumulating at the corners of her eyes. She marvelled that her powerful king's guardsman possessed such tenderness. He held her heart and soul in his strong, yet gentle hands.

Once finished, he lifted her damp braid and kissed her neck, sending shivers through her entire body. Her heart swelled, knowing how much he wanted her, because her passion matched his.

Eyes closed, she whispered, 'You're insatiable.'

'Only with you, sweetheart.' Daien continued nibbling at her neck until she twisted around to claim a kiss.

'We'd better be heading back, I suppose,' Tarienne sighed.

Chuckling at her tone, Daien rose easily to his feet, offering his hand to help her up.

'You know what I'd really like?' Tarienne asked, feigning a look of innocence. 'Let's ride back together on your stallion.'

He sucked in a breath. 'Woman, if we do that, we may never get back to the castle. You really are trying to kill me, aren't you?' He feigned a melodramatic look of pain, hand to his chest.

*   *   *

Daien

Tarienne burst into delighted laughter, the sweet, melodious sound reigniting his desire. Daien's heart swelled with love for his fae princess. He blew out a breath. 'I can't believe I'm saying this but climb onto Lacey so we can return to the castle before nightfall.'

She acquiesced and placed her foot into the stirrup, allowing Daien to help her into the saddle... even though she had been around horses all her life and was an extremely skilled rider.

They cantered along in silence for a while, until Tarienne suddenly pulled Lacey to a halt, frowning. 'Daien, will you help me improve my skill with a sword?'

Surprised by the request, he reined his stallion to a stop beside Lacey and considered for a moment.

'Sweetheart, you are already an excellent swordswoman. I have seen how adept you are when you practice, thinking no one is watching. What could I possibly teach you?'

Tarienne lifted her chin, determination tinged with a touch of sadness lacing her words.

'I wish to improve my skills and become stronger so there will be no excuse for Aidan to leave me behind the next time there's a battle. I'd like you to teach me your fighting style. You're already aware I have my own sword. The one my father gifted to me when I came of age. Please, Daien, will you do this for me?'

He nudged his stallion closer, her plea wrenching at his heart. Tarienne's brow wrinkled. He grasped the back of her neck and hauled her close, almost dragging her off Lacey's back for a long, intense kiss.

Finally, he pulled back, his voice husky with emotion. 'I will do this for you, my love.'

'There's one condition,' she whispered. They were so close; his breath caressed her lips. 'You have to train with your shirt on.'

Daien tipped his head back, laughing heartily. 'You'll have to learn to fight with distractions, but for now, I promise to wear a shirt.'

Surprised by how much it pleased him she was so affected by his shirtless body, he hauled her close for another long, passionate kiss.

Releasing her, Daien's brow furrowed in thought, a small smile playing across his lips. 'Did I distract you that day you arrived at the training arena holding Aidan's hand?'

She groaned. 'I knew you'd noticed... Yes, you did. You smelled so intoxicatingly masculine and looked so incredibly virile. I could barely put a coherent thought together. Do you remember what I said?'

Daien chuckled. 'Yes. You noticed my "condition". After I escorted you back to your chambers, I was so aroused, I rode to the lake and bathed in its icy water for hours. It didn't help a great deal, though, particularly when what I really wanted to do was knock on your door and *demonstrate* my condition.'

Tarienne blushed. 'I always thought you saw me as member of the royal household, nothing more.'

Daien shook his head, enchanted by her honesty, and bemused it had taken them so long to realise their feelings for each other.

'Tarienne, I bathed in cold water so often after being around you. I'm surprised you didn't notice my reaction. I couldn't stop myself from touching you, and when you leaned into me...' He shook his head. 'Gods, sweetheart, it almost destroyed what little self-control I had left.'

Her eyes showed every emotion tumbling through her. Daien desperately wanted to haul her to the ground and make love to her again. She gazed into his eyes for what seemed like ages, and when she spoke, her eyes were damp with unshed tears.

'I loved that you let me lean on you, though I didn't realise at first that's what you were doing. The contact grounded me, helping satisfy my need for touch. You were always so warm and smelled so good.'

'I couldn't have moved away if I'd wanted to, though I didn't want to. You drew me to you. You aren't like any woman I've ever known.'

He drew her to him then, the passion coursing through him overwhelming all rational thought. He kissed her, their tongues duelling, sending fire spiralling through his loins. The horses shifted restlessly.

Finally releasing her, Daien urged his horse forward, a contentment he'd never known filling his soul.

A happy sigh tumbled from Tarienne. She clicked her tongue at Lacey, and they continued their journey back to Castle Therin.

CHAPTER 7

Life in Therin returned to relative normality, except Daien was now able to spend time with Tarienne when his daily tasks were completed. He spent most nights with her, too, slipping back to his own bed in the early hours of the morning to avoid gossip.

Much of Tarienne's time was taken up by helping Aidan with the day-to-day running of the castle. The larders needed to be checked and restocked, the menu for the next week selected, cleaning staff directed to brush down cobwebs and wash floors, not to mention repairs and purchases. It seemed never-ending!

Aidan, she noted proudly, quickly gained a reputation as a very fair and patient king. He ensured he personally heard the grievances of all those villagers who travelled, often long distances, to seek an audience with him. After one particularly long session, where Aidan granted audience to an unusually substantial number of outer villagers, Tarienne decided it was time to implement her plan. There had been many reports of raids on local farms and wild beasts killing livestock. Tarienne didn't know how long Therin would remain at peace, so she didn't want to wait any longer to make her relationship with Daien public.

The king's guardsmen always flanked the aisle where the villagers were admitted, as protection for the king. As usual, after the last of the villagers had been dismissed, Aidan rose from his throne and stretched. Tarienne pulled in a deep breath, determination steeling her resolve. When the king's guardsmen turned to leave, she rose, speaking in a quiet, yet commanding tone that filled the room.

'Daien.'

As one, all in the room turned to face her, questioning looks passing between them. She flowed slowly, yet purposefully, down the stairs toward him. Aidan's mouth quirked into a small smile as she approached Daien. No one else existed for her. He stood perfectly still, his emotions carefully masked, watching Tarienne.

Silence hung heavily in the air as Tarienne and Daien gazed at each other. Tarienne's tongue slid out to moisten her suddenly dry lips and a soft groan escaped Daien. Unable to stop himself, he swooped down, capturing her mouth in a gentle kiss. His arms snaked around her, holding her close, hers sliding around his neck.

A few moments passed before Aidan cleared his throat loudly, grinning, the onlookers beginning to cheer. They smiled against each other's lips and pulled away.

After that moment Tarienne sensed a shift in Daien's soul. The final corner of his heart and mind that he'd previously carefully guarded, opened to her. His thoughts tumbled across her consciousness as though he'd spoken the words out loud. He was deeply touched at her gesture of complete trust, announcing their relationship in front of the king and Daien's fellow guards. She'd brought his dream to life. He was speechless with love... and a burning passion he couldn't sate until later.

Tarienne warmed with the heat of Daien's desire spiralling through his thoughts. He wanted to sweep her away right now and prove the strength of his love for her. Instead, he kissed her hand and bowed deeply as Aidan passed, unable to keep a huge grin from breaking free. Before he followed his king, Daien moved up close to her, fiery desire apparent in his voice.

'Later, sweetheart. Definitely, later.'

Tarienne gasped, her hand fluttering to her chest, a pink flush creeping up her neck and into her cheeks. Daien chuckled as he headed down the corridor with the other guards.

A short while later, as Tarienne walked along the corridors to her chambers, a hand darted out, yanking her behind a stone pillar. She squealed, then instantly relaxed when she recognised the delicious scent of the man sweeping her into his arms.

'I wanted to thank you for today, sweetheart. It was a moment I'll never forget.'

Daien kissed her with such passion, Tarienne wished they were back in her room so they could take it further. When they broke the kiss, she looked into his eyes.

'I'm sorry it wasn't exactly like your dream.'

Daien gifted her with the heart-stopping smile he reserved for her alone. 'It was better. In my dream, *you* kissed *me*. Today, you allowed me the choice.' His voice took on a huskiness, betraying his desire. 'I love you, Ren.'

The nickname used by her family on his lips made her heart clench. *Gods, I love him.*

Daien kissed her, then whispered against her lips, 'Meet me at the training yard in one hour for your lesson.'

Slipping away before she could respond, Tarienne was left breathless and wanting. She watched him stride down the corridor, shafts of sunlight lancing through the windows creating sun-kissed streaks in his brown, shoulder-length hair.

A little unsteady, Tarienne slowly made her way to her chambers. She tried to rest for a while but was too excited at the prospect of training with Daien. Eventually, she gave up and changed into her light brown riding pants and a soft taupe, linen shirt that would allow her to move freely, then left to meet Daien for her lesson. Her heart thumped wildly. She was breathless before the training even started.

As the lesson progressed Daien occasionally slipped his arms around Tarienne to demonstrate a move. He told her that she was a talented swordswoman and a quick learner. Daien demonstrated his pride and escalating desire by moving closer, so their bodies touched, in the guise of helping her perfect a technique.

He groaned as she moved against him. Daien's hands slid down her arms, pulling her back against his chest as he gripped her hands on the hilt of her sword, demonstrating how to spin the weapon. She felt his heart thump erratically to match her own, and she knew that he too struggled to maintain focus. Dragging in a few deep breaths, he managed to finish the lesson.

Tarienne sent him a heated look as the lesson ended, then turned and walked away. She sensed his eyes locked on her retreating form, and heard him pant heavily, knowing it was not entirely due to the exertion of the training.

Unable to resist teasing him she added a sway to her hips, and grinned as it pulled a low growl from his lips. Daring a quick glance over her shoulder she saw his hands fisted at his side and knew that he forced himself to turn away before he followed her. She saw him turn towards the armoury before she dragged in a deep, calming breath and made her way to her room.

*　*　*

Daien

Despite cleaning his sword more vigorously than ever before, then waiting until after the evening meal to return to Tarienne, their passion flared white-hot. Daien marvelled at the heat they shared. She never seemed reluctant, her desire always equalling his own.

He'd heard women often refused their husbands and lovers. Tarienne was different, for which he was grateful. Despite making love often and spending as much time as they could together, Daien couldn't get enough of her. He wondered if she'd cast a spell on him, then quickly discarded the thought. More than anything else, he trusted her.

Whenever they were able, they trained. Tarienne began to gain a strength and agility with the sword that pleased Daien. The rest of her time was spent with Aidan, discussing the running of the castle. Despite her early reservations, she took her role as chatelaine seriously and ensured everything was clean, well-stocked and ran smoothly.

Tarienne was never far from Daien's thoughts, even when they were apart. He found himself uncharacteristically distracted, collecting a few bruises and cuts from his training with the other guards. It helped when he cleared his mind before a match, but never for long.

When the king came to the practice yard to train, Daien forced himself to focus. It took every ounce of concentration he had to remain competitive against Aidan, who was a highly skilled swordsman.

Aidan grinned when he managed to twist Daien's sword from his hand. But Daien, never one to give up easily, dropped low on his haunches and swept out his leg, knocking Aidan's feet from under him. Aidan thudded to the ground... hard. For the briefest of moments, Daien faltered, letting out a breath when his king chuckled, accepting his hand to haul him upright.

He thumped Daien on the back. 'Nice move. I thought I had you for a moment.'

Daien grinned back. '*I* thought you had me for a moment.'

Laughing, they returned inside to clean up before the evening meal.

* * *

Tarienne

Word quickly spread throughout the kingdom that Aidan was a fairer and more tolerant king than his father had been. Tarienne soon noticed fae and elven folk visiting the local market. They were disguised, but she could feel the tingle of their magical presence as they passed her in the streets. Most avoided making eye contact. However, one would occasionally flick their eyes in her direction. When they did, she would smile and nod imperceptibly, hoping to convey they were safe. She couldn't help the sliver of doubt that Aidan would welcome their presence in Therin.

Tarienne had managed to convince Daien to join her while she wandered amongst the stalls. Hand in hand, they sauntered, his thumb absently caressing the back of her hand as they talked.

Noticing a large number of fae and elven folk entering the city, shopping at the stalls, or milling around in groups, she was just about to mention it to Daien when a feeling of impending doom flooded her senses. Quite suddenly, she felt weak and ill. Grabbing at Daien's arm, Tarienne leaned heavily into him for support.

Catching her as she swayed, concern etched his face.

'Sweetheart, what's wrong?'

Pulling in a few deep breaths to steady herself, Tarienne scanned the crowd, trying to find the cause of her reaction.

'I-I'm not sure,' she managed weakly. 'It feels like something,' she swallowed, 'something evil just passed by.'

Daien immediately shifted in front of her, his hand moving to the sword hanging at his side. He narrowed his eyes, assessing the crowd.

'Daien, please take me back to my chambers. I need to speak with Raef.'

He wrapped his free arm protectively around her shoulders, pulling her close as he escorted her through the streets, his eyes scanning for danger, right hand still resting on the hilt of his sword.

When they reached her chambers, he shoved open the door, scooped her up into his arms and gently deposited her onto the bed, sitting beside her, rubbing her back.

'Sweetheart, tell me what happened.'

His voice was filled with both concern and the authority that came with being confident of the ability to protect those he loved.

'I'm... I'm not completely sure. Will you stay with me while I speak with Raef?'

Daien sent her a questioning look.

Tarienne smiled weakly. 'Fae have the ability to project our thoughts to each other over quite long distances. If you hold my hand, I'll project what Raef says so we can both hear. Is that all right?'

He nodded, his trust in her implicit.

Tarienne held out her hand, Daien's fingers entwining with hers. Drawing strength from him, she silently called her brother's name.

'Raef?'

Almost instantly, her brother responded.

'Yes, sweetling?'

*　　*　　*

Daien

Daien jumped a little at the voice in his mind, eyes wide. Tarienne smiled reassuringly.

'Raef, Daien is here with me, listening.'

Raef did not speak, but Daien felt a sense of approval filter through his mind. It was a strange sensation to have someone else's thoughts in your head. He cleared his mind, just as he did when training, so he could focus on what was being said.

Raef chuckled.

'Interesting. You have instinctively cleared your mind to receive my communication. Are you sure you don't have fae or elven blood in you, Daien?'

Daien did not know how to answer, looking at Tarienne for help. She smiled encouragingly.

'Think your words as if you were saying them. Raef's ability in this is strong. He will hear you.'

Daien drew in a breath and pushed out his thoughts.

'It is something I do when I fight to help me focus. I have no idea about my heritage. My parents died when I was quite young. The sensation of communicating like this is odd... yet strangely familiar.'

Tarienne broke into their conversation. *'Raef, can we get back to the reason I contacted you, please?'*

'Sorry, sweetling. Continue.'

Daien was certain he heard a smile in Raef's voice.

'Daien and I were in the marketplace. I noticed a large number of fae and elven folk entering the city and milling around the stalls, then felt something I can only describe as a wave of evil intent. I couldn't identify where it came from, but it felt as if it were sucking the strength out of me. It frightened me, Raef. I've never felt anything like it.'

Raef cursed. *'It's happening sooner than I expected. The balance is failing. Evil creatures have started escaping from the deepest crevices of the land. I've had reports of gargoyles and other blood-sucking creatures terrorising the outer villages. I thought it was only a few but given the influx of elves and fae into Therin, it must be more widespread than I previously believed.'*

'What can we do?' Tarienne asked.

'This is about magical creatures. Evil ones. We can no longer hide this from Therin and its people. Aidan must know, and you must reveal your abilities to help him.'

'How soon must we do this?' Daien interrupted, his concern clear.

He noticed Tarienne smile and felt her pride at how quickly he had accepted this form of communication and learned to project his thoughts.

Raef did not hesitate with his response. *'Now, before it is too late. I will leave for Therin immediately.'*

Daien's and Tarienne's eyes met, before they hastened to find Aidan. They hurried through the practice yard, asking two king's guards, Orien and Elnath, if they knew Aidan's whereabouts, when an explosion ripped through the stone roof over the throne room and an unearthly shriek rent the air.

They both looked up. Tarienne paled.

'Saints preserve us. Gargoyles!'

Daien heard her voice across his thoughts as she contacted Raef. He drew his sword, bellowing, 'Run! Get everyone inside! Now!'

Orien and Elnath sprang into action, swords at the ready, shepherding everyone inside. Tarienne dashed toward the throne room, her cumbersome, long dress swishing around her legs, threatening to trip her.

Daien sprinted along the stone path close behind, wondering what they'd find inside. Battle calm suffused his body, but nothing could have prepared him for what they saw when they burst through the doors of the throne room and skidded to a halt.

Aidan stood in the middle of the room, battling a huge gargoyle with jagged, yellow teeth. It must have stood around eight feet tall. Its skin looked like dark green roof shingles, and its blood red eyes bulged. Its vicious, foot-long claws swiped ever closer, backing Aidan into a corner. Daien swore and ran into the fight.

A deep rumble and cracking drew their attention upward. The roof had started to collapse. Tarienne began chanting, her voice rising above the din as the ancient words flowed from her, her focus on the ceiling above. Realising her incantation was holding the ceiling in place until they could get out, he briefly marvelled at her power before darting in behind the gargoyle and launching himself at its back, sword held high. His blade penetrated its thick, gnarled skin, and an ear-shattering screech gushed from its mouth. The creature swung out with its log-like arm, sending Daien flying across the room, smashing him into the throne.

Pain shot through him as his ribs cracked and his head slammed against the cold, unyielding granite with a *crack*. For a moment, darkness filled his vision, then sparks flashed in front of his eyes, followed by an excruciating pain in his head.

*   *   *

Tarienne

Hearing a loud grunt as Daien impacted with the throne, Tarienne sucked in a sharp breath, waves of fear raising her heart rate and making the hairs on her arms stand up. A sliver of relief rushed through her when Daien shook his head and attempted to regain his feet.

Aidan spun, his sword twirling expertly in his hand, snapping to a stop to stab at the creature's back. Despite its size, it was surprisingly agile, grabbing Aidan before his blade could sink into its flesh.

Cold fury coursed through Tarienne at the sight of those she loved in danger. More creatures arrived, drawn by the smell of blood, she had no idea where they came from.

Tarienne's power surged, an ancient, long-forgotten spell flowing from her mouth. The Spell of Retribution. She didn't know how she remembered the words yet did not question the immense power surging through her as she uttered them.

Allowing the magic to build, she unleashed it, raising her voice over the din of the battle.

'*Gargoyle morden!*'

As the beasts exploded in a bloody mess, Aidan, Daien and Tarienne threw their arms over their heads before they all scrambled out of the way as a part of the roof collapsed, sending choking dust spewing through the now partially destroyed throne room. Daien rose slowly, grimacing, blood dripping down his neck. Holding his sword defensively, he moved up behind Tarienne.

Tarienne frowned, confused at Daien's protective stance, until her eyes focused on Aidan as he rose, covered in gore, expression furious.

Slowly limping toward them, his gaze bored into hers.

'What did you do?'

Tarienne did not answer or flinch from the accusatory tone. Instead, she raised her chin defiantly.

Despite his injuries, Daien moved protectively in front of Tarienne, his sword gripped tightly. 'Sire...' The low warning in his tone unmistakable.

Aidan shook his head, as if waking from a nightmare, and looked around the room, then back at Tarienne.

'You have magic?'

She nodded, an almost undeniable urge to step back from Aidan coursing through her. By sheer force of will, she held her ground and his eyes, swallowing hard.

Aidan seemed to understand, holding up his hands.

'I am not my father, Tarienne,' he offered quietly. 'I was just surprised. Thank you for saving my life, as well as my people.'

Relief almost overwhelmed Tarienne. She reached out, grabbing Daien's arm to steady herself. He turned to her, concern wrinkling his brow. Her attention was drawn to the bloody wound on his forehead. With the last of her energy, she sent a trickle of magic to start healing his wounds, but before she could finish, her legs buckled, exhaustion finally claiming her.

Both Daien and Aidan reacted quickly, leaping forward to arrest her fall. Catching her under the arms, they lifted her gently onto the now half-shattered throne.

'Sweetheart?' Daien's voice was filled with concern.

'I'll be all right. I'm just fatigued.' She smiled wanly at Daien, then looked at Aidan. 'More will come. I need to tell you...'

Before she could finish, she slipped into unconsciousness.

When Tarienne opened her eyes, she lay in her bed, three pairs of concerned eyes staring down at her.

'Raef!' she cried, flinging her arms around her brother's neck as he sat on the side of the bed.

'You gave us all quite a fright, sweetling.'

Raef pulled back, his handsome face breaking into a smile.

Tarienne knew he had ridden hard, and used magic, to reach Therin so quickly. He had smudges of dirt on his clothes, and his shoulder-length, blond hair hung in ratty strands over his eyes and around his face. His bright blue eyes sparkled as he murmured a healing spell.

'It's time we told Aidan everything, sweetling. Rest while we talk.'

Raef stroked her hair tenderly, then stood and pulled up a chair, straddling it backwards.

Aidan perched on the end of the bed; one leg hooked under him. Daien settled into a chair next to Tarienne. He grabbed her hand, planting a gentle kiss on her palm. She smiled at him, eyes full of love. Raef caught the exchange, a pleased grin crinkling the corners of his eyes.

Tarienne looked at him. 'Raef, we need to leave as soon as possible. I can—'

'Hush, sweetling. Our brethren, alongside Orien and Elnath are bringing in the outlying villagers as we speak, along with food and other supplies and the elves are repairing the damage and fortifying the castle.'

His calm demeanour eased the tension in Tarienne's shoulders, as it always had. Temporarily appeased, she pulled in a deep breath, relaxing back onto the pillow, her fingers entwined with Daien's, as Raef began.

'Firstly, Aidan, Tarienne and I are of the fae, the son and daughter of the king and queen of Darewood. As the eldest, we are the crown prince and princess. I tell you this not to intimidate or boast, but to impress upon you the gravity of the situation that would see us both risking our lives to protect you.'

Aidan nodded, his eyes wide. Tarienne could see the tension in his body, but at least he was trying to accept who she and Raef were. She wondered how he would receive everything else her brother was about to reveal.

Raef continued, 'Many years ago, a prophet came to our kingdom, declaring Tarienne and I would be instrumental in helping find the golden stone and returning it to its rightful place, thus restoring the balance of magic to the world.

'The golden stone was created when, several hundred years ago, the Elders of the immortal races fought a deadly magical war against a powerful sorcerer named Rantar. Half-fae/half-elven, Rantar sought to hold the balance of magic for himself. His greatest desire was to destroy the Elders and gather their power for himself. He managed to kill five of the twelve Elder council and, drawing on dark magic, sucked their power from them as they died. This was no easy feat. They are the most powerful and experienced among us.

'The sheer intensity of the power Rantar gathered eventually drove him deeper into insanity than he already was. The rest of the Elder council gathered an army, finally managing to kill him. Unfortunately, many of the creatures he'd created had already escaped. The council spent many years tracking down these fell beasts and, using powerful containment spells, secured them in caverns deep in the bowels of the earth.

'Before Rantar died, the Elders were able to extract the power he had stolen, yet did not absorb it themselves for fear they, too, would be driven mad. They decided to contain this immense power in a precious golden stone and leave it where no one would think to look for it... in the care of a human king. For many years, it was kept safe in the keep here at Therin.'

Aidan's expression was one of surprise. 'My father never spoke of this.'

Raef paused, drawing in a deep breath. 'When your father became king, he buried everything he believed to be magical in a deep cavern several weeks' ride from Therin. Unfortunately, it appears someone or something has found the cavern and, using the power of the golden stone, has begun systematically freeing the creatures trapped beneath the earth.'

'However, it appears the creatures have bred in their dark prison, creating twisted breeds that possess dark magic. The fae and elven folk sensed the change in the balance and began moving to Therin, where they believed their people would be safe. Until recently, they hid their presence, for fear you were like your father and would seek to hunt and destroy them, but the tales they had heard of your tolerance and fair judgment encouraged them to seek safety behind the city walls.

'When we realised it was to be your destiny to return the balance of magic to Therin, we knew we had to protect you at all costs, so Ren and I moved to Ferngrove. As you are aware, your father allowed her to live here believing Tarienne needed royal guidance. We have watched over you to keep you safe until we could help you return the balance of magic to the kingdom. But it seems we must now move with haste to find and retrieve the golden stone before the situation worsens.'

Aidan couldn't speak for a moment, holding Raef's gaze. When he did, he sounded overwhelmed by all he had heard. 'And how– how do you expect me to do that?'

Tarienne finally broke her silence. She knew what Raef had just told him was a shock, a great deal to process at once. 'We will help you the best we can, Aidan. But now you understand why I was so upset when you wouldn't allow me to accompany you to battle Lemere?'

Aidan nodded. 'I did not know...'

'I realise that, but you need to understand. Until the golden stone is found and the balance returned, you cannot exclude myself or Raef from anything. It is our destiny to help you regain it.'

* * *

Aidan

Aidan's head hurt, trying to process all he had been told. His eyes slid to Tarienne. How had she hidden how powerful she was, especially when they'd been so close? He suddenly felt grateful she'd been able to keep it from his father. If she hadn't, she wouldn't have been by his side, to be his pretend love, to support him when his father died. She'd become such a very important part of his life.

Aidan frowned, remembering what they'd said about protecting him, how he always felt better when Tarienne was close. She'd introduced him to warmth and affection. He didn't remember his mother, and his father had rarely touched him, save for a thump on the back if he'd done something well.

Tarienne had listened to him, argued, agreed, laughed with him, hugged him, held his hand, kissed his cheek, massaged his neck and shoulders when he was tense. Had she been using magic on him all this time?

He couldn't stop a small grin from tugging at his lips. A little of the tension he'd felt eased. He wouldn't be alone on this quest.

His attention was dragged back to the present by Raef rising to his feet and yawning widely.

'Now, if you wouldn't mind, Aidan, I need a bath and something to eat.'

*   *   *

Tarienne

Tarienne smiled to herself. Her brother's tall, muscular, lean body was covered in dirt, but he was still so impossibly handsome, the maids would fall over each other to help him. Tarienne knew he would be kind and accepting, and each one would fall a little in love with him. Unfortunately for them, the only woman he would ever be interested in was Elyssia, the exquisitely beautiful half-fae/half-elven woman he'd rescued years ago. She and her brother, Fienn, had settled in Darewood after their parents had both been killed in a bloody battle. They were each other's family now.

Tarienne's focus shifted back to Aidan, who sat regally, proud of his acceptance of everything he'd seen, everything he'd been told.

'The guest chamber next door is currently unused. I'll send someone to draw a bath for you.'

Raef waved his hand. 'No need. I can do that myself, but I would appreciate if you could arrange for some food to be sent up.'

'Consider it done.' Aidan rose. 'I'll also have the kitchen prepare travel supplies. We leave on the morrow.' Aidan's eyes flicked to Daien, nodding almost imperceptibly. Then he left to organise the management of the castle and kingdom in his absence.

Raef kissed Tarienne's forehead. 'Good night, sweetling. Sleep well.' He slipped out of the room.

Neither Daien nor Tarienne spoke for a long time.

'Stay with me tonight, Daien?' she finally whispered.

He moved to sit beside her on the bed, his gaze hooded. His hand covered hers, linking their fingers together.

'You frightened me today,' he whispered.

Tarienne reached for him, placing her hand gently on his cheek.

'I am stronger than you realise, Daien. The spell I worked today drained my strength. That's all. Raef has replenished most of my energy, but I just need to rest some more.'

'You should not have healed my wounds, sweetheart,' he chastised gently. At her stunned look, he smiled. 'I felt your magic flowing into me.'

Tarienne sucked in a breath, then gripped Daien's arms, searching his face. 'You can feel magic?'

He nodded. 'It's like a... tingling feeling. I noticed something similar that day you tended my leg after the boar gored it, after the jousting tournament, then again today, just before you felt the evil at the market. I just didn't know what it was at the time.'

Excitement tinged her voice. 'You sensed the magic of the elves and fae at the market?'

He nodded.

'Raef must be correct. Somewhere in your line is a non-human. I must talk with him about this. Perhaps he will be able to locate a hidden memory or something that might tell us more about your heritage.'

'Enough talk,' he growled, pushing her back onto the pillow, claiming her lips in a dizzying kiss. All thought of anything else fled their minds.

They explored each other's bodies, their passion igniting over and over until the early hours of the morning.

Tarienne had never felt so relaxed, so treasured. Her heart bloomed with love for her warrior. She marvelled at the contrast between the powerful, skilled fighter and the tender, gentle lover.

She finally drifted off to sleep, securely snuggled into Daien, his arm possessively wrapped around her.

The next morning, Tarienne awoke early, feeling warm and achy in the most intimate of places. Daien still slept. Slipping carefully from his embrace so she didn't wake him, she stood then turned back, unable to stop herself from gazing at the gorgeous man in her bed. He looked deliciously tousled, the sheet draped across his taut stomach, one leg casually bent on top of the covers. She grinned.

Mine.

On impulse, she decided to surprise Daien with breakfast, given this would be their last day alone and in a real bed for many weeks.

She tended to her needs, washed her hands and face, warmed the bath water with a whispered spell, just in case Daien woke before she returned with breakfast, then slipped out of the chambers and down to the kitchen. Locating a tray, she grabbed several pieces of fresh fruit, filled a bowl with freshly cooked oats, pouring a little honey over it, and picked up some berry-filled pastries left over from yesterday. Her stomach rumbled as the delicious aroma of hot porridge drifted to her nose.

When she backed through the door of her chambers, Daien swiftly moved to take the tray, placing it onto the small table beside the bed. He was already washed and dressed in deep brown trousers and a black shirt, which was not yet laced up over his muscled torso. He turned back to her, his eyes dark and hooded.

Daien prowled closer, taking her hands in his, dropping a gentle kiss onto her lips. He looked so gorgeous, she desperately wanted him to kiss her again... and again... and again. Drawing her to the chair beside the bed, he motioned for her to sit. Tarienne looked up at him as she did, a question in her eyes.

He dropped to one knee before her, gathering her hand in his. She drew in a sharp breath, her heart pounding.

'Daien...'

'Tarienne,' he interrupted, his voice husky with emotion, 'today we depart on a long and dangerous journey. Before we leave, I want you to understand how much I love you, how much I desire you, how much you mean to me. Before you came into my life, I was happy enough, yet something was missing. You have shown me a depth of love and passion I did not know existed. You are the other half of my soul. I love you so much, sweetheart. Will you marry me?'

Tarienne gasped and slid to her knees in front of him, tears flowing freely down her cheeks. 'Oh, Daien.' She kissed him with every ounce of love and passion she possessed.

When they pulled apart, Daien searched her face, a frisson of concern furrowing his brows. 'Is that an "Oh, Daien, yes", or "Oh, Daien, no"?'

She laughed. 'Yes, my Daien. I love you. Marrying you will make me the happiest woman alive.'

Daien's smile spread wide. He stood, drawing her up with him and wrapping his arms around her so tightly, she could barely breathe. He picked her up and swung her around, making her squeal, planting a bruising, joyous kiss on her lips. Lowering her back to the floor, he fished around in his pocket.

Tarienne struggled to produce a coherent thought. When he produced the most beautiful ring she had ever seen – a gold crest surrounded by rubies and diamonds – her tears began anew. He grasped her hand, tenderly sliding the ring onto her finger.

'Daien, it's beautiful.' Admiring the crest and the setting of the stones, she turned her hand slightly, watching it sparkle in the light. Her gaze sought his. Were there tears in his eyes?

Tarienne flung her arms around Daien's neck, hugging him hard, then kissing her way along his jaw to his lips.

Eventually, he slid her arms from around his neck, grasping her hands. Entwining his fingers with hers, he lifted the ring up to eye level.

'This was my mother's. It's our family crest, though I've never been able to find out more of its history.'

Her eyes filled with tears. 'Oh, Daien. I'm so honoured that you would give me your mother's ring. It is such a precious gift.'

He kissed her fingers one by one, sending a shiver through her. 'I wish we could marry before we leave, but it will be something to look forward to on our return.'

Daien turned her hand over to kiss her palm. Desire flooded her, a soft moan escaping her lips. He worked his way up her arm and to her neck, then the sensitive spot beneath her ear... at which point, all coherent thought left her.

Groaning, she arched against him. Not breaking the kiss, Daien swept her up, shoved everything to the back of the dresser, and set her on top. He moved between her legs, evoking a little whimper from her.

Impatient to feel his skin under her hands, Tarienne grasped the hem of Daien's shirt and dragged it over his head. He broke the contact of his lips with hers, then trailed them down to her breasts, suckling the tight buds through the thin material of her shirt.

Daien pulled her toward him and placed her feet on the floor, then pushed her trousers down her legs, bending to pull them over her feet. Hurriedly, he removed his own trousers, then lifted her back onto the dresser. The silky skin of his manhood strained to enter her.

Her heart thumped, taut nipples rubbing against the material of her shirt. Heat and dampness pooled between her legs, accompanied by a needy ache.

'Daien, please...' she pleaded as he nibbled her lips.

He slid into her heat, sighing with pleasure. Tarienne clamped her ankles around his waist, drawing him in deeper. The shift in position elicited a groan from Daien. Tarienne knew the moment he let himself go, succumbing to the powerful desire coursing through them both.

Their lovemaking was fast and hard, and Daien's climax built quickly. His eyes trailed over her as he thrust. When Tarienne cried out, the intensity too much for her, he sucked in a deep, steadying breath and began a slow, sweet, torturous rhythm, taking them both higher than ever before.

The delicious ache within Tarienne built with every stroke, every touch, every kiss. When her crescendo hit, tidal waves of ecstasy rolled through her. She dug her nails into Daien's back, screaming his name. He slanted his mouth over hers, muffling her cries. Her muscles clenched rhythmically around him as Daien thrust several more times, crying out as his own release hit, his hot seed pumping into her.

Touching his forehead to hers, Daien leaned into her, catching his breath.

They held each other until well after their breathing had eased and heart rates had returned to normal.

Eventually, they parted to clean up and dress, knowing this would be the last time for many weeks they would be able to indulge in such pleasures.

Settling into the chairs by the window to share breakfast, Tarienne lifted pieces of fruit to Daien's lips, eating some herself as they talked.

*　*　*

Raef

After resting, bathing and donning fresh clothes Raef made his way to Tarienne's room and rapped on the solid wooden door.

'Come,' Tarienne called, happiness lacing her voice.

When Raef entered, Daien looked up, smiling. He had one long, leather-clad leg propped up on a chair, the other hanging over the edge of the table where he perched, polishing his sword.

Raef walked to Tarienne, grasping her hands in his, a smile lighting his face as he sensed the waves of happiness emanating from both Tarienne and Daien.

'Is there something you wish to tell me, sweetling?'

Tarienne lifted the ring to where Raef could see it, her face splitting into a huge grin.

Raef whooped, sweeping her up into a hug.

'Congratulations, sweetling, I'm so very happy for you.'

Raef kissed her cheek, then returned her feet to the floor. Striding over to Daien, Raef offered his hand.

'Congratulations, my friend.'

When Daien grabbed it, Raef shook it vigorously and pulled him in for a quick, brotherly hug, then stepped back, surveying them both, his eyes sparkling.

'Raef, would you please have a closer look at the ring Daien gave me? It was his mother's. Perhaps it will tell us more of his heritage.'

*　*　*

Daien

Daien watched as Raef grasped her fingers, carefully examining the ring. Twisting it into the light, Raef frowned, then uttered a few words in what Daien assumed was the fae language that sent a tingle across his skin. When he'd finished his examination, Raef turned to him.

'Would you permit me to look into your mind to see if I can locate any of your childhood memories?'

Daien nodded without hesitation. He already trusted Raef more than some he'd known far longer.

Raef closed his eyes, deep concentration etched across his features. Daien felt him probe carefully and methodically through his memories, sifting back to his younger days. Daien's mother's image flashed into his thoughts, her deep green eyes, flowing long, blonde hair and ethereal beauty catching him by surprise.

Raef opened his eyes, smiling. 'I suspected as much. From what I can tell, Daien, your mother was a druid. I believe your father to have been human. This crest represents a family with deep druid roots. One with the gift of great strength and love for their people. This symbol on the ring,' he pointed to what appeared to be three tiny, interconnected spirals, 'represents strength, the pattern of diamonds and rubies indicates the power of undying love.'

Daien lifted Tarienne's hand to his lips. Deep, unconditional love swirled through the connection they shared. His voice thickened with emotion.

'Then it is perfect for my Ren.'

His eyes shifted from Tarienne to Raef, tapping his head with a finger. 'You found out all that in there?' He whistled through his teeth, making Raef and Tarienne chuckle.

Raef nodded, smiling. 'I assume your parents told you all this at some point, presumably hoping you'd remember your heritage after they were gone.'

'Yes, I believe they did. You seem to have awakened some memories of my mother.' He paused thoughtfully as fragmented flashes of memories long forgotten before this skipped across his consciousness.

'Thank you, Raef.' Tarienne glanced at Daien seeming apprehensive. 'Raef, may I speak with you in the hallway for a moment?'

Daien looked at her curiously but returned to the table and continued cleaning his sword.

* * *

Tarienne

Tarienne drew Raef into the corridor and closed the door. 'I wish to give Daien the gift of immortality, which Father entrusted me with when we left Darewood.' She wrung her hands apprehensively, waiting for his response.

Raef nodded thoughtfully. 'Under the circumstances, I believe it to be appropriate. However, you must explain everything about the spell and its consequences before you bestow this upon him. You should understand he may not agree. It's a difficult thing for mortals to accept, and despite his heritage, Daien is still a mortal.'

'I know. It will change nothing if he does not accept. I need to be with him, Raef. There's a connection I can't explain.' Her heart clenched with the power of her love for Daien. 'It's the same between you and Elyssia, isn't it? I didn't understand before.'

'Yes, sweetling.' Raef smiled, leaned in, and kissed her cheek. 'Now, go to him, but make haste, for the hour of our departure approaches.'

Taking several deep breaths to steady herself, she nodded, then slipped quietly back into the room. Closing the door, she glided toward Daien. He looked up from his sword, his brows drawing together in a small frown. Placing his sword onto the oiled cloth he had been using to clean it, he stood, opening his arms wide. Tarienne walked into his embrace, lingering there for a moment.

'What is it, sweetheart?'

She smiled against his chest. He understood her better than anyone, even Raef. She pulled back and reached for Daien's hands, clutching them tightly.

'Do you remember when I told you I was fae?' He nodded, waiting. 'What I didn't tell you was the fae are immortal.'

She searched Daien's face for a reaction. Seeing none, she assumed this information didn't surprise him. Before her resolve crumbled, Tarienne continued.

'When Raef and I left Darewood, my father gifted me with a very special vial to bestow immortality on my chosen partner, should he not be of an immortal race.'

Barely stopping to breathe, she plunged ahead, her hands trembling. 'I ask you now...' She paused, swallowing down the fear he might refuse. 'Will you allow me to gift this to you with the knowledge, as an immortal being, many mortal friends will age and die before your eyes? It is not an easy thing to do. You should know it does not mean you can't be killed, but it is more difficult to do so. Know that if you do not accept this, how I feel about you will not change. Will you spend the rest of eternity with me, my Daien?'

Tarienne's eyes sought Daien's, attempting to decipher the play of emotions swirling there. Love, joy, acceptance. No hesitation crossed his expression. He pulled her to him, locking her in his powerful arms and gently stroking her hair. Her pulse escalated when he moved her back a few inches, gently grasping her cheeks in his hands to look into her eyes. She was stunned to see moisture in his.

Gods, I love this man.

'My beautiful fae princess, you've already given me the most treasured gift of yourself. To live with you for the rest of eternity is my heart's desire.'

Tarienne's heart soared, tears trickling down her cheeks.

Daien bent his head to kiss them away, his lips trailing down to hers, stealing a kiss. 'What do you need me to do, my love?'

Tarienne marvelled, not for the first time, at the ease with which Daien accepted her magic, the unconditional trust he placed in her.

Walking to her coat lying on the bed, she reached into the pocket and withdrew the vial, removing the stopper. She swirled the thick, clear liquid around, muttering a spell that caused a vapour to rise, then held the vial under Daien's nose.

'Inhale, my love,' she commanded softly.

As Daien closed his eyes and breathed deeply, Tarienne caught the rich, thick scent of the sweet potion.

'*A posse ad esse, citius altius fortius, concordia salus, fac fortia et patere.*'

Her voice was almost unrecognisable to her own ears as she spoke the spell. Laced with the power of the ancient incantation, Tarienne's utterance echoed through the room, enveloping them both in its potency.

She could have just touched him to impart the final part of the magic, but she chose to kiss him instead, letting the spell flow through her into him. Daien inhaled sharply, the power coursing through him, like the lick of a flame around a burning log. Tarienne knew the moment the heat subsided, and the potion had taken hold. She stepped back.

'Is it done?' Daien scanned his body, twisting his head around to search for physical evidence of the change within.

Tarienne chuckled and nodded, flinging her arms around his neck, unable to speak through the intense emotion spiralling through her.

Daien whispered against her hair, sending shivers along her spine, 'What I really want to do now is show you how much I love you, but we must leave soon.'

He held her close, his fingers splayed low on her back. Her heart drummed so fiercely, she was certain Daien must be able to feel it.

When she lowered her hands to rest against his chest, the rapid beat of his heart echoed hers. Daien lifted her chin, dipping his head to kiss her tenderly. She slipped her arms around his neck again, urging him to continue, plastering their bodies together. A growl rumbled through him as he deepened the kiss.

At that moment, a knock sounded on the door. Reluctantly relinquishing Daien's lips, but not their embrace, Tarienne called, 'Come in, Aidan.'

He strode into the room, looking magnificent in full battle regalia, not questioning how she'd known it was him. He stopped midstride, noticing them in each other's arms. Without a word, Tarienne smiled and held out her hand. The ring glistened in the early morning light streaming through the window.

Eyes wide, Aidan strode across the room, smiling broadly at them both. 'Well, congratulations!'

Holding his arms out to Tarienne, he pulled her into a fierce hug and kissed her cheek, then grabbed Daien's hand, shaking it vigorously, before pulling Daien in for a quick hug. Aidan's eyes flew to Tarienne, and she sensed his uncertainty around how she would react to the gesture, given he was king and Daien was a guardsman. He visibly relaxed when she beamed back at him, nodding her approval.

Raef appeared at the door, dressed for battle. 'Are we all ready?'

Daien nodded, sheathing his sword with a resounding metallic ring.

Tarienne buckled on her smaller, lighter fae sword and swung her pack onto her shoulder. 'Ready.'

Aidan nodded, his hand resting on the hilt of his father's sword sheathed at his hip.

They filed out. Tarienne looked back into the room wistfully, then squared her shoulders and followed the others to the stables.

The cobblestone streets were filled with people going about their business, children playing, the clang of the blacksmith's hammer, people chatting as they queued at the food vendors. Women rifled through bolts of cloth to find the one that either appealed to them or they could afford to buy. Those on the street parted respectfully to allow the riders through, bowing low when they realised who rode the majestic war horses draped with gold and maroon.

Tarienne rode in front of Daien. She could feel his eyes roving over her back... and lower. Straightening in her saddle, she spoke into his mind.

'If you continue that train of thought, my Daien, I just might have to join you on your horse and lead Lacey.' She turned in her saddle to see his reaction.

The grin he shot back transformed his face, making him even more breathtakingly handsome. Her heart and body warmed instantly, especially when his gaze filled with sensual heat and promise.

Dragging in a deep breath to steady herself, she turned back, focusing on Raef, who managed to look relaxed and imposing at the same time.

Dressed in the soft green colours favoured by fae of royal blood, her brother looked exquisitely handsome and commanding on his black stallion. Women whispered and giggled, admiring him as he rode past, disappointed when he didn't look their way.

Tarienne's eyes flicked to Aidan riding at the front. He acknowledged his people with a smile and a wave. He was a good king, and she was proud of him for that, but she loved being around him even more when he was "just Aidan"—relaxed and playful, yet still the consummate warrior.

Tarienne worried this quest may be his last opportunity to be himself, without his royal responsibilities. She fervently hoped not.

As the group clattered through the castle gates, Tarienne wondered how long it would be before they returned to their lives behind the walls of Castle Therin.

CHAPTER 8

The group travelled for many miles along the roughly marked, well-worn roads. Tall, straight trees flanked the path, their branches waving majestically in the wind. The smaller branches dipped and swayed, the leaves whispering, telling their secrets to anyone who passed. Tarienne strained to listen, sure she could hear words on the wind. Unable to catch what they said, she slowed Lacey, her brows furrowed in concentration.

Raef dropped back to ride beside Tarienne. 'What can you hear, sweetling?'

'I can't make it out. I feel as if I almost understand the words, then they slip away, becoming just the sounds of the forest. What do you think it is, Raef?'

'It could be that the dryads recognise Daien's druid blood and are trying to make themselves known to him. Let's rest for a while and see if he can tell us anything.'

When Daien and Aidan caught up, Raef motioned them to the side of the road. They dismounted and Tarienne moved close to Daien, leaning into him. He wrapped his arm around her shoulders, kissing the top of her head.

Looking up into his eyes she asked, 'Did you hear anything as we rode?'

His expression turned thoughtful. 'I believed I heard something, but then it disappeared. I feel as if something has been following us for the last few miles. I haven't seen anything, though. Do you have any idea what it could be?'

After tying their horses to a small tree at the edge of the path, Raef and Aidan walked up. 'I believe it to be the dryads trying to make contact with you, Daien.'

Aidan sent him a puzzled look, then looked at Daien. 'Dryads? What on earth is going on?'

Tarienne smiled. Aidan was on a *very* steep learning curve and was handling it incredibly well.

'We have discovered Daien has druid blood. Raef believes the tree spirits recognise this and are trying to call to him. But because the balance of magic has shifted, the dryads are unable to show themselves. Their words are faint, lost in the wind.'

'Druid blood?' Aidan sighed, as though he wanted to ask how many more surprises there'd be. 'What would they be trying to tell him?' A thoughtful expression crinkled his brow. 'I suppose we'll never know, unless they manage to make their words clear to him. Come. Let's rest for a while.'

Shades of regal command flickered through Aidan's attitude. Tarienne supposed it would take him a while to relinquish it.

Raef stretched out under a large, shady tree and took a swig from his waterskin. Daien dropped to the ground beside him, tugging on Tarienne's hand and pulling her onto his lap with a mischievous grin. Aidan plopped down in front of them, cross-legged, and drew a deep draught of water. Then he eyed Daien curiously.

'Druid blood, eh? Does that mean you have magic, too?'

'I have no idea.' Tarienne watched as Daien struggled not to add 'sire' to the end of his comment. She squeezed his hand at the confusion in his tone. His eyes flicked to hers before returning his attention to Aidan. 'I only found out yesterday, after Raef looked at the ring. He took a little,' he wiggled his fingers over his head, 'trip through my memories to determine my heritage.'

Daien's cheeky grin made them all laugh. Tarienne rolled her eyes at him, snuggling happily into his lap.

Raef stood, stretching his long, muscular legs and retrieved his saddlebag. 'Anyone hungry?'

Tarienne laughed. 'Do you know these two *at all*?'

Daien pouted at her playfully, and Aidan let out a reproachful, 'Hey!'

They ate a meal of fruit, bread, and cheese, as if they were on a picnic. Tarienne couldn't help wondering how long the calm and quiet would last.

When they resumed their journey, Daien took the lead, Tarienne and Aidan in the middle, Raef keeping guard at the rear. Aidan seemed to be in a thoughtful mood, and Tarienne was happy to ride silently beside him as they rode up into the foothills of Mount Avalon. The mountain stretched out for many miles to the west of Therin. Tarienne gazed at it, lost in her own thoughts.

The rest of the day was happily uneventful. They rode in silence except for an occasional comment about the woodland creatures scurrying about, the view, or the biting insects that appeared in the late afternoon. When the sun dropped low in the sky, they stopped to set up camp on the edge of an outcrop. Removing their horses' saddles, they rubbed them down, loosely tethering them so they could eat their fill of the lush, green grass.

The camp overlooked a small waterfall and lake that was the beginning of the River Arnon. The valley below was rich with vibrant, green plant life. The pounding of the water on the rocks sent a fine spray over the surrounding vegetation, causing the drops of water on the leaves to glisten like red jewels in the waning sunlight.

Tarienne stood at the edge of camp, enjoying the cool evening air and the beauty of the sunset. Daien's arms slid around her, tugging her back against his chest. Melting into his warmth, she wrapped her arms over his, the contact rejuvenating her after the long journey.

After soaking up the comfort for a few minutes, they searched the edges of the forest, managing to collect a few twigs and small branches for a fire, while Aidan and Raef hunted for small game. They soon returned with two rabbits, cleaned and ready to cook.

Daien and Raef took charge of cooking, tossing the meat into a large, black pot Tarienne had brought with them, along with some wild carrots they'd found and a sprinkling of herbs. Tarienne watched Daien stir the delicious smelling stew, loving that a king's guardsman could cook, wondering where he'd learned.

She smiled, and Daien winked playfully at her as Raef held out the bowls to serve the food. Her brother frowned, shoving Daien's arm gently to gain his attention.

They ate, chatting and laughing companionably.

Raef soon stood to retrieve his waterskin from his saddlebag. 'We're close to the border of Therin. Given we're not certain how far this evil has crept, I think we should take turns on watch. I'll take the watch from midnight, for a couple of hours, if everyone agrees.'

Tarienne nodded. 'I'll take the one before.'

Daien opened his mouth to argue, but she pinned him with a determined look. He held up his hands in surrender, turning to Aidan.

'I'll take the one after Raef until dawn, if you're happy with taking the first watch before Tarienne, sire.'

At the use of the royal acknowledgment, the first since they'd left the castle, Tarienne's eyes flicked from Daien to Aidan.

Aidan responded instantly. 'I'm happy to do whatever suits everyone else, but while we're on this quest, Daien, I am just Aidan, one of you. Not the king.' He looked around the group, earnestly adding, 'Please.'

Yes, s— Aidan.' A mischievous look played across Daien's face. 'Then, since we cooked, perhaps you'd like to do the dishes.'

Tarienne's eyes widened, and she bit her lip to stop herself from laughing.

Aidan paused, opening his mouth to say something, then closed it and collected the plates. He headed down the steep path to the lake below.

Tarienne jumped up, calling out, 'I'll go with you, Aidan.'

She caught up with him halfway down the rocky path, which wound around to the left of the waterfall. The mist rose from the lake, moistening her skin and chilling the air. Tarienne's fae vision allowed her to see in the dark, but a human's vision did not, and Aidan carefully picked his way down the slick, narrow trail. However, given the full moon illuminated the path, she decided against creating a magical ball of light to guide his way.

Tarienne followed him to the edge of the water, taking the plates and beginning to clean them while he filled the large, leather waterskin with fresh water.

When he'd finished, Aidan moved to squat beside her. 'I meant what I said, you know.' He took the remaining plates from her and began washing them. 'I don't want to be the king on this quest. It might be the last time I can be just me. You're all my friends,' he raised his eyebrows, 'though Daien will get payback for this.' He lifted the plate in his hand, chuckling softly, then lowered his eyes back to his task.

Tarienne leaned into him, resting her head on his shoulder for a moment, then sat on the damp grass, her eyes travelling to Aidan's. She could tell he felt like the odd one out of the group, and she didn't want it to continue.

'Aidan?' He looked up at her. 'I'm not sure I would have survived in Therin without you.'

He paused, watching her intently, a slight frown creasing his brow.

She continued, 'Fae need to be touched, to be loved, and though you were initially reluctant, you often hugged me when I needed comfort. Even though we were pretending, I loved being by your side, holding your hand, sharing your life. You have become like a brother to me, and I don't want that to stop. I have room in my life and my heart for all of you. Do you understand?'

Aidan's eyes held hers for a moment more, then he stood, grasping her hand, and pulling her up with him. Gently wrapping his arms around her, he whispered, 'Thank you, Tarienne... for everything.'

Slipping her arms around his waist, she squeezed softly.

After a few moments, Aidan stirred and pushed her back a little, dropping a light kiss onto her forehead. He ran one hand through his short, blond hair, as he often did when thinking. 'We'd better get back, or they'll think we've been eaten by something horrible.'

Tarienne smiled up at him, turning away to collect the dishes from the damp grass, then faced him once again. 'You know, Aidan, I believe you crave touch almost as much as the fae.'

He eyed her thoughtfully. 'Hmm... You could be right.'

In the light of the moon, with his iridescent, blue eyes, light blond hair and pale skin, she thought, not for the first time, how much he resembled an elven prince. She made a mental note to speak with Raef about investigating Aidan's heritage at some point.

Heading back up to camp, they stepped carefully, lest they lose their footing on the slick path. They reached camp and noticed that Daien and Raef had packed away everything except the pot with the leftover stew, which they'd placed a lid over and moved away from the fire to cool. They were both stretched out on their bedrolls, discussing dryads and druids. When Raef made eye contact with Tarienne, she nodded almost imperceptibly. With a smile, he continued his chat with Daien.

Aidan wasn't one to talk much, unless he had something specific to say, but he joined in enthusiastically, asking questions about the druids and their association with the dryads.

Tarienne smiled, pleased "just Aidan" was finding his place in the group.

It wasn't long before Aidan took first watch while everybody else bedded down. He moved to the edge of the outcrop, giving him the best vantage point to keep guard.

'Wake me when it's my turn, Aidan,' Tarienne reminded him.

He nodded and made himself as comfortable as he could.

Daien beckoned to Tarienne, and her heart skipped a beat at the heated look he sent her as she lay on her bedroll beside him. He slid his arm around her, pulling her close.

Snuggling into him, she wiggled to get as close as she could. A barely audible groan reached her ears just before Daien swooped in for a passionate kiss. His tongue stroked hers, setting her body on fire.

After a few moments, they broke the contact, even though they both wanted much more. Daien locked his arms around her, and they settled down to sleep... although Daien had other ideas.

He nuzzled Tarienne's neck, running his tongue down the sensitive area from her ear to her throat, and tightened his grip, pulling her against him. His hard body pressed into hers, his arousal nudging her back. Her body ached with a need she knew she couldn't fulfil right now.

Her eyes flicked to the others. A soft snore escaped Raef's form. Aidan was turned away, keeping watch.

Tarienne swivelled in Daien's arms, so she faced him. They gazed into each other's eyes, knowing they couldn't take their need any further tonight. Turning again so she could snuggle her bottom into his groin, she whispered, 'I love you, my Daien.'

'And I love you, my beautiful fae princess.'

*   *   *

Aidan

While Aidan scanned the landscape, his mind drifted back over the last few months. Not long ago, he'd been a prince, spending his days preparing to be king. Due to his father's decree, Therin had been free of magic... or so they'd thought.

Aidan's only real concern at the time had been to stop his father from presenting him with possible brides. He smiled, recalling his ruse with Tarienne. They *did* love each other, but not romantically. He was happy for Tarienne and Daien, though it raised tiny pangs of jealousy within him. Aidan knew it was because he enjoyed the closeness, the comfort of her touch, as she had suggested earlier today.

Thoughts of comfort raised thoughts of his mother. He wished he could remember more of her. A vague whisper of recollection told him she'd been slender with honey-blonde hair and striking blue eyes, like his, and was very tactile and affectionate. But he wasn't sure if the memory was real or just the way he wanted to remember her.

Now he was the king of Therin and the castle had been attacked by magical creatures. Gargoyles, no less. Tarienne was fae and possessed powerful magical abilities, and his faithful king's guardsman and friend, Daien, was a druid. To top it all off, they were on a quest to retrieve the golden stone, which would return the balance of magic to the world. Until a few days ago, he hadn't known there was magic in his kingdom, let alone a balance that needed to be restored.

Aidan's head swam for a moment. He felt like he was doing the right thing yet had no idea how to achieve their purpose. Reaching for the sword strapped to his side, he rested his hand on its hilt, allowing the familiar chill of the steel to comfort him. Even without magic, he could still protect his friends and his people. He knew it in his heart.

His worry calmed as he looked over his shoulder at the sleeping forms of his companions, coming to rest on Daien and Tarienne, Daien holding her close. He wondered if he'd ever find a deep, all-consuming love like theirs.

* * *

Tarienne

It seemed she had only been asleep for moments before Aidan gently shook her awake to take her turn on watch. Rubbing the sleep out of her eyes, Tarienne slid out of Daien's embrace, careful not to wake him. Hugging Aidan, she walked to the grassy ledge and dropped, cross-legged, onto the hard ground. Before long, Aidan's soft snores reached her ears.

Focusing on the surrounding area and the grassy plain beyond the lake, her eyes swept carefully, checking for any sign of danger.

After several hours, she noticed movement in the distance and strained her eyes and ears for a clue as to what it could be. Her pulse skipped, nervous tension tightening her muscles. When Raef walked up to relieve her, startling her, Tarienne pointed out the distant activity.

He looked, then shrugged. 'Whatever it is, it's a long way off. I'll keep watch. Why don't you try to get some more sleep?'

Tarienne nodded and walked back to Daien, snuggling into his warmth. Unfortunately, she lay there for what seemed like an eternity, sleep eluding her, so she slid out of Daien's embrace again and plopped down next to Raef. Wrapping her arms around her knees, she stared out into the darkness. There was no need for words between them. Tarienne loved her family dearly, but she and Raef were especially close.

Raef pulled her to him to ward off the cold. She leaned into his warmth, both drawing comfort from each other.

'You miss Elyssia.' She looked up at him.

Raef sighed and nodded, eyes sparkling with emotion. 'When I see how happy you are with Daien, I miss her even more, but she is not like you, Ren. She would be neither happy nor safe on this quest.'

'She is a lady—gentle, elegant, beautiful. She is perfect for you.' Tarienne's voice softened. 'I miss her, too. Her soothing ways, her friendship.' She pulled away from Raef and looked up at him. 'When this is over, do you think Lys will come to Ferngrove?'

Nodding, he smiled. 'I wish to ask her to marry me.'

'Oh, Raef, that's wonderful.' Tarienne wrapped her arms around his neck, kissing him on the cheek.

They sat for a while, arms wrapped around each other.

Eventually, Tarienne pulled away. 'I think I might freshen up in the lake.'

*   *   *

Raef

Raef watched as she stood and walked to her pack, quietly gathering a soft cloth and some clean clothes. She disappeared down the path.

Refocusing on the surrounding landscape thoughts of Elyssia slid across his consciousness. He wondered if it was because she was thinking about him, too.

Knowing his mastery of mindspeak was strong enough to reach Elyssia across the distance, he silently called her name. His eyes continued to sweep the area for any signs of trouble as her soft, breathy voice caressed his mind.

'Oh, Raef. It's so good to hear from you.'

He sighed. *'Elyssia, my love!'*

Up on the outcrop, Raef turned away slightly, so he did not intrude on Tarienne's privacy. His thoughts turned back to Elyssia, his body hardening with the memory of her soft cries as they made love. The sound of her voice cheered him more than he believed possible.

'I love you, Lys. Gods, I miss you so much.'

Her tinkling laughter and soft voice rippled across his thoughts, tightening his loins as effectively as if she'd touched him.

*   *   *

Daien

Daien awoke, rubbing his eyes and yawning as he surveyed the area. His body was chilled without Tarienne's warmth against him. Rising, he drank from his waterskin, then sat down beside Raef on the outcrop, looking for Tarienne.

Raef motioned toward the lake, where Daien could just make out her silhouette in the moonlight.

'She decided to freshen up. You know, it's not time for your watch yet.' Raef raised one eyebrow speculatively. 'You could freshen up, too, if you wanted.'

Daien grinned. He scrambled up and grabbed his saddlebag, then trotted down the path, his body hardening at the mental image of the woman he loved, naked and wet.

Tarienne stood knee-deep in the icy water, soaping herself, as Daien prowled up to the bank. He slipped off his clothes, then waded into the water. When he quietly snaked his arms around her from behind, a throaty chuckle escaped her lips as she leaned back into him.

He whispered into her ear, his voice husky, 'Have I told you how exquisitely beautiful you are? Gods, Ren, your body glows in the moonlight.'

'All fae glow in the light of the moon,' she breathed, moulding herself to his hard body, adding, 'when they're naked skin is exposed to its light.'

Slowly turning her to face him, Daien cupped her face. 'You appear ethereal. I have never seen you like this before.'

She was his entire world, could bring him to his knees with nothing more than a kiss from those sweet lips. A soft, possessive growl rumbled through him.

Tarienne plastered herself against him as though she was unable to get close enough. Daien couldn't stop the groan that rumbled through him when she reached up, her lips seeking his.

When she broke the kiss, she grasped his hand, leading him out of the water. Lowering herself to the soft, mossy bank, she tugged at his hand to pull him down too and he willingly settled beside her, his body thrumming with need. Running his eyes over her, his lips curved up appreciatively. He moved his hand between her breasts where her heart hammered, and her body quivered in anticipation.

They made love until the world shattered into sparks of pleasure so intense, he captured her mouth to silence her screams.

As the waves of indescribable pleasure gradually subsided, Daien's entire body hummed. Resting his weight on his elbows, he gazed down at his beloved Tarienne.

'You've never glowed like that when we've made love before,' he whispered in awe.

She chuckled. 'You've never made love to me under the stars before.'

Daien wrapped his arms around Tarienne and rolled over, so she straddled his body, not breaking their intimate connection.

She smiled, caressing the side of his face with her fingers, running them through the stubble on his chin.

'Hmm, note to self... Our house will have no roof.' He chuckled.

Tarienne laughed. 'That might be a problem when it rains. We'd better clean up and get back. It must be nearly time for your watch.'

Daien sighed, his powerful hands circling her waist and lifting her off him. He stood, offering his hands to pull her up, taking the opportunity to pull her against him again. They indulged in exploring each other's bodies a little longer, then washed themselves before dressing and returning to camp.

Raef said nothing as they returned. Looking suspiciously pleased with himself, he yawned, stretched, and lay down on his bedroll. In moments, he was asleep, a smile on his lips.

Tarienne sat next to Daien for a while, his arm draped around her shoulders as he took his watch. When she became sleepy, she retrieved her bedroll, placing it beside him. She snuggled against him, her head in his lap, deep, red tresses falling across his thighs. He smiled to himself, wondering if she realised how much she destroyed both his control and the focus he so prided himself on.

Running his hands through her hair, he scanned their surroundings. He'd never dared to dream he could love, or be loved, with such intensity. His eyes drifted down to Tarienne. His heart clenched with the strength of the emotions swirling within him. Emotions he'd held in check… until she had arrived in Therin. She'd broken through his tight control the very first time they'd met. That day, she'd saved his life and stolen his heart.

His thoughts briefly travelled back three years. After he'd healed from the wounds inflicted by the boar, he'd chanced on her in the great hall, asking permission to escort her back to her chambers. They'd chatted on the way, her arm casually linked through his, Tarienne asking questions about Therin. When they'd reached her chambers, she'd thanked him and gifted him with a smile that made his knees weak. From that moment, he'd been lost.

The first time she'd leaned into him had almost unmanned him. He'd been forced to fist his hands at his sides and grit his teeth to prevent himself from wrapping his arms around her and tasting those sweet lips. After that, he'd sought every opportunity to be close to her, touch her, talk with her.

Daien's mind drifted to the images of her naked body underneath him at the lake earlier. Desire slammed into him, like a punch to the stomach. She was his, yet he still struggled to believe it.

He'd fallen in love, never believing they could be together. Now, he treasured the thought of forever with Tarienne, had confidence in his ability to look after her always.

Daien leaned over, gently touching his lips to hers as she slept. He loved her so fiercely that it hurt.

*　*　*

Tarienne

After Daien finally woke her so they could be on their way, Tarienne lit the fire with a quick spell, warming the rest of the stew for breakfast, while he roused the others.

They all ate in silence, revelling in the closeness of their group. Once finished, Daien washed the bowls in the lake, a penance for making Aidan do it the night before and retrieved more fresh water for the next leg of their journey.

When he returned, everyone was ready to leave. He stowed the bowls in his pack and looped the leather waterskin over the pommel of his saddle. They mounted and cantered back to the road.

Aidan seemed much more relaxed today, chatting amiably with both Daien and Raef, asking them about many things, including mindspeak. When they stopped for lunch, Tarienne decided to explain how they communicated by thought. Aidan quickly caught on to the concept and, much to their surprise, was quickly able to join in when they communicated.

They all chuckled at the intense look of concentration on Aidan's face when he tried to project his thoughts. His mind voice was weaker than Daien's, but nonetheless, he could make himself heard.

After eating, they rode on, teasing Aidan via mindspeak, which he accepted good-naturedly. Tarienne sighed quietly, wishing they could stay like this rather than head into danger.

The next few days passed in much the same way. They settled into an easy pattern of camaraderie and respect for each other's ways. Tarienne was pleased to see Aidan had eased out of his authoritarian persona and into "just Aidan".

Around mid-morning on the fifth day of their journey, Daien noticed they were being followed silently communicating it to everyone.

'Has anyone else noticed that we appear to have company?'

A chorus of agreement filtered back to him.

'Is everyone in agreement that we continue on and see if they mean to intercept us?' Raef asked, riding high in his saddle.

Tiny, almost imperceptible nods of agreement came from everyone. Spurring their horses on, it soon became obvious the trackers were intent on a challenge.

The riders swooped in around them, loosing an arrow that barely missed Raef, whizzing over his head.

All four reined their horses to a halt, leaping down and drawing their weapons. Instinctively standing back-to-back, they faced their assailants. Daien glanced sideways at Tarienne, concern etched across his expression. She briefly met his gaze, nodded and returned her focus to the riders ahead.

Twenty men, all wielding viciously curved blades and wearing filthy, black clothes that appeared to have once been fine leather, tramped through the grass with their knee-high boots made of matted fur, strange bands around their wrists.

When the stench of them reached Tarienne's nostrils, she almost retched. Her heart pounded in her ears, hands shaking slightly around the hilts of her fae knives. Tightening her grip, she dragged in a deep breath. The brush of Daien's arm against her restored her courage, and she raised the knives, crossing them in front of her in readiness.

The attackers smirked, obviously thinking the four riders would be easy prey, until Raef let out a fae war cry that had them pausing mid-stride. Daien, Raef and Aidan surged forward. Swords flashing and twirling, they took down four men before their attackers had time to retaliate.

Tarienne spun with her twin knives, slitting one man's throat, relieving another of his sword. As he groped to regain his weapon, Aidan plunged his sword through the man's heart.

Tarienne nodded her thanks. Aidan spared her a wink, then swung the hilt of his sword in an upward arc under one man's chin, sending him flying backward into several others, sprawling in a crumpled heap.

Refocusing on the battle, Tarienne noticed Daien fighting two men to her left, Raef cutting a swathe through the wall of men lunging and swiping at him to her right. Tarienne spun low, booting one man between the legs. He clutched his groin moments before she slashed his throat with an upward motion. Quickly straightening, she moved to stand at Daien's back.

Holstering her knives and drawing her sword, she emulated Daien's style, exactly as he'd taught her. They became as one, slashing and stabbing, spinning, and ducking, confusing their attackers with their double-team tactics.

Only three of their assailants were left, and they quickly took flight to escape the vicious onslaught of the four warriors.

Looking around at the carnage, panting, Raef, Daien, Tarienne and Aidan finally lowered their swords.

Before they could catch their breath, an enormous pulse of power flowed over them. The earth itself seemed to shake. It throbbed through them, filling their heads with a deafening drumming. The desire to cover their ears was almost overwhelming.

Tarienne fought against it, flinging her hands out to Daien in a silent plea for help. She attempted to chant a counter spell, but blackness quickly filled her mind.

When Tarienne woke, she was facing a thick, wooden post, her ankles and wrists tied around it. The ropes cut into her, congealed blood crusting the skin around her bonds.

She glanced to her right, seeing Daien lashed to a post beside her, unconscious, his head lolling to the side. Dried blood spattered the side of his face. Panic filled her. *Was he still alive?*

She sucked in a few deep breaths, trying to calm herself. Her heart thumped erratically.

Closing her eyes, Tarienne focused on Daien's life force, sighing in relief when he let out a quiet groan. Reaching out with her thoughts, she tried to wake him. She pulled on her bonds, managing to lean against him slightly. Her head cleared a little when she felt the warmth of his skin.

A healing spell formed in her thoughts, disappearing before she could utter the words. Frustrated, she tried again. Something was blocking her magic. She dug deep and held on to the words long enough to allow a tiny trickle of magic to seep into Daien.

The effort quickly turned painful, forcing her to release the incantation, her head spinning. There was no doubt someone with powerful magic held them captive.

Visually sweeping the area, Tarienne searched for Aidan and Raef. There was no sign of them. She could only hope that meant they had escaped.

They were in the middle of a compound surrounded by brown tents. Most were small, however, there were a few larger and highly decorated ones with brightly coloured cloth. Tarienne memorised every detail.

Men, dressed in the same garb as those who'd attacked them, went about their business, leering at her, yet steering clear. Tarienne observed their movements in the hopes of gleaning some information that might help them escape.

When Daien began to stir, her focus flicked back to him. He coughed and winced. A blackening bruise was visible through a tear in the shirt on his right side.

Someone will pay for that.

Daien slowly looked up, his hazy focus settling on her. 'Damn, Ren, what hit us?' he groaned.

'A very powerful pulse of magic I think, but I have no idea where it came from.'

Hearing a sudden commotion to their right, everyone in camp rushed to the source.

Tarienne sensed fear roil over her, curious as to why… until a chilling howl pierced the air. 'Saints preserve us,' she whispered, turning her head to Daien, fear lancing through her. 'Weres.'

'Weres? As in *werewolves*?' Daien asked, frowning, disbelief in his voice.

Nodding, Tarienne drew in a deep breath to steady herself. 'Well to be precise they're wolf changelings. I'm going to try to use my magic to help us escape.'

She closed her eyes, whispering a spell. Nothing happened, but white-hot pain lanced through her skull. She sucked in a breath, moaning.

Once the agony subsided, she slowly opened her eyes to see Daien looking at her, concern etched across his face.

'My magic appears to be suppressed. I can feel it, but I can't seem to access it.' She refrained from mentioning the searing pain.

'What about trying to contact Raef?' Daien suggested, his eyes locked on what was going on over on the other side of the camp.

'Good idea.'

Projecting her thoughts as strongly as she could, she called to Raef, gritting her teeth against the excruciating agony stabbing through her brain.

Shaking her head, as much to dispel the pain as to let Daien know the result of her efforts, she whispered, 'Nothing...'

Before she could say anything else, a tall, powerfully built man, his demeanour one of confidence and authority, strode toward them, a few of his minions trailing behind him, cowering. He was incredibly handsome, with ice-blue eyes and black hair that hung rakishly over one side of his face.

Tarienne scowled, sensing the glamour emanating from him in waves. He moved up so close, she could feel the heat of his body, smell his scent.

Wolf!

'Well, well, well... Tarienne, princess of the fae. It is an honour to meet you.' He bent in a mock bow, laughing as his eyes raked over Daien. 'And who is this? Your human pet?'

Daien showed no sign of irritation, calmly and silently meeting the man's stare.

'I am Lacas, pack master of this group. Now, tell me. What you are doing so far from home, little one?'

Neither Daien nor Tarienne acknowledged his questions. Lacas snarled, 'You *will* answer me, whether it is now or later.'

Without warning, Lacas slammed his lips down onto Tarienne's so hard, it forced her head to snap back. Daien jumped, straining at his bonds, his face taut with fury. When Lacas pulled back, Tarienne spat, trying to rid herself of his taste.

The wolf smirked. 'Ah, your little pet cares for you.' To the guards around him, he snapped, 'Untie her and take her to my tent.' He looked pointedly at Daien, a cruel smirk on his face. 'Then strip her and secure her to my bed.'

Several men rushed forward. Tarienne's heart plummeted, icy fear lancing down her spine. Tears welled in her eyes as she twisted against her captors, daring one last glance at Daien as they dragged her away.

*   *   *

Daien

Lacas laughed. Daien's rage consumed him as he continued to strain and pull at his bonds. He barely noticed the blood trickling down his wrists.

Daien snarled, 'When I get my hands on you, you're dead.'

Lacas walked away, seemingly unaffected by the threat. 'I'll bet your fae is a tasty little morsel.'

Daien wanted to scream in fury. Gut-wrenching nausea roiled through him. He sucked in a sharp breath in a fruitless attempt to calm himself, realising he would not be any help to Tarienne if he didn't. A sliver of doubt about his ability to protect her worked its way beneath his usual confidence. He forced it aside and turned his focus on working the knots binding his hands.

Consumed with fear, Daien continued to pick at the ropes, his wrists painful and bleeding. Without her magic, how could Tarienne protect herself? He jerked violently against his bonds, then began to chew relentlessly at the ropes. Anything to get to her. He'd promised to keep her safe.

He froze as a soft rustling sounded behind him.

*   *   *

Tarienne

Tarienne writhed, kicked, and bit at the men dragging her to Lacas' tent. They laughed, discussing how Lacas liked when they fought and how much he was going to enjoy this one... until she managed to spin out of the grip of one and kick him between the legs. The changeling went down, hard.

The second man released his hold and punched her viciously in the stomach. She dropped to the ground and sucked in panicked breaths of air, trying to fill her screaming lungs. Curling up in the foetal position she wrapped her arms around her knees as she struggled for air.

Lacas stormed up. 'You useless idiots can't even manage to take a woman to my tent.'

He lashed out with his boot, catching the man on the ground in the head. The man cried out, then stilled.

Tarienne briefly wondered if he was dead but felt little sympathy for him.

She turned her attention back to Lacas, struggling furiously as he grabbed her arm and dragged her toward his tent.

Turning, he pinned her with a black stare. The sharp surge in his magical glamour became a physical pain, streaking through her head. When he spoke, his voice was hard and compelling. 'You will *stop* struggling and *will* do as I say.'

Tarienne could do nothing but obey, such was the power of his magic. If only she could access her own, she'd tear him to shreds. Trying to draw on it, she whimpered as white-hot agony lanced through her head again.

Lacas shoved her through the flap of his tent, stepping in after her. He grinned cruelly as she sprawled onto the ground.

'Strip and wash yourself,' he commanded, pointing to a wash bowl and cloth on the table beside the bed.

Although her brain screamed for her to stop, she could not. The power of Lacas' glamour was just too strong, compelling her to do as he said. His eyes raked over her while she undressed, then blatantly watched as she washed herself, his tongue flicking lasciviously over his lips.

Tarienne shuddered, struggling to break through the compulsion holding her. Tears pricked the corner of her eyes when she couldn't.

When she'd finished washing, she picked up her dusty trousers and started to pull them back on.

'No!' Lacas commanded. 'Lie down on the bed.'

Tarienne lay down, albeit reluctantly, her will not her own. Shock filled her at the power of Lacas' glamour. How had he become so strong?

She mentally struggled. A sharp increase in the potency of the magic snapped through her, sending excruciating pain lancing through her again causing her to cry out.

Her chest tightened with panic when Lacas slowly stalked toward her, holding several pieces of rope. Tarienne gasped yet could not move. He tied each of her limbs to a corner of the bed, so she was spread-eagled and vulnerable.

Lacas removed his shirt, adjusted the engraved, leather straps on each of his wrists and flexed the muscles in his arms. Tarienne's entire body trembled violently. She could do nothing to help herself. In her entire life, she'd never felt so exposed, so helpless.

Lacas spoke in a soothing voice, increasing the glamour again.

'Why are you shaking? You want me, don't you? I can feel it, my wolf senses smell your arousal. I can even detect the stench of that human on you. Does he pleasure you, Tarienne? You have never known pleasure until you've been with a wolf. My mate cannot keep her hands off me, yet I'm strangely drawn to you. Your scent is extremely compelling.' Inhaling deeply, his lips curled into a snarl. 'Look at me, little one.'

Her body betraying her, a smile pulled at her lips. When he cupped her breast and rubbed her nipple between his fingers, she arched into his hand, her traitorous body responding even as her mind screamed at her to fight.

He moved down her body to explore her feminine folds. She groaned and bucked, desperate for his fingers to delve deeper, to relieve the growing ache, even while nausea tightened her stomach and tears slid from the corners of her eyes.

'That's it, princess. You're enjoying it, aren't you?' he purred. 'You're delicious, little one. I can see why your human is so addicted to you. I've long heard of the sweetness of the fae.'

Lacas stood, unbuttoning his trousers. Tarienne had never felt such fear, such frustration at not being able to help herself. A moment of utter hopelessness stilled her, threatened to plunge her into blackness Lacas moved closer, unleashing his erection. He straddled her belly, not caring that his weight rested on her. Her breaths came in short gasps, unable to fully fill her lungs with him on top of her, coupled with the sheer terror of what he was about to do.

He regarded her for the briefest of moments, then slid down her body so his hips rested between her thighs, his erection straining to enter her. He shoved her legs apart and circled his hips against her hypersensitive nub, growling like a rabid dog.

Bringing his lips down on hers, he kissed her, hard, biting and drawing blood, then licking it away. He pushed his hands underneath her, his claws protruding, raking down her back, the searing agony making her body rigid with a scream she was unable to voice.

A tear trickled down her cheek. The sensation tugged at her free will, the excruciating pain of the torn skin down her back clearing her head a little.

Somewhere deep inside, Tarienne registered something was terribly wrong. She tasted her own blood, felt the burn of the deep gashes, became aware of sticky fluid trickling down her back. The agony finally broke through her magic-induced stupor.

Bucking beneath Lacas, she fought his intense glamour. He interpreted her movements as eagerness. When he jammed himself at the entrance to her body, Tarienne screamed. Lacas leapt off her in shock.

'How the hell did you break through my glamour?' he snarled as his body tensed, readying himself to pounce, to satisfy his sickening lust.

Tarienne steeled herself. She would fight Lacas every second, likely dying for her efforts. Her thoughts jumped to Daien. If only she could hold him one more time. Another tear escaped and trickled down her cheek. She couldn't even tell him how much she loved him, or that she was sorry.

Her attention snapped back to Lacas when a gurgling sound bubbled from him. Surprise jolted through her when she saw a sword sticking through his chest. As it slowly withdrew Lacas crumpled to the ground in a bloody heap.

Raef stood there, holding his dripping sword high, both terrifying and magnificent in his battle fury. Relief washed over her, tears tumbling down her cheeks.

Slicing her bonds, Raef threw her pack onto the bed and bent to remove one of the leather bands from Lacas' wrist. 'Get dressed,' he ground out, barely contained fury evident in his stiff posture. 'We must get out of here quickly. The wolves are coming.'

Tarienne was sickened by what Lacas had done to her, by her inability to fight his magic. Her stomach roiled. Rolling off the bed, she retched, losing what little food was in her stomach. Her belly clenched painfully.

Raef moved to gather her hair back from her face. He sucked in a sharp breath at the sight of her bloodied back. When she'd finished, he knelt in front of her, offering his waterskin. She rinsed out her mouth, then swallowed a small sip.

Raef's voice softened. 'We don't have time for me to help you now, sweetling. Forgive me? As soon as we are safe...'

Tarienne nodded, gasping in pain when she pulled on the softest shirt she had, which still felt rough against the gashes down her back. She yanked on her trousers and boots, then scooped up her pack to follow Raef, stepping over Lacas' body. Only when they cautiously circled around the back of the tent to avoid being seen did she dare speak.

'Are the others all right?' Her voice sounded small and scratchy, even to her own ears.

Raef responded with mindspeak. *'They are despatching the guards to the right of the compound. Aidan managed to pull me into the bushes and rouse me but not before they took you both. I'm sorry, sweetling... Can you run?'*

Her answer was clipped. 'Yes.'

As soon as they were clear of the cluster of tents, they exploded into a run no human could keep up with. Tarienne desperately hoped the wolves couldn't, either.

*   *   *

Raef

They bolted through the forest, weaving, climbing, splashing through water, anything to disguise their trail. When Raef noticed Tarienne lagging behind, he slowed so she could catch up. What he saw when she did had him chastising himself vehemently. Blood flowed down her back, soaking her shirt, down her legs, into her boots.

His voice was laced with anger, but at himself. 'Damn it, Ren. You should have told me.'

Tarienne stopped, lifting her chin. 'I can run as long as we have to,' she snapped, eyes sparking with determination.

Raef closed his eyes, seeking inner calm. She needed his help, not his anger. When he opened them again, Tarienne stared at him, tears trickling down her reddened cheeks. Her pain hit him like a punch to the gut.

Raef's stomach roiled with anger and disgust at the damage Lacas had caused. He struggled to tamp down the urge to go back and cut Lacas into tiny pieces. He wanted to cry at the pain Tarienne must be suffering, berating himself for not being able to reach her earlier.

*   *   *

Tarienne

'Oh, sweetling. Forgive me. Come here. We have run long enough. I need to begin healing your back.'

Tarienne nodded, swallowing the sobs lurking beneath the fragile thread of her control. She reached for Raef's hands, desperate for his touch. He pulled her closer, touching his forehead to hers, whispering calming words.

When her breathing evened a little, Raef turned her and removed her shirt. He sucked in a sharp breath at the damage inflicted by the wolf's claws, once again having to tamp down his anger.

Leading her over to sit on a large rock, he rummaged through his pack for a soft cloth and his waterskin.

'This is going to hurt, sweetling.' His voice cracked.

She didn't dare turn to look at him as she nodded, afraid to speak and unleash the full force of her distress.

Moistening the cloth, Raef cleaned the blood from her back as gently and carefully as he could. Tarienne had no idea how she held herself still, the wounds burning like fire at the slightest touch.

Clutching her shirt to her breast, she felt exposed and vulnerable all over again. When she heard low voices and saw Daien and Aidan step through the trees, her heart jumped. Daien would hold her. She could fight again now he was here. When they were close enough, their eyes widened in horror at the slashes on her back.

Tarienne watched Daien expectantly, waited for him to come to her. Instead, he grabbed Raef's empty waterskin. Her heart plummeted and shattered, despair filling her as he walked away.

'I'll go fill this,' he growled over his shoulder.

Raef and Aidan exchanged confused glances. Raef frowned, shook his head and continued cleaning Tarienne's wounds.

Aidan crouched in front of her. He grasped her free hand, kissing it tenderly. 'Would any of your special herbs help with the pain?' he asked softly.

Smiling wanly at him, she swallowed against the tears that threatened. 'The one in the red bag, a pinch steeped in boiling water, would help. Can we light a fire here?'

'Yes, Ren. There's no question. I'm lighting it to make the tea for you.' He smiled at her, the love and compassion she saw bringing her undone. Her shoulders began to shake, sobs racking her entire body.

*   *   *

Aidan

Aidan sat next to her and slipped his arm around her waist, away from her wounds, gently pulling her to him. He glanced back at Raef, who shook his head sadly and continued cleaning the deep gashes, muttering a spell as he worked.

When her sobs subsided, Aidan eased back and lifted her chin. He wiped away her tears with his thumb and kissed her on the nose.

'I'm going to light a fire now and make you that tea.'

At her nod, he stood and walked away.

Aidan was incensed by Daien's behaviour. How could he treat this incredible woman that way? Her sobs had almost brought him to tears. How could Daien be unaffected when he professed to love her? And where the hell was he?

Aidan busied himself steeping the tea for Tarienne... partly so she could have something to ease her pain, partly to keep himself busy to contain his ire.

When it was done, he squatted in front of her, holding the cup.

She reached out to accept the brew, wincing. 'Thank you, Aidan. I—'

He leaned in to place a tender kiss onto her cheek. She shivered. Every protective instinct he had urged him to hold her, so he gave in to it and reached around to the back of her neck, carefully pulling her close and pressing his forehead to hers. Tarienne sighed. He held her silently as Raef finished tending her wounds. Aidan's heart ached for her. His anger at Daien stoked higher every minute of his absence.

A little while later, Daien clumped back through the trees, dropping the waterskin beside Raef.

'How far was the damned waterhole?' Aidan asked, anger lacing his voice. 'Bring me some wood for the fire.'

Daien did not respond, grabbing a few pieces of wood and throwing them at Aidan's feet. Aidan glared at him, then thought better of starting something in front of Tarienne in her current state.

*　*　*

Tarienne

Tarienne's eyes followed Daien as he plopped down in front of a dead tree stump. Glancing in her direction, he looked away when he saw her staring at him. Her eyes filled with tears again. The pain of her wounds was nothing compared to the agony of Daien's rejection.

He couldn't even bring himself to look at her, knowing what Lacas had done. Hell, why should he? She couldn't accept it herself. Another tear escaped.

Sipping her tea, the pain eased a little. Tarienne did not speak as Raef finished the healing. She just eased her shirt on and curled up on her bedroll. Closing her eyes, she pretended to be asleep so she didn't have to deal with Daien's disgust. Aidan gently laid a blanket over her.

She soon heard Daien's soft snores. Aidan and Raef moved away, talking quietly. Right now, Tarienne couldn't bring herself to care. Her world had been shattered. The stress and memories of the day had taken its toll. The herbal tea had eased the pain enough that she finally gave in to the bone-deep exhaustion and drifted into a fitful sleep.

Nightmares woke her several times, cold sweat dampening her clothes. Each time, her eyes flicked to Daien. Each time, her heart ached with an almost unbearable feeling of loss, tears trickling down her cheeks until sleep claimed her again.

CHAPTER 9

Tarienne woke the next morning, her body stiff and sore. For the briefest of moments, she wondered why. When she moved to sit up and pain lanced down her back, the nightmare of the previous day returned full force.

Looking around, she saw Daien sitting a short distance away, sipping a mug of what smelled like soup. Aidan and Raef were nowhere to be seen. Carefully, Tarienne rolled onto all fours, gingerly standing up. She grimaced at the pain.

'Is there any soup left?' she asked in as light a voice as she could manage, trying to ease the tension. He nodded but didn't speak. Rummaging through his pack, Daien produced a mug, which he filled and handed to her, not meeting her eyes.

'Daien—' she began.

He jumped up. 'I'm going to wash the mugs,' he ground out, stomping away.

Her heart sank, throat constricting as she fought back tears. Tarienne couldn't blame him for being disgusted with her. She was disgusted with herself for not being strong enough to resist Lacas' glamour. She shuddered at the images of him defiling her, replaying over and over in her brain.

The mug of soup suddenly lost its appeal. Her stomach roiled. Hastily dropping the mug, she ran to the edge of camp. Falling to her knees, she retched until her stomach ached, tears rolling down her face. Alternately sobbing and vomiting until there was nothing left, her stomach cramped, and she rolled into a ball, her arms wrapped around her belly. Despair and agony warred for her attention.

That was how Raef and Aidan found her when they returned. Raef helped her up, dampened a cloth and washed her face, standing beside her as Aidan offered her water to rinse her mouth.

They both glanced around, looking for Daien, then at each other. Raef had obviously hoped leaving them alone would give them time to sort out their problems.

'He's gone,' Tarienne muttered.

Turning to her brother, she swallowed, tears still trickling down her face. 'I need to wash Lacas off my body, Raef. Can you please take me to the lake?'

Squatting in front of her, he brushed the hair from her face. 'I'll take you, sweetling. Don't cry. You know I can't bear it when you cry.'

He gathered her into a careful hug, allowing a healing spell to flow into her.

'I'm sorry,' she sobbed softly, then took a deep breath. 'Can you bring my pack, please?'

Raef nodded, turning to Aidan. 'Could you and Daien retrieve the horses while we're gone?'

Aidan nodded and walked away, mumbling something under his breath that sounded suspiciously like, 'And he's going to get a piece of my mind.'

*   *   *

Aidan

His anger spiked. It was past time to confront Daien.

Aidan found Daien on the other side of the lake, scrubbing at the mugs. 'I think the damn mugs are clean,' he snapped. 'Help me find the horses.'

Daien looked at him sharply but didn't comment. They were silent while they searched for the horses, rounding them up one by one. Luckily, their mounts were well trained, responding to Aidan's whistle, despite having been frightened off by the wolves.

Aidan led Lacey over to his stallion and started to place his foot into the stirrup. Changing his mind, he turned and glared over his shoulder. Daien, head lowered, led both his and Raef's stallion. Aidan's temper finally got the better of him. Standing with his hands on his hips, he drew himself up to his full height.

'You're an idiot, you know that?'

Daien's head jerked up. He glared at Aidan, snapping, 'What?'

'You're... an... idiot!' Aidan mounted his horse, leading Lacey away.

Daien quickly jumped onto his own steed, leading Raef's black stallion. He galloped up beside Aidan, his face taut with anger.

'What the hell are you going on about?'

Aidan reined his horse to a stop, aiming a menacing glower at Daien. He gritted his teeth, barely holding his anger in check.

'One of the sweetest, most beautiful women I have ever known is in love with you, but because of something she couldn't prevent, you push her away. Like I said, you're an idiot.'

Daien glowered at him, looking angrier than Aidan had ever seen him. 'Is that what you think?!'

A dangerous calm laced Aidan's voice. 'Yes, Daien. That's what we *all* think, including Tarienne.'

Shock at Aidan's words clouded Daien's expression, appearing as though he'd been punched. 'Ren thinks I don't want her because of what that animal did to her?' he whispered, the words barely audible.

Aidan nodded.

Daien lowered his head, groaning miserably. 'That's not true. I can't face her because *I* wasn't able to stop it from happening. I promised her I would protect her. I thought *she* wouldn't want *me* because I failed.' He lifted his head, sorrow radiating from him. 'Damn it, Aidan. How can she think I don't want her when she's the very air I breathe?'

Aidan urged his horse closer, his anger dissipating. 'Raef and I couldn't protect her, either, Daien. Don't you think we feel guilt too? Only love can help her overcome this. Talk to her. Tell her how you feel. She also feels shame that she wasn't strong enough to fight Lacas' magic. She's scrubbing herself raw as we speak.'

'I *am* an idiot,' Daien groaned.

Aidan nodded, grinning. 'Yes, you are. Come on.'

Aidan and Daien spurred their horses, thundering toward camp. When they arrived, Daien jumped off his stallion before it had completely stopped, looking back at Aidan.

'Go on. I'll look after the horses.'

Daien nodded, jogging toward the lake, his thoughts racing.

*   *   *

Daien

Raef sat cross-legged on the sandy soil near the water's edge, his eyes averted as Tarienne stood in the waist-deep, icy water, naked, furiously scrubbing at herself.

He watched Daien approach, his expression neutral. Daien held his gaze, desperately hoping her brother would trust him alone with her.

Gods know I don't deserve their trust.

Inclining his head, Raef stood and headed back toward camp. Gratitude spread through Daien that Raef was still willing to give him a chance to make amends, despite the pain he had caused his sister.

Pulling off his boots, Daien waded into the water. Tarienne didn't seem to notice his approach, she was so focused on cleansing her skin. A physical pain slammed into him at the deep, raw gashes across her back. Moisture gathered in his eyes as realisation of what she'd suffered squeezed his chest so tightly, he could hardly breathe.

Stopping an arm's length away, he softly mouthed her name, not daring to touch her yet. Tarienne straightened and turned, excruciatingly slowly, her tear-filled eyes seeking his. The sadness she radiated knocked the breath out of him. He'd done this to her when he'd vowed to love her always, to keep her safe. His heart plummeted. What if she couldn't forgive him?

He drew in a breath. 'Ren, I'm so sorry. I—'

Tarienne's shoulders began to shake. Great, racking sobs rocked her body.

'Ren, don't. Please. Gods, I'm so sorry, sweetheart. I love you so much.'

Daien stepped forward and gathered her tenderly into his arms, careful not to touch her wounds. Maintaining a stranglehold on his own emotions, he didn't move until she began shivering. He led her back to the bank, then carefully wrapped her in the large, soft cloth Raef had left, gently patting her dry. Taking care with her wounds, he helped her dress. She continued to shiver as he pulled her down to sit, so he wrapped his arm around her shoulders, drawing her to his side to keep her warm and provide much-needed comfort for them both.

'Ren, I need to tell you something...'

She lifted her watery eyes to his. Daien's heart pounded. A moment of fear trickled down his spine. He would win her back, no matter what it took.

Clearing his throat, he forged on. 'I was angry at what happened with Lacas, but not at you, sweetheart. At me.' He lifted his hand to cup her cheek. The tenderness, the fierce wave of protectiveness washing over him, brought tears to his eyes.

Tarienne frowned, a question on her lips, but allowed him to continue.

The dam broke, the words spilling from him, tears trailing down his face. 'I was angry at myself because I couldn't protect you, couldn't stop Lacas from hurting you. None of us could. It wasn't your fault, Ren. Gods, Aidan was right. I'm such an idiot. But I'm an idiot who loves you with everything I am. Forgive me for hurting you, please? I...' He swallowed past the lump in his throat.

Tarienne slid her arms around his neck, her lips tentatively sliding over his. He stiffened for the briefest of moments, stunned by her acceptance of his confession. Wrapping his arms around her waist, he carefully pulled her onto his lap, pouring all the love he felt for her into the kiss.

She pulled back, gazing into his eyes. 'Oh, Daien, I thought you were disgusted by me because of what happened. I love you so much,' she smiled, 'even though you are an idiot.'

They both chuckled, then shared a tender kiss which soon became passionate.

No longer able to resist, Daien allowed his hands to roam over Tarienne's body. Although he knew they couldn't make love, he needed her to understand how much he desired her.

He slid his hand under her shirt to the cool, soft skin of her flat stomach, then up to her breast. She cried out against his lips, wiggling on his lap. Daien's responding growl rumbled deep in his chest. The feeling of her breast in his palm sent desire spiralling through him, but he held it in check, albeit with difficulty, as he rolled her nipple between his fingers. Their tongues duelled, his hunger for her growing.

Despite the pain of her wounds, Daien sensed that Tarienne wanted this, needed this more than anything right now. To know he still wanted her, still loved her, was better than any healing magic. She moaned with pleasure as he lifted her blouse and took her nipple into his mouth, suckling. When she arched her back and gasped Daien paused, raising his eyes to check if she was all right. Returning his attention to her taut nipple, he drew it into his mouth again, rolling the other between his fingers. Knowing she was on the edge of a climax, he gently grazed his teeth over the tight bud in his mouth and continued as she cried out tumbling over the peak of pleasure.

He held her until she relaxed against him. 'Daien, I love you,' Tarienne breathed against his lips.

'I love you, my beautiful, sweet, fae princess. I will always love you. I'm sorry—'

Tarienne silenced him with another long kiss. When they pulled back, Daien sighed and lifted her off his lap. He stood, grabbing her hand to pull her up. He wasn't sure how he'd managed to get this beautiful woman to fall in love with him, but he wasn't going to let her go... ever.

He couldn't resist dipping down to her warm, soft lips for another kiss before they headed back to camp, hand in hand.

Raef and Aidan smiled as Tarienne and Daien returned.

'About bloody time,' Aidan mumbled as they passed.

Daien laughed as he gathered his gear. 'Yes, I know. I'm an idiot.'

Before they mounted, Daien waited beside her as Raef checked Tarienne's back again. He spoke a few magical words to speed her recovery and ease the pain. Once he finished, Tarienne grabbed Raef's hand, holding it tightly.

'Thank you, *toror* (my brother). I don't know what I'd do without you.'

Kissing his cheek, she leaned into him. Raef pulled her close, mindful of her wounds. When he released her, Daien was certain Raef's eyes were glassy with unshed tears. Raef glanced at him and Daien nodded as an understanding of how much Tarienne meant to them both passed between them. Moving away to give them a few moments together Daien checked Lacey's saddle and spoke quietly to the mare before Tarienne approached smiling and leaned into him for a moment.

His heart sang as he kissed the top of her head before helping Tarienne into her saddle. He silently vowed never to let anything drive them apart again. As they had headed back to camp, she had made him promise to discuss everything in the future so there would be no more misunderstandings. He chuckled softly, knowing there would still be misunderstandings, but they would work through them together... and the making up would be so sweet. A grin tugged at his mouth.

Tarienne sighed, leaning down for another kiss, which Daien deepened.

Aidan, astride his stallion, coughed loudly. 'Excuse me, but can we get on with our quest, please?'

Smiling, Daien pulled away and mounted his stallion as Tarienne playfully stuck her tongue out at Aidan. Daien guffawed.

Aidan rolled his eyes. 'Charming!'

Raef chuckled too before they all carefully scanned their surroundings and urged their horses back onto the well-worn road. Daien glanced over at Raef's now solemn expression and knew that he suspected they hadn't seen the last of the werewolves.

CHAPTER 10

Late that evening, when they finally made camp in a dark, wooded copse deep in the forest, they were exhausted but had much to discuss. They fed and watered the horses, then ate their fill of the delicious soup Tarienne made with some root vegetables they'd dug up and herbs from her pouch. They finished off with dried bread and cheese.

Their hunger sated, Tarienne piled the dishes next to the fire while the water heated for washing them, then settled down against Daien, carefully snuggling into his warmth, her back still tender. His arm snaked around her shoulders, dragging her closer.

'The weres won't give up so easily. Once they regroup and appoint a new leader, they'll be on our trail.' Raef leaned forward and grabbed another piece of bread. 'We need to determine what they used to negate our magic; otherwise, they will take us as easily as they did the first time.'

Tarienne leaned closer to Daien, trembling, memories of her capture threatening to overwhelm her. He tightened his arm around her shoulders, dropping a kiss onto her head. Aidan grabbed her hand, squeezing, as if willing his strength into her. Tarienne smiled gratefully.

Emerging from her thoughts, she remembered the wristband Lacas wore, the unusual markings.

'I believe their magic may have been contained within the wristbands they all wore.'

Raef nodded thoughtfully. 'Yes. That was what I suspected, too. As we made our escape, I contacted Elyssia with the details of the one I cut from Lacas' wrist. She spoke with her brother, Fienn, to see if he could find exactly what sort of magic it held. He scoured the tomes in the library at Darewood. This morning, he told me he was certain this was the source of the magical pulse we felt, and he provided information about an ancient spell he believes will dampen the potency of the incantation.'

Raef withdrew the black, leather armband from his pack. It was covered in dried blood. Tarienne shivered. She poked at the band tentatively, feeling only a slight magical hum.

'Why doesn't it affect us like it did when they captured us?' she asked, frowning.

'Because all the weres wore them, I'm guessing the spell is amplified by the number of beings wielding it.'

Raef set the band on the leaf-littered ground in front of them.

'Sweetling, you're stronger with this type of magic than I. I've written down the spell. Could you read it so we can see what happens?'

Tarienne nodded, her shaking hands grasping the parchment Raef held. Her heart pounded, and a light sheen of perspiration dampened her skin.

Daien tightened his arm around her, and Aidan scooted closer, lending his support. Raef nodded his encouragement.

She sucked in a deep breath. '*Amoveo ea meiv sina templa kuile!*'

The armband was immediately consumed by flickering, blue flames. When the flames died out, the leather seemed unchanged. Carefully, Tarienne picked it up, examining the band.

'I can't feel the hum of magic from it anymore.'

Raef took it from her. 'Hmm... You're right.' He smiled. 'We'll both need to memorise the spell in case the weres catch up with us. If they do, we'll have to use it quickly, before the magic takes us out.'

Tarienne shivered at the thought of the werewolves returning. She was terrified she'd be paralysed with fear and unable to remember the spell.

Raef handed the armband to Daien, who turned it over in his hands. 'I can't feel the typical tingle I usually can when there's magic in something.'

Daien passed it to Aidan, who shrugged. 'I can't tell the difference, but I'm the only one here without magic.' He returned it to Raef.

'If this spell doesn't work, Aidan, *you're* the only one here who might be able to save us,' Tarienne reminded him.

She turned to Raef. 'How far are we from the caves?'

'I'd say another three days. The closer we get, the more of Rantar's soldiers and creatures we'll likely encounter. We need to be especially vigilant and only stop for short rests. I'll take first watch. Get some rest. We leave before daybreak.'

'What sort of creatures are we talking about?' Aidan rose to his feet, frowning. He didn't seem to mind the fact Raef had assumed charge... for now.

It was easy to forget he had no experience with any of this. Yet he accepted everything as though he'd been born to it. She wondered what Eldan would have done in his place, grateful Aidan was so unlike his father in many ways.

Raef's voice broke through her thoughts. 'I've seen weres that are viciously clawed bears or black crows. Creatures that are part-human/part-animal. Each and every one smells foul and possesses an evil, twisted mind. Some are empowered with magical artefacts, like the armbands. Their plan is to prevent us from retrieving the golden stone, and they will stop at nothing to do so.'

Aidan spoke as he bedded down, confidence in his tone. 'I know nothing of the power of these creatures, but I do know the power of our combined strength, determination, and courage. These creatures will find we are no easy mark. I have every faith in our ability to complete the quest we have been given.'

Raef settled down to take watch, while the others lay on their bedrolls to grab as much sleep as they could. Daien snaked his arms around Tarienne, hauling her close. He was soon snoring softly, but her sore back kept her awake.

Realising sleep eluded her for the time being, she slipped out of Daien's embrace and joined Raef, carefully dropping to the ground beside him.

'Can't sleep, sweetling?' Raef draped his arm loosely around her shoulders, muttering an incantation.

Immediately, Tarienne felt the pain ease. She leaned into him. 'Thank you, *toror*.'

*   *   *

Raef

Resting her head on his shoulder, Tarienne began quietly singing a fae blessing, wishing safe travel and a speedy return. Raef kept watch and listened, soothed by the beauty of the words and the sweetness of his sister's voice.

His thoughts drifted to Elyssia. He missed her so much, his chest ached. She wasn't like Tarienne. She'd never survive what had happened to his sister. His anger spiked at the thought, and he tightened his grip around Tarienne's shoulders.

It had nearly killed him when he looked into that tent to see her tied to the bed, naked, blood on the sheets, Lacas over her. His vision had clouded, heart pounding in his ears, launching him into full battle fury. If it had been Elyssia, Raef knew he would have lost control completely. As it was, he'd barely clung to the last shred of sanity as he thrust his blade through Lacas' back.

Only Tarienne had ever seen that side of him. It terrified Raef

Elyssia might walk away from him if she witnessed his out-of-control battle rage.

He sighed and dropped a kiss onto his sister's head.

*　　*　　*

Tarienne

A short while later, Tarienne shooed Raef away to get some much-needed sleep. Hearing his soft snores almost immediately, she smiled as her focus drifted over their surroundings, keeping watch.

Suddenly, a surge of magic swelled around her. Her chest constricted in fear, making it difficult to breathe. Tarienne rose sluggishly to wake the others, the potency of the magic already weakening her.

Panicking, her mind went blank. She couldn't remember the incantation. Her throat tightened, heart thundering against her ribs.

Like a lantern in the darkness, Aidan rushed up beside her, clutching the parchment containing the spell. Looping his arm around her waist, Aidan's voice was soft and reassuring.

'Ren, I'm here. Just like you were for me when my father died. Let me help you now. I need you to focus, to be strong for all of us.' He tightened his hold on her. 'I don't have magic. I can't do this without you.'

Her eyes flicked to Raef and Daien on their bedrolls, struggling to rise under the power of the enchantment, then back to Aidan.

'I... I can't. What if I fail them?' she whispered.

Panic threatened to overwhelm her when she considered what might happen to Daien, Raef and Aidan if she did fail. Her breathing escalated, remembering what Lacas had done to her. She couldn't go through anything like that again. Her knees buckled. She was certain she was going to pass out.

Aidan firmly turned her to him, clutching her face in his hands.

He met her eyes, his expression full of compassion, yet his voice held authority.

'Ren, you *can* do this. Only if you don't try will you fail them. Read the words, Ren. I have faith in you, my sister.'

His words, his declaration of trust, pulled her back. She hauled in a deep breath, leaning into him as he held up the parchment. '*Amoveo ea*,' she paused, and Aidan squeezed her shoulder reassuringly, '*meiv sina templa kuile*!'

Looking up, they saw the weres approaching in their human forms, heard their roars as their magic-infused armbands erupted into flames. Chaos ensued as they tried to rip off the bands, before their clothes also went up in flames.

Once the magical effect was negated, Raef and Daien roused quickly, jumping to their feet.

Tarienne dropped a kiss onto Aidan's cheek. 'Thank you, Aidan, my brother. You saved us.'

He grinned and stepped away. Drawing his sword, he brought the flat of it to his forehead, mouthing a tribute to his father, before he strode toward the woods and swung it in a wide arc, striking the changelings. Daien joined him, cutting a bloody swathe through their assailants.

Raef and Tarienne joined hands, weaving the Spell of Retribution. Before they spoke the last words, they shouted to Aidan and Daien. 'Drop!'

Though the spell wasn't directed at them, neither Raef nor Tarienne were sure what effect it would have on Aidan or Daien if they were in its path. Aidan and Daien dropped to the ground moments before the fae shouted the final words of the enchantment.

'*...lupus morden*!'

The creatures screamed as the power of the ancient magic blasted through their ranks, searing their skin. They dropped to the ground, writhing in agony, dying a rapid but painful death.

Raef and Tarienne shook with the effort of weaving the ancient spell. Tarienne gripped Raef's hand, swaying against him, her eyes sweeping across the devastation.

Aidan and Daien rose slowly, staring in amazement at the bodies surrounding them, some halfway between wolf and man, dying before they could complete their shift. Many had blood oozing from their ears and vacant eyes.

Tarienne averted her eyes, sucking in some much-needed air to settle her churning stomach.

Stepping over twisted, bloody bodies, Aidan and Daien moved closer to Raef and Tarienne.

'Are you two all right?' Aidan asked, concern lacing his voice.

Raef nodded as Tarienne approached Aidan, placing her hands on his shoulders and kissing him on each cheek.

'Thank you, Aidan. I couldn't have done it without you.'

After hugging him, Tarienne moved into Daien's arms briefly before turning to stand in front of Raef, surreptitiously scanning him for injuries.

A weary grin lit her brother's face. 'Well, at least we know the spell works.'

Tarienne snorted and slipped her arms around Raef's waist, hugging him tightly. He wrapped her in a gentle embrace, resting his chin on her head.

'Well done, sweetling. I knew you could do it.'

Tarienne's heart lifted, and a little of the mental pain she'd carried since her capture eased, knowing that with Aidan's help, she'd been able to do what was needed. Tears moistened the corners of her eyes.

Finally, she slipped back into Daien's embrace, her arms sliding around his neck. She ran her fingernails lightly up though his hair, evoking a low groan from him.

'My *melar* (lover),' she murmured, pressing herself against him.

Daien lowered his lips to hers for a long, passionate kiss.

After several minutes, Aidan groaned and cleared his throat loudly.

'Enough. Let's get moving.'

Strolling over to their tethered horses, they mounted without further conversation. Tarienne allowed her gaze to linger on each of the men she travelled with. She loved them equally, yet each in a unique way.

Riding up beside Daien, she sent her thoughts to him. *'Have I told you how much I love you, my Daien?'*

Daien's warm, dark eyes met hers. *'Yes, but I never tire of hearing it. I love you, too, my beautiful fae princess.'* He fisted his hand over his heart.

She smiled and returned the gesture.

They rode on. Except for a few snarls and growls in the distance, there were none of the usual sounds of the forest. No birds, no skittering animals, no mating calls, not even the sound of rustling leaves. Daien soon became restless, fidgeting in the saddle. She guessed his druid blood called to the trees, but there was no answer. The balance of magic was failing.

An inexplicable tension filled them all. Tarienne noticed Raef, Aidan and Daien often moved their horses to surround her. Raef was quiet and watchful. Aidan's eyes constantly scanned their surroundings, occasionally flicking to Tarienne and sending her a small, reassuring smile. Daien stayed close, ever watchful for any threat.

The group stopped only when it was necessary to rest or eat. The closer they got to their destination, the more the playful banter and idle chatter of the early days of their quest disappeared, replaced by a sense of foreboding. They could no longer light a fire when they made camp, fearful it would draw attention to their whereabouts. They dared not separate to hunt, so their food supply was running low. Tarienne knew it was time to spare a little magic in order to steep some medicinal, herbal tea to improve everyone's mood.

After they finished a meagre meal of stale bread, cheese, and dried fruit, Tarienne retrieved her pack from her saddle. She opened her satchel of herbs, selected a few and dropped them into a pot, which she then filled with water. Raef, Aidan and Daien watched with curiosity. She smiled, pulling out four metal mugs.

Murmuring a few words in the ancient language, she quickly heated the water. Using a thin piece of cloth, she strained the liquid into each of the mugs, then handed them out.

Raef sniffed the concoction suspiciously. He scrunched up his nose at the odour, evoking a giggle from Tarienne.

'It's St John's-wort, milk thistle and gingko biloba to help boost your mood, along with dried berries and ginger for flavour. Try it, you big baby.'

Raef raised his eyebrows and sipped. Everyone watched expectantly. 'Hmmm, not bad... if you can get past the smell. Pee-ew.'

Tarienne swatted him playfully, chuckling.

Aidan and Daien sipped the brew, making appreciative noises.

Tarienne smiled and settled next to Daien. He moved the mug into his other hand and slipped his free arm around her shoulders.

Too soon, they were on their way again, fearful of staying in one place too long. Tarienne felt the separation from Daien like a physical ache, relieved slightly by riding as closely as she could to him and communicating through mindspeak.

Three days after their encounter with the weres, they came upon a large, grassy plain with no cover. Reining their horses to a stop, they peered out from under the mantle of the trees. In the distance, they saw what appeared to be an encampment with a great deal of activity going on. Smoke rose from huge fires, and even across the great distance, they could hear the din of an army, one made up of evil men and creatures.

As they watched two of the great bearlike beasts began fighting, ripping at each other with their huge claws and biting viciously as they roared their fury over some perceived affront. A group of men standing nearby laughed at the spectacle until the creatures came too close. Shouting angrily, one large man in the group who seemed to be dressed in black garments hanging in tatters around him, withdrew a crossbow, loaded it and shot one of the bears. Stunned, it roared, then toppled onto its back, dead. Wolves and other foul creatures quickly converged and began devouring the fallen beast.

Even from their hiding place across the plain, amongst the trees, Tarienne could feel the evil hanging in the air like a thick fog. The weight of malintent and the stench of the malodorous army stretched its evil fingers across the plain threatening to engulf the companions as they observed.

'Now what?' Tarienne shuddered and turned to the others, moving Lacey closer to Daien as she spoke.

'We must cross the plain to the left in order to reach the caverns where the stone is buried,' Raef answered after a long silence.

'How do you propose we do that?' Aidan asked, a frown wrinkling his brow.

'Let's take a short break and discuss our options.'

Raef dropped smoothly from his horse. His hand ran along the animal's flank as it backed up a few steps, its ears flicking nervously. He spoke quietly close to its ear to soothe its agitation. Aidan did the same, pulling half a semi-dried apple from his pocket. His steed happily took it, munching contentedly, its anxiety momentarily forgotten.

Daien slid from his horse. Walking around Lacey, he held his hands up to Tarienne to help her off the mare's back. Placing her hands on his shoulders she slipped into his waiting arms. His large hands circled her waist possessively as he slowly lowered her to the ground.

Seeking his hand, she entwined her fingers with his. He smiled reassuringly, chasing away the unwelcome feeling of impending doom invading her senses.

Raef grabbed a chunk of apple from his pack and began munching on it.

'We need to cross to the left of the encampment. They'll probably have scouts spread out in the forest, surrounding the plain. Any suggestions?'

While Raef addressed everyone, Tarienne noted that he focused on Aidan, knowing he was the one with the most experience strategising.

Aidan paused thoughtfully before he spoke.

'I believe the only course of action is to take the path through the centre of the plain. To ride as quickly as we can in the hope we can outrun the sentries most certainly placed around the tree line. If they follow, we'll need to decide whether to stand and fight or continue pushing the horses as hard as possible.'

Raef nodded, looking at Tarienne and Daien for their opinion.

Daien's gaze was unwavering.

'I'd normally say stand and fight, but they'd quickly outnumber us. So, I agree with Aidan. Run as fast and hard as we can in the hopes of reaching the caves before they reach us. Hopefully we can get in and out with the golden stone before all hell breaks loose.'

Tarienne nodded. 'I agree. I believe it's our only chance.' She moved closer to Daien, the real possibility of losing him crushing her chest. Breathing as evenly as she could, she tightened her grip on his hand.

Daien turned to her, a tiny frown creasing his forehead, then sent her a reassuring smile. Tarienne forced herself to smile back.

'So, we're all agreed.' Raef strode to his horse and removed his pack. 'Let's rest for a bit, then we can formulate a more detailed plan.'

He gave Tarienne a confident smile.

Do not worry, sweetling. We have the power of the prophecy with us. We are equal to this battle, including Daien and Aidan.'

Aidan's eyes flicked between Raef and Tarienne, a small frown on his brow, as though he'd heard their silent conversation. Turning away, he busied himself with brushing down his stallion.

Raef sat on the ground, cross-legged. Daien grabbed his pack and sat on the soft grass, his back resting against a gnarled tree, branches spreading up high forming a leafy canopy. Tarienne suspected his druid heritage instinctively drew him to the trees for comfort. Smiling, she joined him, leaning into his hard, muscled torso, his heat chasing away the cold.

Aidan sat on her other side, linking his fingers with hers, both seeking and giving comfort. He grinned, his handsome face slightly drawn, his eyes a little too bright.

Tarienne leaned over to place a kiss on Aidan's cheek. She loved this man. He was her brother in every sense of the word except by blood.

Aidan leaned in close and whispered, 'Do not fear for me or Daien. We have trained all our lives for something like this.'

Squeezing his hand, Tarienne again wondered if Aidan had heard her conversation with Raef.

Sharing some rather dry bread and cheese, they washed it down with fresh water as they discussed what to do if they were attacked. All agreed, they would fight together to the end.

If needed, Raef and Tarienne would draw on an ancient spell requiring them to combine their magical strength. Should that be the scenario, Daien and Aidan would ride beyond the tree line, as far as necessary to be safe, and await their arrival. Of course, Aidan and Daien strenuously argued against this.

Raef eventually convinced them it was the best course of action, explaining he couldn't guarantee their safety if they were in the path of the spell when it was unleashed. It would cost Tarienne and himself more energy to shield them magically, which could negatively affect the potency of the incantation. In the end, Aidan and Daien agreed, albeit reluctantly.

*   *   *

Daien

Daien still struggled with the possibility of having to leave Tarienne to face the enemy without him. His warrior's blood pulsed like a drum. He had promised Tarienne he'd protect her. He'd failed her once. He wouldn't allow it to happen a second time.

He knew she was nervous. He could feel her body trembling slightly. It wasn't due to a lack of skill with her weapons, because she was as fierce and talented with her sword and twin knives as anybody he'd ever trained with. No. It was because Lacas had robbed her of her confidence. Raef's and his sister's power combined was immense, but two against a whole army? He glanced at Aidan, who sent him a look of resolve, seeming to sense his struggle.

Slowing his breathing, Daien reached deep for the calm he needed. Tarienne's intoxicating scent of vanilla and cinnamon teased at his senses. He drew it in, allowing it to soothe him.

After finishing their meagre meal in silence they rested for around an hour, then prepared to leave once again.

Daien approached Tarienne and drew her to him for a long, tender kiss. 'No matter what happens, never forget how much I love you.'

Tears welled in Tarienne's eyes and she stifled a sob, clenching the front of his shirt. 'Don't you dare leave me, Daien. I'm not sure I could go on without you.'

He sighed. 'Nor I you. You are the very air I breathe, and I plan to spend forever loving you.'

*   *   *

Tarienne

Tarienne's heart felt as though it was on the brink of breaking at the possible outcome of the upcoming fight. Pulling herself together, she smiled through her tears. 'See you in the forest on the other side, my love.'

Daien kissed her again. When they pulled away, Raef and Aidan, in turn, each hauled her into huge hugs, then clasped elbows with Daien, both pulling him into brotherly hugs.

They mounted their horses.

'Ready?' Raef asked. He held Tarienne's eyes for a brief moment. His usual vivid blue eyes had turned dark, like an ocean in a storm they barely contained the battle fury welling within.

'Courage, sweetling.'

At his nod, they erupted from the cover of the trees, thundering across the grassy plain.

Tarienne leaned low over Lacey's neck, whispering, 'Run like the wind, dear heart. Our lives depend on it.'

Seeming to understand the dire need, Lacey's hooves flew across the green grass, keeping pace with the larger stallions. The horses snorted, chests heaving.

Halfway across the plain, riders broke from the forest. The small army thundered toward them, horses covered with black armour, white, painted markings along the animals' sides. Not one of the approaching riders was remotely human. Aidan's, Raef's, Daien's and Tarienne's horses bolted forward as the disfigured creatures bellowed and shrieked.

The rhythmic thud of their horses' hooves streaking across the now crushed grass of the plain created the sensation of moving in slow motion.

Assessing the situation, loose tendrils of hair whipping around her face, Tarienne released her bow from its clasp, thankful she'd grabbed it from the castle armoury, even though she hadn't used it once since she'd left Darewood. Gripping Lacey tightly with her knees, she grasped an arrow from the quiver on her back and loosed it at the closest of the beasts hurtling toward them. It thumped straight into its chest. Black-red blood bloomed around the arrow as the creature fell, to be trampled by its own steed.

The armoured horses quickly flanked them, too close for her to use her bow. Slinging it across her shoulder, Tarienne lay low across Lacey's neck again, urging her to run even faster. The beasts leaned forward, brutally whipping more speed from their horses. Long, cruelly curved swords glinted in their enormous, hairy hands.

When Tarienne lifted her eyes, her heart slammed into her throat. A wall of archers stood ready to unleash a barrage of arrows in their direction.

She screamed above the din, '*Raef!*'

His attention snapped to her, then upward, swearing under his breath. Time slowed as he hooked his reins around the pommel and rose in his stirrups. Tightening his knees against his stallion's flanks, he raised his arms, chanting a spell. Aidan, Daien and Tarienne closed in around him. The arrows slowed in the air, then stopped, dropping harmlessly to the ground. He blew out a long, heavy sigh of relief.

The rabble whooped as their quarry slowed a little, assuming they were close to defeat. Surrounding the companions, they forced them to a halt.

The stallions snorted and stomped nervously, trapped within the circle of evil. Lacey stood completely still, sides heaving, her nostrils twitching, ears back. Terror threatened to consume the mare. Tarienne leaned low over the horse's neck, whispering a soothing spell into her ear. She calmed as Tarienne moved her into position with the other horses, facing outward toward their aggressors.

Tarienne focused on Raef as he let the battle fury build within him, holding onto it tightly. He grinned wildly. Everything was going according to plan. So far. Still standing high in his stirrups, he gathered his magic, letting it build, then broke into a chant, the force of the spell seemed to rumble the very foundations of the earth.

Tarienne stood in her stirrups. Raising her arms, she joined Raef's chant, which had shifted to the incantation they'd discussed. The power coursed through her, throwing everything into sharp focus. The ancient magic pulsed in her veins, fuelling her resolve, escalating her power.

Aidan and Daien sat, unmoving, swords raised. Their faces were a mask of determination, their battle fury temporarily leashed.

Their assailants smirked, not yet realising their peril. Their horses' sides heaved, flecked with foam from their frothing mouths.

*　　*　　*

Aidan

Aidan breathed evenly, focusing on the faces of the enemy, vaguely registering the unfamiliar words flowing from Raef and Tarienne. Their magic shimmered through the air, buzzing in his ears like a swarm of angry bees. Ignoring the hum, he raised his sword, aware of Daien doing the same beside him.

Raef continued chanting, speaking into Aidan's mind as he wove the spell with Tarienne. *'When we release the magic and clear a path, push your horses as fast as you can. Don't look back or stop, no matter what you hear.'* Raef's voice was commanding, his eyes sliding between Daien and Aidan.

Aidan nodded, glancing at Daien, knowing he wouldn't want to comply, despite their earlier agreement.

Daien started to protest, but Tarienne turned toward him, pinning him with a powerful glare. Her green eyes now iridescent, she wore the magic she held like a mantle. She shook her head imperceptibly. Reluctantly, he yielded.

Aidan and Daien beheld Tarienne for the briefest of moments, her body glowing with the immense power she wielded.

Aidan watched Daien as he wrenched his mind back to the present. This was not the time for distractions. He allowed Daien another second to take in the sight of her before he forced him to refocus, shouting for him to prepare to move.

As they waited Aidan noted the contrast between Tarienne and Raef as they wielded their magic, Raef's power was terrifying. His body sparked, fed by the booming fae words unfamiliar to Aidan's ears. A deep blue-red glow grew between Raef's and Tarienne's hands, like a fireball. Aidan realised then why they wanted him and

Daien to flee, to ensure they would not be in the path of their power. How could they battle against such a force with nought but a sword? He fervently hoped that, if the need arose, he'd find the strength within himself to fight an opponent who possessed magic.

The enemy, suddenly realising their mistake in assuming the group was weak and cowed, wheeled around, scrambling to retreat.

Aidan sent up thanks that the fae were on their side as the power flowed between them, the air crackling like a lightning storm. Daien nodded in Aidan's direction. Riding away from Raef and Tarienne would be one of the hardest things they'd ever have to do, but they knew there was little choice.

Once he and Tarienne completed the powerful incantation, Raef shouted a battle cry. The retreating beasts crashed and bumped into each other chaotically. Aidan and Daien exploded out of the centre of the confusion, their swords cutting a swathe through the riders too slow to escape.

*   *   *

Daien

Daien risked a glance over his shoulder to see Raef and Tarienne sparking and crackling with the power of the enchantment they'd unleashed. The cloud of magic swept toward the terrified creatures and their mounts.

Dragging his attention back to their escape, Tarienne's whisper reached Daien on the wind, above the clamour of the battle.

'Stay safe, my love, and keep Aidan safe for us.'

Urging his stallion on, Daien kept pace with Aidan. His heart torn in two, he had to force himself to continue moving away. He whispered back, *'I love you, Ren. Hurry back to me. We'll be waiting.'*

Now he knew how she'd felt when they rode away to battle Lemere. He swore that neither of them would ever feel that way again.

Aidan and Daien drove their stallions across the plain and into the forest, almost to the point of exhaustion before they dared slow their pace. Finally, they stopped, dismounting beside a small lake, breathless and filled with worry. Allowing the horses to graze and drink, they brushed them down quickly before making camp in a leafy copse of young trees close to the water's edge.

Collapsing onto the cool, damp grass, they drank deeply from their waterskins, listening for signs of pursuit or any indication Tarienne and Raef followed. Daien's heart thumped loudly against his ribs as he fought the urge to go back.

He turned to Aidan. 'This doesn't feel right. We're trained as warriors, to stand and fight.'

He jumped to his feet, pacing around the campsite. 'Damn it, Aidan. I can't wait here while Gods knows what is happening to them out there.'

'You're making me dizzy, Daien. Sit down and breathe. Do you think I liked leaving them? We'll wait for a while, then decide whether to go back. Give them a chance to do what they need to do.'

Daien responded to Aidan's commanding tone without question, dropping cross-legged to the ground beside a young elm tree. He'd been a king's guardsman so long, it was second nature to obey his king, but it didn't stop the rising growl. Aidan's eyebrows rose in challenge, but he refrained from commenting.

*   *   *

Tarienne

When they knew Aidan and Daien were safely out of range, Raef and Tarienne unleashed the power they had gathered. The creatures directly in front of them dropped to the ground, dead. The rest panicked, trampling their own comrades that had tumbled to the ground when their horses reared. Horses screamed in terror, their riders struggling to maintain control to save themselves. The bolder beasts amongst their ranks that had survived by shielding themselves behind others, continued their approach. Several groped and clawed at Tarienne's feet and legs, trying to pull her off her mare.

Tarienne drew her long knives, the battle fury burning through her like wildfire. She quickly despatched the creatures grasping at her ankles, slashing their necks with a wide arc of her twin blades. Thick, black blood spurted onto the ground and Lacey's flank as the hideous creatures gurgled, surprise registering on their disfigured faces before their lifeblood slickened the trampled grass and they crumpled to the ground.

Tarienne glanced at Raef. He'd jumped off his stallion so that he could wield his sword more easily. Eyes wide, his blade flashed, his body tense.

Raef circled, spinning his weapon easily in his right hand then snapping it into his fist in readiness for the next attack. His sword was covered with black blood, headless corpses littering the ground around him.

A vile smell rose from the dismembered carcasses. The stench and grisly sight momentarily caused Tarienne's stomach to roil. She swallowed hard, refocusing her attention on Raef and the power pulsing between them.

Raef swung himself back onto his stallion, moving closer to Tarienne to maintain the enchantment as long as possible to allow Daien and Aidan time to ensure they were as far away as possible. Exhaustion threatened to claim them, but they fought on, holding onto the incredible potency of the spell.

When Tarienne thought she might collapse, the air suddenly pulsed. Raef had opened himself up to the power coursing through him, allowing his immense strength to combine with the ancient magic. Tarienne wondered how he had anything left to give when she was so exhausted.

She watched as those caught in the blast flew backwards and slammed to the ground, writhed momentarily, then disintegrated into a bloody mess. The few remaining creatures that had somehow avoided the shockwave ran for their lives.

Relaxing a fraction, Raef and Tarienne settled back down onto their saddles, panting. Without warning, a black cloud swooped toward them, temporarily blocking what little warmth the sun provided.

'Saints preserve us. Crow changelings,' Tarienne breathed, not sure she had anything left to give.

'Courage, sweetling. We still hold the ancient power. Focus on me and recite the words to reinforce the spell.'

She sighed. Neither of them could wield the magic needed alone. She was close to collapse. The strain of holding the ancient magic for so long had sapped most of their energy. Calling on their reserves, they loosed the last of the power they held.

The giant, coal-black creatures plummeted through the sky, their razor-sharp beaks aimed at their prey. One managed to break through Raef's defences. A cry of pain broke from his parched lips when the creature's beak slammed into his right shoulder. His sword clattered to the ground.

Tarienne knocked an arrow and sent it whizzing past him, straight into the bird's throat. It dropped to the ground, lifeless. She sensed that Raef fought to hold onto the power long enough to destroy what was left of the flock.

As the last of them plunged to the ground, unmoving, his focus drifted over to Tarienne, her bow in hand.

'Thank you, sweetling.'

Breathless, they sat silently for a moment, wondering what else would come. When it became clear that they were victorious, for now, Raef slipped to the ground, bending awkwardly to pick up his sword. Grabbing it with his left hand, he wiped it clean on the grass, re-sheathing it with a wince at the pain in his other shoulder. Tarienne dismounted, wiping her blades on the grass before returning them to the twin leather scabbards on either side of the belt around her waist.

With what little strength she had left, she moved to Raef's side, examining his wound. It was deep and filthy from the foul matter on the carrion crow's beak. When Tarienne reached out to place her hands over the wound and heal it, Raef pulled away.

'Not here, sweetling. We'll need all our remaining strength to ride to safety.'

Tarienne nodded, too spent to argue. Supporting each other, they hobbled back to their horses.

Sighing as she settled into her saddle, Tarienne leaned down and whispered into Lacey's ear, 'Thank you, dear heart. Do you have the strength to take us to the trees, where we can all rest?'

Lacey snorted and trotted off toward the tree line, as if offended at the suggestion she was tired. Tarienne managed a tiny smile at the stubborn pride of her mare. She turned to see Raef following slowly, slumped over his stallion's neck.

Tugging gently at Lacey's reins to slow her, Tarienne waited for her brother to catch up. She'd never seen him so fatigued. Concern stabbed at the edge of her thoughts. Could she protect him if she needed to? Nudging Lacey close to Raef's stallion, they moved slowly. Tarienne's impatience to tend Raef's wounds stabbed at her, despite her bone-deep weariness.

When they finally reached the forest, they didn't have the energy to move too far in. Thankfully, their horses' thirst led them to a small waterhole close to the edge of the heavily wooded forest. They slid from their saddles, exhausted.

Raef barely managed a few steps before collapsing onto the cool grass. He rolled onto his back and groaned. Tarienne rushed over to him. His face was flushed, and she feared his wound was already infected. His skin was warm, and his eyes glazed.

Concern rippled through Tarienne again. She could barely function herself, yet she needed to tend to his festering wound. Uncapping his waterskin, she lifted his head and encouraged him to drink deeply. He complied then fell back onto the grass.

Her heart clenched with fear. Raef had always been the strong one. Always looked after her. Tears pooled in her eyes as she stared at her brother, more vulnerable than she'd ever seen him before. She dashed away the tears.

Stop being such a baby. She rallied the last of her strength.

Knowing she couldn't move Raef on her own, Tarienne retrieved his rolled-up bedding from beside his saddlebag and bunched up a soft cloth she found there to serve as a pillow. She lay his bedroll out beside him, then shoved him until he responded, rolling onto it with a groan. She covered him with a blanket to ward off the chill of the evening air. Raef heaved a deep sigh, falling into a fitful sleep.

Tarienne walked over to the nearby waterhole and filled a container, then grabbed a bowl from her pack and tipped a little into it, warming it magically. After steeping a pinch of goldenseal, which would start the healing process, she cleansed his wound. Once finished, she placed a clean, damp cloth onto his forehead and lay down beside him on her own bedroll, too tired to keep watch.

Managing a brief spell to conceal them, she closed her eyes. The trees rustled, whispering. Tarienne strained her ears trying to decipher their words, before exhaustion claimed her and she drifted off to sleep, her hand laying protectively across Raef's chest. Her last thoughts before her eyelids flickered closed were of Daien and Aidan. She prayed they were safe.

CHAPTER 11

Aidan awoke with a start, unsure where he was for a moment. Daien still slept, his back against a young oak tree, its tiny leaves on the thin, lower twigs brushing the top of his head. Aidan crawled over and shook his shoulder.

'Daien, wake up.'

He opened his eyes and rubbed them, trying to focus. Bewildered for a second, he looked around, then jumped up, agitation making him pace.

'Damn it, I fell asleep. Aidan, we must find them.'

Aidan stood, resting his hand on Daien's arm. 'Calm down. Let's eat, then we'll go back.'

Despite his outer calm, Aidan's heart thumped. Tarienne and Raef should have found them by now, unless... He wouldn't allow himself to finish that train of thought.

'Why don't you try to contact them using your mindspeak?'

Daien visibly calmed, blowing out a breath and grinning. 'Yes. Of course. Forgive me.' He sighed. 'I have no trouble thinking clearly in battle, it's second nature to me, but I'm an idiot where Ren's concerned. Any sensible thought completely flees.' He looked pointedly at Aidan, who smiled.

Their friendship had strengthened during this quest, and Aidan treasured the bond they'd forged. He reminded himself to tell Daien that when the opportunity arose.

Aidan watched while Daien concentrated on contacting both Tarienne and Raef, knowing Raef was more likely to pick up his mind voice if they were a long way off.

After several moments, Daien growled, grief clouding his expression. 'Nothing.'

'They're likely exhausted and asleep somewhere safe. Come on. We'll eat as we ride.'

*   *   *

Daien

Aidan rested his hand on Daien's shoulder, his expression resolute. 'I promise you. We'll find them.'

Daien met his eyes and nodded, pulling in a deep breath to calm himself.

They strode over to saddle the horses, then fished some dried biscuits out of their packs, munching on them as they rode through the forest. The trees rustled as their branches swept toward Daien, seeming to reach out, trying to brush at him as he passed.

After a while Aidan reined his horse to a stop. 'Daien, halt for a moment.'

Daien pulled his horse alongside Aidan's, his hand automatically settling on the hilt of his sword. 'What's wrong?'

'Do you see how the trees move?'

Daien looked around, frowning, not exactly sure what Aidan meant. 'It's the wind... isn't it?'

His gaze swept around as he lowered his voice, his heart beating an erratic rhythm. 'There is no wind.'

Daien concentrated on the whispery sound the trees made, stunned to hear a soft, breathy voice.

'*Follow me...*'

An ethereal figure appeared in front of them, beckoning. Aidan and Daien jumped yet held their tongues for fear of startling the creature. It was tall and willowy, with wispy, green hair that almost reached the ground, glossy leaves twined around its arms and legs, pristine, white flowers woven through its hair.

In awe of the creature he'd only heard of in stories, Daien whispered, 'A tree spirit.'

The spirit turned, its whisper little more than a rustle of the leaves but its words carried to them on the wind

'*Come, friends. I am a dryad of the forest. Follow me. Your fae have need of you.*'

Daien turned to Aidan, whose eyes were wide. Aidan nodded. Daien wanted to ask if Tarienne and Raef were all right but dared not. His heart thumped erratically, a drumbeat in the sudden stillness of the forest.

They followed silently, moving more slowly than they would have liked. Even the horses barely made a sound in the quiet calm of the heavily treed forest. The fresh scents of the flowers and leaves revitalised them, filling them with pure, clean strength, clearing and enhancing their senses. Calm infused them, soothing their fears, reassuring them.

Almost an hour later, the dryad faded and disappeared.

Daien looked around, calling softly, 'Lady of the Wood, where are you?'

Her voice drifted to them from the surrounding trees. '*I can take you no farther. The evil is too strong. Continue north, and you will find the waterhole near the forest's edge. Do not give up. Their lives depend on it...*'

Her words trailed off, almost blown away in the breeze. Daien shoved aside the fear threatening to overwhelm him, knowing it wouldn't help them find Tarienne and Raef.

Not wanting to waste a moment, they urged their horses on. The trees seemed to part for them, guiding their way. When they reached the edge of the forest and looked out over the plain, Daien's heart pounded at the destruction.

The grass was brown and burnt, pools of thick, black blood surrounding the dismembered bodies of the creatures that had attacked them, as well as those of huge crows with viscous yellow beaks. The stench was overwhelming causing both Aidan and Daien to cover their noses.

'How could they have survived this?' His eyes met Aidan's, his own fear reflected there.

They sat motionless for a while, the stink of death unsettling the horses. Turning back toward the forest, they dismounted and led their stallions, silently looking for tracks.

After searching for almost an hour, their frustration rising, Aidan called out, 'Over here.'

Daien rushed over, finding Aidan crouched pointing at two sets of tracks, one lighter than the other, indicating a smaller horse.

'Lacey.'

Daien's spirit lifted. 'They can't be far then.'

Mounting their stallions, they moved slowly, their eyes glued to the tracks. When they heard a horse nicker, their heads snapped up. Lacey trotted over to them, her saddle still on, snorting, as if to say, *Well, it's about time.*

Scanning the area, Daien's eyes finally settled on the outline of Raef and Tarienne lying in a clearing beside a small waterhole. Relief washed over him. He leapt off his horse, sprinting to where they lay.

Quickly checking them, Daien noticed dried blood on Raef's shirt, as well as a deep wound on his shoulder, the skin surrounding it, fiery red. Tarienne showed no visible wounds and a little of his tension drained away.

Daien crouched beside Tarienne, grasping her shoulder gently and shaking. She did not respond immediately, then quickly leapt up, drawing her knives.

He held his hands up. 'Ren, it's me.'

Slowly, she focused on him. Letting out a sob, her knives clattering to the ground, she fell into his arms. Warm relief spread through Daien.

A moment later, she drew back slightly and pulled Aidan into the embrace. He slid his arms around them both.

She pulled away suddenly. 'Raef was injured, and we were both so exhausted, we couldn't ride any farther. Thank the Gods you're both here and unhurt.'

Glancing down at her brother, tears pricked her eyes. 'I need to help him. He's burning up with fever.'

Aidan crouched, feeling Raef's forehead.

'Daien, could you light a fire and fetch some water? Ren, fetch the herbs out of your pack to help with the infection, then rest beside Raef while I cook some food for you both. You're going to need your strength to heal him.'

Daien rolled his eyes and mouthed to Tarienne, *Bossy*!

*　　*　　*

Tarienne

Tarienne chuckled, thankful Aidan had taken charge, as Daien hurried to the nearby waterhole, soon returning with a waterskin filled with fresh water. Grabbing her pack, she sank down beside Raef. Daien handed her a clean damp cloth, which she used to wipe her brother's forehead, then his face. Once the water had been heated over the fire, she made a tea with some herbs she had selected and whispered a healing spell.

Daien sat behind her, his legs on either side of her, providing support as she worked. Aidan prepared a stew with the last of their meat and a few dried vegetables, then asked Tarienne which herbs would enhance the flavour. The aroma wafting from the cooking pot made her mouth water. She hadn't realised how hungry she was, unable to remember how long it had been since they'd last eaten.

When Tarienne had finished the incantation and cleansed Raef's wound, the tea had finished steeping.

She called softly to Raef. '*Toror*, come back to me. Open your eyes.'

It was a few moments before he began to stir. A collective sigh of relief rippled through the group. He slowly opened his eyes, taking a moment to focus on the concerned eyes scrutinising him.

'How did we do?' he croaked.

Tarienne rolled her eyes and snorted. '*That's* the first question you ask? Sit up and drink this, dear heart.' She held out the tea as Aidan helped him sit up, Raef taking the cup with shaky hands.

Tarienne answered his question while he sipped the hot tea.

'We won the battle, took out three-quarters of the army, and would have gotten away unscathed if the crow changelings hadn't attacked. One crow somehow penetrated our defences and drove its beak into your shoulder, but you managed to hold onto the magic. We threw everything we had left at them. They fell from the sky, dead, some half-changed. It was disgusting.' She shuddered. 'We managed to make it just into the forest, and that's the last I remember until Daien woke me.'

Aidan handed them each a bowl of stew and they ate in silence. Tarienne was relieved to see Raef eating, albeit slowly. Once she'd finished, she placed the bowl down then jumped up, wrinkling her nose.

'I need to bathe.'

Aidan smiled. 'I'll sit with Raef. You two go freshen up. When you're finished, I'll bathe.'

Tarienne and Daien wasted no time collecting the rough lumps of soap from their saddlebags, some soft cloths to dry themselves and clean clothes, then disappeared through the trees past the small waterhole to the lake beyond. Raef, whose colour was slowly coming back, and Aidan settled down to chat about the events of the last few days.

*   *   *

Daien

When they arrived at the lake, Daien swept his arms around Tarienne, kissing her, reassuring himself she was here and safe. Knowing how tired she was, he pulled back.

'Sweetheart, take off your clothes. I'll help you wash.'

Even through her exhaustion, she managed a cheeky smile. 'Only if you take yours off, too.'

He huffed in frustration but couldn't deny he desired the feel of her skin against his. 'All right, but I'm just washing you. You're exhausted.'

They undressed, shivering as they walked into the cold, waist-deep water. Tarienne stood still while he soaped the front of her, a testimony to how tired she was. Sliding the soap across her skin, Daien barely contained the urge to slip his hands between her legs.

His resolve hanging by a thread, he ordered her, his voice husky with desire, to turn around so he could lather her back. When she complied, he wrapped his soapy hands around her and could not stop himself from caressing her breasts as her body slid enticingly against his.

She swayed into him, and Daien grabbed her waist, supporting her. Lowering them both into the water, he rinsed her off, then swept her into his arms, carrying her back to the bank.

'Can you dry yourself, sweetheart, while I quickly wash?'

She nodded, and he felt the heat of her gaze as he strode into the water. He quickly rubbed the soap over his body then dipped under the water to rinse himself. As he walked back, he chuckled quietly to see that the cloth she held to dry herself hung limply from her hands as she watched him.

He walked to her, snagging her hand, and sank onto the soft grass, pulling her with him. His body partly covering hers, he leaned in for a tender kiss.

Daien shifted to cover her with his body, supporting his weight on his elbows. When he bent to kiss her, she whimpered, greedily devouring his lips. Holding himself still, he fought an inner battle against the powerful love and desire battering at his wavering control.

Groaning, Daien circled his hips against her. When she wrapped her legs around his waist, he lost control. Meeting his fierce passion with her own, she moaned as he dropped kisses down her neck and across her breasts. When he pulled her nipple into his mouth, she arched into him, moaning again as their passion escalated.

A groan slid from his lips before he rested on one arm, his fingers moving down her body to her sensitive nub bringing her close to her peak before centring himself over her and sliding into her heat. Within moments Tarienne's climax hit hard. He smothered her cries with a deep kiss, then soared to his own crescendo, groaning loudly.

After they both managed to catch their breath, Daien smiled.

'If that's what you do to me when you're exhausted, I can't wait for you to be fully rested.'

She chuckled, swatting him playfully. 'We'd better wash again and return to camp.'

Reluctantly, Daien lifted himself and stood, his eyes sweeping over her body appreciatively.

When they'd washed off the evidence of their lovemaking and dressed, Tarienne turned to him, looping her arms around his neck.

'I didn't realise something until today. I physically draw strength from you. It must have something to do with your druid blood.'

Daien pulled one of her hands to his lips before he remembered the dryad who had helped him find her.

'With everything that has happened, I forgot to tell you. When we were in the forest looking for you and Raef, a dryad appeared. She's the only reason we found you.'

Tarienne stilled, eyes wide. 'That means the balance of magic has started to tip back our way. We must tell Raef.' She grabbed his hand, pulling him with her.

They rushed back into camp, and Tarienne's words tumbled out, her eyes sparkling. 'Raef, Daien and Aidan saw a dryad. She helped them find us. That means the balance is changing, doesn't it?'

Raef chuckled. 'Yes, sweetling. It's a good sign. I gather you enjoyed your bath?'

Tarienne's face flushed with the heat of a blush, but she grinned. 'Yes, we did. Thank you.'

They all chuckled, relaxed in each other's company. Daien briefly wondered if they were sometimes a little too comfortable. Danger stalked them, which had been proven many times over the course of their journey. His mood sobered a little, wondering what their next challenge would be.

Aidan rose. 'I think I'll freshen up, too.' He gathered some soap, clean clothes, and a cloth, then disappeared through the trees.

Raef lay back on his bedroll, wincing slightly. Kneeling at his side, Tarienne placed her hands over his wound. He started to pull away, but she speared him with a determined glare, eyes narrowed. He chuckled and acquiesced, visibly relaxing as her ministrations eased the pain.

Daien poured some tea and handed it to Raef, who downed it quickly.

'Is there any stew left?' Raef asked, sitting up.

Tarienne beamed at her brother and hastened to retrieve a bowl of the tasty stew Aidan had prepared. Raef ate with surprising zeal, finishing in mere moments.

When Aidan returned from his ablutions, they all settled down to sleep, confident the magical wards Tarienne had set would keep them safe until morning.

CHAPTER 12

By first light, Raef had recovered enough to continue their journey. Tarienne forced him into one more healing session before they left, to ensure he had strength enough for the ride. He rolled his eyes at her fussing but conceded it would make travelling easier.

The final leg of their journey led them up the cold, grey side of the mountain to the caves, one of which held the golden stone. The path was steep and winding. On one side was a narrow, grassy plain. On the other, a sheer drop down to a rocky, fast-moving river.

The river, a tributary of the River Arnon, bubbled and swirled through the narrow course edged with black stone worn smooth by the constant thrashing of the water. Jagged rocks poked up through the water, dividing the river's path, creating white froth as it hurtled along. In the distance, they heard the tell-tale sound of a waterfall. Tarienne urged Lacey away from the edge, her fear of heights causing her pulse to race.

Daien moved up beside her. *'Are you all right, sweetheart?'*

Tarienne smiled. *'Yes, my love. I just truly dislike heights.'*

Without a word, Daien slowed his stallion, then reined it between her and the drop. His thoughtfulness brought dampness to her eyes.

'Have I told you today how much I love you?'

He grinned. *'Yes, but I will never tire of hearing it. I love you, too, and always will.'*

He returned his attention to scanning the area for danger as Tarienne marvelled at how fortunate she was to have a fierce, yet tender warrior by her side. She couldn't help but smile at the contradiction that was Daien. A battle-hardened warrior who could kill a man one moment, then make such tender, passionate love to her the next. Fearsomely protective and loyal, he also had a wild side and a wicked sense of humour. And he was hers.

They were all on high alert, expecting the caves to be guarded. Tarienne and Raef swept the area with their heightened magical senses, not sure if they were relieved or disturbed, however neither of them could identify any immediate threat. There appeared to be no sentries monitoring their approach.

Pulling their horses to a halt, the group scanned the tree line. Still nothing. They exchanged worried glances. It was too quiet.

Raef closed his eyes and straightened in his saddle obviously searching for something he had perceived. Tarienne focused on her surroundings too, sensing a wisp of magic that was there and then gone. Exchanging glances, she noted Raef's frown and sensed he was trying to locate it again. He met her gaze and shook his head; it had disappeared as quickly as it had come.

Nudging their horses into motion again, they moved slowly.

Abruptly, a black blur sprinted parallel to them, close to the edge of the precipice, then a huge, midnight-black wolf shot out, startling the horses.

Lacey panicked, screaming as she took off, galloping away from the creature as quickly as she could. Tarienne frantically tried to calm her and rein her to a halt. The mare ignored her and thundered on, eyes rolling, ears back, sides heaving.

Tarienne's breaths came in gasps. Her heart thundered and arms ached with the effort of trying to control her mare. She managed to lean forward over Lacey's neck, whispering calming words into her ear. As the mare began to respond, Tarienne lifted her eyes... and screamed, the edge of the cliff nearing quickly. Terror coursed through her.

Yanking on the reins as hard as she could, Tarienne shrieked, 'Lacey, stop! Please! Oh Gods! *No!*'

*   *   *

Daien

The huge animal crouched, blocking Aidan's, Daien's and Raef's paths, its wolfish stare momentarily holding their focus. Raef roared, 'Let us pass, wolf. We must stop her!'

The animal hesitated for a moment, looking over its shoulder in the direction Lacey had gone, then its form shimmered, golden sparks radiating from its body. It shifted into a tall, muscled, very naked man. His skin was tanned, his black hair short and spiky, his eyes a bright, ice blue.

He quickly moved aside, shouting, 'Hurry! There's a precipice ahead!'

Raef kicked his stallion into action. Daien spurred his horse forward, Aidan close behind. He vaguely registered the wolf-man shimmering again, but his focus was on getting to Tarienne, his stallion flying across the stones and grass of the narrow plain. Finally, he spotted Lacey standing at the edge of the cliff, sides heaving, but Tarienne was nowhere to be seen.

Daien's heart slammed against his ribs. In his peripheral vision, he saw Raef and Aidan jump to the ground, their mounts snorting and stomping. He launched himself from his horse's back before it stopped, scrambling to the edge. Leaning over, he frantically called her name. '*Ren!*' Rational thought fled in the wake of the terror engulfing him. A sob ripped from his lips.

The waterfall thundered onto jagged rocks hundreds of feet

below. Daien's voice was swept away by the sound of the pounding water, his face wet from the fine spray. Thumping his forehead into the wet grass in desperation, he sensed the wolf approach.

Incensed and driven by grief, he sprang up, drawing his knife from his boot, attacking the beast, both tumbling to the ground. The wolf snarled and snapped. Daien swung his arm in a wide arc, attempting to sink his blade into the animal's flank. They rolled over and over, fur, man, and blood blurring together.

Despite his fury, Daien was much smaller. Not pausing to consider the wolf could have easily ripped his throat out if it wanted, he fought like a man possessed. Surprisingly, the wolf chose not to bite Daien, just protect itself from his ferocious attack. Daien was beyond caring, fury and despair blending to remove all rational thought.

*　　*　　*

Raef

Instead of intervening, Raef closed his eyes, searching for Tarienne, trying to contact her with his mind. He knew locating her was the only way to calm Daien. Swallowing hard, he drove back the same despair he knew the warrior felt.

Finally, Tarienne's mind voice, faint and filled with agony, penetrated his brain. Relaxing a fraction, he sent a calming pulse through their sibling connection.

'We're coming, sweetling. Hold on.'

He turned toward where Daien and the beast fought. *'Daien!'* Raef shouted, authority lacing his voice. Not pausing, Daien swung his head in his direction. 'Desist. Ren needs you. She is alive somewhere down the side of the cliff. *Wolf!* Stop!'

The changeling's eyes met Raef's. Daien faltered as Raef's words penetrated his anger-fogged brain. The animal jumped back, panting, cautiously eyeing Daien, ready to defend if attacked again. A trickle of blood from a nick on its ear dripped down its muzzle.

Daien sank onto the damp grass, panting, arm bleeding, the knife still clutched in his hand. 'She's alive?' He dropped his blade and let his head fall into his hands, his shoulders shaking as tears of relief coursed down his cheeks

Eventually, he raised his head and swiped at his eyes, rational thought slowly returning. 'Where is she?'

Aidan stood next to him, sword drawn, staring at the wolf. Daien nodded his thanks, and Aidan sheathed his weapon offering his hand, assisting him to his feet.

The wolf once again shimmered into a man and strode into the bushes. He returned moments later, dressed in black, leather trousers and torn, grey shirt.

Without uttering another word, they all crawled to the edge, searching for Tarienne. They carefully scanned each ledge below, A strangled cry slipped from Aidan when he spotted her and pointed about a third of the way down to the right.

'There!'

Tarienne hung by her hand. At first, they thought she had a grip on a huge thorn sticking out of a crack in the side of the cliff, but they soon realised her hand was impaled on it. Face contorted in pain, her feet scrambled for purchase on the slippery cliff face, trying to take the pressure off her bloodied hand.

Aidan rested his hand on Daien's shoulder. 'We'll get her back.'

Raef shouted down to her, but the thunder of the waterfall was too loud for her to hear them. He nodded at Daien, tapping his head, silently telling him to use his mind voice and heard Daien's gentle words though his mind, reassuring Tarienne.

'*Sweetheart...*' Daien said softly into her mind, *'I'm coming for you. Hold on, my love.'*

Anchoring one end of a rope they'd retrieved from Aidan's saddlebag to a nearby tree, Aidan tied the other end securely around Daien, while Raef positioned himself at the edge of the cliff. Aidan took up position behind Raef, both men digging their heels into the dirt and gripping the rope tightly as Daien moved slowly. He widened his stance and leaned back, slowly making his way toward Tarienne.

*   *   *

Tarienne

She vaguely registered someone scrambling down the side of the cliff toward her andmanaged to duck her head when some small stones dislodged and hurtled down, almost hitting her face. Raef spoke into her mind in an effort to distract her.

Raef's voice filtered through her waking moments. As she drifted in and out of consciousness, Tarienne dreamed fitfully of hurtling over Lacey's head, scrambling to grab onto something as she plunged over the cliff, the sharp rocks battering and bruising her body as she fell. When she'd glimpsed a huge thorn growing out of the side of the cliff, she'd thrust her hand out to grab it. The only thing she remembered after that was pain. Excruciating, debilitating pain.

Now she hung there, her hand impaled on the thorn, her body weight hanging on it. The only saving grace was a small niche she'd located where the tip of her left boot now rested. Blood trickled down her arm, and she could no longer feel her hand. The pain shooting down her arm, however, was intense.

*   *   *

Daien

Daien eased himself down the sheer cliff face. His hands threatened to slip on the rope, which was wet from the fine spray rising from the waterfall. His eyes did not stray from Tarienne. The woman who had saved him from himself. Letting her die was not an option.

Daien's teeth clenched as he noticed the bright, red blood oozing down her arm, her beautiful face contorted in pain, her eyes glazed.

When he finally reached her, she was barely conscious. His heart ached, and his throat tightened. He needed to be strong, so he forced himself to drag in several deep breaths, seeking the inner calm he always drew on in battle. He contacted Aidan and Raef through mindspeak, asking them to let the rope out slowly so he could move closer.

Swinging toward her, he positioned his feet on either side of her body and leaned in, gently gathering Tarienne to him. Supporting her weight, he tried to snap the giant, wickedly barbed thorn. Tarienne screamed in pain, immediately going limp in his arms.

Daien hated that he'd hurt her but took advantage of her unconscious state to slowly slide her hand off the thorn, blood oozing down her arm.

He secured her to his chest, wrapping his arms protectively around her limp body.

'I have her. Pull us up.'

Daien was distantly aware of another, unfamiliar presence listening. Shoving the feeling aside, he concentrated on ensuring Tarienne did not bump into the cliff while they painstakingly inched upward. He gently pushed off the jagged wall with his feet when they moved too close.

As they neared the edge, a hand reached down. Daien looked up, seeing the changeling. He hesitated for a moment. Now was not the time for anger. He reached out and firmly clasped the changeling's hand, who hauled them back over the edge. The minute they were back on solid ground, Aidan and Raef dropped the rope, rushing to their side.

Raef sucked in a breath at the sight of Tarienne's hand. 'We're going to need a fire, but we can't light one here. We'll have to head back into the cover of the forest so we can tend to her wound.'

The changeling cleared his throat. 'I know where there's a cave that's safe... if you'll trust me.'

Raef stood; arms crossed. 'Why should we trust you?' He pointed down at his sister. '*You* caused this!'

Anger emanated from Raef surrounding him with a powerful and intimidating aura as he waited for a response.

The changeling stood, facing Raef, not looking the least bit intimidated. 'My name is Tere. I am not with the local pack ruled by Lacas. In fact, they're trying to kill me. I was escaping from them when I saw you. I didn't mean to startle your friend's horse. Let me help you. Please.'

'Lacas is dead,' Raef responded in a flat tone. 'I know this, because I killed him.'

Tere blinked then nodded and waited.

Raef glanced at Aiden and Daien, they both nodded in silent acknowledgment before he turned back to Tere, his voice laced with authority.

'Take us to this cave but be warned. If this is a trick, your life is forfeit.'

Tere nodded and moved behind a tree, returning in his wolf form. Daien mounted his stallion, and Aidan and Raef carefully lifted Tarienne into the saddle in front of him. He looped his arm around her, pulling her limp body into his so she rested with her back to his chest, her head leaning back on his shoulder. Tucking her injured hand into her shirt to protect it until they could tend to it properly, he urged his horse forward to follow the changeling, who loped ahead of them in wolf form.

They moved slowly and both Aidan and Daien exchanged a glance as a warning from Raef entered their thoughts.

Remain alert. The wolf might yet betray us.

*   *   *

Raef

Less than half an hour later, they passed through a heavily wooded area, then took a sharp turn down and to the left of the waterfall. The extremely narrow path spiralled around until they came to a partially concealed cave. Once they cleared the bracken away, the opening was large enough to allow the horses to enter.

Raef quickly dismounted and carefully gathered a still unconscious Tarienne from Daien's arms. Daien slid from his mount and gently took her from her brother, holding her close while Raef helped Aidan create a makeshift bed.

After they'd piled all their bedding on top of some soft, dry moss they'd gathered, Daien carefully lowered Tarienne's limp body onto it. Aidan lit a small fire in the corner of the cave, tending it carefully so it produced as little smoke as possible.

Raef knelt beside his sister, concern in his eyes. Smelling smoke, he turned to where Aidan tended the fire. He spoke a few soft, unfamiliar words, dissipating it. Aidan nodded his thanks, grabbing some dried meat from his saddlebag.

Daien rummaged in his pack and produced his waterskin, a bowl and a clean cloth so they could cleanse Tarienne's wound.

After Daien carefully washed her broken and bloodied hand, Raef used his sensory magic to gently probe the wound to determine the extent of her injuries. Sitting back on his heels he pulled in a deep breath. Besides the large hole in the middle of her palm, the skin, and muscles around it were torn, the small bones shattered. Unbelievably, though, her arm, which had supported her weight until they freed her, was strained but not severely injured.

Pushing his magic into her, Raef felt the cuts and bruises on her body respond, healing, but her hand showed no improvement. He frowned, sitting back on his heels.

'I can't heal her,' he growled.

Daien met his worried glance, his brow furrowed. Aidan turned from the fire, where he stirred the stew.

'What do you mean?' he asked.

Raef launched to his feet in frustration. 'There's something I can't identify holding back the healing process.'

Tere moved up from where he had been standing at the front of the cave. The three men turned to him.

'The thorn...' he offered quietly. 'I fear it was planted there with changeling magic. Will you allow me to try?'

Daien leapt to his feet, circling around Raef, getting into Tere's face. 'You will *not* touch her, wolf!'

Aidan and Raef grabbed his arms, pulling him back. Aidan growled, 'Peace, Daien. He's trying to help.'

Daien whipped around to argue, but Tarienne coughed violently, her body shuddering. He rushed to her, quickly placing his hands behind her back, and raising her into a sitting position. Settling behind her, he wrapped his arms securely around her.

'It's all right, sweetheart. I've got you. Lean on me.'

The coughing subsided and Tarienne's eyes flicked open. Raef crouched, feeling her forehead, gently touching a red welt likely caused by a sharp rock during her fall. Checking her eyes for any signs of a head injury, he was pleased to see her green gaze staring back at him, clear and alert.

He smiled. 'Welcome back, sweetling.' Raef linked his fingers with Tarienne's good hand briefly, then handed her the herbal brew. 'Aidan has made you some tea to ease your pain.'

Managing a weak smile, Tarienne accepted the tea. She sniffed, identifying the herbs she'd taught Aidan to blend. Her eyes trailed to Raef's... then she jumped, almost spilling the hot liquid over herself at the ice-blue eyes of the stranger standing behind him. The eyes of the wolf that had spooked Lacey. Her body began to tremble.

Daien tightened his grip around her waist and pulled her closer, whispering, 'It's all right, sweetheart.'

Turning slightly so she could see Daien's face, she relaxed back into him, draining the warm, soothing tea.

Raef took the empty mug from her and grabbed her hand, rubbing his thumb gently across her knuckles. She focused on him, brows furrowed.

Raef released her hand and stood. 'His name is Tere. He helped us rescue you, then showed us this cave where we could safely tend your wounds.'

Daien growled, 'We wouldn't be here if he hadn't scared Lacey.'

Aidan threw him a sharp look. 'Peace, Daien...'

* * *

Tarienne

Raef motioned to Tere to come forward. Tarienne felt a possessive growl rumble from Daien's chest. Placing her uninjured hand over the one wrapped around her, she caressed it lightly. He settled a little, and she tipped her head back to claim a chaste kiss.

Tere stepped closer, crouching down so he could meet Tarienne's eyes. 'Forgive me. I did not mean to startle your mare. I am Tere, from the Inare wolf pack many miles west of here. I am pleased to make your acquaintance...' He paused.

Despite the pain in her hand and exhaustion etched across her face, Tarienne responded graciously. 'I am Tarienne.' She glanced at Raef, who nodded imperceptibly. 'This is my brother, Raef. Over there is Aidan, and behind me is Daien.'

Tarienne knew better than to tell Tere too much yet. If he knew Aidan was the king of Therin and Raef and herself crown prince and princess of the fae, he could try to use the information against them.

Tere nodded. 'It's a pleasure to meet you all. Your brother is having some difficulty healing your wound, Tarienne. I believe the thorn was forged with changeling magic. I'd like to help.'

She met his eyes, carefully assessing this stranger. He was very handsome, his bronzed skin contrasting with his shiny, black hair and ice-blue eyes. His arms were muscled, chest broad.

Her attention returned to his face, his full lips curving into a smile at her perusal, eyes sparkling with mischief. He looked mildly amused when Daien scowled. Tarienne pressed herself back against him, reassuring him.

'If you're willing to try healing my hand, I would appreciate it; however, you need to know Raef will monitor what you're doing.'

'I'm willing, given I inadvertently caused your injury, but your brother can be the only one present while I do this.' He looked pointedly at Daien.

Tarienne felt Daien's anger and caressed the back of his hand.

'All right but could you all give Daien and me a moment alone, please?'

They rose, walking outside.

Daien grasped her chin and planted a soft kiss on her lips. She smiled at him weakly.

'We can't finish what we have begun if I'm not well enough to help. I'll just hold you all back. You know this. Let Tere try to heal me, please. Raef will be here to ensure he doesn't do anything else, and you will be just outside.'

Daien opened his mouth seemingly to protest, but instead, blew out a breath and nodded. 'You are my heart and soul. I will acquiesce to this only so you can be well again.'

He eased himself away from her, kneeling to look into her wide, green eyes. He sighed, kissing her tenderly, before rising to leave.

When he reached the cave entrance, he looked back and blew her a kiss. Catching it, she held it to her heart. Daien brushed through the tendrils of ivy hiding the cave entrance, as Tere and Raef re-entered.

Raef smiled encouragingly at Tarienne as they lowered themselves to the ground on either side of her. Tere held his hand out, nodding reassuringly. Tarienne nervously lifted her injured hand with a wince, placing it in his. She flinched at the first tingle of his magic.

Tere's fingers and magic gently probed, feeling for the extent of the damage. Suddenly, Raef straightened, likely sensing as Tere's scent swirled around her. He growled a warning, settling as the changeling quickly withdrew it.

Tere sent Tarienne an apologetic glance. His natural fragrance had affected her more than she had anticipated. She felt confused yet refrained from looking away. Sensing Tere's physical response to her, she frowned sightly as he returned his attention to her hand, circling his fingers lightly around the wound. Gently massaging her hand to stimulate blood flow, a warm tingle infused her fingers as he released tiny amounts of magic into the damaged bone and muscle. She scented his arousal again, fainter this time, but her body still responded. Tere paused, meeting her gaze.

Glancing at Raef, Tarienne realised he hadn't noticed this time. Her focus snapped back to Tere as he carefully wrapped another wisp of his scent around her. She sucked in a small breath, her heart thumping harder than it should.

Tarienne spoke, voice wavering slightly. 'Raef, could you get me some water, please? I'm so thirsty.'

He rose at once, glancing down at her before exiting the cave. The moment he was out of sight, Tarienne placed her hand on Tere's thigh. Sliding her thumb up and down, perilously close to his groin, she whispered, 'Thank you.' Tere jumped a little then grinned.

When Raef entered again, carrying a waterskin, she quickly slipped her hand back into her lap and gratefully accepted the cool liquid, closing her eyes as the water slid down her parched throat.

Raef dropped to the floor again and smiled at Tarienne before turning to Tere. 'The healing is proceeding well. Thank you, Tere.'

Tere nodded but made no comment. Spending a few more moments infusing her hand with his magic, he finally finished the healing session and shot to his feet, stomping outside. Tarienne's eyelids drooped, and she drifted into a pain free slumber.

When she woke a few hours later, a pair of deep brown, concerned eyes watched her. She smiled lovingly at Daien, who captured her lips in a gentle kiss. Wrapping her arms around his neck, taking care not to bump her injured hand, she deepened the kiss. Daien groaned, pulling her into a strong, possessive hug.

When he pulled back, he tenderly brushed her hair away from her face. 'Are you hungry, sweetheart?'

Tarienne's stomach rumbled in response.

Daien smiled and stood, grabbing his pack. Finding a bowl, he filled it with the scrumptious smelling stew Aidan had made. It was not the first time she had wondered where Aidan had learned to cook so well... or at all. As Daien handed her the bowl and positioned himself behind her, she noticed Tere sitting near the entrance of the cave, staring at her. Sending him a small smile, she turned her attention back to the food, leaning into Daien as she ate.When she finished eating, Tere approached her. 'If you're up to it, I'd like to try another healing session.'

Tarienne took a moment to respond. 'If you think another session so soon will help...'

She turned to Daien. 'Would you leave us for a short while, dear heart?' She ran her fingers down the side of his face.

He captured them and kissed her palm. 'Are you sure you don't want me to stay?'

'No, my love. Tere says he works better alone.'

Daien narrowed his eyes at Tere, as if in warning, then stood and walked outside, Aidan following.

Raef crouched in front of his sister. 'Do you want me to stay?'

'No, *toror*. I'll be fine.'

Tere dropped down to the ground in front of Tarienne, cross-legged, and held out his hand. She placed her hand in his without meeting his eyes. Slowly, he began to massage around the wound, his magic trickling through her healing the bones and muscles. Initially, he kept his attention on her hand, then lifted his eyes to meet hers. His scent coiled around her again.

Tarienne inhaled sharply, a frisson of arousal spiralling through her. Confusion clouded her thoughts as Tere glanced over his shoulder toward the cave entrance. He slowly moved closer and lowered his head, continuing to massage her hand.

Her eyes languidly met his and she licked her lips. A deep growl rumbled through Tere as he captured her lips for a hot, wet kiss. She softened, opening her mouth to accept his probing tongue. After a few moments the haze lifted from her brain. And she stiffened, pushing Tere away. Furious, she hissed at him, 'What the hell do you think you're doing?'

He looked at her for a moment, as if confused, then a smirk curled his lips. 'I didn't hear you protesting, and I could scent your arousal.'

Tarienne gritted her teeth, knowing Tere spoke the truth. 'Your magic affects me, but I don't know why. Do not take advantage of it again.'

A tiny frisson of fear slid through Tarienne as she remembered the power of Lacas' glamour. She eyed Tere, a vague feeling of familiarity tugging at her memory.

Tere huffed out a frustrated breath and wordlessly returned to healing her hand. Once he finished, he stomped toward the entrance of the cave, stripping and dropping his clothes on his bedroll before shifting into his wolf mid-stride as he burst outside.

Tarienne's eyes followed Tere's rapid exit and wondered what his story was. There would be time to learn more when he returned to the cave. *If* he returned. It wasn't long before she drifted into a deep, restful slumber.

Several hours later, Tarienne awoke to find her three favourite males sitting, watching her. Her face broke into a smile. She rose, still a little unsteady, and bent to kiss Raef and Aidan on each cheek. She then knelt in front of Daien and wrapped her arms around his neck, pouring every ounce of love she had into the kiss.

Daien's arms wrapped around her, his lips crushing hers. Tarienne swayed, scooting closer. Daien chuckled, sliding his hands down to her bottom and pulling her onto his lap.

Aidan and Raef exchanged grins, stepping away to stoke the fire, allowing them a little privacy.

Eventually, they all stretched out on their bedrolls. Daien and Tarienne snuggled happily, murmuring quietly to each other. Tere had still not returned.

*　　*　　*

Tere

They were all fast asleep when Tere slipped quietly through the cave entrance. His eyes ran over Daien and Tarienne entwined in each other's arms. He closed his eyes at the sudden onslaught of emotion. Opening them again, he derided himself flopping onto his bedroll, frustration welling within him. The sky outside was just beginning to lighten when he finally succumbed to slumber, dreaming vivid, erotic dreams of Tarienne.

Her curvaceous, naked form stretched out on top of him, as she trailed hot kisses down his body. She grasped his arousal, caressing and stroking, then ran her tongue along the length of him, circling the tip of his rock-hard erection. His back arched to meet her as Tere groaned loudly at the exquisite pleasure.

Surrounding his member with her lips, she sucked hard, sliding him in and out of her hot mouth. His hips moved in unison with her motion as he buried his fingers in her hair. With a shout, his climax surged, long and powerful, Tarienne greedily swallowing his seed. Taking a few moments to catch his breath, Tere deftly flipped her beneath him.

Settling between her legs, he returned the favour, pleasuring her with his tongue until she screamed with release. He slid up her body, entering her moist heat with one satisfying thrust. Tere couldn't resist dipping down for a long, passionate kiss as he pumped into her tight sheath. He groaned against her lips as he increased the tempo until another blistering climax ripped through him, rocking his entire body...

Unceremoniously, Tere was yanked awake. Jumping to his feet, he shook his head to clear it, a menacing growl rumbled through his chest. Aidan took a defensive stance, waiting. Tere's sleep-fogged brain finally registered where he was.

Quickly glancing down, he was grateful his shirt was long enough to cover the evidence of his dream.

'Damn it, man,' Tere bit out. 'Don't ever wake me like that.'

Aidan relaxed slightly, holding up his hands. 'Sorry. I just wanted to ask if you were hungry.' He stomped away, grumbling about ungrateful wolves.

Tere flopped back onto his bedroll, scrubbing a hand down his face, trying to wipe the dream from his thoughts. He knew the only way to clear his head was to run.

Noting that Aidan was the only other person in the cave, he stood, turned away and pulled down the soft trousers he wore to bed. Quickly wiping away the evidence of his climax with a soft cloth, he stripped off his shirt, shifted and hurtled out of the cave.

Sprinting to the closest waterhole, he intended to banish the dream in the icy water but froze when he saw Tarienne and Daien standing in waist-deep water, naked, wrapped around each other.

The wolf watched from the cover of the trees, unable to tear his eyes away. He transformed in a shower of gold, still incapable of forcing himself to leave. His body reawakened as he watched Tarienne and Daien make love, and he was sorely tempted to seek relief by his own hand when Tarienne cried out her release.

Tere's body ached with desire. Clamping his mouth shut so he didn't make any sound to alert them of his presence, he crouched, unmoving. Tarienne gracefully walked out of the water, her wet skin glistening in the sunlight. She was a glorious sight to behold. Tere rose, involuntarily taking a step toward her. He caught himself, swore silently, then shifted again, bolting through the trees on the silent pads of his wolf.

When Tere finally stopped running, exhaustion demanding he stop, he shifted into his human form. Dropping to the cool grass, he stared out over the precipice, his knees drawn up, arms wrapped around them to ward off the cold of the early spring morning.

What the hell did Lacas do to me?

Tere sat for what seemed like hours, going over and over his captivity in his head. Why would he react to Tarienne like that when he loved his beautiful Ileia with every fibre of his being? It must have something to do with what they'd subjected him to during his captivity. But what? Abruptly, he remembered the bitter liquid they'd forced him to drink. It had caused vivid hallucinations, which continued to haunt his dreams. That, combined with the magic Rantec had used on him, must have affected him more than he realised.

Tarienne looked so much like his beautiful Ileia. He broke down, sobbing into his hands.

Ileia...

A magnificent reddish-brown wolf who transformed into a stunning woman with long, wavy red hair and the most beautiful, compelling green eyes, just like Tarienne.

Ileia had been captured by Lacas' minions as she and Tere had attempted to escape from the pack. One that had turned from a prosperous, happy pack into one living in fear of its leader, Lacas, who had murdered his mate – Tere's mother – and tried to kill Tere.

Tere had not been able to prevent Ileia's capture or find her since. Believing Lacas may have murdered her as revenge, his heart had been broken and empty... until he'd meet Tarienne, Raef, Aidan and Daien. For some inexplicable reason, they'd accepted him, despite their difficult start.

He was starting to feel better, more like his old self, guessing the run had helped his body burn off whatever was in his system. He shifted into his wolf form again, knowing what he needed to do.

When Tere arrived back at the cave, he slipped inside, shifted, and dressed quickly while the others were outside. When Tarienne walked into the cave to pack her things, he approached, standing a respectable distance away.

'Tarienne?'

She met his gaze, head cocked.

'I wanted to say I'm sorry for what happened earlier.' He blew out a breath. 'My captors gave me a potion. I'm not sure what it was, but it made me feel and act out of character. I think I've burned off most of it by running.' He stepped forward and grasped her uninjured hand. 'Can you forgive me?'

Tarienne paused for a moment then smiled. 'I believe you, Tere. You are forgiven.'

Relief flowed through him.

'Just don't let it happen again.'

Tere's body tensed as he spun, ready to defend himself, seeing Daien leaning against the cave entrance, arms crossed. He pushed off the wall and strode over, a grin on his face, giving Tere a friendly clap on his back before moving to Tarienne's side.

Astonishment spread across Tere's face. 'You knew?'

Daien nodded. 'We don't keep secrets.'

Tere ran one hand through his hair. 'And you don't want to pound me into the ground?'

Daien smiled. 'That's initially what I wanted to do when she told me, but Ren can be *particularly persuasive* when she wants something...' Daien raised his eyebrows at Tarienne, who rolled her eyes and laughed. 'Not to mention, despite everything, I happen to believe you.'

Aidan walked through the entrance of the cave. 'Come on, you lot. We'll never complete this journey if you all keep jibber-jabbering.'

Daien raised his eyebrows again. 'Jibber-jabbering?'

They all laughed heartily, and Tere realised his acceptance into the group was assured.

CHAPTER 13

Before continuing with their quest, they gathered to discuss their strategy to retrieve the golden stone. Tere offered the information he'd gathered.

'The stone lies in the heart of the largest cave, guarded by ten huge beasts. They are half-man/half-oxen and over seven feet tall. Strong, yet not overly intelligent. I'd say there are close to one hundred men and beasts, heavily armed and led by the very powerful sorcerer, Rantec, son of Rantar.'

Raef and Tarienne startled, eyes wide.

'Rantec?' Tarienne asked, disbelief tinging her words. 'Rantar's offspring? But how?'

Tere nodded. 'The legend says Rantar took a human woman. She bore a son, then died, or was killed, immediately after the birth. They say he was raised by Lacas' pack, but I never saw any evidence of a human in the pack while I was there.'

Raef swore. 'How did we miss this? If it hadn't been for Tere, we would have ridden to our death. Damn it. The prophecy mentions nothing of a son.'

His voice was tinged with an anger Tarienne had rarely seen him allow to surface, except during battle.

Tarienne reached over, placing her hand on his arm to quell his anger. 'Raef, you are not omniscient. We just need to rethink our plan of attack. Aidan?' She turned to see him rubbing his chin thoughtfully.

'We are vastly outnumbered, so we must be clever about this. Daien, what say you and I set a series of traps? We can draw the men and beasts out and take down as many as we are able. Tarienne and Raef can use their magic to disable the rest and enter the cave to retrieve the stone.'

Daien nodded. 'What part will Tere play in this?'

Tere's expression one of surprise, he responded, 'They're looking for me. I can be your decoy, lead them right to your traps.'

Aidan nodded approvingly. 'You can help us set the traps so you know exactly where they are and can avoid them.'

Tarienne nudged Daien and smiled, pleased with his inclusion of Tere into their plans.

Raef smiled, his usual assurance returning. 'Ren, we need to take care using our magic. We must not exhaust ourselves before we reach the stone. It's highly likely Rantec is in there, and we do not know how powerful he is.'

Tarienne thought for a moment. 'If he *is* in there, he'll know the moment we use any magic, so we need to make it count, destroy as many of the guards as we can at once. We'll need to combine our magic, like we did on the plain, if we are to have any hope of defeating him without exhausting ourselves too quickly.'

Tere nodded. 'As soon as I've cleared the last of the traps, I can return and back you up.' He looked around the group waiting.

Raef acknowledged the plan so far. 'Perfect! Aidan and Daien can follow when they're finished. The last thing we need to decide on is which incantation to use.'

Tarienne, Raef and Tere stood silently, deep in thought, Aidan and Daien watching them, waiting.

Tarienne spoke quietly, almost reluctantly. 'There... There is one spell we could use. We could summon the Blade Spirits.'

Tere's eyes widened, a touch of fear in his voice. 'You would summon the Spirits to aid in destroying Rantec and his followers? How do you know they won't turn their magic on you? They are ancient warriors so powerful magically, they swore to fight evil for eternity, even after their death. Over time they have become dangerously unpredictable. There are times those who summon them are also destroyed, though it is suspected those who died called the Spirits for their own gain.'

Raef sighed. 'We don't know they won't turn on us, but Ren is right. It's our best chance. While it will take both of us to call them, it won't overly tire us. Aidan, Daien, I know you do not know of the Blade Spirits, so I cannot expect either of you to agree to it.'

Aidan looked at him with determination. 'I trust you with my life, so I will agree with what you believe to be right. I know I can speak for Daien, as well.'

Daien nodded. 'We have already agreed we stay together no matter what, so I'm in.'

Tarienne smiled at them both, then turned to Tere. 'You do not have the bond we possess, Tere. Do not feel compelled to do this.'

His gaze slowly swept over everyone. 'Despite our difficult beginning, you have accepted me as a friend. I will stand by you and do what I can to help.'

Raef's voice held power. 'Then let us be on our way, and may the Spirits be with us all.'

Reaching into the middle of the circle and placing their hands together, they united in their battle cry. '*Gurith geoth riam laie,*' then repeated in the common tongue for Tere's benefit, 'Death to our enemies!'

Aidan, Daien and Tere left to set their traps, while Raef and Tarienne slipped around to the wooded area close to the cavern entrance. They waited and watched to determine how many guards were posted. There appeared to be only four, so they decided to eliminate them without magic.

Tarienne pulled in a deep breath and glided out from the cover of the trees, approaching them, hips swaying, smiling provocatively. Almost gagging from the stench of the *men*, a term she used loosely, she forced a suggestive smile onto her face, sidling up closer.

Like a silly chit, she called out, 'Ooo... Soldiers. I love soldiers. Wanna play?'

She fluttered her lashes, blowing a kiss in their direction. The men ogled her salaciously, the ugliest of them swaggering toward her, leering.

'I'll play with you.' He grinned, revealing yellow teeth, huffing fetid breath in her direction.

Tarienne forced herself not to gag and take a step back. Gritting her teeth, she held out her hand. He slapped his filthy palm into it, and she made a show of pulling him toward the trees. Repressing a shudder, she allowed him closer.

'Give us a kiss.' He grabbed her head, trying to pull her lips to his.

She skipped away, calling over her shoulder suggestively, 'If you follow me, I'll give you more than a kiss.'

Tarienne was grateful to see Raef quietly despatch the other three guards while they were distracted by watching her lead their friend away. She allowed the man to catch up again. He grinned lecherously as she approached, swinging her hips.

She allowed him to pull her close, albeit reluctantly, and he roughly grabbed her breast. Bile rose in her throat. She slowly slid her knife from its hiding place at her hip and thrust. His eyes widened in surprise when her knife penetrated the thick blubber of his stomach. Quickly withdrawing it, she swung it up in one smooth, practised arc, slicing his throat open.

Gurgling softly, he fell to his knees, then crashed forward, thumping to the ground. Blood poured from his wounds, soaking the ground beneath him, his life force draining into the parched soil.

Tarienne hurriedly joined Raef, her stomach churning. They crept along the cold, damp walls of the cavern, pressing themselves into the shadows. A raucous stomping and clanging emanating from the deep recesses of the cave heralded a large group of what sounded like foot soldiers approaching.

Tarienne and Raef pressed themselves against the wall, hardly daring to breathe when around fifty creatures trudged past. They were just as Tere described – half-man/half-beast, all close to seven feet tall – but there were many more than they'd anticipated.

Dressed in oily, black leather pants and black, studded boots, their bare chests were covered in coarse, dark hair.

Tarienne shivered, panic thundering in her ears. There were so many. How could they possibly defeat them?

Raef met her eyes, an unspoken question of readiness in his eyes. Tarienne swallowed hard and nodded. The moment the creatures passed their hiding place, Raef and Tarienne stepped out, faced each other and began summoning the Blade Spirits.

'*Yahalla onnia Blenidae en'i Lyuhta* (We call on the aid of the blade spirits),' they chanted in unison, their arms spread wide, their fingers touching.

The air around the beasts shimmered as the tall, lithe, powerful figures of the blade spirits solidified. Clothed completely in shiny black leather, long, white-blond, braided hair and piercing grey-blue eyes the only things visible beneath their hoods, they presented a fearsome sight.

Confused, the beasts turned, clumsily drawing their weapons as the ethereal warriors cut a swathe through them. The creatures had little hope of survival, quickly hacked to pieces by the unrelenting blades of the ancient warriors. In only moments, the last of them died, bathed in their own red-black blood.

The Blade Spirits then turned to face Raef and Tarienne.

Raef stepped forward, confidence written in every movement. Boldly meeting the eyes of the warriors, he bowed low. 'We thank you for your assistance, great blade spirits. You honour us with your presence.'

Then he uttered the words to reverse the summoning spell, '*Kyoshonia, i'Lyuhta* (Return home, blade spirits).'

The Spirits straightened, snapped an unexpected salute with their swords, then shimmered, disappearing in a shower of bright sparks.

Tarienne let out the breath she hadn't realised she'd been holding.

Tere bounded up in his wolf form, whining softly. His wolfish gaze swept over the bodies of the beasts.

Tarienne kneeled, stroking the soft fur on his head. 'The blade spirits aided us,' she whispered. 'Were the traps successful?'

Tere cocked his head sideways in what appeared to be a nod. Tarienne chuckled, rising, her hand resting on the head of the huge black wolf. Running her hand through his thick, silky coat provided an unanticipated comfort. Tere's wolf leaned against her leg.

Raef motioned them farther into the blackness of the cave, his finger on his lips, pausing briefly as Daien and Aidan quietly joined them. Hiding in the cold, damp shadows just beyond a deep, dank chamber, they watched a small, insignificant looking man with long, silver hair reverently holding a huge, golden orb. The sphere sent out shards of amber light as he chanted in the old language, the language of magic. They guessed him to be Rantec. Several more of the beasts guarded him, positioned around the walls of the chamber.

Raef dropped his hand, signalling them to attack. Tarienne was so focused on the enemy, she did not hear Tere's soft, warning yip until it was too late. The moment she stepped from the shadows, Rantec's hawklike focus shot to her. Before anyone could react, he launched a ferocious blast of magic in her direction. Tere leapt in front of her, the full force of the powerful spell slamming into his flank. He yelped, landing hard on the ground, motionless.

Tarienne bit back a cry, her heart slamming against her ribs and ripped her attention from Rantec for a split second to check on her friend. There was no movement, no rise and fall of his chest. A tear escaped, despite the fury roiling within her.

Sparing a glance at Raef, Aidan and Daien embroiled in battle with the great, hairy beasts, Tarienne sucked in a deep breath and began chanting the Spell of Unmaking, which had the power to send a soul to the Underworld while simultaneously eliminating their physical body.

Raef spared a glance in her direction and shouted a warning.

'*Ren, no!*'

Tarienne ignored his plea and unleashed the full force of the ancient incantation. Rantec attempted to deflect it, but its potency was fuelled by her anger, overpowering him. A blood-red glow spread around him, then a narrow, black slit opened in the rock behind him and began sucking him in. His agonized scream filled the cave. His human body began to shrivel, like a grape drying in the sun, as his spirit was being wrenched free.

Too late, Tarienne realised her mistake. She'd underestimated him. Rantec fell to the ground and lunged at her, grabbing her ankle. Her eyes flew to the incandescent red glow creeping up her leg. Panic lanced through her, squeezing the breath from her lungs.

Pain ripped through her body. Tarienne screamed as Rantec's vice-like grip on her leg unbalanced her and she fell to the ground. She scrambled for purchase in the dirt, frantically struggling for her freedom. She kicked hard at his groping hands, trying to dislodge him, to no avail. His filthy nails bit into her leg, drawing blood. It trickled onto Rantec's knuckles, hissing, steam wafting up. Her eyes rolled as her muscles began to spasm. The searing agony burned her insides like flames igniting kindling.

The insidious glow continued its excruciating journey up her body. She fought with every ounce of strength left to stay conscious. Rantec finally disappeared into the blackness of the spell, but his grip had not loosened. Tarienne's chest tightened, and she gasped for breath. Icy fingers of terror raced up her spine as darkness took her. The last thing she heard was Daien's anguished plea.

'*No!*'

*　　*　　*

Raef

As Aidan felled the last of the creatures, both he and Raef spun around to see Tarienne convulsing on the ground. Daien stood a few feet away, surrounded by an eerie light, chanting unfamiliar words. Raef started to rush forward, but Aidan stopped him, motioning to Tarienne, who had already stilled and breathed more easily.

Raef reluctantly forced his attention to Tere's limp body. He was in wolf form, which told him he still lived. Raef and Aidan crossed to him quickly and knelt, Raef resting his hand on the wolf's flank.

'He's alive, but gravely injured. I'm not sure I can heal him, but I'll try.'

He focused his healing power on Tere, placing his trust in Daien to take care of his sister. It was one of the hardest things Raef had ever done. Every instinct told him to go to her, to hold her, to make it better, just as he'd done when they were children. But if he couldn't do that, he'd do everything in his power to heal the wolf that had saved his sister's life.

Tere's wolf remained motionless as a warm glow emanated from Raef's hands, feeling for the extent of his injuries, then tentatively beginning to heal them. His eyes continually flicked to Tarienne, bathed in the glow of Daien's magic. Raef wasn't surprised he possessed the gift of earth magic. He thought he'd caught a spark when he'd filtered through Daien's early memories, but he hadn't been certain. He was thankful he had found his power when Tarienne needed it most.

Raef glanced up momentarily to see Aidan making his way to the golden stone nestled in a shallow crevice in the cave wall. He pulled a soft cloth from his pocket and dropped it over the stone. Wrapping up the glowing orb, he carefully nestled it in his pack, cushioning it with his folded cloak.

As Raef concentrated once more on healing Tere, Aidan slowly walked up and touched his shoulder, his eyes flicking to Tarienne. A soft moss had crept across the bloodied ground to cushion her crumpled form. Ivy gently wove itself around her, cradling her body with fresh, green leaves. White flowers sprouted from the stems, encircling her head like a crown.

The colour slowly returned to Tarienne's face, and Raef heaved a sigh of relief. He dragged his attention back to Tere again.

After a few minutes, the wolf opened his eyes, whined, and struggled to stand. Raef and Aidan gently held him down, urging him to take a few moments.

Tere's ice-blue eyes focused on them as he gave a little whine of thanks, he then dropped his head back to the ground. They both stood and turned, seeing an exhausted Daien stagger to Tarienne's side, his eyes damp with unshed tears.

'Ren, sweetheart, come back to me.'

No response.

Daien's pleading gaze met his friends' eyes, despair etched across his face, shoulders slumped. His control shattering, tears tumbled down his cheeks. 'Rantec has pulled her spirit into the afterlife with him. I... I was too late.'

Raef dropped to his knees at his beloved sister's side. Placing his hands on either side of her head, he sent pulses of magic through her, panic taking hold of him when she did not respond.

He hung his head and whispered, 'My sweet baby sister, don't leave us. We need you.'

Aidan scooted over, grasping Tarienne's hand then turning to Tere. 'Her heart still beats. Tere, you helped her before. I know you are injured, but can you do anything now?'

* * *

Tere

A shimmer of gold sparks indicated Tere's shift to human form.

Ignoring his nakedness, he dragged himself to Tarienne's side, placing his hands over her heart. He closed his eyes, sending his wolf in search of her spirit.

'She does not yet walk the afterlife. Her spirit wanders, lost. I think we can pull her back if we work together. Place your hands on her so she can feel you, then call to her with your mind voice.'

Tere moved his hands to her abdomen. Closing his eyes, he drew in a deep breath and sent his spirit wolf to find her. Raef took one hand, Aidan the other, and Daien cradled her head in his lap, caressing the side of her face. They were all distantly aware of each other's unspoken words calling her back.

Daien pleaded with her. '*My beautiful Ren. Come back to me. Please don't leave me to an eternity without you. I love you. You are my soul, my life. Walk toward me, sweetheart. Be with me always. We all need you...*' He broke off, swallowing back tears, barely able to form a thought. '*I can't go on without you, sweetheart. Please...*'

Tere's spirit wolf could see that Tarienne wandered alone, confused, as she called to a shadowy figure.

'Daien?'

The shape wavered but Daien's voice reached out to her for a few more moments.

'*I love you. You are my soul, my life. Walk toward me, sweetheart. Be with me always. We all need you...*' The voice faded, disappearing.

'Daien? Don't leave me here. I'm lost.'

Sensing her panic Tere approached slowly through the foggy landscape on silent paws. Raef's and Aidan's voices floated in the void. Her eyes searched the foggy landscape, straining to see them.

Tarienne squinted as Tere approached as though she attempted to bring him into focus. She walked forward, tentatively approaching the shadow.

'Tere?'

The wolf yipped, padding toward her. Gently, he grasped her hand with his mouth, leading her down the path, toward the voices.

'Hello?! Where are you all?!' she called, hope in her voice.

Tere pulled more firmly, his mouth gentle, yet strong around her wrist.

Finally, Aidan, Daien, and Raef appeared in the fog, standing together. Tere's wolf released her hand, nudging her toward them.

*   *   *

Tarienne

Tarienne gasped and her eyelids fluttered open to see three pairs of worried eyes gazing down at her. Her attention was drawn momentarily to a now fully dressed Tere approaching from the direction of the cave entrance.

'Sweetheart...' Daien pulled her attention back before gathering her to him and hugging her so hard, she could barely breathe. He pulled away, and Tarienne watched a myriad of emotions play across his face... fear, love, protectiveness. When she noticed his damp cheeks, her own eyes welled with tears. Daien placed a gentle kiss on her lips.

Tarienne returned the kiss then pulled back to look into the eyes of the man she loved. She smiled happily before turning toward Raef and reaching for his hand. He lifted her fingers to his lips, then held her hand to the side of his face, closing his eyes against the emotions threatening to overwhelm him.

Reaching out with her other hand, she squeezed Aidan's, noting the dampness in his eyes.

Sitting up slowly, she turned her attention to Tere. 'Your wolf brought me home.'

Daien, Raef, and Aidan exchanged confused glances.

'I heard Daien calling, but I only saw him for a moment before he was gone. Not knowing which way to go, I walked toward where I'd seen him. Then I heard you all, but I couldn't seem to reach you. Tere's wolf took my hand and showed me the way. Thank you, Tere. You saved me... again.'

Tere smiled. 'Daien put you on the right path. You just needed some encouragement to continue.'

'You have earned our trust, Tere.' Aidan's stern expression let them know this was the king speaking. 'As such, you should know us for who we really are.'

Raef, Tarienne and Daien nodded.

Aidan continued, placing a hand on his chest. 'I am Aidan, king of Therin. Raef and Tarienne,' he gestured toward them, 'are the fae crown prince and princess of Darewood.' He nodded at Daien. 'This is Daien, the most trusted of my king's guardsmen, a dear friend of druid blood and betrothed to Tarienne.'

Tere's eyes widened with shock. Eventually, he bowed slightly. 'I am humbled and honoured to be in your presence—'

'No, Tere,' Tarienne interrupted.

He frowned, blinking at her.

She continued, 'As Aidan said, you have earned your place. We told you who we are to prove our trust in you, not change your attitude toward us. We are still Tarienne, Raef, Aidan and Daien. No more, no less.'

Tere nodded. 'I very much appreciate your trust and friendship.'

Glancing around the cave, he asked, 'In all the confusion, do we know what happened to the stone?'

Aidan smiled and produced a cloth from his pack, which he unwrapped to reveal the golden stone. It glowed brightly, pulsing in his hands. Quickly, he covered it again.

'We should get as far away from here as we can before reinforcements arrive. Ren are you well enough to travel?'

She nodded. 'Yes, I think so.'

Daien and Raef helped her up. She stood for a moment, bending her knees, and shifting from one foot to the other, testing her legs. 'I feel quite all right, considering.' She eyed Daien speculatively. 'What did you do?'

Daien shrugged, snorting. 'Honestly, I don't really know, but I somehow called the Earth Spirits. I had no idea what I was doing. It just,' he flung out his hands, 'flowed out of me.'

Daien paused before he spoke again turning to Tarienne. 'I have never felt such fear as when I thought I'd lost you. The words of the incantation just filled my mind, followed by a swell of magic, the power of which almost drove me to my knees. A vague feeling of familiarity filled me as I spoke, and I wondered if my mother had tried to teach me at some stage how to wield the magic. I was very young when she died so I do not remember much about her, but I am certain that you would have been great friends.'

Tarienne grinned. 'My wonderful druid.' Wrapping her arms around his neck, she lifted onto her tiptoes to claim a kiss.

Aidan shook his head and looked at Tere. 'Take no notice. They're always doing that.'

Laughing, they made their way out of the cave in readiness to leave.

As they reached the horses, Raef quietly moved up beside Tarienne, grasping her hand. She turned to face him. Frowning at the residual fear and pain reflected in his eyes she wrapped her arms around him tightly.

Raef hauled in a deep breath, burying his face in her hair, his voice breaking as he whispered, 'I thought I'd lost you, sweetling. Please, never do that to me again.'

Tarienne hugged her brother fiercely, allowing her courage and love to flow through their sibling bond. She spoke across Raef's thoughts. *I love you, dear brother, and I have no intention of leaving you... ever. You'd never manage without me to boss you around!*

Raef snorted out a laugh. Releasing her, he roughly wiped his arm across his eyes, then dropped a kiss onto her cheek.

Raef and Aidan untethered the horses, while Tere stepped behind a tree and stripped, handing his clothes to Daien. Tarienne smiled at the unlikely friendship developing between the two.

Tere shifted, breaking into a run to put distance between himself and the horses. Tarienne admired the sleek gait of the wolf, wondering again what his story was. She supposed he'd tell them eventually.

Aidan gently placed the wrapped golden stone into his saddlebag and hauled himself up onto the black leather saddle cinched tightly around his stallion's girth.

They rode off at a gallop, alert for a potential ambush, and thundered down the side of the mountain, distancing themselves from Rantec's headquarters.

Almost an hour later, as the landscape started to level out and trees appeared on either side of the track, they heard a chilling howl. Reining the horses to a halt, they listened and waited. Daien nudged his stallion closer to Tarienne, his hand on the hilt of his sword. She sent him a worried glance.

Tere's wolf suddenly burst from between the trees, panting hard. His tongue lolled out of the side of his mouth as he hurtled toward them, speaking into their minds.

'Run! Wolves!'

The group wheeled their horses and took off, pushing them as fast as they could go. They followed Tere down the side of the incline, through a thick stand of trees.

Emerging onto a short, grassy plain leading down to the river, they reined their horses to a skidding stop. Tere faced off with a huge, slate grey wolf. The hackles along Tere's back stood erect, his lips drawn back into a snarl. At least thirty other wolves were fanned out behind the grey.

Across the river behind the wolves, close to one hundred horses, ridden by all manner of creatures, stomped, and snorted. The riders all held crossbows, aimed in their direction. Tarienne pulled in a steadying breath, nudging Lacey closer to Daien's stallion.

Aidan and Daien both swore and drew their swords, yanking their shields from where they were strapped to their saddlebags. But Daien's wouldn't release, snagged on one of the straps. He cursed as he struggled with it. Raef murmured the beginnings of a spell.

Several things happened simultaneously.

Tere and the grey launched into a vicious battle, snarling and snapping. The riders across the river loosed their arrows, the collective *twang* echoing in the clearing. Raef stood in his saddle, shouting the final words of his incantation, and Aidan dove off his horse toward Daien, as an arrow hurtled toward him, while he continued to struggle to release his shield. Horror froze Tarienne as she watched the scene play out, seemingly in slow motion, before her.

When the reality of the drama slammed into her brain, she screamed a spell, flinging a blast of power from her fingertips to halt the arrow's trajectory.

She held her breath, watching as Aidan shoved Daien off his mount and out of the arrow's path. It slammed into Aidan's chest. He grunted as he fell to the ground, landing beside Daien with a bone-crunching thud. The air left his lungs with a *whoosh*, bright red blooming across his chest. His hand went to his chest before he pulled it back and looked at it, seemingly puzzled at the sight of blood, before his eyes rolled back into his head.

Tarienne jumped off Lacey's back and ran to him, dropping to her knees and cradling his head, frantically muttering a spell to arrest the bleeding.

Daien groaned and rose to his knees, his eyes widening when he saw the arrow protruding from Aiden's chest. Crawling over, he grasped Aidan's hand in his. Tarienne's eyes met Daien's and the horror and fear she saw mirrored her own as she continued to attempt to save Aidan's life.

'Daien, place your hands on Aidan's chest around the arrow and press down as hard as you can. We must stop the bleeding.'

Raef flung his hands out, unleashing his invocation. The thunderous boom created a shockwave, rocking the ground beneath them. The surrounding trees shuddered against the immense blast, creaking, and groaning in protest. Many of the wolves and riders fell to the ground, confusion scattering the rest of them.

Raef leapt from his stallion and dashed toward Tere, still locked in battle with the grey wolf. Plunging his hands between them, Raef grabbed the huge, grey wolf by the scruff. He grunted, the muscles of his arms and chest bunching as he hauled the wolf off Tere and hurled it toward the closest tree. The wolf slammed into the trunk, bones cracking, the breath expelled from its lungs with a rasp. The grey dropped to the ground in a bloodied heap, motionless.

Raef's hawk-like gaze flicked back to Tere, who had transformed and lay on the ground, chest heaving. His attention then snapped to Aidan, an arrow in his chest. Tarienne cradled his head in her lap, frantically uttering healing spells. Daien knelt at his side, his hands pressing around the arrow, trying to arrest the flow of blood pouring out around it.

*   *   *

Raef

Battle fury engulfed Raef's calm. Magic swirling around him, Raef sensed Tere's magic gathering as he rose, joining the maelstrom.

The power of Daien's rage, coiled tightly, like a snake ready to strike penetrated Raef's awareness as he moved up beside them. Drawing his sword, Daien brought the flat of the blade up to his forehead, and the words he used to call on the Earth and Tree Spirits for aid whirled around them.

The immense, combined power they wielded crashed into their attackers as they unleashed it. The small army spun to retreat, realisation of the power they faced driving them back.

A thick, churning mist surrounded them before they made it far. Beasts and men alike coughed violently. Horses reared, dumping those still on their backs to the ground, choking. The viscous, magical fog crept up their bodies. Raef watched fear cloud their eyes before the mist enveloped them completely.

The ground rumbled as Raef's chanting escalated. Magnificent and terrifying in his wrath, he shouted a triumphant battle cry.

Daien raised his sword and jammed it into the ground, shouting, '*Bás* (Death)!'

A crack in the earth spread from Daien's feet, soon opening to a wide chasm. Screams of the men and beasts falling into its depths pierced the dense cloud of fog, before the chasm closed with a loud *crack*. The mist quickly dissipated; the army gone.

Yanking his sword from the ground, Daien resheathed it. Raef spun toward Tarienne and Aidan, he and Daien sprinting over and dropping to their knees on either side of the king's still form. Tere dragged his battered body to Aidan's feet.

Tarienne lifted her eyes to his for a second, quickly returning to her attempts to heal the extensive damage the arrow had caused. Raef's sent his magic through his sister, boosting her healing power and sensed her ragged nerves calm a little

Finally, they both sensed they were making some progress. Aidan's internal bleeding had slowed to barely a trickle. Raef grasped Tarienne's shoulders reassuringly as her thoughts filtered through their connection. *She wondered if her healing abilities would be enough, knew a wound like his had the potential to be fatal. She could not – would not – lose Aidan.*

Tears sprang to her eyes as her hands trembled violently. Daien moved closer, gently wiping them away with his thumbs. Giving her a gentle smile, he stood, moving away to gather wood for a fire. Despite his injuries, Tere joined him.

Tarienne spared a quick glance at the changeling. Raef knew she wanted to check on him, make sure he wasn't too badly injured, but she knew his body would heal on its own, unlike Aidan's.

Daien and Tere worked silently to build a makeshift camp, light a fire, and cook a meal.

What seemed like hours later, Tarienne and Raef beckoned Daien over. Tarienne's tight smile revealed her exhaustion.

'When we tell you, pull the arrow out, straight up, as quickly as you can.'

Tere moved closer as Daien stood over Aidan, one foot either side of him, his hands wrapped around the arrow shaft.

Tarienne nodded. 'Now, Daien.'

Daien exerted such force on the arrow that he almost lost his balance and tumbled backward when it broke free from Aidan's body. Blood oozed out of the wound. Tere quickly grabbed Daien, halting his backward trajectory.

Daien straightened, inspecting the bloodied shaft of the arrow. He held it out to Tere, smiling.

'Thank you, Tere. I'd have landed flat on my backside if you hadn't caught me.'

Tere nodded and took the arrow, examining the tip. He sniffed it. 'I can detect no evidence of any poison.'

A sliver of relief flowed through Raef, although Aidan was still in danger of succumbing to his injuries, despite their tireless efforts.

*   *   *

Daien

Daien stared at Aidan's still form, an overwhelming sadness threatening to consume him. He raked his hands through his hair, which was stringy with perspiration and dirt. His thoughts drifted back to the pleasure he'd shared with Tarienne in the cool, clear lake only a few days ago. How quickly things changed.

He sighed quietly and walked over to the fire, settling against a young field maple.

After making him as comfortable as possible and covering him with clean bedding, Tarienne and Raef eventually moved away from Aidan, having done all they could, and collapsed near the warmth of the crackling fire. Tarienne snuggled into Daien's side.

Daien's brow furrowed. 'How is he?'

When Raef responded, his tone was flat, exhausted. 'He's alive. That's all we can say for now. We need help. We can't heal him completely.' Raef settled on the bedroll Daien had laid out for him.

Daien stood, untangling himself from Tarienne. Walking closer to the fire, he filled a cup of hot soup from the cooking pot and returned, crouching beside her, offering her the cup. Her face was drawn, her eyes holding a deep sadness.

'Drink this, sweetheart. There's no more you can do right now.'

Tarienne looked up, her eyes shadowed. She absently accepted the cup, wrapping her slightly shaky hands around its warmth. Daien covered her hands with his own, willing his strength into her. She smiled weakly at him, taking several sips, before Daien took the cup from her freezing hands and placed it onto the ground. He sat and hauled her onto his lap, resting his back against the nearest maple and gathering her hands in his, rubbed them gently to warm them. Tarienne curled up and lay her head on his chest. He enveloped her in a strong embrace, the instinct to protect her burning through his body. Grasping the cup of soup again, he handed it to her, curling her fingers around it.

Tarienne sipped the hot liquid, sighing. Daien smiled down at her and kissed the tip of her nose, feeling her sag a little in his lap. Slowly, her eyes closed. Grabbing the almost empty cup, he tossed it several feet away, then settled a sleepy Tarienne against his chest, leaning back against the tree and closing his eyes.

*　*　*

Tarienne

Having slept for a few hours Tarienne opened her eyes with a sigh and rose from Daien's lap to check on Aidan, placing a hand on his brow.

'He is so hot. He needs a cool compress,' she mumbled, her gaze sliding over the others as they stirred, concern creasing her forehead.

Daien rose, fishing around in his pack for a clean cloth. Tere took it from him and poured some water onto it from his waterskin, then wrung it out and handed it to Tarienne. She folded the cloth and dabbed at Aidan's face, laying it on his forehead.

Tarienne's dismay escalated as a distressing thought occurred.

'Do you think there could have been something on the arrow?'

Tere blew out a breath. 'Changelings often poison their arrow tips, but the riders were not changelings. Plus, Daien and I checked it thoroughly. There didn't seem to be anything on it.'

Raef sat up. 'Whatever the cause, we need to get Aidan to someone who can help more than we are able. We're about one week from Darewood. We need to get there as quickly as possible.'

'I agree,' Tarienne answered, 'but how are we going to transport him?'

'We can build a litter and I could ride his horse,' Tere offered.

They all considered for a moment, then Daien asked the question on everyone's minds.

'So, you can ride a horse with the,' he waved a hand around Tere, brows furrowed, 'wolf thing?'

Tere chuckled, glancing at their mounts. 'The horses don't seem to mind me in human form. I can mask my scent, so I don't frighten them.'

'Right. We'll rest for a few more hours, then build the litter and be on our way.' Raef lay down again and closed his eyes. 'You should all get some sleep. I've set some wards to warn us if anything approaches.'

Tarienne curled up on Daien's lap again. His arms snaked around her, tucking her into the protection of his body. She sighed, drifting into a deep, yet fitful slumber, haunted by nightmares of an arrow slamming into Daien's chest.

CHAPTER 14

Once they'd finished building the litter, they strapped Aidan on securely. His skin still felt very warm, so Raef and Tarienne spent a few moments on some more healing spells. Tarienne wiped his face with a cool cloth, dribbled some water into his mouth and checked the bindings. She talked to him as she worked, desperately hoping he would give some sign he could hear her.

Tere slowly moved in front of Aidan's stallion, running his hand along its muzzle, and quietly speaking a few words in a language no one else understood. The horse nudged him and nickered, as if giving him permission to ride. He then hauled himself into the saddle, grimacing slightly. Tarienne wanted to check his injuries, they obviously still caused him some discomfort, but she knew his body would heal them quicker than anything she could do.

They rode more slowly than they would have liked so as not to injure or cause Aidan further discomfort. Every so often, Raef projected his thoughts to their father, letting him know what had happened, where they were and that they required help.

Three days into their journey, they spotted a lone rider heading toward them. They halted, Daien's hand resting on the hilt of his sword. Tarienne focused on the rider and sucked in a breath.

'Arivaelle!'

Raef's face split into a huge grin.

Daien and Tere looked between them until Tarienne explained excitedly.

'Rivi's our sister and the best healer there is.'

Tarienne urged her horse forward, Raef close behind. The siblings leapt off their mounts and hurtled into a three-way hug.

Tarienne gifted Daien with one of the smiles she reserved for him alone as she rushed over. Grasping his hand, she squeezed it as she led him to meet her sister.

'Arivaelle, this is Daien, my betrothed.'

Daien bowed slightly. 'It is indeed a pleasure to meet you, Arivaelle.'

She smiled. 'And you, dear Daien. Welcome to our family.' Arivaelle hugged him softly, then turned to Tere.

Tarienne smiled. 'This is our friend, Tere.'

Arivaelle paused, assessing Tere for a moment before she spoke. 'It is a pleasure to meet you, Tere.'

He bowed low, his voice wavering slightly. 'T-The pleasure is all mine, milady.'

'Now, where is King Aidan?' Her focus quickly snapped back to the purpose of her ride.

Tarienne led her to Aidan strapped to the litter. Arivaelle placed her hands over his weeping wound, closing her eyes. Tarienne watched as she worked, pleased at the immediate change in Aidan's colour.

After a few minutes, his eyes fluttered open. Arivaelle requested some water and supported Aidan's head, allowing him a small drink. He licked his lips appreciatively as his gaze focused on Arivaelle.

'I must be dead, for I'm being cared for by an angel,' he whispered, his voice scratchy. Grinning weakly, he drifted back to sleep.

Tarienne chuckled. 'I think he's going to be fine.'

Arivaelle blushed furiously as the relieved friends laughed.

She continued her healing spell for some time, then wiped down his face and neck. 'We must get him to Darewood as soon as we are able.'

Raef nodded. 'When you are finished, we'll move on.'

*　*　*

Daien

Arivaelle made them stop every couple of hours to tend Aidan. Each time she did, he looked better and stayed awake a little longer.

After almost a week since they had left camp with a severely injured Aidan, the group arrived in Darewood to a joyous greeting. Entering the inner circle of the fae city, Daien couldn't hide his amazement at the beauty. It was ethereal, like its inhabitants.

When a tall, willowy, elegant woman with deep blue eyes appeared between the columns of silver trees lining the entrance to the royal rooms, Daien's eyes widened wondering who she was.

Stunning in soft cream robes that floated around her slim body and bare feet, her soft, blonde hair curled around her face, like a halo. Daien's question was answered moments later.

Raef's focus drifted in her direction, and he sucked in a breath. 'Elyssia.' A smile transformed his face as he all but ran to her, scooping her into a crushing hug. He lifted her off the ground and held her close as they shared a kiss that left no doubt of their love.

This was a side of him Daien hadn't seen before. He understood how Raef felt being separated from his love for so long. The realisation of how deeply he'd fallen in love with Tarienne frightened him a little.

Leaving Raef and Elyssia to their reunion, Tarienne, Daien, Arivaelle and Tere carried Aidan to a room where he could rest and recuperate. Once they had him settled, Tarienne showed Tere to a room not too far from her own, promising to show him around after they rested. She then led Daien to her sleeping quarters.

As they walked hand in hand, he glanced around in awe. He marvelled at the golden leaves and silvery branches that entwined to create shimmering, leaf-covered walls, the long corridors adorned with colourful flowers woven together, creating intricate patterns.

Tarienne laughed as she drew him into her room. Daien felt Tarienne's gaze on his back like the heat from the sun as he walked around, reverently touching the walls and furniture. Finally, he shifted his focus back to her.

She held her breath when he prowled toward her, her eyes darkening with passion. Tenderly pulling her into his arms, he captured her lips.

Tarienne ran her hands over his hard muscles, settling them over his heart. Daien's hands slid down to her bottom, pulling her close, his desire pressing against her.

Drawing back for a moment, Daien turned to look at the bed. 'Hmm... A warm, soft bed. I hope you're not planning to get much sleep tonight.'

*   *   *

Tarienne

The sensual timbre of his voice turned Tarienne's insides molten. Her heart slammed into her ribs, her body reacting instantly. Barely able to breathe, Tarienne managed to push him away just enough to look up into his eyes. In a low, husky voice, she delivered an invitation she knew he could not refuse.

'Bathe with me first, my Daien.'

He groaned loudly. 'Whatever you want. I want to show you how much I love you for as long as we can stay awake.'

Leaning close, she whispered, 'I love you so much, Daien. I look forward to eternity with you.'

He hauled her against him, covering her lips with his in a long, passionate kiss, then scooped her up and carried her to the bed. Placing her gently onto the soft, cream-coloured coverlet, he stretched out next to her, silencing her protests with his finger on her lips.

'We'll bathe in a moment. I want to enjoy being with you, taking our time for a change.'

He drew in a breath when she licked his finger, then drew it into her mouth, softly sucking on the tip. Withdrawing his finger, he replaced it with his lips.

Daien moved his body over hers until the evidence of his desire pressed between her legs. Her body arched into him, and Daien swore under his breath.

'I wanted to take this slowly, but you stir my blood so.'

Leaning down, he dropped light kisses along her neck, trailing down to the exposed skin of her breast. Sliding his hand up her stomach, he continued his exploration, until he reached the hard bud of her nipple. It beaded under his touch, and he groaned.

When she raised her arms over her head, his entire body shook with the lust he'd held in check. Dragging her blouse over her head, a growl rumbled through him. He licked her nipple, watching her as her lips parted on a gasp. She writhed beneath him as he suckled each tight bud in turn, her soft moans urging him on.

Sliding to one side, Daien trailed one hand down her body. Tarienne moaned and pushed at her riding pants. Daien slipped off the bed, unfastened the buttons and yanked them off. He pulled his shirt over his head, flung it to the side, then dropped his trousers. Climbing back onto the bed, his hand trailed up her inner thighs. Tarienne's hips bucked, wanting more.

Daien obliged, slipping his fingers underneath her undergarments to circle her sensitive nub. Tarienne cried out, arching into his hand. He captured her lips, sliding his tongue into her mouth.

Tarienne moaned again as Daien eased his fingers into her warm wetness, sliding them deep then withdrawing slowly. Sensing her tension rising, he increased the pace. When he shifted his thumb to massage her sensitive nub, she whimpered, then thrashed beneath him, calling his name as her climax exploded.

Her body still shuddering, Daien lifted himself over her and slid into her heat, the sheer pleasure sending shivers of primal lust lancing through them both, propelling his hips in a punishing rhythm. For the first time since they'd made love in her chambers in Therin, Tarienne sensed Daien completely let go of his tight control, giving in to the all-consuming desire driving him.

When Tarienne wrapped her legs around his waist, pulling him deeper, they both shattered into a million shards of white light, his hot seed pumping into her on the tidal wave of the most intense pleasure she'd ever experienced, robbing her of all coherent thought.

Supporting himself on his elbows, he rested his forehead on hers, gasping for breath. Daien kissed her tenderly, then reluctantly slid off her gorgeous body, pulling her to her feet.

'Now, where do we bathe, sweetheart?'

Tarienne's knees wobbled a little before he snaked his arm around her waist. She pointed to a room off to the side of her chambers.

*   *   *

Daien

Daien felt the gentle tingle of magic as she led him to the bathing area. He stopped, whistling through his teeth. The large, round bath was surrounded by white, cut stones and nestled in a thick bed of soft moss. Steam already rose from the gently bubbling water. Daien turned to Tarienne, his mouth agape.

She smiled seductively, stepping closer. He lifted one of her hands to his lips, kissed each finger in turn, then led her into the water.

Sighing as he sat, the warm water enveloping them, he dragged her back between his legs, his hands wandering over her luscious body. With the way she writhed against him, moans falling from her lips, desire consumed him once again. She suddenly twisted out of his grip and took his lips in a punishing kiss. He smiled against her mouth, loving how much she craved him, amazed how she could awaken his body again so soon after such an intense climax.

Her green eyes, dark and wide, met his. She gave him a bewitching smile. Daien growled and pounced, splashing water onto the rocks and moss. His hands slipped around her lean body to cup her tight bottom. Tarienne slipped her hand between them, circling her fingers around his throbbing manhood to guide him into her tight sheath.

All coherent thought was lost as he set a slow, languorous rhythm, encouraged by her whimpers and gasps. Moments later, her muscles clamped around him at the same time another earth-shattering climax surged through his body. They cried out, not caring if they were heard.

They lay back in the warm water, catching their breath, when Tarienne motioned for him to listen. Daien frowned. Then a shout and a loud moan reached his ears.

'Raef! Oh, Raef!'

Tarienne giggled quietly. 'I think they're pleased to see each other.'

They chuckled, then stepped out of the tub. After drying each other with deliciously soft cloths, they climbed into the warm, downy bed and fell into an exhaustion fuelled sleep.

The next morning, everyone was summoned to the meeting hall by Tarienne and Raef's mother and father, Queen Aistarenne and King Thalion. Daien was a little nervous at the prospect, but Tarienne entwined her fingers with his and squeezed gently to reassure him.

'Do not fear, my Daien. They will love you as I do.'

He took a deep breath and nodded. As they were about to enter the hall, a figure so fast it appeared as a blur launched at Tarienne. Daien's hand flew to the hilt of his sword, ready to draw it. Tarienne burst out laughing, enveloped in a giant hug.

'Kyre, you almost knocked me over.' She hugged him fiercely.

He pulled back and kissed both her cheeks. 'Ren, you've been gone for so long. Damn, it's good to see you.' A grin split his face.

Tarienne turned to Daien, motioning him over. 'Kyre, this is Daien. Daien, my brother, Kyre.'

Kyre eyed him for a moment, then clapped him on the back and pulled him into a quick hug, whispering loudly, 'Good luck with Ren. She has quite the temper.'

Daien laughed as Tarienne scowled and swiped playfully at her brother.

Kyre was as tall as Raef, his long, wavy blond hair hanging loose down his back and his shining eyes a deep, sea blue. He moved with grace and assurance yet had an air of mischief about him. Daien noted his muscular build and fearless demeanour, certain he would be a dangerous enemy, yet an extraordinary ally. The looks he garnered from the women walking past told him Kyre, like Raef, was extremely popular with the ladies.

Daien turned slightly to see a younger man standing several steps back, waiting. He approached Tarienne with a quiet dignity, though the hug he gave her was no less fierce.

'I've missed you, dear sister. I'm so pleased you're home.'

'Authion, my brother, I have missed you too. This is Daien.'

He turned his attention to Daien. 'Welcome to our home and our family.' He extended his hand. When Daien accepted it, he pulled him into a brotherly hug, his smile warm and genuine.

Daien noted how different Authion was compared to the others. He was as tall as the rest of his family, but his hair was black, secured in tiny braids, his eyes a vivid green, like Tarienne's.

Tarienne led Daien over to meet more of her family.

'You've met Arivaelle,' she continued, then turned as Raef and Elyssia entered behind them, hand in hand. 'And this is Elyssia.'

Elyssia moved gracefully from Raef's side to greet Daien, reminding him of a swan gliding on a lake.

'It is a great pleasure to finally meet you.'

When his brows furrowed, she smiled.

'Tarienne and I have spoken much of you through our mind connection.'

Daien glanced at Tarienne, then smiled at Elyssia. 'It is a pleasure to meet you. The woman who captivates Raef must be special indeed.'

Raef laughed as Elyssia blushed, smiling sweetly, and moving back to his side. He tucked her safely under his arm, a calm contentment settling around him.

They all turned to face Queen Aistarenne and King Thalion, who stepped down from their thrones. They approached Tarienne and Daien first. Daien thought how noble, yet kind, they both looked. The queen took Tarienne's hand in hers, her long, red hair not unlike her daughter's, yet tamed into a long braid.

'Welcome home, my beautiful daughter. We have missed you.'

Tarienne hugged her mother, tears in her eyes. 'I have missed you all so much.'

Aistarenne kissed Tarienne affectionately on the cheek, then turned her attention to Daien, holding her hands out to him. He grasped them gently, smiling nervously.

She beamed. 'Do not fear, dear Daien. You are most welcome here. You are part of our family now,' Aistarenne looked around at her children and raised an eyebrow, her eyes twinkling with amusement, 'though you may not wish it so at times.'

The others chuckled as Daien grinned at her. 'I am very happy to be here and meet Tarienne's family.'

She smiled at him again, then looked around. 'Where is Tere, the wolf changeling?'

He answered nervously, 'H-Here, Your Majesty.'

They all turned to see Tere, looking small and apprehensive, standing with Authion. Authion nudged him forward. Tere took a step and dropped to one knee, bowing his head.

'Your Majesty, it is an honour to meet you. To be granted entry into your kingdom is a great gift.'

Aistarenne moved forward and placed her hand on his head. 'Rise, Tere. You are most welcome here. We have heard of your deeds to protect our children and wish you to be at ease with us. We would be pleased if you would treat Darewood as your second home.'

He rose slowly, fleetingly meeting the queen's eyes. 'I no longer have a true home, so I would be honoured. You are most gracious, Your Majesty. Thank you.' Tere bowed low.

Aistarenne stepped over to speak with Raef, while Thalion introduced himself. Daien couldn't help thinking how alike Thalion and Tarienne were. The king was quite imposing and regal, but down to earth, like his daughter. Aistarenne was elegant and serene, possessing a strength her daughter had inherited. Suppressing a chuckle, Daien wondered from which of them Tarienne acquired the stubbornness.

*   *   *

Tarienne

Later that afternoon, they went to visit with Aidan. To their relief, he looked much improved. They found him sitting with Arivaelle, her hand in his, his thumb absently caressing her fingers. Tarienne rushed in and threw her arms around his neck, noting her sister quickly withdrew, busying herself with tidying the room.

'You look so much better. Rivi has done a wonderful job.'

Aidan grinned at her. 'Yes, she has.' His face softened, his eyes flicking to Arivaelle.

Tarienne looked between them, a smile spreading across her face.

She walked over to Arivaelle, pulling her into a hug.

'I don't know what would have happened without you.' She lowered her voice so only she could hear. 'It seems you have healed his wounds and stolen his heart.'

Kissing Arivaelle on the cheek, Tarienne pulled back, grinning at her blushing sister. She was pleased for sweet, shy Arivaelle and Aidan. They were perfect for each other.

Daien, Raef and Tere joined them, gently clasping Aidan's shoulder. They sat and chatted, catching up on everything that had happened, filling in the gaps for him.

When Tarienne reminded Tere she'd promised him a tour around Darewood, Aidan straightened and smiled.

'I wouldn't mind taking a walk. I'm getting tired of sitting.' Aidan looked hopefully at Arivaelle.

She nodded with a smile, shooing the others away from the bed so she could help Aidan up, despite their offers of assistance. He wrapped his arm around her shoulders for support, their eyes locking momentarily, before she slipped her arm around his waist. Tarienne smiled, warmth and happiness bubbling within her.

They all walked slowly through the grove of silver and gold trees that formed an archway along the centre of Darewood. Not long into their walk, Authion approached, beckoning to Tere, who excused himself and strode away, their heads close as though deep in discussion. Tarienne and Daien dropped back beside Raef and Elyssia, watching Aidan and Arivaelle, arms wrapped around each other, chatting animatedly.

Raef stopped and slid his arms around Elyssia, kissing her passionately.

Daien turned Tarienne to face him. Desire burned in his eyes. Tarienne swept her arms around his neck, breathing in his delicious, masculine scent. When she licked her lips, he groaned, lowering his mouth to hers for a long, sensual kiss that built a slow burn deep within her.

*   *   *

Aidan

Aidan and Arivaelle, as if sensing both couples stopping, turned around to see them locked in a passionate embrace. Aidan's heart thumped erratically as he contemplated doing the same with Arivaelle. Their eyes met. Before he could act, her hands slowly made their way to his chest.

His heart drummed under her fingers. Arivaelle smiled encouragingly. Aidan drew in a sharp breath as her lips parted, her tongue sliding out to moisten them. Slowly, he lowered his head, allowing her time to move away, feeling her sweet breath on his lips. The scent of cinnamon and honey, with a hint of vanilla, teased his senses.

To his surprise, she rose up on her toes, brushing her lips against his. He kissed her gently, carefully, as though she might break, then pulled back to gaze into her eyes. When she smiled, he couldn't resist dipping down for a longer, deeper kiss. He ran his tongue over her full, soft lips, his pulse skittering in response. Arivaelle softened, parting her lips in invitation. Aidan allowed a groan to rumble through him.

Aidan slid his hands to her tiny waist, savouring the feel of her slim, curvy body against his. Arivaelle slipped her hands around his neck. Her nails skimmed his scalp. He shivered, pulling her against his overheated body. Losing themselves in the sensuality and heat of the kiss, they were oblivious to their surroundings.

When they finally pulled apart, a little breathless, they saw the others staring at them, jaws slack. Aidan grinned and shrugged. He wrapped his arm around Arivaelle's shoulders again. She slipped her arm around Aidan's waist and threw them a pleased grin.

They watched, stunned, as Aidan and Arivaelle passed them and returned to the castle.

Raef, the first to recover, chuckled. 'Well, what do you know. Our little sister has fallen for the king!'

Tarienne smiled. 'Actually, I think she's fallen for "just Aidan".'

CHAPTER 15

For the next few days, they rested, secure in the knowledge the golden stone was temporarily safe in the deepest vault of Darewood.

Tarienne enjoyed spending time at home. She knew it would end too soon, so she spent as much time as she could with her family, and relaxing with Daien.

One week after their arrival, Queen Aistarenne and King Thalion summoned them all to a meeting in the great hall to discuss their plans to return the golden stone to Therin.

Raef, Daien and Tarienne entered together, sitting with their family at the front of the room. Authion and Kyre, on either side of their mother and father, no longer looked like Tarienne's easy-going brothers. They both had a regal bearing and an almost stern look she knew indicated their total focus on the problem at hand.

Aidan arrived moments later, Arivaelle on his arm. He kissed her as she untangled her arm from his, leaving him to his meeting. Aidan followed her departure, his attention lingering on her as she walked away. Sighing happily, he moved farther into the room, bowing slightly as he approached the king and queen seated at a long table at the front of the long hall.

Tere entered next and bowed deeply, glanced around at the rows of seats, then sauntered over to sit next to Aidan.

King Thalion spoke first. 'We have called this meeting to discuss how best to proceed with the problem of the golden stone and the creatures called with it. We believe the best way is for you all to return to Therin and place the stone deep within the keep. Be warned. It will require powerful wards to protect it.'

Raef listened to his father, his elbows resting on the table, fingers steepled in front of his face. 'And what of the creatures summoned by the magic of the stone?'

His voice was calm and measured, yet Tarienne sensed Daien's awareness of the tingle of power radiating from him. When he glanced at Tarienne, she smiled and winked.

'Authion and Tere have come up with what they believe to be a viable plan and wish to discuss it with you here today,' King Thalion replied.

Raef nodded his approval.

Queen Aistarenne serenely watched the proceedings. Tarienne smiled as Aidan's thoughts drifted to her. He fleetingly wondered if she had the ability to spread calm, because he felt quite relaxed. She grinned and watched as her mother turned to him, smiling sweetly, also reading his thoughts. Aidan returned the smile, then refocused on Authion and Tere, who stood, ready to present their plan to the group.

To Tarienne's surprise, her brother gestured for Tere to start. She wondered if the changeling understood the measure of respect Authion had just afforded him by allowing him to speak first. Raef raised one eyebrow at her, which she acknowledged with an almost imperceptible nod.

Tere moved to the front of the room his gaze drifting around his audience. 'Aidan has spoken with us about Therin and the ability to lock it down, its people safely inside, to create a stronghold. Authion, Aidan and I have devised a plan to draw Rantec's minions to Therin, ambush them, then return them to their prison beneath the earth.

'We believe the best approach is to send two groups to Therin to confuse the enemy. One will transport the golden stone, the other will be a decoy, taking a route closer to Rantec's army and drawing focus away from the group transporting the stone, who will leave first. When they reach Therin, they will ensure the people from the outlying areas are moved within the castle walls. The army of Darewood will dispatch a day later and attack Rantec's army from the rear as they attempt to capture the stone and take Therin.'

Once finished, he made eye contact with Authion, nodded, and sat down.

Authion's vivid green eyes swept the room. 'As Tere has indicated, we believe we can recapture these creatures by moving the people behind Therin's walls and strategically placing an army of fae, elves and men at enough distance from Therin so they are not detectable. We need Rantec's followers to believe they are on the stone's trail and allow them to almost catch up with it. The army will then move in, overpower the creatures, then summon the elder council to return the beasts to their prison.'

Aidan stood. 'Then I must return to Therin, bring my people within its walls and ensure there is enough food and water to sustain them through this. I would ask for one of you to go with me.'

Without any hesitation, Daien shot to his feet. 'I'll go with you, sire.'

Aidan smiled. 'Thank you, Daien.'

Tarienne and Raef stood. Raef glanced at Tarienne, then spoke for them both.

'We, too, will accompany Aidan back to Therin. Authion, who do you suggest as the decoys?'

Authion eyed Raef for a moment. 'Well, seeing as the creatures expect the stone to be with the four of you, I can't think of better decoys. Tere has offered to be part of the group transporting it.'

Raef waited, a slight frown on his face, knowing there was more. 'And?'

'I will accompany Tere.'

Every eye turned to the strong, determined, feminine voice from the back of the room. Arivaelle stood in the doorway. The room erupted with shouts of protest.

She strode to Aidan's side, who protested as loudly as Raef and Tarienne. Holding her hands up, she shouted into their minds.

'*Stop!*'

Stunned, they all halted mid-sentence.

'I have discussed this with Mother, Father, Authion and Kyre, and I fully intend to accompany the party transporting the stone!'

Arivaelle held all their gazes in turn, daring them to protest.

Daien snorted and spoke quietly but loud enough for Aidan to hear, 'And who does *that* remind you of?'

Tarienne glared at him, then chuckled, realising he was right. 'You should be used to this, Aidan.'

He stared at Tarienne for a moment, then turned to Arivaelle. 'Rivi, are you sure about this?' Lowering his voice, he added, 'I couldn't bear to lose you now that I've found you.'

Arivaelle stepped closer and wrapped her arms around his neck. 'Oh, Aidan, you're not going to lose me. I want to do this for you. For us. I want to come to Therin... if you'll have me.'

Without thought as to who was in the room, Aidan lowered his lips to hers for a scorching kiss.

Tarienne grinned, gazing around the room mischievously. 'Don't worry. They're always doing that!'

Aidan chuckled against Arivaelle's lips as Raef, Tere and Daien laughed heartily. Everyone else just looked at each other, confused.

Tarienne grinned. 'I'll explain later.'

Authion spoke, bringing them all back to the task at hand. 'Are we in agreement then?'

Raef sat again and leaned forward on the table. 'That's only two.' Raef eyed Authion, waiting, authority in his demeanour.

Authion eyes held his brother's, unfazed. 'Myself, Kyre and Father will make up the rest of the second group.'

Raef's attention jumped to his father, who stood, a smile hovering on his lips. 'I am not a decrepit old man yet.' In truth, he looked barely older than Raef, his body still sculpted and strong. 'It may have been many years since I've been in battle, but I *was* the leader of the army of Darewood long before you were all born.'

Before Thalion could say more, Elyssia swept into the room, stopping by Raef's side.

'I wish to come with you.' Her eyes pleaded with Raef, seeing denial hovering there. 'You have been gone for so long. I don't want you to leave me again.' She placed one hand on Raef's chest, her eyes pleading, voice wavering. 'Please, Raef, don't leave me behind again.' A single tear slipped down her cheek.

Raef cupped her face in his hands. He wiped the tear away with his thumb and leaned down to place a tender kiss on her lips.

Tarienne watched Raef's expression change from indecision, to love, to determination.

'Oh,' she squeaked out, clamping her hand to her mouth and leaning into Daien, knowing what her brother was about to do.

Confused, Daien wrapped his arm around her shoulders, tucking her into him.

When Raef dropped to one knee in front of Elyssia, she gasped, hands flying to her mouth.

'My darling Lissy,' Raef began, 'this wasn't quite the way I'd planned it, but I love you. You are my heart, my reason for being. I want to be with you always. Will you marry me, my beautiful, sweet Elyssia?'

She dropped to her knees, tears of joy streaming down her cheeks. 'Yes, Raef! Oh yes!'

Raef captured her mouth in a passionate kiss, the room erupting in cheers.

Tarienne's eyes swam with tears. Daien pulled her closer, smiling broadly. Aidan snaked one arm around Arivaelle's waist and hauled her to him. She reached up to kiss him lightly, tenderly. When they drew apart, gazing into each other's eyes, Arivaelle blushed.

Tarienne wondered at the change in Aidan. He would have never shown so much affection in public previously, and the fact it was in front of her parents was even more amazing. Aidan's happiness filled her with joy. Only Tarienne and Daien knew how far Aidan had come emotionally. She smiled.

Daien leaned into her. 'What are you smiling at, sweetheart?'

She snuggled into him. 'I was just thinking how different Aidan is to the man who left Therin only a few weeks ago.'

Daien ran his hand up and down her back affectionately. 'I wonder what his subjects will think when he returns?'

'They'll think him a better king for his travels. He always had far more compassion and empathy than his father, but now he's happy and more confident. I can't help thinking what Eldan would have made of "just Aidan".'

Daien snorted. 'I can't imagine Eldan being very happy about it.' He glanced down at Tarienne. 'He found true love... Like us.'

She smiled. 'Yes. Like us.'

Tarienne looked into his eyes. Her body responded to the virile heat of his hard body pressed up against her. Her breasts strained against the material of her shirt. Lips parted slightly as her heart began to thud against her ribs. Her breathing quickened.

Daien grasped her hand. 'We're done here. Let's go back to your chambers.'

'*Our* chambers,' Tarienne corrected as they bowed quickly. Her mother and father nodded their assent with knowing smiles.

Raef chuckled as they hurried off, laughing heartily when Kyre scrambled up and ran after them, almost barrelling into her when he tried to block their exit. Tarienne was too quick, sidestepping, her brother sprawling onto the floor.

Tarienne laughed. 'You've never been fast enough, Kyre.'

He chuckled as he picked himself up. 'I'll succeed one day.'

She called back over her shoulder, 'In your dreams, little brother!'

*　　*　　*

Tarienne

They'd decided to travel under the cover of darkness, so their movements weren't detected and their whereabouts remained unknown. Once night fell, they said their farewells.

Tears in her eyes, Tarienne hugged her family fiercely, then mounted Lacey, quietly cantering into the darkness of the forest with Daien, Raef, Elyssia, and Aidan. Daien drew his horse up beside her, blowing her a kiss. Tarienne smiled and reached over to squeeze his hand. She wished the journey to Therin wasn't so long and fraught with peril.

Tarienne looked at each member of the group, coming to rest on Aidan. There was more than one reason to be grateful to Arivaelle, both for his life and the happiness radiating from him.

Shifting her focus to Raef and Elyssia, Tarienne smiled. They were so happy. But a sliver of concern pierced her joy. Would sweet, fragile Elyssia be able to cope with the rigours of the journey? What if they were attacked again? Would Raef be distracted protecting her?

Daien's voice across her thoughts brought her back to the present. *'Sweetheart, you're frowning. What's wrong?'*

Tarienne beamed at him. *'Have I told you today how very much I love you?'* His answering smile stole her breath. *'I'm just a little concerned about Elyssia and how she'll cope with travelling.'*

Daien leaned over and grasped her hand, bringing it to his lips. *'She's not fierce like my warrior princess, but she'll manage. Raef will ensure her safety.'*

Tarienne's eyebrows lifted in surprise. *'Warrior princess?'*

They both chuckled softly, and her concerns slid to the back of her mind.

They rode in silence until they reached the borders of Darewood, pausing for a moment to look back, already missing the comfort and familiarity of home. Pushing forward, they kept to the edge of clearings and to the deepest part of the forest.

Just before sunrise, they made camp deep within the forest, where the foliage was so dense no sunlight penetrated. Raef lit a small, magical fire that emitted heat but no smoke, then they settled in to eat and rest.

The dynamics of the group had altered, and Tarienne experienced a fleeting sense of sadness at the lack of the usual banter. She dropped into Daien's lap as he rested, his back against a tall tree.

His arms snaked around her. She turned her head to kiss him, then wiggled to get comfortable, evoking a low groan from Daien. Wrapping her arms around his neck, Tarienne kissed him passionately. Then she pulled away and glanced at their group.

Raef and Elyssia cuddled on Raef's bedroll. Aidan poked the fire with a stick as he stared into the depths of the forest, seemingly distracted.

Tarienne snorted softly and looked at Daien. 'I guess we're on sentry duty.'

'I'll take second watch,' Aidan said, still gazing into the distance.

'And I'll take the last,' Raef responded. When Tarienne stuck her tongue out at him, he grinned. 'You should know we're always alert, Ren, even if our focus appears elsewhere.'

Tarienne projected her thoughts to Raef. *It's just different now. I love having Lis here, but we had settled into such a great pattern, it's difficult to adjust. Not to mention we're not really being sympathetic to Aidan. He doesn't have Rivi here with him.*

Raef untangled himself from Elyssia and scooted over beside her, pulling her from Daien's lap onto his in one swift movement.

She sighed. 'I'm sorry. I sound like a petulant child, don't I?'

Raef held her to his chest, like he used to when they were young. They all sat quietly for a while. Then he broke the silence.

'Ren's right. We need to discuss group dynamics as we did when the four of us left Therin.'

Raef released Tarienne, who kissed him on both cheeks before clambering to her feet. 'Thank you, *toror*.'

They talked for almost an hour, settling on how best to work together. Instead of being focused on their partners, they decided to interact more as individuals, and things soon began to settle into a more comfortable pattern.

The next night also passed without incident, but when they stopped to make camp as the sun rose, Aidan pointed out how unnaturally quiet it was. There were no bird sounds, no animals skittering across the dried leaves of the forest floor. On high alert, they spread out from camp, weapons drawn. The trees began to rustle, though there was no wind penetrating this deep.

Wolves slowly materialized between the trees, snarling, and snapping as they backed the companions into their campsite. The wolves circled yet did not attack.

Daien closed his eyes for a moment. The trees began to sway, then started to move violently, their branches cracking around the wolves like whips, knocking some off their feet with a yelp.

Daien, Aidan and Raef took advantage of the distraction, moving forward, careful to keep their backs to each other. Tarienne and Elyssia also stood back-to-back. Tarienne wielded her twin knives, and Elyssia loosed arrows from her bow, which they were now glad she had the presence of mind to fling over her shoulder before leaving home. Tarienne was surprised at her accuracy, each shot deadly.

With the trees attacking from behind and the group attacking from the front, the remaining wolves began to retreat, but not before Tarienne flung out her hands, blue fire pouring from her fingertips.

When the last of the wolves either lay dead or had fled, Daien placed his hands on either side of the closest tree. Resting his forehead on its damp bark, he whispered his thanks. Tarienne joined him, placing her hands beside his. The others followed suit on the trees closest to them. A soft rustle of leaves and branches whispered through the forest, seemingly in acknowledgment before all was still once more.

Tarienne removed her hands, wrapping her arms around Daien.

'That was amazing.'

He grinned, sweeping his arms around Tarienne, and pulling her close for a kiss. When Aidan rolled his eyes and groaned as he walked away, everyone chuckled. Tarienne grinned against Daien's lips, kissing him again before they pulled apart to pack their belongings.

To reach Therin before it was besieged, they now knew they'd have to travel day and night, only stopping briefly as needed. After calming their still skittish horses with a few soothing words, they mounted and urged them into a gallop. The trees seemed to part as they thundered through the forest, then snapped back into place behind them, guarding their back. Tarienne caught Daien grinning as he leaned low over his stallion's neck. She suspected he had orchestrated their rear guard.

A few hours later, they stopped for food and drink, allowing the horses to rest. Aidan prowled around the perimeter of the area. They couldn't afford to be taken by surprise again.

For three more days and nights they travelled, stopping only when necessary.

On the fifth day, stumbling upon a shallow cave only two hundred feet from a narrow creek surrounded by long, green grass, they made camp, exhausted.

Unsaddling their steeds, they allowed them to graze as they dumped their gear into the mouth of the damp cave. Elyssia retrieved her bedroll from where it was secured behind her saddle, rolled it out and flopped down onto it, unused to travelling long distances, let alone at the punishing pace they had set. She was totally exhausted, though she had not complained once.

Raef dropped to one knee beside her, brushing her hair back from her face.

'Sleep, my love. We're safe enough here.'

Elyssia smiled up at him then quickly drifted into a deep, fatigued slumber.

Raef glanced at Daien and Tarienne, then Aidan. 'Get some sleep. I'll keep watch for a while.'

The fact none of them argued was testimony to how tired they all were.

Aidan spread out his bedroll and lay down, propping himself up on one elbow. 'Wake me for the next watch.'

Raef nodded, positioning himself at the entrance to the cave, a silent sentry in the inky blackness of the unnaturally starless night.

CHAPTER 16

When they'd all managed to catch a few hours' sleep, they saddled their horses and headed out once more. As they approached the plains of Therin, there was evidence a large army had camped nearby, food scraps and horse droppings marring the usually fresh, green grass. They pushed their horses harder trying to beat the army to Castle Therin.

Aidan rode in front, Raef, and Elyssia in the middle, Tarienne and Daien bringing up the rear. Tarienne glanced over at Daien, her face obviously betraying her concern because he spoke into her thoughts.

'We'll make it, sweetheart. I love you.'

A small smile curved her lips. *'I love you, too.'*

They turned their focus to what lay ahead, but Tarienne couldn't deny the nagging fear nipping at the edges of her awareness.

*　　*　　*

Aidan

Several miles from Therin, it became obvious they were being tracked. Alerted by the occasional glimpses of riders racing through the distant trees, the barely audible, far-off howl of wolves, they urged their exhausted horses on, hooves flying across the fresh, green grass. Thundering along, the horses flicked up small stones littering the well-worn path, turning them into tiny projectiles.

A small flicker of relief coursed through Aidan when the castle came into sight, but it fled when he turned and saw their pursuers forming a solid wall behind them.

Aidan spared another glance over his shoulder calling out. 'Faster. They're gaining on us.'

Leaning over his horse's neck, he pushed his stallion as quickly as it could go. When he was close enough, he prayed the guards would recognise his cape and armour, he straightened in his saddle and shouted, 'Open the gates!'

Nothing.

Frustration flooded him. This was his stronghold. He stood in the stirrups as he hurtled along, bellowing, 'By order of your king, open the damned gates!'

They were so close now, if the gates weren't opened, they would be trapped between them and the thundering wave of their pursuers.

Finally, amid shouts of recognition the heavy, iron gates began to creak upward slowly, lifting just enough so they could duck through. Aidan let out the breath he'd been holding and raced under the gate, clinging to his stallion's neck.

The moment they were all through, Aidan leapt off his destrier, shouting, 'Close them! Close them now!'

The guards responded without hesitation, but a handful of the pursuing riders breached the opening before it closed. Aidan drew his sword, the metallic ring resonating around the courtyard. He lunged forward.

Tarienne and Daien jumped to the ground and fought back-to-back, spinning, and thrusting in a choreographed display of destruction. They had become a deadly team.

Elyssia, still mounted, nocked, and loosed arrows in rapid succession. There was a *whoosh* and a *thud* as one of their attackers fell dead in front of her, an arrow in his chest. Elyssia deftly nocked another, felling a tall, thick warrior dressed in what looked like black rags. The man's eyes went wide as he dropped to the ground in front of Aidan, dead, her arrow buried deep in his back. Aidan nodded to her in acknowledgment.

Raef, looking fearsome as he fought – jumping, rolling, slashing – despatched the last of their assailants, lopping off his head. Chest heaving, he let the tip of his sword drop to the ground and scanned the grisly devastation. They were all covered with splatters of their attackers' blood and breathing hard.

Aidan looked around, seeing no visible evidence of an increased number of villagers within the castle walls. Despair clouded his expression.

'My people... I'm too late!'

Tarienne moved toward him. 'Aidan–'

Hearing movement behind them, they turned to see Orien skidding to a halt in front of Aidan and dropping to one knee. 'Sire, it is you.' His face split into a grin. 'We have the people inside the castle walls. They started coming in a few days ago amid reports of rogue wolf packs roaming the countryside. The elves brought in the rest, despatching any wolves they found. We've collected as much food as we could manage.'

'Everyone is here?' Aidan breathed out. At Orien's nod, his expression brightened. 'Well done, Orien. Well done! Please, get up.'

'Thank you, sire.' Orien stood, clapping Daien on the back. 'Welcome home, my friend.'

Daien clasped Orien's hand in a two-handed grip, grinning. 'It's good to be home.'

Turning back to Aidan, Orien continued, 'Wolf sightings have become more frequent in the last two weeks, and there have also been some dark, hideous beasts roaming the countryside – some on horseback, some on foot. The people are afraid. Now you have returned, sire, it will raise their spirits.'

Aidan nodded, pulling off his gloves and tucking them into his saddlebag. 'I must call a gathering to reassure the people. Orien, could you arrange for the horses to be cared for, please? We have ridden hard for many days, and they deserve special care.'

'Of course, sire.' Orien called some guards over to help.

Aidan strode off, his mind racing with what needed to be done. Breathing deeply, he settled his thoughts, allowing the relief that his people were safe, for now, to soothe the savage beating of his heart. As he walked away he overheard a conversation between Tarienne and Daien.

'And the king has returned,' Tarienne observed.

Daien replied, 'I wonder if that's the last we'll see of "just Aidan".'

Tarienne sighed. 'I sincerely hope not.'

Hearing their words Aidan made himself a silent promise to ensure he was "just Aidan" as often as possible.

Busying himself with the tasks at hand Aidan noticed Raef and Elyssia slipping off to the room near Tarienne's chambers, as Tarienne and Daien headed into hers to get some much-needed sleep.

Aidan didn't have time for sleep. He was busy ensuring everyone was housed and distributing food when he heard shouting outside.

Racing to the gates, he found Arivaelle, panting hard, sliding off her mare, the horse's sides heaving. Aidan rushed to her, worry stealing his breath. Arivaelle flew into his arms.

'Rivi, I thought you were with Tere.'

She nodded, pulling out of his embrace. 'I was. But I volunteered to be a messenger to let you know they're close. Father cloaked me in a spell of invisibility, so I didn't alert Rantec's army to my presence. I let Raef know via mindspeak that I was coming, and he told the guards to let me in. The spell only lasts a short while, so I had to ride like the wind.' She chuckled softly. 'I think I scared your guards when I suddenly appeared at the gates.'

Aidan grinned, hugging her hard, before leading her to his chambers. He ordered a bath and some food, then encouraged her to rest while he continued to deal with ensuring his people were safe, fed, and relaxed.

He found her several hours later, bathed, fully clothed, legs dangling over the side of the bed, sound asleep. Grinning, he noted the barely eaten food and moved closer to gently lift her feet, sliding her body around so she was safely in the middle of the bed. Covering her with a blanket, he slipped off his boots and jacket and lay down beside her, looping his arm loosely over her body. He inhaled the sweet scent of her hair, smiled happily and slipped into a deep sleep.

When Aidan awoke the next morning, Arivaelle was still asleep, cuddled up against him. Stroking her hair gently, he carefully rolled her onto her back, leaning over to gaze at her. His heart thumped wildly at the sight of this stunning woman who was all his.

Her eyes fluttered open and a beautiful smile lit her face as her eyes met his. Aidan leaned down to her soft, full lips for a kiss. She was deliciously warm, and he barely stifled a groan.

Reluctantly, he started to lift himself off the bed, but Arivaelle quickly grabbed his arm, unbalancing him. Aidan fell back onto the bed, laughing.

Arivaelle quickly moved to straddle his hips, silencing him, her tousled hair sweeping across his face and chest as she leaned forward to kiss him. 'Please, do not go. Not yet.'

Aidan's heart thundered. His arms snaked around her as he flipped her beneath him. His body ached with desire, his arousal straining against his trousers.

Arivaelle wiggled beneath him, making him grit his teeth, fighting for control. 'Aidan, please. Make love to me,' she whispered.

Aidan sucked in a breath. Closing his eyes, he struggled to formulate the words to explain his feelings.

'Rivi, not like this. I want you so much, but I want to show you how much I l–' He stopped, blinking at her, an inner debate taking place. Then he blew out a breath. 'Arivaelle, I love you and want to show you how much, but I want to spend all night showing you. Do you understand?'

Arivaelle's eyes glistened with tears. 'Aidan… I love you, too. More than I would have believed possible in the brief time we've known each other.'

His eyes searched hers, his face slowly lighting with a huge smile. His heart soared. Leaning down for a long, sensual kiss, he couldn't believe his dream for a love as wonderful as Tarienne and Daien's had come true. He couldn't ever remember feeling this happy, this contented.

Stretching himself out next to her, his body hard with desire, he stroked his knuckles down her cheek. 'I really must go, but I'll be back as soon as I can.'

Arivaelle slipped her arms around Aidan's neck and pulled him down for a light kiss, but when she ran her tongue over his lips, he couldn't help deepening it.

She giggled and pushed at his chest. 'You'd better go. I'm going to eat some of the food that was left last night and freshen up.'

Aidan lifted himself off the bed, gazing longingly down at her, eyebrows raised.

She laughed. 'Go!'

Aidan smiled and sat on the edge of the bed, pulling on his boots. Grabbing his jacket, he blew her a kiss and left. Now he understood Tarienne and Daien's need to be together, always touching, kissing. He sighed as he made his way down the corridor.

The second he finished checking on preparations for the impending battle, Aidan returned to Arivaelle. She flung herself into his arms. He was overjoyed at the reception and allowed himself time with her – kissing, hugging, caressing – before they left to meet with

Raef, Elyssia, Tarienne and Daien in the guest room. When they saw Arivaelle, there were gasps of surprise and a great deal of hugging.

Elyssia and Raef sat on the bed, thighs touching, fingers entwined, the sheets tangled. Aidan's eyes locked with Rivi's. His body responded to the need he could see there. Her breathing quickened, her breasts rising and falling seductively.

Aidan shifted, his leather trousers suddenly too tight and uncomfortable. He almost groaned aloud when her tongue flicked out to moisten her lips. He placed an arm around her shoulders and hauled her to his side. But instead of appeasing his desire, her closeness escalated it.

Aidan forced his attention back to the others. Daien sat on the lounge chair, Tarienne sitting in front of him. His hands rested on her shoulders, thumbs absently caressing her neck. Daien raised his eyebrows, a knowing smirk on his face, as though understanding exactly how he felt.

Aidan cleared his throat to gather everyone's attention and to help himself focus. 'Raef, I assume you contacted Kyre?'

'Yes. They're close, so it shouldn't be long before they're ready.'

Aidan released Rivi and paced around the room, thinking. 'Until they contact us to let us know they are, I'm posting double guards around the walls and archers in the towers. We'll prepare the army for battle and ensure everyone has food and accommodation. There's not a great deal more we can do. Daien, could you assist Orien in readying the army? I'll brief them all tomorrow.'

When Daien nodded, Aidan clapped his hands together with a smile. 'Now, I'm starving. Let's head down to the kitchen.'

There was a chorus of agreement. They made their way to the kitchen and ate heartily of the roast meats and sweet cakes. Laughing and chatting, they allowed themselves to forget the impending battle for the moment.

After they'd eaten their fill, Daien excused himself to find Orien.

Raef and Aidan headed off to check the armoury and discuss the battle plans.

*　　*　　*

Tarienne

The three women disappeared into Tarienne's room to talk about their role in the upcoming battle. Tarienne loved having Elyssia and Arivaelle at Therin and wished they both could stay, though she knew it was unlikely.

They all agreed Tarienne would take part in the battle, Rivi would stay at the castle, ready to help with the wounded, and Elyssia would position herself on the castle walls with the archers.

Tarienne knew Aidan and Daien wouldn't be happy about their decision, but this was not negotiable. Tarienne needed to be close to them both, especially during the battle.

When the men returned, the women told them their plans. All three pinned them with determined glares, daring them to argue. The men looked at each other, then all raised their hands in silent defeat, knowing there was little chance of dissuading the ladies once their minds were made up.

Tarienne almost chuckled at their easy capitulation, yet knew Daien and she would discuss it later to ensure she wouldn't put herself in any unnecessary danger.

Three days after they'd arrived at Therin, Raef heard from Authion and Tere. He let them know of the battle plans, and they informed him they were in position.

On the fourth day, the army of Therin was ready. Mounted soldiers on restless horses filled the streets. The villagers gathered to cheer them on as they clattered down the narrow paths through the city. The banner of Therin fluttered proudly in the wind. Aidan led the cavalcade, his appearance both fierce and regal as he sat tall and confident, his gold-edged, red cloak flapping around his thighs. His armour shone in the sun, and he rested one hand on the ornate hilt of his sword, the other holding his stallion's reins. He was flanked by Daien, Orien, Raef and Enrith.

Tarienne rode a little farther back on Lacey, only agreeing to ride behind them after a huge argument with Aidan. He believed if she was determined to fight in this battle, she would at least be a little safer amongst the soldiers. She knew she was safer at Daien's side than anywhere else yet did not want to argue on the eve of the battle.

Daien swivelled in his saddle to search for her amongst the riders. Locating her, he smiled, his voice penetrating her thoughts.

'I love you, Ren. Stay safe, my warrior princess.'

Tarienne's eyes held his.

'I love you, too. Never forget, I will hold you in my heart always. Stay safe, my handsome druid warrior.'

Daien turned, urging his horse up close to Aidan's stallion in readiness for the battle ahead.

She and Daien had also argued over her insistence on participating. She understood he feared for her, but she could not ignore the prophecy. He knew she needed to do this, but with tears in his eyes, he had confided in her he had a nagging feeling someone close to them would die.

When they exited the gates, they formed into two parallel lines behind Aidan and stopped. He reined his horse up and down the line, finally halting in the middle. Standing in his stirrups, he addressed his army.

'Today, we go into battle for Therin, to ensure its inhabitants can live safely and in peace. Do this not for me, but for the families of Therin, for your own families, for yourself, and ride with honour.'

The army raised their weapons high and shouted as one, 'For Therin.'

Aidan smiled, allowing his **gaze** to sweep along the lines of soldiers, pausing momentarily on his elite king's guardsmen, then Raef and Tarienne.

Aidan's soft voice entered her mind as his eyes met hers.

'Stay safe, dear heart.'

'And you, my brother.'

Aidan paused. Tarienne could feel his emotions swirling. Nodding almost imperceptibly, his eyes held hers for a moment longer, then turned his stallion to face the forest and wait.

An army of wolves, beasts and men soon appeared from the thickest part of the forest, forming a semi-circle. A small group of men appeared to be in charge, shouting orders. Aidan did not flinch as they continued to pour out from between the trees.

The Therin army was badly outnumbered, but they knew Authion and Tere approached, the fae army close behind them, waiting for the signal to attack. The grunts and growls of the creatures they faced carried across the open space. Aidan breathed deeply, steadying himself, his focus on the gathering forces.

He raised his hand, urging his army slowly forward, everyone knowing to await his signal before attacking.

Lined up on the castle walls, the elves who had brought in the outer villagers stood in silence, their arrows nocked in readiness, Elyssia with them.

Without warning, the wolves launched forward.

Aidan dropped his hand, signalling the attack. The horses leapt forward, thundering toward their foes. Tarienne urged Lacey ahead, so she was directly behind Daien's stallion. Swords drawn, the men shouted their battle cries, ready to plunge into the approaching wolf pack. Before they were too close, Aidan raised his sword, signalling the archers to fire.

Tarienne heard the *whoosh* of arrows as they hurtled over her head, hitting their targets with deadly accuracy. Beasts and wolves dropped, bellowing and yelping. Aidan's army advanced, reaching their foes as the barrage of arrows ceased.

Tarienne's short sword slashed and spun, slicing at the remaining wolves as they leapt, snapping and snarling. She could hear the screams of terrified horses, the howls of dying wolves, the grunts, and bellows of the beasts as they lumbered between the horses, swinging their maces, ripping open both armour and skin.

Her heart pounded. Fear rippled down her spine. Straightening in her saddle, she fought on, pushing the panic aside, keeping Aidan, Daien and Raef in sight as best she could.

At the centre of the battle, riding became impossible.

Tarienne leaned forward and whispered into Lacey's ear, 'Back to the castle, dear heart.'

She leapt off Lacey's back, landing beside Daien, and slapped the horse's rump, sending her home. He stepped in front of her. His sword twirled skilfully in his hand as he moved with deadly grace, slicing his way through the enemy.

When she caught sight of a mace hurtling toward her head, Tarienne swung her sword upward. She managed to deflect it, but the force of the blow ripped her sword from her hand, twisting her wrist painfully. She grimaced but quickly drew her twin knives and began fighting at Daien's back.

Aidan briefly glanced down when her sword landed at his feet, then quickly bent, and picked it up. Calling her name, he tossed it to her. In one smooth movement, Tarienne caught the hilt, sheathed the blade, and spun, launching a sideways kick at a wolf about to attack Raef.

Caught unawares, the brown wolf flew sideways, yelping when it smacked hard into a nearby tree trunk. Tarienne braced, ready for the wolf to launch itself at her. When it didn't, she looked closer, noticing a long, sharp branch protruding through its ribs, a pool of blood growing beneath it. Despite the bloody battle around her, Tarienne shuddered, then turned her attention to a particularly ugly beast lumbering toward her.

Half-man/half-oxen, one of the creature's eyes was larger than the other, drool dripping out the side of its large mouth. It stood at around seven feet tall, and Tarienne knew she was no match for it physically. Swiftly, she launched one of her knives in its direction. The creature's face went slack when the knife lodged between its eyes. Teetering on its huge, hoof-like feet, it crashed to the ground, face first, driving the knife into its brain.

Tarienne heaved the beast onto its back, retrieving her blade. She had no time to wipe its blood off on the grass before several enormous men, all with black hair, beards and clad in animal skins, barrelled toward Daien, Raef and Aidan.

Tarienne threw both of her blades simultaneously. Two of the men dropped without a sound – one with a knife in his eye, the other with one protruding from his throat. He gurgled, shock registering on his face as he died in an increasing puddle of his own blood. She quickly retrieved the blades, wiped them on the grass and sheathed them and yanked her sword from its scabbard before she resumed ducking and weaving around Daien.

It wasn't long before a horn sounded, heralding the arrival of the fae army. Her heart lifted a little; however, the fighting only increased in intensity, and she found herself being swept away from Daien.

Fear pierced her heart as the battle forced her farther away. Tarienne could do nothing but focus on her next quarry. She was bruised, bleeding, filthy, not to mention exhausted. She prayed the others were safe as she fought on, switching from her sword to her knives again to relieve the soreness building in her shoulder from wielding the heavy sword.

*   *   *

Raef

They fought long into the night. Raef and Daien managed to keep Aidan in sight, fleetingly catching sight of Kyre cutting a bloody swathe through the beasts. Briefly, both Authion and Tere appeared at their side, but the fighting quickly dragged them away.

Raef worried for Tarienne. He had not seen her for hours. As he knocked a huge beast to the ground and plunged his sword into its chest, he reached out for their sibling bond. There it was, shining like a beacon, settling his worry a little.

Refocusing on an enormous, hairy man hurtling toward him, Raef sidestepped. When his attacker tripped, Raef spun and swung his blade at the man's head. The head rolled away, almost in slow motion. A macabre sight, even in the unrelenting bloodshed of the fierce battle.

Raef hauled in a deep breath, then noticed Tere shifting into his wolf form and sprinting to their right.

*   *   *

Tarienne

Tarienne had lost sight of her brothers, as well as Aidan and Daien, but she could do nothing about it right now. Three men surrounded her, leering. She moved warily, twirling her knives in her hands as she quickly assessed her assailants, selecting the weakest.

Just as she readied herself to attack, Tere bolted up in his wolf form, launching himself at two of the men, tearing their throats out before they realised what had happened. The third, momentarily distracted, forgot about Tarienne just long enough for her to seize the opportunity. She spun and slashed high, slicing his throat and opening his chest on the downward stroke.

Relaxing slightly, Tarienne sucked in a deep breath. Panting, tongue lolling out, his muzzle bloodied, Tere leaned against her legs as she patted the fur between his ears.

'Thank you, Tere, my friend.'

He looked up into her eyes, a wolfish grin on his face, then dashed back into the battle.

Tarienne wiped the perspiration from her face, exhaustion setting in. Sucking in a few steadying breaths, she strode toward where she'd last seen Aidan and Daien. Peering around the seething mass of bloody soldiers, beasts, and wolves as they fought, weapons clanging, Tarienne thought she spotted Daien. Her momentary distraction almost cost her life.

Hearing a faint sound behind her, she reflexively ducked as a beast swung its mace toward her head, one of the spikes catching the side of her face. Spinning and falling hard, Tarienne's head smashed into a rock. Her vision blurred and stomach roiled. When a huge, black wolf with ice-blue eyes approached, limping, she managed to mumble, 'Tere.' Pain knifed through her head as Tere nuzzled her face. Then she knew nothing but blackness.

CHAPTER 17

As the first light of dawn crept over the horizon, the army of Therin, along with the elves and fae, had destroyed the majority of Rantec's army. Those not killed or mortally wounded had fled.

The sun began to rise, an eerie mist hovering above the battlefield. Bodies and bloodied weapons littered the ground, blood staining the once green grass a slick, dark red. The stench of death permeated the air, shafts of sunshine glinting off the armour of the dead, their cold, lifeless bodies never to be warmed by the sun again.

Aidan crouched to wipe his sword on the ground, then resheathed it, the metallic ring echoing in the eerie silence. He stood and surveyed the gruesome scene, sighing, hating the senseless destruction, saddened by the deaths of so many of his men.

Spotting Daien, Orien and Raef not far away, talking quietly, he walked over. They all wore concerned expressions.

Aidan frowned. 'What's wrong?'

Daien held his gaze, fear in his eyes. 'We can't find Ren.'

Despite bone-deep tiredness threatening to overwhelm him, Aidan reacted. Pointing to several soldiers, he commanded, 'You three. Lady Tarienne is missing. Gather others and search the battlefield. Do not return until you find her.'

The soldiers bowed. Grabbing a half-dozen others, they began their search. Daien, Raef, Orien and Aidan spread out, stepping over bodies as they went. Each time they recognised one of their own, either injured or dead, they called for others to take them to the castle.

They called Tarienne's name, both out loud and through mindspeak, getting no response. They soon met up with Authion and Kyre, telling them their sister was missing. Their faces creased with worry, they joined in the search.

Authion suddenly yelled. The others rushed to his side to find Tere in his wolf form, a deep gash in his flank oozing bright red blood, an arrow protruding from his chest.

Crouching, Authion spoke to him softly. Raef contacted Arivaelle through mindspeak, asking her to come quickly. Tere's ice-blue eyes looked pale and glazed, his breathing was ragged. He managed to shift into human form, the effort evoking a loud, pain-filled groan. Blood poured from his wounds.

Aidan unclasped his cloak, draping it over Tere's naked form to keep him warm. Kneeling beside him, he laid his hand on Tere's shoulder. 'You fought like a true warrior today, my friend.'

Arivaelle rushed to Tere's side, her relief obvious at seeing Aidan and her brothers safe. She dropped to the ground behind Tere, lifting his head gently to cradle it in her lap. He began to cough, grimacing, his spittle bright red and viscous.

As he tried to speak, Arivaelle commanded gently, 'Shh, stay quiet.'

When she began to chant a healing spell, he tried again, his voice coming out as a hiss. 'Tarienne...' It was all he managed before he had another coughing fit.

Raef's heart skittered wildly. Did he know where she was?

Arivaelle lifted her sad eyes, shaking her head. Aidan closed his eyes for a moment, then moved closer.

'Tere, we can't find Tarienne. Do you know where she is?'

He did not respond for a moment. Then he lifted a shaky arm, pointing toward the far edge of the battlefield where a large, grassy mound led down to the forest's edge.

Tere's arm dropped, and eyes closed, his final breath leaving him on a sigh. Arivaelle choked out a cry of despair as she lifted his head and gently placed it on the ground. Aidan let out a deep, mournful groan. He wrapped his arm around Arivaelle's shoulders, pulling her up and holding her tightly. Their heads all hung low as they stood over Tere for a brief moment.

'He shall be buried as a warrior of Therin,' Aidan said quietly, then directed two of his men to protect Tere's body.

He looked at those standing around him. 'We must find her.'

*   *   *

Daien

Heading in the direction Tere had pointed, they fanned out, loudly calling her name.

Daien's heart pounded as he searched. His throat burned, his eyes gritty. His fear for Tarienne threatened to steal all sensible thought.

Just as despair began to settle heavily on his chest, Daien looked up, sucking in a sharp breath. A shadowy figure shrouded in mist appeared on top of the large, grassy mound.

Tarienne...

He called her name, emotion making his voice waver. The others turned as he broke into a run. Tarienne started toward him, but she suddenly crumpled. Falling forward, her limp body rolled down the hill, coming to rest against a heap of bloodied wolf corpses.

Daien cried out as he ran. 'Ren, *no!*'

Aidan, Raef, Kyre and Authion bolted in his direction. He heard Raef call Arivaelle with mindspeak as they ran, alerting her they'd found Tarienne and needed help.

When they reached her, Tarienne was cradled in Daien's lap. She was spattered in blood and dirty. Tears rolled down Daien's face as he rocked her. 'Ren, no. Don't leave me. Please. Please.'

Arivaelle ran up and dropped to her knees. 'Ren... No, Ren,' she cried.

Raef grabbed Arivaelle's shoulders, shaking her. 'Focus, Rivi, please.'

Arivaelle closed her eyes for a moment, trying to call on the healing calm, sobs still escaping as she sucked in a large breath and hovered her hands over her sister's body. 'Let me feel for injuries.'

Aidan squatted beside her, his own eyes damp with unshed tears. After a few moments, Arivaelle sat back on her heels, brows furrowed.

'Other than a bump on her head, I can't find anything wrong. I think she's just exhausted and her body has shut down so she can recuperate. I've never seen this happen before, but I've heard about it.' She looked at Daien, hope in her eyes. 'Talk to her. She may be able to hear you.'

He scraped the back of his hand across his eyes and focused on the woman in his lap. Gripping one of her hands, he lightly circled his thumb across her palm.

'You're safe now, my love. Wake up, Ren. We're all here. Talk to me, sweetheart.'

Raef crouched beside her, grasping her other hand. 'Ren, you promised you wouldn't scare me like this again. Come on, sweetling. Come back to us.'

A few anxious moments passed before Tarienne's eyelids fluttered open, slowly focusing on the people looking down at her. With a wince, she tipped her head back slightly to see Daien's face just above hers, immense relief flooding through him.

'I thought I'd lost you,' he whispered, caressing her cheek.

She slowly sat up and turned around, wrapping her arms around his neck. Daien buried his face in her hair.

Aidan tapped Daien on the shoulder. They looked up. Aidan grabbed her hand and helped her stand, pulling her into a hug, serving to reassure himself she was safe. Each of her brothers and Arivaelle pulled her to them in turn, all needing to touch and hold her after their scare.

As Kyre released her, a look of worry passed across her face. 'Where's Father?'

Raef took her hand. 'He's all right. He was slightly injured. Elyssia is with him in the castle. I've let him know you're safe.'

'What about Tere? He saved my life. One of the beasts caught the side of my head with a mace. Before I blacked out, I saw Tere's black wolf standing over me, protecting me. He must have dragged me over here to keep me safe. Where is he?'

No one responded for a moment. Tarienne's eyes met Daien's. He pulled her into a hug, whispering, 'I'm sorry, my love. He's gone.'

She pulled back, eyes wide with shock, before she broke down in Daien's arms, sobbing. 'He saved my life, Daien. He saved me.'

He held Tarienne to him, stroking her hair and rocking her as she unleashed her grief.

The others drifted away to determine how many casualties their own armies had sustained and to organise the funeral pyres for the dead. Aidan ordered a detail to begin piling up the bodies of their enemies in preparation to burn them. He personally saw to collecting Tere's body to prepare him for his burial as a warrior. Another detail was sent out in search of survivors they would take to the castle.

The great hall soon became an infirmary littered with makeshift beds. Those who had any healing abilities flitted from bed to bed, doing what they could for the injured.

Daien led Tarienne into the castle. 'You need food and rest. No arguments.'

She had no energy to argue anyway, leaning into him as they walked. Daien wrapped his arm around her shoulders, pulling her close.

When they reached her chambers, Daien helped Tarienne undress, washed her as best he could with a bowl of water she managed to warm, slipped her nightgown over her head, and tucked her into bed. Within moments, she was asleep.

Daien quickly washed, changed into some clean clothes, then sauntered off to the kitchen to find something to eat. Restless after the battle, he instead made his way down to the infirmary to see if he could help, but Arivaelle shooed him away, telling him to get some rest. Exhaustion overtaking him, he decided to do as she asked, figuring food could wait until they were rested.

A few minutes later, Daien slipped, naked, into bed beside Tarienne. He pulled her body to him, looped his arm over her and fell into a deep sleep.

* * *

Tarienne

The next morning, Tarienne woke to find herself alone, but knew Daien had slept beside her, because his scent lingered.

Slipping out from beneath the covers, she padded over to the window, pulling on her bed jacket against the chill of the morning. Rows of covered bodies lay in the courtyard. Daien and Orien oversaw the treatment of the deceased soldiers of Therin, ensuring they were handled with the dignity they deserved. Tarienne watched for a while, a deep sadness descending over her.

Daien glanced up at the window, as if sensing her watching. His rich voice slid into her thoughts.

'Good morning, sweetheart. I'll finish up here shortly and bring you some breakfast. Rest, my love. You deserve it. I love you.'

The immense power of his love reached out to her, warming her heart and bringing a smile to her lips. *'I'll be waiting, my Daien.'*

Daien held his hand over his heart for a moment, then strode away to help Orien.

Tarienne's thoughts drifted to Aidan, she didn't envy his position at all, knowing he would personally speak with every family who had lost a loved one. Her heart ached for them all, but most of all for Tere, who had become a friend to them all in the brief time they'd known him.

She turned away from the window, deciding to take a long bath to see if it would help ease her tired, sore muscles and aching head. Using her magic to warm the water she stripped and sank down into its heat, sighing. The small cuts on her arms stung, the bruised lump on the side of her head throbbed and the small gash on her face burned but the warmth enveloped her and began to ease some of her aches.

After dipping her head and body beneath the soothing warmth, she rose up just enough to rest the back of her neck on the edge of the bath, taking care not to bump the side of her head. Little rivulets of water ran down her neck and between her breasts, and her dripping hair hung around her face. She closed her eyes, allowing the heat to seep into her muscles, and drifted into a light sleep.

*   *   *

Daien

Daien quietly entered the room, sucking in a breath and almost dropping the tray of food he held when he spied her in the bath. *My woman...* He placed the tray on the dresser. He couldn't tear his eyes away from her firm, round breasts bobbing up and down in the water as she breathed. His body tightened and his heart thumped a staccato beat. With his last shred of sensible thought, he turned, bolting the door to her chambers.

As he walked to the bath, he grabbed a damp ball of fragrant soap and lathered his hands, kneeling on the floor behind her. Tarienne jumped a little as his soapy hands began to slide over her skin. She tipped her head back, her face lighting up in a smile. Daien dipped down for a gentle kiss, his hands sliding down her body to massage her breasts.

He pulled back and tenderly lathered Tarienne's hair, massaging her neck and shoulders. When he'd finished, she slid under the water to rinse the soap from her hair Desire coursed through him, his gaze sweeping over her. Her expression issuing a silent invitation he could not resist.

Tarienne's lips curved into an appreciative smile as he undressed. She warmed the water again with a few words of fae magic and lowered herself into one end of the tub, her knees drawn up, so Daien had room to join her.

'Gods, you're delicious,' she breathed.

Daien chuckled and dropped down into the water, splashing some over the side. Hauling her onto his lap, his lips frantically captured hers. His hands roamed her body. She wriggled impatiently on his lap, rubbing against his hard length. A low growl rumbled through his chest.

Slowly urging Tarienne onto her knees, he lowered himself behind her, moving her hair aside so he could kiss and nibble her neck. Daien's hands slid around to her breasts, moving from one to the other until she wriggled and pushed her bottom against him, the movement and her moans fuelling his desire.

He slid his hand between her legs, cupping her mound, then slipped two fingers into her slick wetness.

It wasn't long before Tarienne's body clenched around his fingers as she moaned his name.

Before the sensations subsided, Daien positioned himself at her entrance. She lifted up, eager, as he eased into her, her muscles tightening around him, pulling him in deeper. Daien groaned and set a torturous rhythm.

The tingling ache at the base of his spine built quickly. He slipped his fingers between them and massaged her sensitive nub, her climax taking hold, her clenching muscles evoking a groan from deep within his soul. He plunged into her over and over, finally crying out her name as his body hummed and his seed pulsed into her.

Gasping for breath, he withdrew and collapsed back against the bath, water splashing over the edge. Tarienne giggled as she turned and sat on his lap in the warm water.

'Daien?'

He responded languorously as he trailed his hands up and down her back. 'Hmm...'

Tarienne stroked his damp hair. 'I love you. Let's get married.'

Lifting his head, he looked into her eyes. 'I thought we'd already agreed.'

'I know, silly.' She smiled. 'I mean, let's get married now... Well, not today, but very soon.'

'Sweetheart, you know how much I love you. I'll marry you today if you want to.'

Tarienne hugged him hard, shaking her head. 'Mother would never forgive me if she wasn't here for the wedding, but very soon. Right now, I want to warm up the water and spend some more time together.'

Daien smiled and waggled his eyebrows, then pulled her closer. He began a sweet, slow torture, his hands and mouth exploring, rubbing, gently tweaking her most sensitive places.

Tarienne's hand drifted down into the water, and she whispered the spell to heat it again. Daien's passion heated, too, and he swept them both into sweet ecstasy again...

*   *   *

Tarienne

When they finally dressed and headed downstairs, they found Aidan standing in the repaired throne room, one arm casually looped around Arivaelle's shoulders. Raef sat on a low table with Elyssia tucked into his lap, his arm around her. They all looked bathed and somewhat refreshed, though the burden of being king obviously weighed heavily on Aidan today. His brow was creased, his expression one of deep concern and he looked a little pale, as though her hadn't slept enough.

Tarienne walked over to him, slipping her arms around his waist in a reassuring hug. He held her tightly, then eased her away a little. Looking profoundly serious, he asked something that tore at her heart.

'Do you feel up to singing the lament at Tere's funeral tomorrow?'

Tarienne swallowed hard and took a few deep breaths, her voice coming out as a whisper. 'Yes. I'd like to do it. For Tere.'

Aidan pulled her to him again, holding her for a long moment, then released her into Daien's arms. She snuggled close to his chest, drawing strength and courage from the man she loved.

Arivaelle and Elyssia crowded around her, slipping their arms around both Tarienne and Daien in a group hug.

'We'll sing the lament with you if you'd like,' Arivaelle said softly, Elyssia nodding in agreement.

Tarienne nodded, unable to speak past the lump in her throat. Their support meant everything to her.

When they separated, Raef strode over and slid his arm around Tarienne's waist, holding her tighter than she expected. Frowning a little, she looked up at him as he sucked in a breath.

'Before we left Darewood, Tere asked me to give you something.' Producing a little package of soft hide tied with string, he placed it into her hand.

Tarienne unwrapped it carefully, her hands shaking. She pulled at the last of the string holding the package together and the hide fell open, revealing a small black, hand-carved wolf with tiny, ice-blue, gem eyes.

Eyes welling with tears, Tarienne breathed, 'It's beautiful.'

Her watery gaze met Daien's. He smiled reassuringly, and Tarienne sucked in a deep breath as she struggled to control the overwhelming sadness rolling through her. Closing her hand around the little wolf and raising her eyes to the heavens, she whispered, 'I'll treasure it always, Tere. Thank you, dear friend.'

'He was a friend and has left his mark on us all. He fought valiantly.' Aidan added.

He waited a few moments before he stepped forward, Arivaelle's hand held tightly in his. He brought her fingers to his lips, dropping a light kiss on her knuckles. A big grin split his face as he met Arivaelle's eyes.

'It is with that in mind, amidst all the sadness and destruction of the last few days, that I carefully considered the timing of this. However, I feel it does not show disrespect to those who have passed, rather that life moves on, and we all have a future to look forward to. So, I wanted you all to be the first to know I've asked Arivaelle to marry me, and she has accepted.'

Elyssia and Tarienne squealed, hurtling forward to envelop Arivaelle and Aidan in bone-crushing hugs.

'What wonderful news!' Tarienne gushed.

Raef stepped forward, pulling his second youngest sister into a tight embrace. Kissing her on the cheek, he released her, grasping Aidan's hand and pulling him into a brotherly hug, slapping him on the back.

'Well done, Aidan.'

Daien extended his hand, grabbing Aidan's elbow and pulling him in for a quick hug.

'I'm so pleased for you both. You deserve to be happy.'

Despite the lingering joy of their news, the next day was difficult. The acrid smell of smoke from the piles of burning bodies invaded every room in the castle.

At dusk, Tarienne and Daien joined the mourners lining the square at the centre of the castle. Aidan and the others already waited at the front of the assembled crowd. Daien slid his hand into Tarienne's as they assembled around Tere's funeral pyre.

Aidan's arm tightened around Arivaelle's waist. The gathered crowd waited in silence. Orien handed him a flaming torch, which he touched to the wooden structure holding Tere. The fire quickly took hold, blazing in the darkness. Tendrils of smoke drifted upward, filling the air with the sweet scent of fresh hay and the musky oils used to cleanse the bodies.

Tarienne drew in a deep breath and began the fae lament, her voice not as clear or as strong as she wished, softened by barely contained emotion. She knew very few could understand the words, but the mournful tune pierced the silence, speaking of bravery and love.

The words evoked a deep sadness yet spoke of the joys of life beyond death. They wished the traveller well on their journey, pledging undying memories and eternal love.

Tarienne's sorrow welled up, tears spilling down her cheeks. The loss of Tere, who had managed to become dear to them all in a truly brief time, was a physical pain. Her chest tightened, her throat constricted, her voice wavered.

Elyssia and Arivaelle joined in, moving up close beside her. They stood together, united in their grief, hands outstretched as the pyre burned. Even those who did not understand the words responded to the sorrow in the strains of the lament.

The three women linked arms, holding the last note, until they saw the hazy figure of a huge wolf rise above the flames. It paused, looking back at the assembled group. Its ice-blue eyes glowed, then it disappeared into the darkness. The crowd gasped. Tarienne stared into the blackness a moment longer, her heart aching with the loss of a dear friend.

Tarienne, Elyssia and Arivaelle turned back, tearfully, to the awaiting arms of the men they loved. They watched the flames in silence, huddling close, lost in their own thoughts until most of the crowd had wandered away. Finally, they headed back into the castle to share a glass of wine and toast lost friends.

*　*　*

Aidan

Several weeks had passed since the burials. Friends and family had arrived from Darewood – kings, queens, lords, and ladies from outlying kingdoms entering the castle for the royal wedding.

Therin was ablaze with colour and filled with expectation. Market stalls and brightly clothed entertainers lined the streets. The people were excited, not only because their king was to marry a half-elven, fae princess, but there would also be two other fae weddings. Lady Tarienne was to marry one of the king's guardsmen, and her brother was marrying his long-time fae love. Therin was abuzz.

Aidan could not remember being so happy, finding himself uncharacteristically emotional. A few months ago, he would not have believed he could love someone so much. Now he couldn't imagine a life without Arivaelle.

*   *   *

Tarienne

Tarienne found it difficult to believe the day of their wedding had finally arrived. She was so happy, she wanted to cry... and did several times, as did Elyssia and Arivaelle.

Arivaelle was nervous to become queen of Therin, but she'd confided in Tarienne that she loved Aidan so much, she couldn't envision a life without him. Seeing them so happy and in love brought immense joy to Tarienne and Daien.

Tarienne bathed and slipped into her cream, narrow waisted gown, flowing fae lace tumbling down the full skirt. Her mother had thankfully brought it and Elyssia's stunning, snow-white gown with her from Darewood. Her mother, Elyssia and Arivaelle worked her hair into an intricate braid at the back with tiny cream-coloured flowers woven into it. The rest of her hair was curled softly around her shoulders.

Staring into the mirror, Tarienne smiled, her thoughts drifting to Daien. She couldn't wait to see him and his reaction to how she looked. She wondered if he was nervous because the two emotions coursing through her right now were love and excitement at wedding her soul mate.

She turned to see her mother's, Elyssia's and Rivi's eyes all glistening with tears. Walking up to them, she stretched her arms out and they all hugged each other. Stepping back, she smiled.

'No tears today, everyone, just happiness and love.'

Nodding they set to work, first on Elyssia's spun gold hair then on Rivi's white-blonde locks. They both looked so beautiful that Tarienne had to hold back tears despite her own earlier decree.

When the music began King Thalion swept in beside her, a very proud father-of-the-bride while Fienn grinned and offered his arm to his sister, Elyssia. Fienn's words to his sister whispered across Tarienne's thoughts before they began.

'Mother and father would be so proud of you Lys, you look wonderful.'

Elyssia turned to him for a moment with a watery smile and mouthed, 'Thank you.' Then the four of them began their journey, side-by-side down the aisle. Tarienne smiled at the guests as they traversed the long aisle decorated with garlands of white flowers. She briefly met Elyssia's eyes, and tears threatened again at how happy Elyssia was and, how happy she was for Raef.

Lifting her eyes they locked on Daien and a little gasp escaped her lips. Dressed in the crimson and gold of Therin, he was heart-stoppingly handsome, but it was the joy in his expression that took Tarienne's breath away. He stepped forward to claim her as she approached on her father's arm, with a smile that made her heart jump and whispered next to her ear making her shiver.

'You are so beautiful.'

Taking his arm, she turned to thank her father before settling next to Daien at the altar and whispering back.

'And you are so handsome I can barely breathe.'

His hand slipped into hers and he lifted it to his lips, his eyes holding hers, showing the depth of love he felt for her.

Breaking the spell, she forced herself to turn away and watch Raef and Elyssia step up beside them. They too had eyes only for each other and the love emanating from them was palpable. Tarienne had never seen Raef so happy and content.

The priest began the dual ceremonies and before they knew it, they were married. Daien let out a little whoop and pulled Tarienne close for a deep kiss. Before she closed her eyes, she saw Raef hauling Elyssia against him, locking lips with her. When the priest cleared his throat, a little chuckle went through the guests as the couples reluctantly broke apart.

Turning together, Raef, Elyssia, Tarienne and Daien walked back down the aisle to the cheers of the guests. They were all so exquisitely happy as they made their way to sign their marriage documents. But the day was not over, and the four of them soon returned to sit in the front pews to witness the kingdom's much anticipated wedding of their king, Aidan, and the soon to be, queen, Arivaelle.

It was the highlight of the day for everyone. Aidan looked magnificent at the altar in the royal colours of Therin. His face split into a huge grin as Arivaelle entered the church on her father's arm. She was breathtaking in her pale blue, low-cut dress woven with silver and gold, cinched at her tiny waist, and flowing into a full skirt that spread out behind her as she glided down the flower-strewn aisle. A dress fit for a queen, worn by Aidan's mother when she married his father.

His eyes glistened with love as she walked toward him on her father's arm. Tarienne leaned into Daien for support, intense emotion whirling through her. Her sister was exquisite, and the ladies of the court gasped at her ethereal beauty.

When the ceremony concluded and Aidan kissed his bride, a great cheer went up from the guests. Soon after, an even louder cheer was heard from the crowd gathered outside.

'Long live the king! Long live the queen!'

Aidan's expression was one of pure happiness as they headed toward the great hall for the wedding feast.

Raef, Elyssia, Daien and Tarienne followed close behind, anxious to be the first to congratulate Aidan and Arivaelle. Tarienne paused, looking into Daien's eyes. He lowered his head to steal a quick kiss, filling her with a sense of completeness. They were finally married.

They moved into the great hall where the wedding feast was set up. Serving staff stood in readiness to present plates of the finest succulent pheasant, beef, chicken, the freshest of vegetables, followed by delicious fruits and decadent desserts. It was unparalleled, the likes of which Therin had never before seen. The celebration continued until the early hours of the morning when the final guests trailed away to their quarters.

Visitors from the elven kingdoms had been keen to confirm the return of the balance of magic as they congratulated Aidan and Arivaelle, presenting them with invaluable, magical gifts as a sign of respect and confirmation of their allegiance. Tarienne suspected Aidan did not know the significance of the gifts given. She would ensure they were placed in the keep for safety.

The next morning, the castle was extremely quiet. Tarienne decided to take a walk in the sunshine, leaving a softly snoring Daien to sleep. Smiling happily, she gently kissed him on the cheek.

'Sleep well, my wonderful husband.'

Shutting the door, Tarienne glided into the gardens. Surprised to find Aidan there, looking incredibly pleased with himself, she walked up to him. He turned, his face lighting up when he saw her. Tarienne walked into his arms and hugged him tightly.

'I gather you had an enjoyable night?' she teased.

Chuckling, Aidan released her, grasped her arm, and tucked it through his. They walked along the cobblestone path, through the sweetly scented garden.

'It was the most wonderful evening of my life. I wanted to thank you.'

Tarienne frowned, confused. 'Thank me? For what?'

Aidan paused. Turning Tarienne to face him, he grasped both her hands gently.

'If you hadn't come to Therin and changed my life, challenged everything I believed in and supported me unconditionally, I would never have met your most incredible sister. A few months ago, I would not have believed I could love and be so deeply loved, with the most amazing friends. Friends I trust with my life. So yes, thank you.'

He drew a breath and, looking uneasy, continued. 'Ren, would you do one more thing for me?'

She cocked her head, smiling as she waited for him to continue.

'Would... Would you and Daien stay here at the castle and make it your home? Please?'

Tarienne blinked back tears. 'Aidan, you already know I love you as my brother. Daien and I have spoken at length about this. We'd love to stay here with you. Daien also wishes to remain as one of your king's guardsmen, if you agree.' She chuckled. 'He said you need him to keep watch over you.'

Aidan laughed. 'Nothing would make me happier.' He sobered. 'Were you aware that Rivi's wedding gift to me was immortality?'

Tarienne smiled. 'That's the most wonderful news. I did the same for Daien when he proposed. Now we can all spend eternity together.'

Aidan mused, 'Hmm, eternity... I don't think I want to be king forever.'

'You won't have to be, Aidan.' She chuckled. 'In time, you can hand over the rule to your children.'

He hugged her hard, then they walked back inside together, reminiscing about the previous day. This was the real Aidan, his compassion and tenderness the attributes that made him such a wonderful king.

By the time Tarienne returned to their chambers, Daien had

bathed and was pulling on his boots. His face lit with love, lips curving into the special smile he reserved only for her. She walked into his arms for a long kiss.

'Good morning, my beautiful wife.'

Tarienne grinned. 'And good morning to you, my gorgeous, sexy husband.'

Daien captured her mouth in another passionate kiss. Tarienne slipped her arms around his neck and leaned into him, savouring the feeling of belonging to each other.

Two days later, Tarienne, Daien, Raef, Elyssia, Aidan and Arivaelle were ready to ride to Ferngrove to begin their honeymoons. Tarienne was anxious to leave, though she loved Therin. At Ferngrove, they could relax and enjoy each other's company, without the pressures of royal life.

The triple wedding only a few days earlier was still fresh in the minds of the people of Therin. The streets were lined with well-wishers throwing flowers in front of the cavalcade. Tarienne prayed the celebrations had begun to erase the memories of the fear and death the people had seen over the last few months.

They were all eager for a glimpse of their new fae queen, their beloved King Aidan, and the fae royalty, including Tarienne's parents and brothers, who were returning to Darewood.

Tarienne waved and smiled as the crowd cheered, noting Daien's discomfort at the attention. She smiled. He was a king's guardsman at heart and unused to the scrutiny.

As the horses cantered through the huge iron gates separating Castle Therin from the surrounding villages, Tarienne glanced back at the place she now called home, then allowed her gaze to drift over each member of her family. She fervently hoped the next few months would not be as eventful, or dangerous, as the last.

Her eyes alighted on Daien, her heart swelling with love. He turned, as if sensing her scrutiny, and smiled. His eyes darkened, then his warm voice washed across her thoughts.

'Are you certain you don't want to ride up here with me?'

Heat suffused her body and her pulse quickened. *'Yes, I do want to...'* She chuckled. *'But we'd never make it to Ferngrove.'*

Daien barked out a laugh. Her eyes travelled appreciatively over his very enticing body as he pulled his horse over to hers, covering her fingers with his on Lacey's reins. Lacey nickered at Daien's black stallion as they stopped.

Daien leaned down from his much taller mount to capture Tarienne's lips. She fisted the front of his shirt to hold him to her, desperate for the contact. Vaguely, she registered the *clip-clop* of the others passing as Daien's lips slid seductively over hers. The rich, spicy taste of him sent warmth and desire flooding through her.

Aidan chuckled. 'They're always doing that.'

Laughter rippled through the group.

Tarienne smiled against Daien's lips, released him, and whispered, 'Later, my Daien. Later.'

The look he sent her was full of heat and promise. She suddenly wished they were already at Ferngrove.

Tarienne absently rubbed Lacey behind one ear as they moved on, cantering along the grassy edge of the well-worn road. She scanned the forest, an odd feeling they were being watched sliding through her. She frowned.

Probing carefully for a mind connection, she smiled broadly as she recognised the familiar thought pattern.

'Welcome back, dear friend. I don't know how you're here, but we've missed you.'

From the cover of the forest, a large, black wolf with ice-blue eyes stood quietly watching. A wolfish grin curled his lips as her thoughts reached out to him.

'It's good to be back, Tarienne.'

CHARACTERS:

Aidan (fiery) –pronounced *ay-den* – Prince of Therin. Six feet tall with bright blue eyes and short blond hair, Aidan is handsome and takes pleasure in honing his body as he hones his skill with a sword.

Aistarenne (blessed and gracious in high elvish) – pronounced *ay-eest-ar-enn* – Queen of Darewood and mother to Raef, Tarienne, Kyre, Arivaelle and Authion. Tall with dark red, waist-length, wavy hair, and pale skin, Aistarenne is a serene, calming influence, yet a strong warrior in times of need. Her skill with the bow is renowned.

Authion (war in high elvish) – pronounced *awth-i-on* – Youngest son of Aistarenne and Thalion. He is six feet tall with long, black hair tied in many small braids around his head and vivid green eyes. He is the leader of the fae army of Darewood and a formidable warrior.

Arivaelle (sunlight in high elvish) – pronounced *ar-ee-vay-ell* – Second youngest child of Aistarenne and Thalion. Nicknamed Rivi by her family. Gentle and always happy, Arivaelle is tall and beautiful with pale skin, white-blonde hair, and vivid green eyes. She has a very ethereal appearance, like her mother, and a formidable latent power in times of need. She is also the most skilled healer seen in recent times. Her chosen weapon is the bow and arrow.

Daien (gift in Druid) – pronounced *day-en* – King's guardsman. Around six-foot-two with shoulder-length, chocolate brown hair and deep brown eyes. He has druid blood from his mother's side, though he knows little about his heritage as his parents were killed when he was quite young.

Eldan – pronounced *eld-aan* – King of Therin, six-foot-two with greying hair and grey-blue eyes. Prince Aidan's father. The king is a powerfully built man who commands attention and whose courage and strength are forged in battle for his kingdom.

Elyssia – pronounced *el-is-ee-ya* – Nickname, Lys. Half-fae, half-elven, she is Raef's lover and soul mate. Tall and blonde with blue eyes, she is passionate, elegant, extremely gentle. Exquisitely beautiful, even by fae standards, and lives in the fae kingdom of Darewood with her brother, Fienn.

Enidar – pronounced *en-y-dar* – King's guardsman. A big, friendly man. Built like a bear, he is a formidable enemy, fiercely loyal to all those he calls friend.

Enrith – pronounced *en-rith* – King's guardsman. The oldest of the king's guardsmen at thirty-eight, Enrith is a married man with a wife, Lenore, and two little girls. He is six feet tall and strongly built with brown eyes and short, deep brown hair. He has a ready smile and is a courageous warrior.

Fienn (fair in high elven) – pronounced *fin* – Elyssia's brother. Fienn came to Darewood with Elyssia after the death of their parents. He is also half-fae and half-elven, and like his sister, is exquisite to look upon. He is fair-skinned and six feet tall with violet eyes yet finds his looks more of a hindrance. He holds the key to the chambers where the history of the fae of Darewood and many other magical tomes are housed.

Janek – pronounced *ya-nek* – King's guardsman. A small, wiry man with dark skin, the best hand-to-hand fighter ever seen, other than Daien. His loyalty, as with the other guardsmen, is unquestionable.

Kyre (flawless in high elvish) – pronounced *keer* – Third child of Aistarenne and Thalion. Like his siblings, Kyre is tall, his long, blond hair falling to his waist, his eyes a deep, sea blue. He moves with grace and certainty, and his muscular build and fearless demeanour make him a dangerous enemy but an extraordinary ally.

Lacas – pronounced *lay-cas* – Werewolf changeling. Tall with short, black hair and ice-blue eyes. Lacas is alpha of the pack.

Orien – pronounced *or-y-an* – King's guardsman. Orien is tall and muscular with a tanned complexion and hazel eyes. At around five-foot-eleven, he is Daien's best friend amongst the king's guardsmen and often trains with him.

Raef (strong in high elvish) – pronounced *ray-f* – Tarienne's eldest brother. Crown prince of the fae of Darewood. Over six-foot-three, muscular, with light blond, shoulder-length hair, and bright blue eyes. He is incredibly handsome yet has eyes for no one but Elyssia. He is a valiant and intimidating warrior, yet patient and compassionate. He also has strong magical and mindspeak abilities.

Rantar – pronounced *ran-tar* – A powerful sorceror, half-fae and half-elven, who tried to hoard the balance of power by killing five of the twelve members of the elder council several hundred years ago.

Killed by the remaining elder council, the power he had gathered was contained in a golden stone and left for safekeeping with a human king.

Rantec – pronounced *ran-tek* – The son of Rantar. His mother was a human who died when Rantec was born. He was raised by Lacas' wolf pack for the sole purpose of using the golden stone to gain power.

Rouan – pronounced *roo-arn* – King's guardsman. At twenty-two, Rouan is the youngest of the King's guardsmen. Around five-foot-ten, he is also the shortest, but what he lacks in height, he makes up for in tenacity and technique.

Tarienne (adventurous in high elvish) – pronounced *tar-y-en* – Nicknamed Ren by her family and close friends. Crown princess of the fae of Darewood. At five-foot-ten, she has waist-length, deep red hair, and vivid green eyes. Her skin is pale, but she is less ethereal than her sisters. She has a quick temper and is, like her mother, a strong and formidable warrior, as well as an accomplished swordswoman.

Tere – pronounced *t-air* – Wolf changeling with ice-blue eyes and black fur in his wolf form. In human form, he is six feet tall, his hair black and spiky. He is extremely handsome and extraordinarily strong.

Thalion (strong in high elvish) – *pronounced Tha-lion* – King of Darewood and father to Raef, Tarienne, Kyre, Arivaelle and Authion. A strong and fair king to almost one thousand fae, Thalion is around nine hundred years old, but because immortals age extremely slowly, does not look much older than Raef. He is six feet tall with twinkling blue eyes and shoulder-length, dark blond hair.

GLOSSARY OF TERMS

Gurith geoth riam laie – Fae battle cry meaning 'Death to our enemies.'

Kyoshonia, i'Lyuhta – Dispels previously uttered incantations. You can only undo those spells you cast yourself, not those cast by others.

Melar – 'Lover' in both fae and elvish.

Toror – 'Brother' in both fae and elvish. Often used as an endearment.

Yahalla onnia Blenidae en'i Lyuhta – A spell to summon the blade spirits, fearsome ancient warriors who swore to fight evil for eternity, yet have been fighting so long, they have become dangerously unpredictable.

Darewood (pronounced *de-ara-wood*) – The birthplace of Tarienne and Raef. It is home to the fae ruled by King Thalion and Queen Aistarenne. There are approximately one thousand fae in Darewood.

ABOUT THE AUTHOR

Kathryn's love of reading and writing began during her school years, where she earned many awards for her poetry and short stories. On leaving school, Kathryn put aside her dream of writing, opting instead for the more stable choice of a nursing career.

When fate brought her to a job in a University library, her dreams were rekindled, but put on hold once again to raise her family. She contented herself with reading widely, always searching for new authors' works to devour. From Narnia to the Lord of the Rings, magic, shifters and highland romances, her book collection has always been one of her greatest treasures.

Now retired from her career as a librarian, when Kathryn isn't writing she enjoys quilting, travelling, spending time with her family, looking after her grandson and catching up with friends.